NO TURNING BACK

"I'm sorry," he murmured. "Sorry for the way I've treated you—sorry for the life I've led. I wish we could meet again and start over. Most of all I wish I could be the man you want me to be."

"I wish you could, too." She sighed.

She tried to picture him dressed like Roger—in fashionably cut clothing complete with the proper embellishments—and almost laughed out loud. It would never work. Matthew Stone *belonged* in his molded buckskins, or a breechclout and high moccasins. No matter how other men dressed, they paled in comparison. She didn't really want to change him; she loved him the way he was.

"Can you forgive me—accept me—as I am?" The question reflected her own inner debate. As his hot breath stirred her hair, she turned in his arms to see his face in the dim morning light.

"I don't know," she answered honestly. "But you're not a fool, and I'm sorry I called you one. Can you forgive me?"

"I'm not sure you were wrong!" he said, laughing softly. "Sometimes I think I'm the biggest fool who ever lived. Despite our differences maybe *because* of them—I can't stay away from you."

"And I can't stay away from you," she whispered. "God help us both."

BOOK YOUR PLACE ON OUR WEBSITE AND MAKE THE READING CONNECTION!

We've created a customized website just for our very special readers, where you can get the inside scoop on everything that's going on with Zebra, Pinnacle and Kensington books.

When you come online, you'll have the exciting opportunity to:

- View covers of upcoming books
- Read sample chapters
- Learn about our future publishing schedule (listed by publication month *and author*)
- Find out when your favorite authors will be visiting a city near you
- Search for and order backlist books from our online catalog
- Check out author bios and background information
- Send e-mail to your favorite authors
- Meet the Kensington staff online
- Join us in weekly chats with authors, readers and other guests
- Get writing guidelines
- AND MUCH MORE!

**Visit our website at
http://www.zebrabooks.com**

PAINTED HORSE

Katharine Kincaid

Zebra Books
Kensington Publishing Corp.
http://www.zebrabooks.com

ZEBRA BOOKS are published by

Kensington Publishing Corp.
850 Third Avenue
New York, NY 10022

First Printing: November, 1998
10 9 8 7 6 5 4 3 2 1

Printed in the United States of America

From mother to daughter to granddaughter
The circle of life goes 'round. . . .
We are bound by love,
A family forever.

This book is dedicated to Mariah,
Born July 11, 1996.
Beloved Granddaughter

One

Indian Territory, 1872

The screams of women and children echoed across the prairie, shattering the deep night silence. Wreathed in smoke, eyes glinting with terror, white-gowned figures tumbled out of doorways and fled burning cabins. Men scrambled to defend the settlement, but they might as well have tried to stop the charge of a maddened buffalo. On this night of the full moon, what the whites called a Comanche Moon, the warriors of the People meant to destroy their enemies and return Comancheria to those who rightfully owned it.

Painted Horse refused to feel pity. He was *Kwerharrehnuh* now—and had been for a long time. The whites deserved to die. They lied and they stole. They butchered the buffalo and desecrated Mother Earth. They swarmed across the prairie in ever-increasing numbers, claiming all they found and all the People cherished.

Urging his horse forward, he eagerly joined in the killing. When he ran out of bullets he threw down his carbine and reached for his war club. Clinging to a thong tied around the neck of his best buffalo runner, he rampaged among the fleeing whites—felling them one by one. It was easier than hunting buffalo, where a brave risked tumbling to the earth and being trampled by the huge, lumbering beasts.

Arrogant and secure in their greater numbers, the whites

hadn't anticipated the attack. The men fought poorly, while the helpless women and children offered easy targets on the moonlit plain. Silver light poured over all of them, making blood glisten like oil. Some of the women lifted their hands and turned pleading faces toward their attackers. Painted Horse didn't hesitate. His own blood surged hotly through his veins; he had a destiny to fulfill, and he was merely fulfilling it.

Then he came to the girl, a child of no more than four or five summers. In her arms she clutched a cloth doll as if it might spare her from destruction. Her long white nightdress billowed about her in the light breeze, and he glimpsed bare feet and legs. She panted softly—out of breath from running. Tears streaked her plump cheeks as she gazed at him through a cloud of tousled, silver-spun hair.

She stood there, waiting, watching . . . concluding it was useless. She could never outrun him; death had come for her. He read all this in her upturned face as he bent low over his pony's neck, lifted his war club—and froze, halting before her. A distant memory stirred, like the soft summer wind whispering its secrets.

God in heaven! The child reminded him of Isabella, his long-lost sister. Dressed like this little girl and clutching the cloth doll made by their mother, Isabella had often come creeping to his bedside in the loft and begged to crawl beneath the heavy quilt to sleep beside him and Thad.

"It's too cold in my bed," she had murmured. "And too lonesome. Can I come in with you, Matt, just for a little while?"

Grumbling, he had peeled back the quilt. Thad had stirred and muttered, protesting the sudden chill, as Isabella hopped into bed and snuggled against him, a soft, squirming body burrowing close for warmth and comfort in the cold dark night.

She's not Isabella, a voice chimed in his head. *She's the enemy. Kill her.*

But her eyes were Isabella's eyes—wide and frightened, yet resigned at the same time. This was how Isabella had looked on that day when the Comanches had come for them, snatching

up first him and Thad, shooting Pa and Ma as they ran screaming from the soddy house, and finally . . . axing Isabella, standing there in the field, knowing she couldn't run far enough or
fast enough to escape.

The hot wet sides of his pony heaved in and out against Painted
Horse's thighs. He sat still for a moment—unnerved and debating. Just as he decided to take the child up on his horse and
protect her from the violence exploding all around them, another
horse crashed into his, almost unseating him. A war club swung
high in the air, hovered there a moment, then . . .

Enraged, Painted Horse spun around and swung his own war
club. The warrior looking back at him laughed in his face; it
was Stalking Wolf, his brother, once known as Thaddeus, or
Thad. Painted Horse slowly lowered his club. He didn't return
his brother's grin, and it disappeared as quickly as it had come.
A fierce scowl replaced it.

"Remember my Comanche wife and son," Stalking Wolf
sneered. "The whites ran them down like dogs and killed them.
They showed no mercy, and neither must we."

He spoke in the language of the People. Painted Horse wondered if his brother could even remember the white man's
tongue. Thad had been too young when he was taken to retain
many memories of his previous life, but Painted Horse remembered; images often flashed in his mind like lightning, illuminating people and places from his far distant past.

He resisted them; they were too painful.

*Remember my Comanche wife and son—but remember Isa-
bella, too! How could he have forgotten Isabella and his own
parents? . . . . Was there no escape from this unending madness?*

Bathed in sweat and shaking from head to foot, Matthew
Stone struggled to awaken from the nightmare that had plagued
him for years. This terrible nightmare had driven him to abandon the Comanches and return to the world of the white man.
Like a cobweb it clung to him, refusing to let go, and he thought

of how unfair it was that after four long years he should still
be dreaming it, when he had done all any man could to right
the wrongs he had committed as an Indian.

So much pain. So much guilt and anger. He had endured
enough to last a lifetime, and still could not escape it. He would
never forget the look in his brother's eyes when he had told him
he was leaving the *Kwerharrehnuh*. Disbelief, sorrow, anger,
and disgust had all been etched there.

His Comanche mother, shriveled and bent in her old age, had
mourned as if he were already dead. His Comanche father had
turned his face away, pretending he had never existed. His closest friend, Quanah Parker, himself the son of a white woman,
had shamelessly begged him to stay.

He hadn't needed to explain things to his Comanche wife;
after he'd refused to participate in any more raids, she had left
him and given herself to a more deserving warrior, one whose
courage could not be questioned.

Matt had turned his back on all of them, yet his spirit still
longed for the freedom of the plains. Savagery seemed to linger
in his soul, making it impossible for him to fit into the world
he had chosen. The whites avoided him; they sensed he was
different—not truly one of them. After four long years of trying
and failing to win acceptance his life remained a lonely hell,
beset by nightmares and painful doubts.

Once he'd been a proud free Comanche who claimed an entire
tribe as his family, and the whole of the *Llano Estacado* as his
home. Now he was an isolated, would-be rancher confined to
his small, barren acreage and carving out a meager living cap-
turing wild mustangs and selling them to the U.S. Cavalry. The
army then used the horses to hunt down his Comanche brothers.

I'm doing the right thing, he told himself for the thousandth
time. *But if he was doing the right thing, why did peace elude
him, and happiness seem a distant dream?*

As he did so often, he lay sweating in his narrow bed in his
crude little shack on the fringes of Comancheria and grimly

wondered what was right and wrong, and why he alone of all the people he knew had so much trouble sorting it out.

Life made no sense.

He had taught himself to read and write better English than the officers at the fort. He now wore white clothing and followed white ways. He spoke, acted, and looked like a white man, no longer staining his skin with berry juice or darkening his hair, so that he might blend more perfectly with the short, dark-complected, bandy-legged Comanches.

His height, light skin, greenish-colored eyes, and sunstreaked copper curls had always set him apart from the Indians, but now that he bore a greater physical resemblance to his chosen people he still couldn't make himself think like them.

He had tried not to condemn them, but he nurtured a seething contempt for the beliefs and behavior of most white men. When they killed a buffalo they took only the hide, leaving the meat to rot. Some killed only for the sport of it, and didn't even take the hide or the tongue, which the Indians considered a delicacy.

Nor were white men any more careful of other wildlife. Matt had seen them shoot waterfowl by the dozens, for no other reason than to watch the birds fall from the sky. He could not understand their careless destruction of the world around them. Wherever they crossed the plains they left a trail of trash and ugliness—and of course, abandoned graves. Their wagon wheels cut deep scars on the breast of Mother Earth. Deeper still were the wounds they left on the hearts of those who loved the plains and never wasted the land's precious bounty.

Frowning into the darkness, Matt admitted to himself that he sorely missed his Comanche family, his brother, his friends—even his pretty faithless wife, Sweet Water. He could understand why she had left him. To a Comanche, courage was everything. A man—and his wife and children along with him—lived or died based on his eagerness to confront his enemies. Among all Indians, men of courage were revered and women sang their praises, while cowards were shunned, and no Indian maid would knowingly marry one.

Matt had taken enough scalps to prove he was no coward, but Sweet Water had rejected all other explanations for his refusal to slay more whites. He had tried once to tell her about his recurring nightmare, derived from an actual experience, but she couldn't understand. Her grandfather, an uncle, and a brother had been slain by white men. Several female relatives had been raped and abused by army soldiers. To her, vengeance was the only answer to these tragedies.

At first, believing he was ill, she had diligently dosed him with herbs. When that failed to work, she had alternated between berating him and ignoring him. At last, she had left him. Whenever Matt closed his eyes he could still see her image—tall and slender for a Comanche female, with huge black eyes, a waterfall of night-black hair, and a body whose contours made him ache with frustration and longing, as much now as when he'd first met her.

Where was she now? Was she still alive? If so, she was probably starving. Most of the Comanches had already been rounded up and forced onto a reservation near Fort Sill. In captivity they didn't get enough to eat, but usually fared better than the ones being hunted by the army. The most rebellious band still roaming the Staked Plain was the one to which he and Sweet Water had belonged. Quanah Parker, the man he had called his closest friend other than his brother, was now the band's leader.

Rolling off the bed, Matt stood and walked to the single small window in the room. Outside, a full moon made the prairie bright as noon. The wooden shutter stood open, admitting the smell of parched earth and grass. He inhaled deeply, identifying the underlying odors of dust, manure, leather, horse, and prairie dog.

Not for the first time, Matt fervently wished he still lived among the Comanches. On nights such as this, when a Comanche Moon rode high in the star-spangled sky, he'd be riding alongside his brother and Quanah, headed out on a raid, fighting for a way of life that made far more sense to him than this one.

The hell of it was he could never go back; it was only a

matter of time before Quanah Parker and Stalking Wolf were either killed or forced onto the reservation to join the Comanches already bowed, beaten, and held in captivity. Towns were growing fast, and railroads now snaked across the wilderness. Despite the "Indian menace," the whites kept coming, building more towns, killing more buffalo, herding more cattle. . . . There was no end to them.

And Matt had seen the faces of the Indians confined to the reservation and forced to survive on what little the whites provided. Their spirits were crushed, their pride ground into the dust. Resentful and unhappy, accustomed to following the buffalo instead of waiting for handouts that rarely came, they were mere husks of their former selves. Even those willing to try farming, as the whites advised, gave up in disgust when drought killed their fledgling crops, or passing herds of cattle en route to the railhead in Dodge trampled them.

To the Indian, wielding a hoe was squaw work, hardly fit labor for former warriors and hunters, the lords of the plains. So the reservation Indians brooded, drank whiskey when they could get it, plotted vengeance, and rotted inside. They reminded him of dried gourds, empty of life, bereft even of souls. They had died but didn't yet know it . . . or maybe they did know it.

Yes, he had done the right thing. He had made his choice; he must now live with it—but oh, how he wished it could be otherwise!

Turning back to the bed, disgusted by his divided loyalties, Matt lay down again, closed his eyes, and resolutely sought sleep. The dream didn't usually occur twice in one night. If sleep came to him now, it would last until morning and be deep and dreamless, the only escape possible from the turmoil churning inside him.

He was just dozing off when he heard the distant tinkling of bells. This time he leapt from the bed and grabbed the always-loaded rifle standing in the corner. The chiming of the bells signaled that someone was trying to steal his mustangs, penned in several corrals not far from the house. As a deterrent to theft, either by Indians or unscrupulous whites such as the buffalo hunters, he had looped coils of the new invention, "bob wire," through the long grass around the corrals and tied bells to the wire. Anyone trying to penetrate the barrier couldn't do so without alerting him.

As he rushed from the house, the bells chimed furiously, and the pent-up mustangs neighed and stomped. Crouching Comanche style, Matt zigzagged toward the sounds and stopped just short of revealing himself to whomever was caught in the wire. Peering around the back of the lean-to near the closest corral, he spotted the source of the wild clamor: it wasn't a human, but another horse.

A large white horse with patches of dirt or dark coloring splashed across his body like paint—a painted horse.

As Matt watched, the animal struggled frantically to free himself from the barbed wire. Apparently he had stepped into the middle of a double coil, and in his exertions had only succeeded in hopelessly ensnaring his body. The barbs on the wire bit deeply into the horse's chest and front legs, causing more damage than Matt would have imagined possible in so short a time. Even given the fact that horses could do foolish things and injure themselves in the process, this one's eagerness to hurt himself astonished Matt.

As Matt moved closer, the horse reared up on its hind legs and snorted a ringing challenge. The wire gouged it further, but the horse paid no attention. Had it not been restrained, it would have charged Matt.

Matt warily retreated. Perhaps the animal had gone mad from fear and pain. Or it might have eaten loco weed, but animals so inflicted seemed dazed and disoriented, while this one was alert and very much aware of his surroundings.

Snorting and blowing, the horse watched Matt until he again slipped from sight behind the lean-to. When he emerged on the other side of the structure, the horse was still watching and still enraged by his presence. He shrieked and again pawed the air.

Blood dripped down his chest and legs as the wire lacerated flesh and muscle.

"Whoa . . . whoa, my friend." Propping the rifle against the building, Matt held out one hand to the horse, but it continued bucking, rearing, and screaming with fury. Affected by the excitement, the mustangs in the nearest corral whinnied, stomped, and milled about in a tight circle. Several squatted and urinated, and Matt suddenly realized that the enraged captive was a stallion.

The horses in this particular corral were all mares or young fillies. He had already separated out the young males and either turned them back out on the plain to mature, taken the older ones to Fort Sill to be gelded for use by the army, or confined them in another corral downwind of the mares. This fierce bold stallion had intended to steal himself a ready-made band, some of whom were prime for mating.

Squinting in the dim light, Matt studied his uninvited guest. The stallion had blue eyes, not brown, and a patch of brown covered his head and ears. Matt noted that the patch of dark on the stallion's bloodied chest was color—not dirt—and his heart pounded in sudden excitement. The horse was a true "painted horse," as the Comanches and *Tejanos* called them. He was also a Medicine Hat, an animal whose unique markings proclaimed that he possessed strong medicine.

Among the Comanches—and the Cheyenne, too—all "painted horses" were prized, but a horse marked like this one could be owned and ridden only by a great warrior. So highly did the Indians regard such a horse that they believed they couldn't be killed while riding one. No bullets would ever bring down a warrior mounted on such a fine horse.

Matt recalled seeing a poster at Fort Sill warning that a young stallion of this description was running free on the plain and stealing mares from soldiers and settlers alike. The poster said the horse, claimed to be a dangerous rogue, had killed a man, and should be shot on sight. Even worse than that, he was exactly the sort of horse to incite the reservation Indians to warfare by evoking memories of past glories.

Smiling to himself, Matt shook his head. The poster hadn't lied. This horse could definitely arouse dispirited Indians and encourage them to resume fighting. Had Matt himself encountered him in his former life, he would have considered the occasion a momentous visit from his namesake and guiding spirit—and so would the rest of the Comanches.

They would have believed he'd been sent a message and only needed to fast and pray to discover its meaning.

Matt ignored the sense of hope and exhilaration sweeping over him; he steadfastly resisted the feeling of impending destiny. He was a white man, now; he no longer believed in superstitious nonsense. The color of a horse's hide could not prevent its rider from being killed by a bullet. The Indians had foolish notions about trains, too. When Matt had finally "tamed the Iron Horse" by riding in one he had realized how ignorant the People were about many things.

That didn't mean he didn't feel a strong empathy for this wild injured stallion. Whether or not it was because the horse was a Medicine Hat and his Comanche namesake, Matt knew he wanted to free him, doctor his wounds, slowly win his trust, and make a friend and servant of the splendid creature. He desperately wanted to ride him—not to break his spirit, but to capture his essence to replace the spirit he himself had somehow lost.

He stood a long time watching the stallion's struggles and waiting for him to grow calmer. Any hurried movement on his part risked driving the horse into complete panic. He would then struggle and fight to his death. When caught and held fast—with no time to adjust—some horses would break a leg or even their own necks in a desperate bid for freedom. This one was already seriously injured, and seemed perilously close to that final crazed effort.

Matt slipped back to the house to retrieve a tool for cutting the wire. He also fetched a bucket of water, a pail of grain, some strips of cloth for bandages, and a few other things he thought he might need. Thirst, hunger, and the stallion's own struggles would eventually sap his strength. Matt planned to go to work when that happened. He'd use every trick the Comanches had taught him to heal the horse's wounds and transform him into a trustworthy loyal companion. The Comanches were the best horsemen on the plains, and Matt had learned their lessons well. Even among the Comanches, he had excelled.

Now, for the first time in a long time, if indeed he had ever known such a sense of joy and purpose in his troubled life, Matthew Stone relished being alive.

Boston, 1873

Seated at the long candlelit table in the dining hall of the mansion left to her by her late parents, Grace Elizabeth Livingston smiled at her elegantly clad guests. The tinkle of fine crystal and clink of sterling made a muted music underlying the conversation, and on this cold late winter evening, Grace found little to merit complaint.

The setting was gorgeous, the company congenial, the food superb. Best of all, tonight she would announce her impending marriage to Roger Clairmont, who was beaming at her from the opposite end of the lavishly laden table. A fine-looking gentleman with impeccable manners and a ruthlessness to match her own, Roger had finally overcome her objections and convinced her that at twenty-seven, she was entitled to seek personal happiness, not merely success. Having spent the last seven years consolidating the shipping empire left to her by her father, Grace had believed she would never marry. At her age, and considering her devotion to business, who would want her? In Roger she had found the ideal mate—or if nothing else worked out, the perfect business partner. A successful textile manufacturer, he was one of the few men she'd met who didn't seem put off by her energy, ambition, and moneymaking skills.

She knew what everyone called her behind her back: Amazing Grace. The woman who wouldn't take no for an answer, believed she was smarter than most men, and had made enough money to prove it. The woman who enjoyed bringing her male competitors to their knees and making liars of everyone who had ever claimed that a woman couldn't run a family business by herself.

She had to admit there was some truth to these assertions; she enjoyed her work and had learned not to agonize over every difficult decision. These days she surprised even herself with her ability to take a tough stand on issues fraught with conflicting emotions.

At their very first meeting, Roger had declared he admired her. He claimed to covet not only her money—this, he said jokingly—but her knowledge and drive. In any case, he had all the right connections and was eager to exploit them to further both their interests. When he had finally proposed to Grace, he had sworn he didn't expect her to be the conventional, stay-at-home wife. Such a mate would only bore him, and Roger hated above all to be bored.

In view of all this, it mattered little that Grace had great difficulty imagining herself in bed with him. She would never admit it to anyone, least of all Roger himself, but the few kisses they had shared had roused nothing more than a sensation of emptiness and disappointment. She had expected the earth to shudder with some great inner cataclysm, and it hadn't even trembled. She dreaded her reaction—or lack of one—if and when he attempted to go *beyond* kissing. She doubted she could hide her distaste for the whole sorry business.

She hadn't yet discussed this unfortunate situation with Roger, but she felt certain they could reach some accommodation in regards to her marital duties. Assuming they could, Roger would most certainly fulfill her most important prerequisite for a husband: that is, he would allow her to go her own way. She wanted a husband who would cherish her femininity but not demand more than she could give or use it to control her. Most of all, she needed a husband to shield and protect her from greedy grasping competitors who resented her success and schemed to topple her.

Over the last seven years, she had discovered what a cold, cruel, lonely world it could be, and she no longer wished to be alone in it. As for children, she secretly yearned to have a few— at least someone to inherit the Livingston legacy. Since Roger didn't appeal to her in "that way" and seemed to possess few paternal qualities, she had to forego the possibility and concentrate on friendship, instead. Since he had never mentioned children, she didn't think he would mind separate bedchambers, or at least, *beds*.

A surge of affection for this man who had rescued her from lonely spinsterhood swept over her, and Grace took a sip of wine and met Roger's glance over the rim of her wineglass. In his usual witty way, he was entertaining the lady to his right with a tale about the perils of manufacturing and the difficulty of obtaining loyal dependable workers. Grace had often thought that if he would just pay his workers more, he wouldn't have so much trouble, but she never argued the point, because Roger's success spoke for itself. His rise to fame and fortune had been nothing short of astonishing, especially considering the fact that he had started with almost nothing ten short years ago.

Roger gave her a sly knowing grin and lifted his own wineglass in silent salute. Soon, at the end of the meal, she would announce their plans: a June wedding sure to set all Boston on its ear. Ah, if only Ellie were here tonight, to share this moment of happiness and triumph!

Thinking of Eleanor, her younger sister, Grace suffered a stab of melancholy. She hadn't seen Ellie in eight years, not since the foolish girl had broken their parents' hearts by running off with a charming, ex-Confederate army officer headed West to make his fortune. Judging from Ellie's letters, which arrived several times a year, her husband, William, hadn't yet found his life's work, but their union had produced two children, Emily, now six years old, and Jonathan, four.

Ellie's letters always centered on the children; she rarely mentioned William and never answered Grace's questions about where they were living or in what manner of hardship. The last Grace had heard, Ellie and her family were headed for California by the Santa Fe trail, an arduous undertaking from all reports, and Grace devoutly wished her sister were still living in Boston, where at least she could keep an eye on her and help out when help was needed. She had never even seen her niece and nephew, and if she never had children of her own, she intended to make Emily and Jonathan her heirs.

Ellie had written that little Emily was Grace's "mirror image." Poor thing. The child would have been far luckier if she had inherited her mother's ravishing looks.

"So what do you hear from your dear sister?" Adele Delamere, the lady seated to her right, suddenly asked. An old family friend, Adele had apparently guessed the direction of Grace's thoughts.

Grace focused on the elder woman's wrinkled face. Two bright splotches of color high on her cheekbones indicated too much wine, an overly generous application of cosmetics, or both.

"Not much, I'm afraid. I received a letter last summer, but have heard nothing since."

"Pity," Adele sniffed. "Such a pretty child, Ellie was. And so delicate. Much too young and frail to go running off to the wilderness. Too bad she got only the beauty, while you got the brains, my dear."

"Why, thank you very much, Adele—I think."

Suddenly self-conscious, Grace touched the creamy lace spilling from the bosom of her outrageously expensive gown. Her sister's ethereal beauty had always been a source of pride and a tribulation. Grace couldn't begin to count the number of times people had remarked upon Eleanor's loveliness, while rudely ignoring Grace's less notable features.

Eleanor had the palest blond hair, bluest eyes, and creamiest skin imaginable, while Grace's tresses were an unfashionable wheaten color and somewhat unmanageable. Her eyes were her best feature, but still only a nondescript hazel. Her skin was ruddy hued, a far cry from the pale porcelain or alabaster over which men sighed. Both girls had always been slender, but petite Eleanor seemed to float when she moved, while tall raw-boned Grace bustled about with brisk purpose. Grace sometimes tripped over the hem of her own gown, and could only hope little Emily hadn't been burdened with her clumsiness, along with her common appearance.

"Now, my dear Grace, I didn't mean to imply that you aren't attractive. As you've matured, you've certainly found your own sense of style, but Ellie . . . well, she was a natural beauty. Quite breathtaking. The girl always put me in mind of an angel descended from heaven."

Yes, Grace thought. That was the way she remembered her, too. Longing to see her sister again, Grace wondered where Ellie was tonight, and what she was doing. Despite their differences—and they were as different as day and night—she did so miss her only sibling!

Ellie had failed to mention when she expected to reach California, and whether or not she and William were embarking on the hazardous journey before or after the onset of winter. Even as a child, doted upon by their parents, Ellie couldn't be bothered with details. Unlike Grace she never seemed to worry; surrounded by adoring adults who granted her every wish, she had basked contentedly in their affection and allowed others to grapple with unpleasantness.

The single rebellion in her entire serene and perfect life had been running off with William Barrington. It was typical of Ellie never to question whether or not she was cut out for a future of adventure and possible danger. William's charm and dark good looks had thoroughly captivated Ellie; she had also loved his Southern drawl, and been certain he was destined for great things.

"I, too, always thought Ellie resembled an angel," Grace murmured, half to herself. "And I wish she would suddenly float down from the clouds and join us here tonight."

"Why tonight, especially?" Adele avidly inquired. "Is there something special about this evening?"

"Restrain yourself," Grace chided. "I'm not going to tell you before anyone else. You'll find out soon enough."

Dessert was served: poached pears in Madeira sauce. Grace's cook, Mrs. Hugg, had informed her earlier that it was all the rage in Europe. That's why Grace employed her—to prepare unusual delicacies that made invitations to her table much sought after by all the important people in Boston.

As spoons delved into the aromatic offering, Roger suddenly leapt to his feet and raised his glass. Grace had seen her servants refill that glass several times already—not that she was counting.

"Wait a moment, everyone," he said gleefully. "I know Grace has this all planned, but I'm weary of waiting."

He eyed Grace proudly, if a bit unsteadily. All eyes turned from him to her. Beneath the scrutiny, Grace's cheeks burned, and her heart fluttered absurdly.

"I wish to propose a toast," he announced.

"The champagne," she murmured. "At least wait until the champagne is poured."

"Ah, yes, the champagne." Roger waved his glass, slopping red wine on the immaculate lace tablecloth.

Grace signaled to a waiting servant who raced to fetch the champagne. Roger was rushing things a bit, but his enthusiasm couldn't be faulted. He was grinning so widely she feared his lower lip might split. He was also swaying, and she feared he might topple over if someone breathed on him. Perhaps she shouldn't have sent for the champagne, after all.

"My dear Amazing Grace!" He paused to chuckle at his own humor. "That's what they call you, and I quite agree. You *are* amazing. I've thought so from the day I first met you—actually, even before that. I'd heard about you before I ever laid eyes on you, and I thought to myself, 'Now, there's the perfect woman—the one I've been waiting for all my life.' "

Her guests exchanged glances, and Grace tried to swallow the lump that had suddenly popped into her throat. Such fervent public admissions embarrassed her. Roger was making fools of both of them.

"Roger, do sit down, and wait for the champagne," she implored. "This isn't how I'd planned to tell everyone. . . ."

"But what do you mean to tell us, dear?" Adele burst out. "I can't stand the suspense. Can it really be what I think it is?"

She rolled her eyes, and everyone laughed. Grace was spared the shame of having to admit the obvious by the sudden flustered arrival of Jenkins, the butler, in the doorway.

"Miss Livingston, forgive me for interrupting, but you have a caller. He is most insistent that he see you immediately."

Grace resolved to give Jenkins a raise in pay at the earliest opportunity. "Who is it, Jenkins?"

"A Colonel Marberry, Miss Livingston. From the army," he added, as if that clarified everything.

It didn't. Grace knew the current and past presidents of the country, numerous senators, congressmen, and generals, but she couldn't think of a single army colonel of close enough acquaintance to be so bold as to interrupt a Livingston dinner party.

"You may show him to the green salon." Rising, she set down her napkin and nodded to her guests. "I had best see what the colonel wants. The army mustn't be kept waiting."

"Shall I accompany you, dearest?" Roger had a drunken gleam in his eye, and he swayed dangerously in her direction.

"No . . . no, Roger. See that the champagne is poured, will you? We'll have a toast and share our good news when I return."

"Splendid! Assuming we can wait that long for the champagne."

"And the news," Adele added.

Again, everyone laughed.

Why did they all find the idea of her marrying Roger—or

anyone else—so funny? Grace was annoyed. She wasn't *that* old or eccentric, was she?

She pondered the question as she followed Jenkins to the green salon.

Two

Colonel Marberry was a dour-faced, middle-aged man with a mustache. His blue uniform looked travel-worn, and his boots were wet and muddy. As Grace entered the green salon, he glanced down in dismay at the dirty puddle he had made on her beautiful, green and gold Aubusson carpet, imported only recently from France.

"Sorry, Miss Livingston. I didn't realize—"

"Never mind, Colonel. Obviously you have more important matters on your mind. What brings you here this evening? I don't believe we've met before, have we?"

The colonel shook his head, his gaze baleful. "No, Miss Livingston, we have not. I regret to inform you I am here on official business. I have news regarding William and Eleanor Barrington and their children."

For a moment, the names didn't register.

"Ellie? You have news of Ellie, my sister?"

"Yes, Miss Livingston." The colonel nervously cleared his throat. "You asked Senator Blessing to secure news of your sister's whereabouts."

Grace had almost forgotten the incident; it had happened so long ago. "Why, yes . . . yes, I did. I saw him at a tea just before Christmas, and mentioned that I hadn't heard from Ellie since summer. She *never* writes as often as she should. Either that or the mail is terribly slow and subject to losses. Even given that, I . . . I had an uneasy feeling, as if something might be wrong.

I've since decided I must have been mistaken, and shouldn't have bothered the senator with family matters."

"Yes, well . . . the senator took your concern quite seriously and corresponded with my superiors. I was assigned the task of seeing what I could discover about Mrs. Barrington. . . . Alas, the news is not good, Miss Livingston."

"What is it? What's happened?" Grace felt a surge of panic.

"Your sister, brother-in-law, and their children were members of a small party of whites passing through Indian Territory. Comanches set upon their wagon train, killing most of the party, including William Barrington, and . . . and grossly mutilating them. They then took your sister and her children captive, and no one has seen or heard of them since."

Grace grasped the back of a Louis Quatorze chair upholstered in green velvet. Leaning against it to still her sudden trembling, she blinked at the colonel. His somber face had gone all fuzzy. "Ellie and the children have been captured by Indians, and William is dead," she repeated. "Did I hear you correctly?"

"Perhaps you should sit down, Miss Livingston. I know this must come as a great shock."

"There must be some mistake! How can you be so sure my sister and her family were victims of this dreadful attack?"

"Someone who knew him positively identified William Barrington's body. The party was only a few days out from the last fort they had visited, you see, and people at the fort remembered them."

"But . . . but . . ." Grace could not believe it. She was sure she must be dreaming the entire conversation. "I thought travel to California was safer now than it used to be!"

She wasn't sure of this, but she desperately wanted to believe it. Ellie had assured her that she and her family would be perfectly fine.

"Ignorant Easterners often claim it is, but those of us who have spent some time there would never say so. Most of the Comanches have been confined to a reservation near Fort Sill in Indian Territory, but a few unruly, wild bands still roam the plains, preying on settlers and unwary travelers. Until *all* the Indians are removed from the region or confined to reservations, travel through the area will remain dangerous and uncertain."

He paused, giving Grace a chance to grapple with her horror and disbelief. "When did this occur?"

"Early last fall."

"Last fall! Then why am I hearing about it only now, in the middle of February?"

"Begging your pardon, Miss Livingston, but your name isn't Barrington, and your sister didn't go around informing people of her maiden name. Besides, so many whites have been killed—so many atrocities committed—it's impossible for the army to keep track of them all or to notify the relatives involved. Had it not been for Senator Blessing—"

"I might never have heard the news at all! Why, that's monstrous, Colonel—forgive me—I can't remember your name."

"Marberry. Yes, I agree. Unfortunately, we're very shorthanded, and much too busy pursuing the red devils to take the time to track down next of kin."

"But Ellie and the children!" Lifting a hand to her throat, Grace tried not to picture her angelic sister in the clutches of a bunch of fiends from hell. "Did the army go after them? Have you heard where they were taken or what happened to them after their capture?"

The colonel shook his head regretfully. "I'm truly sorry, Miss Livingston, but you must consider them dead. The little girl was only six-years-old, the boy, four. And in your sister's delicate condition—"

"What do you mean? Was Ellie ill?"

"No . . . not that I know of." The colonel colored to the tips of his ears. "A woman your sister met at the fort told me that Mrs. Barrington was expecting another child when they set out. Your sister confided that she was worried it might be born before they reached their destination."

"Oh, no! She never mentioned her condition to me in her last letter!"

"Nonetheless, it's true. Perhaps, she simply didn't wish to worry you."

Yes, that must be it. Had Grace known Ellie was pregnant, she would have been frantic. When Ellie hadn't said much about the births of her first two children, Grace had surmised that she'd had a hard time of it. Under prodding, Ellie had finally admitted that yes, she'd almost died bearing Emily, and Jonathan's birth hadn't gone any better. A doctor in Missouri had advised her to avoid having any more children.

"Colonel, you must explain to me why the army didn't go after my sister and her children. Is it military policy to simply abandon white captives to the wretched Indians?"

The colonel's color deepened. "Hardly, Miss Livingston. But you must understand that the country is exceptionally harsh and wild, and captives are brutally treated. We can almost never locate them. When we do find 'em, they're often half-dead or in imminent danger of dying, poor devils."

"So you've washed your hands of them," Grace accused, not in the least sympathetic to *his* problems.

"Absolutely not. We attempt to negotiate the return of *all* white captives held by the Indians. When we capture Indian women and children, we're sometimes able to trade them back to the Indians in exchange for whites. Many have been returned this way. It's just that we've no way of knowing who's still out there, waiting to be found. We made inquiries regarding your sister and her children, but no whites meeting their description have been seen by any of the captives returned to the Indian agency at Fort Sill in recent months."

"That doesn't mean they're *dead.*"

"True, but it's doubtful they could have survived those first few weeks of nonstop travel across the plains. When the Indians are on the run they don't take time for food and water, or to look after whites who may be injured. Often they leave the weak to die on the plain—or kill them, rather than be detained by their slow progress."

"I refuse to believe they are dead! If the army can't be bothered, I'll go there myself and conduct my own search."

"That's impossible, Miss Livingston. You've no idea how wild the country is—or how savage the Comanches are. Anyone setting foot inside Comancheria risks losing a scalp. Hardly anybody comes out alive. Why, most of the region is still unexplored. The savages can hide in hundreds of places, and they're always on the move, which is why the army can't catch them. We do the best we can, but—"

"Excuses, Colonel. You have an abundance of excuses, but all I care about is rescuing my sister and her children, assuming they are still alive. I'm a wealthy woman. I'd be willing to furnish the army with whatever they need to—"

"Out of the question! Forgive my bluntness, but the army can't be put at the disposal of a single person searching for captives who are probably dead by now, anyway. Even as we speak, the Comanches, Cheyenne, Apaches, and Kiowa are making war on white settlements in Texas and along the Mexican border. I only took time from my own responsibilities out of respect for Senator Blessing."

"You're returning to Indian Territory?"

"Not immediately. From here, I'm traveling to Washington. The president desires firsthand information regarding the Indian conflict. Bleeding heart do-gooders pleading leniency for the savages beset him on every side, but what the Indians really need is a dose of good hot lead in their backsides. . . . Forgive me, Miss Livingston, but the Office of Indian Affairs is made up of missionaries trying to protect the Indians from the whites, when it should be the other way around."

"It's all right, Colonel. After hearing your news, I quite agree with you. Thank you for coming here. Please pay my respects to President Grant when you see him. However, if you wouldn't mind, before you go I have a few more questions."

"I'd be pleased to answer whatever I can."

Twenty minutes later the colonel departed and, armed with all the information she needed, Grace marched back into the dining hall to rejoin her neglected guests. They were all drinking champagne and laughing uproariously at one of Roger's inane jokes.

As soon as he saw her, Roger sprang to his feet. Swaying even more precariously now, he offered her a glass of champagne. "Sorry we couldn't wait for you, Gracie, love—but you were gone such an awfully long time."

Grace had never been called Gracie in her life, and she wondered why he couldn't see by her demeanor that something was terribly wrong. She waved away the champagne.

"Roger, I've something to tell you—indeed, all of you."

"What, love?" He leaned toward her, making a visible effort to focus his bloodshot eyes. "If it's about our weddin', guess what? I already told 'em. But I didn't set the date yet. I left that for you, Gracie, old girl."

Grace had never seen Roger drunk before, and she didn't like what she was seeing. Around the table, her friends and business associates all raised their glasses.

"Congratulations and best wishes, Grace! . . . Here's to a lovely wedding and many years of marital bliss. . . . Why didn't you tell us sooner, you sly old thing?"

The comments slid off Grace like a brief inconsequential rain shower. Gradually, her champagne-befuddled guests realized that she wasn't celebrating the occasion.

Roger broke the sudden silence with a question: "Gracie, love, is something wrong?"

"Indeed there is, Roger. I'm sorry to have to tell you this, but there's been a change of plan."

Rejecting Roger's arguments, along with those of nearly everyone else she knew, Grace made arrangements to travel to Fort Sill in Indian Territory. There she hoped to hire someone competent to conduct a search for Ellie, Emily, and Jonathan. Failing that, she herself would go after them.

Over the past seven years, Grace had learned that money—

combined with enough grit and determination—could accomplish anything. In this case she prayed it would buy freedom for the only family she had, if indeed she still had them.

Her decision meant breaking her betrothal to Roger. With his every protest against her plans, he convinced her he wasn't the man she had hoped he was. Grace waited in vain for his offer to take on all the Comanches single-handedly in order to help find her relatives. Not only did he refuse to accompany her or play the gallant hero, but he told her she was a rash, feather-headed female; if she insisted on this foolhardy venture, she should at least sign everything over to him in case she never made it back to Boston.

She wound up telling him their relationship was over, and that from now until her return, her solicitor, Mr. Bartholomew Gumby, would be handling all her business affairs.

Even her cook and butler pleaded with her to reconsider, but Grace had made up her mind. She had to find out what had happened to Ellie and the children and, if they were still alive, rescue them. She could never live with herself, wondering if members of her own flesh and blood were wearing deerskins and living in tipis, perhaps starved and mistreated, believing themselves forgotten and abandoned by those who'd once known and loved them.

Grace was sure she could persuade the army commander at Fort Sill or the Indian agent stationed nearby to assist her. She herself intended to question every white captive returned to the agency; someone was bound to remember a slender blond woman and her two young children. In an Indian village, Ellie's blond coloring couldn't possibly be overlooked.

Grace had always cultivated the ability to get things done in short order. With this new motivation she moved heaven and earth—and a few stubborn humans—to reach Dodge City in a matter of weeks. From there she traveled across country by army freight wagon and arrived at the Indian agency near Fort Sill on the breezy sunny morning of April 1, 1873.

Fort Sill was a modest collection of clapboard buildings

which had been thrown up in haste on the windswept prairie several years previously. The agency was three miles away. Fortunately, the freight train was headed there with a load of supplies for the reservation Indians.

Upon their arrival, a noisy smelly horde of Indians descended like locusts upon the wagon. Ignoring the angry faces and outstretched hands, Grace held a scented handkerchief to her nose, climbed down from the wagon, and mounted the two sagging steps to the shabby wooden structure.

The close proximity of the clamorous Indians intimidated and repulsed her. She regarded them with the same deep loathing she normally reserved for cockroaches, rats, spiders, snakes, and other lowly vermin. When a baldheaded, paunchy, stern-faced gentleman dressed in a severe black suit came forward to greet her, she gasped in relief.

"Miss Livingston?" Apparently, he had received the message she'd sent ahead to inform him of her impending arrival.

"You must be Mr. Lawrie Tatum, the Indian agent," she responded. "The man I've come so far to see."

"I'm not the Indian agent for long, Miss Livingston. I am being replaced by someone whose political beliefs more closely correspond to the expectations of the people who sent me—The Society of Friends."

"You are a Quaker, then?"

Lawrie Tatum nodded and ushered her into the building. In Tatum's spartan office, Grace heard his whole story over tea and stale bread. Like so many other agents employed by the Office of Indian Affairs, Tatum belonged to a religious denomination who considered it their duty to protect the mistreated aborigines from the vengeful army and western whites.

He had arrived at the agency in July of '69, knowing nothing about the Indians but believing God would provide all the needed information. He had done his duty and tried hard to protect his charges from those who believed "The only good Indian is a dead Indian."

Over time, as the Indians committed one atrocity after another, he had come to realize that force was the only thing they respected and understood—hence, the only way to deal with them.

As they sat stiffly on plain, hard, wooden chairs and balanced their cups on their knees, Mr. Tatum revealed his earnest agitation. "Since I've been here my charges at Fort Sill have stolen sixteen thousand, five hundred horses and mules out of Texas, and shamelessly boasted about it. They have burnt, raped, pillaged, plundered, and massacred all over the region, sometimes taking captives for the sole purpose of returning them to me for a reward, or to use them as pawns to obtain the release of their own relatives held by the soldiers."

"That's terrible! No wonder you were forced to change your views."

"I dare not tell you some of the awful things they've done," he said, and told her anyway, describing in vivid detail how the Indians had tortured a wounded teamster during an attack on a freight train. Imagining what they would have done to *her* if they'd attacked the wagon outside, Grace gagged on the stale bread he had provided.

"While I cannot condone reprisals," he continued, "I have tried in my own way to control my charges by withholding their annuities and food supplies, which are hardly enough to feed them, anyway. Sometimes they don't even arrive. The new agent, who should be here any day now to take my place, will have his hands full, I can promise you."

"But what precisely led to your dismissal?" Grace prompted, anxious to hear of recent events at the agency.

"Why, I allowed the arrest of the three leaders who conducted that wagon train massacre and *bragged* about it in my presence. I permitted army officials onto the reservation to arrest the culprits, and they've been taken back to Texas to stand trial. Furthermore, I asked the army to help round up the bands who still refuse to come into the reservation. As a result, I've been dismissed. My superiors were incensed. They've never approved of having army guards here at the agency. Yet how else am I to control these savages? Perhaps, had I acted sooner—sided with the army, instead of the Friends—I might have averted these tragedies before they happened. Unless one has lived here and witnessed the problems firsthand, one can't possibly understand."

He almost broke down in tears, and Grace leaned over and patted his arm in a comforting manner. "There . . . there, Mr. Tatum. I understand. I truly do. You came here with such high ideals, believing that gentleness and honesty would solve all problems, and instead discovered that force was needed. But then you are dealing with ferocious unprincipled heathens, not timid lost lambs from a wayward flock."

"That's it exactly, Miss Livingston. As I've tried to tell my superiors, I can't stand idly by preaching peace when war is waging all about me. In time, and with proper education of their young—the removal of small children from the influence of their elders, for example—future generations of Indians may come to see the error of their ways and be ready to embrace our teachings, but for now . . ."

"They must be hunted down like wild dogs. The price of their crimes can only be extermination."

Lawrie Tatum swallowed hard. He looked at Grace as if she'd suddenly reared up and stabbed him. But Grace had heard enough by now to convince her that the savages must be subdued, by whatever means necessary. Whenever she thought of gentle Ellie and her innocent children among them, she felt a rage so bone-deep and ravenous that it blotted out all other considerations. If only she could rescue Ellie she didn't care what happened to the Indians; they deserved whatever suffering befell them.

"Mr. Tatum," she said gently. "I've come all the way from Boston to try to rescue my sister and her children from the murdering Comanches. Please, can you help me? Can you tell me how best to go about it?"

But Lawrie Tatum couldn't. Instead he gave her a stern lecture on all the reasons why she must remain at the fort in company with the few officers' wives in residence, until her relatives were returned or some word was heard about them. She certainly couldn't set off on her own looking for them, and he could think of no one who'd be willing to take her. No whites except the soldiers—and the buffalo hunters, who were every bit as wild and vicious as the Comanches—dared venture into Comancheria these days; the Indians loved nothing better than to kill trespassers.

"What about the soldiers?" Grace demanded. "They should have mounted a search for my family as soon as they heard of the attack on their wagon train."

"My dear, there are too many of these attacks for the army to handle. Fort Sill has barely enough soldiers to defend it properly. Why, until Colonel Mackenzie took over command of the 4th Cavalry, the soldiers received hardly any training."

"Colonel Mackenzie?"

"Yes, Colonel Ranald S. Mackenzie. He's the one who took the three Indian leaders—they were Kiowas, not Comanches, by the way—back to Texas. He's currently scouring the plains for the rebellious bands who refuse to honor the treaty of 'sixty-seven, wherein we granted reservations to the Indians and promised them annuities in exchange for their lands."

"If he's out scouring the plains, why can't he conduct a search to find my relatives?"

"Miss Livingston, he's the only one who could possibly find your relatives. However, his mission is one of destruction, not rescue. He tries to burn villages and capture the large horse herds of the Indians, so that they can't hunt or roam the plains at will. Of course he attempts to save white captives when he finds them, but, as you can imagine, in the heat of battle it isn't always easy to distinguish between whites and Indians. White captives are often killed instead of rescued. In any case, it will be months before Colonel Mackenzie returns to Fort Sill so that you can even discuss the matter with him. By next winter, perhaps—"

"I cannot wait until next winter, Mr. Tatum. You must think

of someone else who can help me. These buffalo hunters you mentioned . . ."

"Filthy loathsome butchers, Miss Livingston. In my opinion, a lower class of people than the Comanches."

"I have money. I'm willing to pay—"

"Don't mention money! Not to anyone. All the buffalo hunters care about is money. If you attempt to deal with them, you're apt to lose both your fortune and your life."

"But surely there's *some*one who knows the Comanches, understands their language and their ways, and could guide me into Comancheria." His sternly disapproving expression gave her pause. "Or go himself, to see if he can locate my sister and her children . . ."

"It's not possible for a single man to enter Comancheria and come out alive, Miss Livingston. Come to think of it, I do know someone who knows the Comanches. Indeed, he once lived among them and adhered to their ways."

"He sounds like the ideal person!"

"No, I wouldn't say that! I only mention him because he could verify everything I'm telling you. However, he may be unwilling to do even that."

"For heaven's sake, why?"

Mr. Tatum shrugged. "Matthew Stone is a strange hard man. As boys he and his brother were captured by Comanches. They grew up among them and were adopted. One day not long after I first arrived here, Mr. Stone walked into the agency and declared in halting English that he had left the Indians, including his brother, and was now going to live as a white man. . . . He wouldn't say why. Refused to discuss the matter. All he wanted was a job so he could earn his keep. I took him over to the fort commander, who sent him out to catch wild horses for the army—to replace the ones the Indians are always stealing. . . . He works long and hard, catching horses and breaking them. Learned the skill from the Comanches, who can do anything they please with a horse. Mr. Stone finally bought himself a ranch on the edge of Comancheria, but he hasn't done much with it. Costs a lot of money to purchase cattle and put in crops."

"Why do you insist he's not ideal? He sounds exactly like the person I'm looking for." Indeed, Grace thought, if he were poor, so much the better for her purposes.

"Well, as I said, he's strange. The Comanches left their mark on him. To my knowledge he's never harmed anyone, but he presents the appearance of being fierce and savage. Doesn't talk much and drives strangers away from his land with a gun. He used to come and borrow books from me. Taught himself to read, write, and speak proper English—better than most around here. Said he'd forgotten most of what he learned as a child, so he had to start over. I invited him for supper a couple times, but he never wanted to stay long. His eyes are . . . troubled, as if he's seen more horror in life than most folks. If he has, he won't discuss it. It can be terribly lonely out here, Miss Livingston, and Matt Stone is the loneliest man I know."

Grace set down her cup. "Where does he live? How do I go about meeting him?"

"Oh, you don't want to go all the way out to his place. It's a two hour ride south of here, in an area unsafe for traveling. And Mr. Stone is usually out rounding up wild mustangs for the army, not sitting at home waiting for visitors. You'll have to wait to meet him until he comes to the fort to deliver a batch of horses."

"I can't waste time sitting around a fort." Grace rose with a swish of her skirts. "Thank you so much for the tea and information, Mr. Tatum, but—"

Mr. Tatum also rose. "Miss Livingston, forget about Matt Stone and wait for Colonel Mackenzie's return. It may take a while, but your safety is more important than . . ."

Just then, a soldier burst through the doorway. Red-faced and gasping, he blurted: "Painted Horse has struck again!"

Mr. Tatum turned pale. "That thieving rascal! What's he done this time?"

"Broke up a camp of buffalo hunters and stole all their

horses. Just rode right in and took 'em. Happened a couple nights ago. The hunters only just made it back to the fort."

"Who is Painted Horse?" Grace glanced from one agitated man to the other.

The soldier—a mere boy with freckles and protruding front teeth—turned to her excitedly. "Why, some say he's a phantom Comanche, a vengeful spirit. Others insist he's real."

"He's real, all right." Mr. Tatum set down his cup with a clank. "He performs astonishing feats of horsemanship on his big painted stallion, while stealing cattle and horses that often turn up right here among the reservation Indians when their annuities come late, or not at all. His particular mission is harassing the buffalo hunters, because the buffalo are the mainstay of the rebel Indians still refusing to come onto the reservation. In short, he's a criminal, and one more good reason why you must remain at the fort and leave the search for your family members to the U.S. Army."

"There are no such things as phantoms, Mr. Tatum," Grace scoffed. "And if the army permits this Painted Horse to break the law right beneath their noses I can hardly expect them to succeed in the task of finding my relatives, can I?"

"You've no other choice, Miss Livingston. The freight wagon that brought you here will leave for the fort soon, and you must be on it. When you arrive there, the women will look after you until Colonel Mackenzie's return."

"Thanks for your good advice, Mr. Tatum." *Which I utterly reject.* "If you'll excuse me, gentlemen, my business here is concluded. Good day to both of you."

Maneuvering her chocolate velvet skirt, which was trimmed with silk, chenille, and moire in the latest fashion, Grace left the two men earnestly discussing the army's most recent failure to meet its obligation of protecting U. S. citizens in Indian Territory. Marching outside, she discovered that the men aboard the freight wagon were still unloading its contents to the grabbing Indians, who seemed to be grumbling about the quantity—

or quality—of the goods they had thus far received. Such in-
grates!

Fortunately, her own belongings had been separated from the
supplies and now stood at the back end of the wagon, awaiting
transport to the fort. No one noticed Grace as she strolled
around the side of the building.

There stood a hitching post with three saddled horses tied to
it. Grace eyed the horses with great interest and only a little
misgiving. Back home in Boston she kept two carriages, but
had never had occasion to mount a horse. Now seemed a good
time to learn to ride; no one was watching the horses, either.
Mr. Tatum had said that Mr. Stone lived south of the fort. The
angle of the sun peeking through the puffy white clouds overhead suggested that it was only noon. Grace figured she ought
to be able to ride out to Mr. Stone's, talk to him, and still return
to the fort before dark.

She chose a horse that looked sleepy and unlikely to give
trouble. It was brown and matched her gown and bonnet. Taking
its reins, which were only looped over the railing, anyway, she
led the animal around to the back of the furthest building that
made up the agency compound.

She didn't see a soul, so she hitched up her skirts, fought her
undergarments into submission, and climbed aboard. She immediately realized she wasn't dressed for the occasion. Her stylish garments made straddling an army saddle almost an
impossibility. But Grace hadn't earned her nickname for nothing; lifting her skirts, she yanked out a couple of steel half-
hoops, tossed them on the ground, then determinedly sat on the
rest of her unwieldy clothing and set out across the prairie.

Her horse had only one gait: a jarring trot that bounced her
all over its back. The slower she tried to get the animal to go,
the faster it went, but Grace managed to steer it in a southerly
direction. The feather of her bonnet dipped low over her eyes,
obscuring her vision, but she didn't dare let go of the reins long
enough to push it away.

Threatening the horse with dire consequences should it fail

to obey her commands, she hung on for dear life and rode away
from the agency to find Mr. Matthew Stone, the only man who
could possibly help her find her sister, niece, and nephew.

Three

Matt rubbed his hand along the colt's sweaty neck, praising it for a job well done, then swung down from the saddle. It was getting late; he should quit for the day. Besides, the sorrel colt had had enough. He was pleased with its progress. The youngster was now ready to be turned over to the army, along with a dozen others Matt had been training for them. When mounted the colt no longer bucked, though he still laid his ears back and threatened to bite when the girth was drawn tight around his mid-section.

Matt made a mental note to warn Grierson at the fort to assign the colt to somebody with a little patience who didn't demand too much, too soon, from a young horse. Given more time, this one would make a willing trustworthy mount.

Looping the reins around one hand, Matt opened the gate to the breaking pen and led the colt across the yard.

Watching his approach from his own private turnout, his stallion, Renegade, nickered and leaned against the top railing. He flattened his ears at the colt, letting him know who was boss at the ranch. His actions told Matt he was jealous of the attention the newcomer was getting. It had only been a couple of nights since Matt had ridden him to rout a bunch of hunters trailing the buffalos headed for the northern grasslands, but Renegade was greedy.

The stallion would happily have gone out every night, for he relished the long gallops across the open plain as much as Matt did. He also enjoyed rounding up stolen horses and driving them south toward the Staked Plain for the Comanches to find; Matt had done that with the horses belonging to the buffalo hunters. He hadn't dared risk bringing them back to the ranch or passing them onto the reservation Indians; the hunters had been riding easily recognizable painted horses.

None had been as fine as Renegade, but a couple were decent, Comanche-trained buffalo runners, which had only increased his fury. He resented it when white men rode Indian horses to catch and slay the very animals that had once supported the plains tribes.

This year the hunters had started early in the season, and Matt hoped that his pre-dawn raid would serve as a warning to others yet to come. The hides weren't even worth much at this time of year; it could only be pure spite that drove the hunters—and a desire to kill every last buffalo so the free Indians must surrender at last.

Renegade nickered insistently while Matt put away the colt. Depositing his saddle on the porch railing of the house, he walked over to the stallion and scratched along his neck beneath his mane, which Renegade particularly enjoyed. Renegade responded by sticking his head over the railing and playfully butting Matt in the chest. Ears pricking forward, the stallion suddenly paused and gazed out onto the plain. Matt turned to see what had captured the horse's interest.

Far out on the horizon, a solitary figure trudged in their direction. Unaccustomed to visitors, especially on foot, Matt expelled a low whistle of surprise. Even at a distance, he could tell the figure was a female; she wore a long full skirt and a feather-trimmed bonnet. And she was limping, as if she'd come a long way.

She surely needed help, but Matt couldn't dash to her assistance until he'd taken time to disguise Renegade. He couldn't risk having someone recognize the stallion. Blue-eyed horses weren't all that uncommon, but few were Medicine Hats like

Renegade. The wanted posters for Painted Horse contained a good description of the stallion's distinctive markings.

Quickly, Matt climbed over the railing and entered the pen. Thinking he had come to ride, Renegade followed him around the enclosure like a well-trained hound. Matt led him into a corner out of sight from the approaching woman, where the house blocked her view. Scooping up dirt in both hands, he rubbed it into the stallion's white coat, making it blend with his patches of color. Matt preferred using ashes and dye made from berries, a trick he had learned from the Comanches, but he had no time for that now.

He worked fast, and had just finished when he heard the woman calling him—by name! Somehow she knew his white name, an ominous sign.

"Mr. Stone? I know you're here. I saw you. And I'm sure you saw me. . . . Mr. Stone! I'm not going to go away, so you might as well come out and face me."

Whoever she was, she was mighty determined. And angry. Her voice had a knife's edge quality, as if she intended to cut out his heart when she saw him. Wiping his hands on his buckskin trousers, Matt left Renegade's pen and walked around the house to meet her.

Grace was furious. She *knew* that man had seen her; he'd been petting his horse, stopped, and glanced in her direction. Then, for no apparent reason, he had completely ignored her, climbed into the pen with the horse, and moved out of sight.

She could see him now—walking toward her around the side of his shack and behaving as if he'd only just discovered her presence. She watched him come, his long, lithe body moving in a way she had never before seen a man's body move. Every joint, muscle, and tendon appeared to have been oiled to make it more supple.

He wore buff-colored, fringed buckskins, and his long, copper-colored hair was pulled back from his temples and secured at the back of his neck. Like hers, his eyes were hazel, but his had glints of pure green. She thought them cold—cold as winter, and as unfathomable as an Indian's.

Nowhere near as dark as the Indians she had seen at the fort, he still reminded her of a savage, not merely because of his dress and hairstyle, but because of his expression. He looked as if he spent all his time outdoors; the elements had streaked his hair with red-gold highlights and etched character lines deep into his face. She saw no gentleness in him, no tolerance, no suggestion of humor, no inclination toward kindness. This man was as hard as the country that had bred him. She could only guess at the life he had known, and she didn't want him to see that he intimidated her. The fact that he *did* angered her. She had learned to converse easily with men who governed nations and industries; who was this prairie lord to make her shiver in her too-tight shoes?

"Mr. Stone!" She infused his name with all the loathing and fear he inspired in her.

His brow lifted ever so slightly. He didn't have the courtesy to acknowledge his own name! Or to wonder what a woman on foot was doing all alone on the plain. She wasn't about to confide that she'd been dumped on her backside by an unruly horse and forced to hobble the rest of the way there to see him. Nor would she reveal that she was weary, footsore, hungry, thirsty, and incredibly relieved to encounter another human being. She had so feared he might be off somewhere, tracking horses, and her long walk would be for naught. "Don't you want to know why I'm here?" she burst out, annoyed by his silence and lack of curiosity.

"I expect you'll tell me when you're ready."

His voice didn't surprise her; like the man himself, it suggested danger.

"I came to offer you employment." She resorted to the haughty tone she used when it became necessary to impress a man who considered himself grander than a mere female. It usually cut the fellow down to size; he would suddenly realize he wasn't dealing with some country bumpkin.

Matthew Stone didn't look impressed. Didn't even ask what employment she was offering. Turning on his heel, he silently walked—glided—away.

"Mr. Stone!"

He stopped, but didn't bother to face her. "I already work for the army. I don't need another job."

He resumed walking, and Grace completely lost her temper. Running after him, she raised her fist and gave him a good hard thump on the shoulder—a shoulder that was higher than hers by a good three inches. With the speed and force of lightning, he spun around and seized her wrists.

"Don't ever do that to a man you don't know, lady. It's a good way to get yourself killed."

Staring up into his cruel green eyes, Grace conceded that death was a distinct possibility. He looked on the verge of killing her. "My name is Grace Elizabeth Livingston, and I'll thank you not to break my wrists, Mr. Stone."

Releasing her, he stepped back, but not before she saw a flicker of something on his face. Could it be admiration? He must have been expecting tears, pleas, or other evidence of female weakness. He didn't know her very well. She had learned years ago to submerge all evidence of her sex. Once a man sensed softness in a woman, he only used it to his advantage.

"Your house is little more than a poor man's shanty," she sneered. "On my long walk to your ranch this afternoon, I saw no cattle grazing on your land or crops growing. I can only conclude that the army doesn't pay very well."

"And you *do?*" The question reeked of sarcasm.

"I could turn this pitiful excuse for a ranch into the biggest, richest spread in all of North America," she boasted without a shred of shame. She intended to breech his wall of indifference any way she could.

"Where's your horse?" he suddenly demanded.

The change of subject startled her. "My horse?"

"How did you get out here? Don't tell me you walked all the way from Fort Sill."

"I didn't walk all the way. I rode, or tried to. The beast I chose to carry me wasn't very cooperative."

His eyes narrowed. Apparently he'd never experienced such a problem. "Where did you get the animal?"

"I . . . borrowed it."

"Borrowed it?" His hard-eyed gaze cut her like a whip. "I'd never let you near my horses. The way you're dressed doesn't inspire confidence that you know what you're doing."

Grace disliked the direction of the conversation. Somehow, he had taken control of it. "You're quite right, Mr. Stone. I've never before ridden a horse. Moreover, whoever owns the beast—I believe it's the army—hasn't the faintest idea I borrowed it. No one even knows I'm here."

She wondered if she ought to admit that, then decided it showed confidence.

"Why *are* you here?"

At last, Grace thought, they were getting somewhere. "I want to hire you to find my sister and her children. The Comanches captured them late last summer. If they're still alive I wish to rescue them. The savages killed my sister's husband. Now she has no one but me to care what happens to her and the youngsters."

"If she's still alive, she has the Comanches. By now she's someone's wife or slave. Her children have been adopted into someone else's family. They're as good as dead, Miss—or is it Mrs.?—Grace Elizabeth Livingston. Didn't they tell you all that at the fort?"

"It's *Miss* Livingston, and I didn't get as far as the fort. I only got as far as the Indian agency. Mr. Lawrie Tatum told me much the same thing. Like you, he failed to understand that I'll go out and find the Comanches myself, if I have to, but I *will* discover what happened to my sister and her children."

"More likely the Comanches will find you first and lift your scalp before you ever get a chance to ask them about your relatives."

"I don't doubt it. That's why I need you. You could take me. The Comanches know you. You know them. I realize the idea may not appeal to you, but my sister and her children—who are still quite small—will need my assistance. Like it or not, I *must* accompany you. As the result of her ordeal, Ellie may be distraught. And the children will require the care and comfort only another woman can give."

Matthew Stone heaved a deep sigh. He studied the setting sun. The western horizon was now aglow, painting the tips of the distant mountains a fiery red. His frown told Grace he wasn't admiring the spectacle. At last, his gaze skewered her, his eyes showing no sympathy or willingness to assist her.

"My services as a guide through Comancheria aren't for sale, Miss Livingston. I refuse to take you. What's more, you're a fool to have stolen someone's horse and ridden out here when you don't even know how to ride. You're lucky you made it this far. The Comanches or a bad fall could have killed you. It's too bad about your sister, but if she's as headstrong and foolish as you are, she probably asked for the trouble she found."

"She didn't *ask* for anything! She and her husband were just passing through Indian Territory on their way to California, and the bloodthirsty savages attacked them for no good reason. They *hacked* poor William to death. The good Lord only knows what they've done to Ellie, Emily, and Jonathan. . . . What kind of man are you that you can deny my request? I'd be willing to pay you almost anything—and it's quite obvious you need the money!"

He again seized her wrists, his grip so punishing that her bones creaked in protest. Confronting her nose to nose, he spoke in a tone so low she how wondered she could hear him, yet each word fell like the blow of a hammer.

"Listen, you little eastern snob. The Comanches have good reason for attacking people who trespass on their land. White men have starved them, lied to them, and stolen all they own.

I may be a white, too, but in my eyes, Quanah Parker is a hero, not a bloodthirsty savage. Whatever he's done he's been forced to do. He's the finest human being I've ever known."

"This Quanah Parker," she shot back. "Is he the leader of the rebel Comanches?"

"Yes. He's one of the few your kind haven't yet managed to kill or capture."

"Then he's the man I want to find. If anyone knows what's happened to Ellie, he will. Take me to him, and I'll stock this sorry excuse for a ranch with five hundred head of prime cattle, the best available."

He shoved her away from him. She tripped over her skirts, but managed to maintain her footing by sheer force of will.

"Go back to Fort Sill. Take it up with Colonel Mackenzie. From all I've heard, he's the only man capable of bringing whites out of Comancheria alive."

"That's what Mr. Tatum said, but I don't believe it." Grace rubbed her aching wrist. "You could do it if you wanted to."

"I don't want to."

"Why not? Haven't I offered you enough? All right, I'll also replace your shack with a house that wouldn't be out of place in Boston on the street where I live. I'll build you a proper barn, too, and supply all the fencing you could ever want or need."

His upper lip curled contemptuously. "Just how rich are you, Miss Livingston?"

"Rich enough to do all I promise and never feel the pinch. . . . Have we a deal, Mr. Stone?" To her great astonishment, he again spun on his heel and strode toward his house. "Mr. Stone! I demand an answer, sir. If you don't want what I've offered, what in heaven's name *do* you want?"

He halted and very slowly turned back to face her, his expression so fierce that the muscles of her abdomen contracted. "I want you and every other white—opportunist and do-gooder alike—to go back east where you come from. I want you to leave this land to the people who love it, the ones who've lived here for centuries before you ever discovered it. I want to hear the thunder of buffalo hooves on the plain again and be able to ride from the Arkansas to the Rio Grande without seeing a single ranch, fort, settlement, or piece of trash left by a white man. *That's* what I want, Miss Livingston. Can you give me that?"

"I can't stop progress, Mr. Stone."

"Progress? I'm not talking about progress. I'm talking about *destruction.* Like most whites, you don't know the difference."

"Just what do you expect me to do—leave my sister and her children to starve among your precious, misunderstood savages? I'm not responsible for whatever wrongs have been done to the Indians, but *they* are responsible for depriving me of my relatives. I want them back, or at least to find out what happened to them. Is that so terrible? . . . . We don't have to *like* each other to do business. I don't care if you hate me. I don't think too much of you, either. That's beside the point. Just say you'll help me, and I'll make you a very rich man. If you want to, you can give all the cattle to the starving Indians. When it's all over, I intend to take my family back to Boston and forget I ever saw this wretched country."

"Go see Colonel Mackenzie. Maybe he'll appreciate your generosity. I sure as hell don't."

"Colonel Mackenzie is out killing Indians and won't return before Christmas. While he's killing Indians, he's probably also killing white captives. He's gotten permission to do whatever he pleases, and apparently his main goal is destruction, not rescue."

"Permission . . . ? Just what do you mean—*permission?"*

Sensing a crack in Mr. Stone's armor, Grace quickly took advantage of it. "I overheard some soldiers talking at the agency. It seems Colonel Mackenzie has been given approval to exterminate the rebel Comanches as if they were rodents. I asked Mr. Tatum about it, and he confirmed that Colonel Mackenzie is deliberately razing Indian villages and shooting Indian horses in a concerted effort to bring the Comanches to their knees."

A muscle leapt in Matthew Stone's jaw. The news greatly

disturbed him, and Grace realized she'd been using all the wrong weapons. "If you care so much for the Comanches, why don't you avail yourself of this opportunity to persuade them to surrender and come into the fort before they are all dead—and their white captives along with them?"

He scowled at her a long moment before answering. "Mackenzie will never find their villages. They have hiding places all over the *Llano Estacado*. If the worst happens they can always head down to Mexico."

Grace slipped her hands behind her back and crossed her fingers, praying that the Almighty would understand why she had to lie and forgive her for it. "The soldiers said Mackenzie was headed for Mexico. Do you mean to say he's not permitted to pursue the Indians across the border? It seems to me Mexico would appreciate some help in dealing with the savages. Their experiences with the Indians must be as bad as ours."

"You heard that? You actually heard that Mackenzie was headed for the border?"

Mr. Stone avidly watched her.

"I . . . I refuse to answer that. Perhaps I've revealed more than I should. Perhaps the soldiers were merely gossiping, or I . . . I misunderstood what I overheard."

He took a step toward her. "Miss Livingston, if you have any hope of persuading me to help you, you'd better answer me truthfully. Did the soldiers or Tatum himself say that MacKenzie has permission to pursue the Indians into Mexico?"

"Why is it so important to you, Mr. Stone? If I answer yes, will you change your mind about accompanying me into Comancheria? And if I answer no, will you still refuse?"

"I want to know the truth, damn you. Tell me the truth."

His hands were clenched at his sides. He looked as if he wanted to grab her by the neck and throttle the truth out of her. Grace almost admitted she was making it all up. Then she remembered Ellie and decided that anything she did or said, any lies she told, were fully justified. Her usual honesty wasn't working. Out here all the rules were different, and money hardly seemed to matter.

"I don't know if the colonel has *orders* to go into Mexico, but I'd say he's been given tacit approval. No matter what laws he breaks or atrocities he commits, his superiors will look the other way. The savages have gone too far, Mr. Stone. The country, the president, and the army have had enough. So have I and every other decent, law-abiding citizen."

His eyes reminded her of a wild animal's, how she imagined they might look, especially if the animal was being hunted. It was time to end this.

"Do you accept my offer of employment?"

"I'll think about it! But if I do decide to go after your sister, I won't take you along. You'd only slow me down and cause a bellyful of problems. You can't even stay on a horse."

"If you don't take me, the deal is off," she calmly countered. "I've told you. Ellie and the children will need me. Now that I've met you, Mr. Stone, I realize I could never entrust their well-being on the homeward journey entirely to you." When his brow arched menacingly, she hastily added: "You'd drive them too hard, I'm sure."

"No one could drive them as hard as you could, Miss Livingston. I've never met a woman so determined."

The air between them vibrated with tensions Grace could not identify. She'd never before experienced such intensity with a man—or anyone. Certainly not with Roger. She was even acutely aware of him physically. Mr. Stone was so tall, so broad-shouldered and slim-hipped. So powerful and predatory. In his formfitting buckskins, he exuded masculinity and made her uncomfortably conscious of her own deeply buried femininity. He could easily overpower her, and the thought simultaneously thrilled and scared her.

But he can't out-maneuver me; I won't allow it.

"If you wish, I'd be willing to purchase half the cattle I promised you now, before we depart, and the other half when we return," she said, to break the silence stretching awkwardly between them. "However, if you leave without me, you won't get a thing."

His response was to fold his arms across his formidable chest and laugh in her face She had thought him incapable of laughter, but this bitter amusement suited his volatile, unpredictable nature. A green sparkle lit his eyes, and his mouth curved sensuously, giving him, for a brief moment, a devastatingly handsome aspect that quite unnerved her.

"I haven't said I accept your bargain, Miss Livingston. I've only promised to think about it, so don't celebrate your victory too soon."

"When will you make up your mind? I'm not prepared to wait very long, Mr. Stone."

"A couple of days, at most. In the meantime, go back to Fort Sill and harass the soldiers for more information on Mackenzie's plans. They'll be no match for you."

Once again Grace noted her surroundings. By now the sun had set, and the air had a bite to it. The wind had died down, but she could sense the cold lying in wait. In twenty minutes or less, it would be completely dark.

"How do you expect me to get back to the fort at this late hour?" She was hoping he would offer her the loan of a wagon or a cart. She hadn't driven before either, but driving had to be safer than riding, especially in these wide open spaces where there was no danger of tight corners or traffic.

"Why, I don't know, Miss Livingston. The same way you got here, I guess."

Grace snapped her head around so fast to look at him that she got a crick in her neck. "You can't be serious."

He was. The look he gave her was long and challenging. He wanted—*expected*—her to beg. His desire to prove his superiority and force her to admit she was only female and therefore weak, needy, and inferior, was stronger than most men's. Sooner or later men just *had* to demonstrate that they were the stronger, wiser, more competent sex.

Grace hadn't met anyone as infuriating as Matthew Stone,

but she had encountered hundreds of men who had underestimated her on first meeting and been forced to revise their opinions later. She sincerely doubted that Mr. Stone would actually permit a woman to walk all the way back to the fort by herself in the middle of the night. She would call his bluff by pretending she didn't care in the least what he did.

"All right, Mr. Stone, I'm going. Don't keep me waiting long for your answer, or I'm apt to leave for Comancheria without you—in which case you'll *never* get those cattle I promised or a brand new house."

Shivering from the cold but determined not to let him see it, Grace picked up her skirts and headed back toward the open plain. She forbade herself to limp, and managed to conceal the discomfort from the blisters on her toes and heels. She didn't know how far she'd have to walk before Matthew Stone relented and came after her, but she was determined to remain calm, dignified, and self-possessed, whatever happened.

Unfortunately, the ground was rocky and uneven, and she stumbled frequently. The gathering darkness hid rocks and prairie dog holes. Briars snagged her skirt and tore at her petticoats. For a long time, Grace didn't look back to see if Matthew Stone was watching her uncertain progress. By the time she succumbed to curiosity, she could no longer see his ranch, and she certainly couldn't see *him* coming after her.

Night had swallowed the prairie. Only the distant illumination of stars lit her way. All she had to do was keep walking north. Eventually she would reach Fort Sill and the Indian Agency. She mustn't become confused and forget which way was north, because if she deviated too much from the proper direction, Mr. Stone could never find her when—*if*—he came. *What if he didn't come?*

Grace imagined herself crawling into Fort Sill on her hands and knees, her feet bloody stumps, ground down to the bone. She wondered if she would be so eager to do business with Mr. Stone if he forced her to walk all the way back to Fort Sill. A two hour horseback ride translated into twice that much walking or more, depending on whether the horse was walking, trotting, or galloping for two hours. Before being dumped, she had managed to stay on the horse for at least an hour; she had the sore muscles and backside to prove it. Given time, she knew she could master riding—but she suddenly wasn't at all sure she could manage trudging back to Fort Sill alone in the cold night.

She wasn't accustomed to such vigorous exercise. Moreover, she'd had nothing to eat since Mr. Tatum's stale bread and tea. Longingly, she thought of the simple but hearty meals the soldiers had prepared on her trip from Dodge City. One specialty had been fluffy biscuits prepared in an iron skillet. Combined with strong hot coffee and a kind of porridge made from corn meal, the biscuits had kept her from starving in her haste to get to Fort Sill.

Unbeknownst to anyone, she had slipped the soldiers a generous sum of money to get her there as fast as possible, and they had hardly stopped except to camp late at night.

That was another thing . . . her money. With every step she took, it weighed her down. Her private seamstress had sewn large inner pockets in her gowns, so she could carry money at all times on her person and be prepared for anything. She didn't have enough on her at the moment to buy Mr. Stone's cattle, but it felt as if she did. The weight had hampered her riding, and without the hoops she had discarded, her full heavy skirts now dragged at her.

Grace debated whether or not to leave a trail of discarded gold coins and paper bills on the prairie. Despite her reckless boasts to Mr. Stone, she was the sort of woman who never spent the smallest coin without calculation. Frivolous expenditures held no appeal, and she disliked the idea of tossing good money to the four winds.

Grimly, she pressed on, ignoring the heaviness of her skirts, the soreness of her feet, and the tiny kernel of fear swelling in her stomach. She was Grace Elizabeth Livingston—Amazing Grace. And once she had set her mind on something, she *never* gave up.

Four

Matt had no intention of going after Grace Livingston until at least a couple hours after moonrise. If he were to seriously consider taking her with him to search for her relatives among the Comanches, he might as well find out now what kind of backbone she had. He would never agree to haul her around Comancheria without first testing her ability to handle danger, fear, and hardship; how she behaved tonight would tell him whether he dared risk it or not.

As he made his preparations, dressing as a Comanche, carefully grooming Renegade, then painting himself and the horse with war paint, Matt thought about Grace Livingston and her amazing offer.

Regardless of her arguments or any possible financial rewards, he was only willing to consider going at all because of the information she had brought. Time was running out for the Comanches; if Mackenzie *had* been given permission to cross the Mexican border to destroy them, Quanah would have to act *now* to salvage the bargaining power he had already lost by refusing to parley in the past. He must be induced to surrender before Mackenzie caught up with him; only then would the Comanches stand a chance of retaining control over any portion of their ancestral lands.

If, however, the Comanches continued fighting and staunchly refused to make an effort to form a lasting peace, Matt knew what would happen. Most of the Indians would die; those who somehow managed to survive would have no say whatever in their futures. In all likelihood they wouldn't be allowed to live anywhere *near* their ancestral lands.

Even Lawrie Tatum—a man of religion, sworn to peace, who had tried to befriend the Indians—had finally decided the Comanches were doomed and could no longer be protected. Tatum had allowed soldiers onto the reservation to arrest the Indians accused of crimes they might or might not have committed.

Matt had done all he could to feed the starving Indians, but he could no longer prolong the inevitable or fight their battles single-handedly. Like so many other tribes who occupied land the white men wanted, the Comanches had arrived at the point where they had to concede defeat and negotiate for the best terms possible. It was time for Painted Horse to return to the People and persuade them to see reason before it was too late.

While he was at it he might as well rescue some poor white woman and her kids, but he'd be damned if he'd accept Grace Livingston's money! This was something a man did for his own reasons. The thought of getting paid for it, by a bossy female yet, did not sit well with him.

Miss Livingston thought her money could buy anything, but no man he respected—white or Indian—would agree to take orders from a woman in exchange for money. Men provided for women, not the other way around. Among the Comanches when a man wanted to marry, he brought horses to a girl's family to pay for the privilege. After marriage he provided meat, hides, and trinkets. Even in the white world women depended on men for food, shelter, clothing, protection—indeed, their very survival. Just who did Miss Livingston think she was, offering to *buy* his services?

She had insulted him by remarking on his poverty and flaunting her wealth in his face. Matt had only held his tongue because he had wanted to see how far this uppity spoiled female would go. With every word she uttered Grace Livingston had further infuriated him. Assuming he accepted her offer, he'd let her think he was doing it for the cattle and the fine house. But when the time came for her to deliver on her promises he would coldly inform her that Matt Stone wasn't for sale, and never had been. He wouldn't touch her damn money if she begged him to take it!

Oh, he wanted the cattle. And the big house, barn, and fencing. But he didn't want those things from *her;* he preferred to get them for himself. If she wanted to express her gratitude, she could do it in the time-honored manner of women since the dawn of time. She could give him . . . softness. Femininity. Gentleness and yielding flesh.

Considering his experience with his Comanche wife, he no longer expected loyalty or faithfulness from women, but an hour of warmth and intimacy beneath a blanket or buffalo robe was something he still craved. He'd be willing to accept *that,* even from a woman who didn't appeal to him otherwise. Unfortunately, Grace Livingston didn't seem to realize she *was* a woman and capable of affording physical comfort. She might wear a huge, ridiculous skirt and a silly hat totally unsuited to her environment, but she had learned to think, act, and talk like a man. A white man, at that.

For all her posturing, though, she hadn't been able to conceal her basic femininity; in her huge, greenish-gold eyes Matt had glimpsed fear, uncertainty, and the desire for protection. Her bravado was a sham. She was afraid of him, the Comanches, and of going into Comancheria. So he had to know before he took her with him whether she was capable of surviving the journey or likely to panic and get them both killed.

He didn't want the responsibility for bringing two small children and another female—possibly an injured one—out of Comancheria by himself. If Miss Livingston's sister were still alive, she could very well be a crazy woman by now, used and abused by every lusty brave in the tribe.

Her children had probably fared better. Often mistreated in the first days of their captivity, children were quickly absorbed into tribal life. Exhilarated by their newfound freedom, children adopted by the Comanches—especially boys—soon did not want to leave. It had taken Matt a full year or so to stop wishing he could return to his own people, but within a few months, Thad had switched his loyalties and begun behaving as if he'd always been a Comanche. The younger the child, the sooner he forgot his origins and adapted to his new life. Miss Livingston's niece and nephew might already be reluctant to bid farewell to the Indians.

Dealing with these possibilities would be Miss Livingston's responsibility. Once he found the Comanches and delivered his own message, Matt would be ready to return to his ranch. Miss Livingston, her sister, and her sister's children could accompany him or not, as they chose. His duty would be done—and maybe at last he'd be free of the nightmares that continued to plague him.

Once the Comanche problem was solved—one way or the other—Painted Horse could quietly disappear, and Matt could concentrate on making his ranch a success with*out* the bribes of a bothersome female. One day cattle would cover his land, and he'd breed fine horses and build a big house. Perhaps he'd even marry. While his brother and Quanah Parker still fought the whites, these things were beyond him. He was going into Comancheria for himself and the Comanches, not for Miss Livingston. And now he would discover just how brave and determined his would-be companion really was.

As Matt applied dark blue hand prints to Renegade's now groomed and gleaming white coat, he couldn't help grinning. He'd gone out of his way to make himself and the horse look more savage than usual. Black war paint streaked his own face and bare chest. He had removed his buckskins, and wore only a Comanche breechclout and tall fringed moccasins made of soft deerskin with tough, buffalo hide soles.

He had darkened his hair to subdue any possible copper high-lights, entwined feathers in it, and attached two long dyed braids made from the hair he had shorn upon his return to the white world. The distinctive Comanche war helmet secured all this. Made from a bison scalp, the headdress consisted of the great, thrusting horns of the bull buffalo, which now protruded from his head in all their menace and magnificence.

He also sported his favorite necklace of bear's teeth and silver ornaments, along with silver armbands and a wicked-looking knife strapped to his thigh. By the time he finished disguising both himself and Renegade, a nearly full moon had risen, lighting the plain for his surprise visit to Miss Livingston. He only needed to fetch his lance and war shield, emblazoned with the emblem of a painted horse, and he was ready to strike terror into her female heart.

At the last moment, Matt decided to forget the lance and war shield, and keep his hands free. He had already allowed for Renegade's ease of movement; the stallion wore only a Comanche war bridle made of braided horsehair half-hitched about his jaw and a lightweight Comanche back pad with attached stirrups that allowed for great maneuverability. Matt much preferred the back pad to a conventional, heavy saddle. And of course, Renegade had a sturdy thong around his neck, so that Matt could hang off his side while the stallion galloped. To an onlooker, it would appear no one rode him, a favorite Comanche trick.

Matt mounted his horse Comanche-style—from the right. One of the hardest adjustments he had to make when he gave up his Comanche ways had been to start mounting his horses from the left side, as most white men did. Only some Mexicans, in imitation of their Spanish forbears, retained the custom of mounting a horse from the right. Matt suspected that the Indians had copied this custom, along with many other aspects of horsemanship, from the very people from whom they had first stolen horses many long years ago.

The similarities between the way the Mexicans handled horses and the way the Comanches did things still amazed him. Alone among the Indian tribes, the Comanches practiced gelding their young stallions, initially a Mexican custom, to make them more tractable.

Fortunately, no one had gelded Renegade. Probably no man had been able to get near enough to try. For whatever reason,

Matt was grateful. He intended that the stallion should one day provide him with an entire herd of painted horses. When the Indians were gone, Matt meant to keep the breed alive. The swift colorful horses of the plains deserved to be spared extinction. They were symbols of a way of life that would never come again—to either red man or white.

As Matt rode out to find Miss Livingston, he released a bloodcurdling war cry. At the signal, Renegade joyously reared, pawed the air, dropped to all fours, and broke into a flat-out gallop. White men had nothing to equal *this*, Matt thought, as the wind whistled past him and the grass flattened beneath the stallion's pounding hooves. He felt a pang of sorrow for the fast approaching day when he, too, would cease to thunder across the plain, a painted warrior on his painted steed, a man unique among men, fearing nothing, not even death. For an Indian, dying was an act to be courted, not feared; it was *how* one died that mattered. Like his brother and Quanah Parker, Matt hoped to die free and proud on his beloved plains.

Grace couldn't stand it any longer. She sat down on the hard ground and removed her shoes—those ridiculous impractical shoes! Whatever they were made for, it wasn't walking. Her feet were bleeding; she'd had a wet squishy feeling in her stockings for some time now. And that wasn't her only discomfort. Her skin had been rubbed raw in several places by her corset; the spring-latch undergarment constricted her breathing. Why did women torture themselves this way?

Back home in Boston she had never once questioned the dictates of fashion; she had prided herself on being properly attired for every occasion. The way she dressed affected people's opinion, so she had chosen simple but stylish garments and slavishly adhered to quality in their cut and construction. Now she didn't care what *any*one thought; she wished she had never worn the requisite corset that ensured a nineteen inch waist, or shoes that looked good but felt terrible.

She stripped off her wet stockings along with her shoes and flung them into the cold, prairie wind. She was so miserable that she wanted to weep. Instead she slowly got to her feet, wriggled her bare toes in the icy grass, and resumed her journey. If she made it back to the fort in one piece, she promised herself to change her wardrobe—and tell everyone there what a horrible man Matthew Stone was.

No . . . no. This predicament was *her* fault; she mustn't blame him for the agony she had brought on herself. Her success in Boston was based on a willingness to assess her own weaknesses and find a way to overcome them, or at least to compensate. Blaming others was self-defeating; it prevented one from learning from bad experiences and discovering how to avoid them in the future. She must summon all her hard-won knowledge about how to be successful in the strictly male world of business and apply it to surviving in the wilderness while rescuing her family from the Indians. If Matt Stone refused to help her, she would find someone else. While she was looking, she would learn new skills, such as riding a horse and dressing properly for long hikes across the prairie.

At least the moon had risen, and she could now see where she was going. She knew which way was north—or thought she did. Instead of dwelling on the cold or how much her feet hurt, she tried to concentrate on the beauty of the prairie. The star-studded sky arched overhead like the vault of a European cathedral, and the wind played the song of an organ, sonorous and deep. Earlier she had heard wolves calling in the distance. Fortunately they hadn't approached, nor was she aware of any other living creature save jackrabbits and occasional deer moving on the plain.

Though scared, Grace could appreciate the grandeur of the scenery. Picking her way carefully, she wondered if it would take all night to reach Fort Sill. More than ready to try riding again, she kept a sharp lookout for the horse who had unseated her. Thinking she might find the animal grazing along the way, she stopped occasionally to peer in all directions.

Suddenly, a dark shape far out on the plain caught her eye. Moonlight glinted on horns, suggesting a buffalo. As the shape drew closer, she saw it was a horse, carrying a man wearing a set of sharply-curved horns on his head—a Comanche!

Another thought occurred: *Painted Horse.*

Her bones shuddered with the certainty that this horn-bedecked figure galloping across the plain was the phantom Comanche she'd heard about at the fort . . . and he was headed straight for her!

Grace assessed her vulnerability as she had never before assessed it in her life. Not only was she shockingly unprepared—barefoot and ill-dressed—for her present circumstances, but she lacked a pistol, rifle, or other weapon to ward off attack. How had she allowed herself to come here so deficient in survival skills?

The impulse to flee thrummed in her veins. She wanted to pick up her skirts and run—anywhere, as fast as she could. But running would accomplish nothing except to betray fear; she couldn't outrun a man on a horse. But if he meant to trample her or strike her down with a club, she could make his task more difficult. If she were lucky, she might disable him.

Rocks and stones littered the plain. As she stubbed her toe against one, Grace considered the offending object as a possible weapon. Stones weren't much, but they were all she had, so she bent over and began gathering as many as she could find. Making a pouch with her skirt, she scooped them inside.

The sound of hoofbeats grew louder as the Indian swooped down on her with deadly intent. Rising, her skirt weighted with stones, Grace hurled the missiles at him as he came. Her aim was terrible, and his laughter rang out, mocking her puny efforts and devastating her self-confidence. In no time she had depleted her small arsenal.

Moments before trampling her, the Indian's horse skidded to a stop. Before Grace comprehended what was happening, the Indian himself leaned down, hooked a powerful arm around her tightly-corseted waist, and hauled her aboard the horse to sit in front of him, with her legs dangling off one side The horse leapt forward, and Grace would have toppled beneath its flying feet had the Indian not held her to him, clamped like a second skin to his nearly naked body.

She struggled a moment, then thought better of it. She'd fallen off a horse once today, risking broken bones, and didn't want to push her luck any further. Besides, fighting this Indian would be like trying to whip an oak tree. Entwining her fingers in the horse's mane, she clung to it and prayed for divine—or human—deliverance.

The horse ran for a long time, during which the Comanche's arm remained locked like a vice around Grace's midriff, just below the swell of her breasts. Her left arm and shoulder were crushed to his chest. She could feel his heartbeat, an unavoidably intimate sensation. The thought flashed in her mind that she had never before felt or heard another person's heart beating against some part of her, but then, no one else had ever embraced her this tightly.

The Indian's heart beat steadily. Her own heart raced. It seemed to be pounding in her throat, not her chest. In all the commotion her bonnet had been knocked askew, and she couldn't see, which probably accounted for the acuteness of her remaining senses. She fancied she could also hear the Indian breathing. While she gasped and panted with fear, he breathed normally, as if he kidnapped women every day of the week.

Whenever she inhaled, his scent filled her nostrils. There were no disgusting body odors, as she might have expected. Instead he smelled masculine but clean, the predominant odors being that of leather and horse. An elusive herbal fragrance also clung to him, emanating perhaps from his minimal garments—or his hair.

She didn't want to think about the wicked buffalo horns he wore on his head. She was glad she couldn't see his face. Before he'd grabbed her, she'd had only a quick impression of harsh, painted features, and darkly shadowed eyes. He was the fiercest sight she had ever beheld, and she trembled to think of being his prisoner. Trying not to panic, she wondered where he was taking her, and what he would do when they finally got there.

All at once he leaned back slightly, and the horse plowed to a stop. Again the Indian's arm kept her from falling. In the next moment, he shoved her away from him, so that she tumbled off the horse and fell heavily to her knees. Scrambling to her feet, Grace pushed back her bonnet and spun around to face him. Brimming with insults, she never once considered the wisdom of her actions; all she cared about was telling him exactly what she thought of him.

"You . . . you savage beast! You hideous, painted vermin! You fiend from hell! . . . What do you want with me? Whatever it is, I'll fight you 'til my last breath! I'll claw out your eyes! I'll bite off your nose. I'll steal your knife and carve up your vitals!"

The Indian sat back and laughed. As if he'd never heard anything so amusing, he roared with laughter. The response silenced her as nothing else could have. She doubted that he understood what she had said, but he couldn't possibly mistake her contempt; she had expressed her feelings clearly enough, and her own brashness horrified her. Would he make her pay for every foolish threat she'd uttered?

He urged his horse closer. She fought the urge to retreat. The one thing she wouldn't do was run from him; Grace Livingston didn't run from anyone. Once again he leaned down. This time his hand grasped the back of her head. His mouth crashed down on her mouth in a savage kiss that rocked her foundations.

She raised her fists to hit him, but she couldn't see, couldn't think . . . not when he was kissing her so fiercely. The intimacy froze her in place, as surely as if he'd suddenly reached inside her body and squeezed her heart.

Holding her head in place, he kissed her with a brute thoroughness that shattered her will to fight. Somehow his tongue found hers, and slowly, almost gently, caressed her. The contact so shocked her that she quite forgot about hitting or biting him; she could hardly keep her knees from buckling. She inhaled his breath, which was sweet and pleasant, then drank his kiss, accepting it as she had his heartbeat, because she had no choice. For all the control she had over what she was doing, she might have been dreaming.

When he finally released her, her knees *did* buckle. Sinking down in a puddle of skirt and petticoats, she stared at him. He stared back. A moment later he whirled his horse on its haunches and galloped off into the night.

Arms and legs trembling, heart thudding, she wrapped her arms around her waist, bowed her head, and wrestled for control. She attempted to wipe the overpowering kiss from her mouth. When that didn't work, she leaned over in the grass and spat out the taste of him. But the taste and feel of him lingered; his kiss had seared her soul as well as her lips. He had violated her as surely as if he had stripped her naked or beaten her senseless.

No one had ever kissed her like that. She had never imagined such a kiss was possible. It couldn't have lasted very long—a few moments at most—yet it had seemed like an eternity.

Grace lifted a shaky hand to the bodice of her gown. Her breasts were tender and swollen, her nipples engorged. With every small movement she could feel the prickle of lace against her skin, scraping and abrading it. How could a single kiss have done this to her? . . . . And a kiss by a savage. A heathen wearing buffalo horns and little else.

Tears stung her eyes. She gulped, swallowed, and lurched to her feet. He had disappeared, but that didn't mean he wouldn't return to finish what he'd started. She didn't understand why he hadn't ravished or killed her. Or taken her with him to serve as his slave. Maybe he simply preferred she die a slow, agonizing death from thirst and hunger on the open plain. Or that the wolves find her. Or a snake bite her. Or lightning strike her dead.

She had no idea where she was, and the moon had soared so high in the sky that north could be any direction. She wasn't good at directions, anyway. She had no business even being here; she had only come to this part of the country for Ellie's sake, and Ellie might be dead by now.

A single tear rolled down her cheek. Grace sniffed loudly and dashed it away. This was how Ellie must have felt when she was captured. Taken against her will, knowing her husband was dead, fearing for the lives of her children, she must have been terrified to discover herself a prisoner somewhere on the trackless, neverending prairie. Had Ellie, too, been abandoned and left to die? Whatever the case, no doubt she had occasion to stand barefoot on the plain and wonder what would become of herself and her children.

Thinking of Ellie's trials and tribulations helped Grace overcome her own sense of hopelessness and helplessness. Ellie's plight had been far worse. If Ellie still lived, she had endured suffering Grace couldn't even imagine. She mustn't allow her courage to falter. She must look on the bright side; she had survived an encounter with Painted Horse. Now she must figure out which way was north and start walking in that direction.

The man who had kissed her *had* to be Painted Horse. Even in her fear she had noticed a few things about him: He had been riding a many-colored animal—mostly white, with a few dark patches of color. Blue handprints and a dark circle around one eye had given the horse a bizarre, frightening appearance.

The soldier at the agency had described him perfectly. Having once seen him, no one could forget him; Grace knew she would never forget him—not for as long as she lived . . . which wouldn't be very long if she didn't get moving.

Feeling slightly better now, she peered in every direction, debating which way was north. A light immediately drew her attention. In the far distance was a soft glow, such as lamplight spilling through a window might make. Whatever it was, it deserved investigation. She hardly dared hope it might be someone's cabin or shanty.

She resolved to conceal her presence until she knew for certain what the light was, and where it was coming from. She mustn't make the mistake of escaping one danger only to plunge headlong into another. This impossible country overflowed with dangers, ardent Indians being only one of them. From now on she must keep her wits about her. No more succumbing to impulse. After all, this wasn't Boston; she was a long way from home.

Five

The house belonged to Matthew Stone. Grace recognized it as soon as she got close enough to see the shack and corrals. This was the worst place the Indian could have picked to drop her off. Mr. Stone would think she had returned in defeat to beg his assistance in getting to the fort.

Grace sighed with weariness. It had taken her almost an hour to get there. On the prairie, distances were deceiving. She had estimated no more than a twenty minute walk to reach the light, but like everything else she'd had to deal with recently, this was another humiliating mistake. Of course, she'd been limping at the speed of a turtle; still, it didn't seem fair. Having used up all her energy fretting over Painted Horse, she was in no mood to face Mr. Stone again. She suspected the Indian had known all along where he was taking her: to the only bit of civilization around, if indeed Mr. Stone's ranch could be called part of "civilization."

She should be grateful she still had her scalp—and her virtue. Instead she was profoundly irritated. Why couldn't he have dumped her near the fort? She supposed he didn't want to get that close to the soldiers. Whatever his reasons, she was here now, and not about to start trekking back to Fort Sill at this time of night.

She started toward the house, changed her mind, and headed for Mr. Stone's outbuildings. She preferred remaining outside to confronting the odious man when she might burst into tears at the least provocation. Relief at not being lost on the plain wasn't enough to banish exhaustion, cold, hunger, thirst, pain, and emotional trauma. At the moment all she wanted to do was lie down somewhere—anywhere—to curl into a ball and lose herself in sleep. A little rest would give her the strength to tackle Mr. Stone in the morning.

Bypassing the corrals, she settled on a three-sided structure that afforded shelter from the ever-present wind buffeting her unmercifully. As she passed the first corral, several horses whinnied. One snorted and trotted excitedly along the railing. Grace hoped Mr. Stone would ignore the commotion they were making. Gingerly, she entered the black depths of the lean-to and discovered a mound of dried grass in one corner. Apparently Mr. Stone kept a supply of prairie grass to feed his horses when they weren't turned out to find their own sustenance. She wished he were as thoughtful of people as he was of his animals.

He probably had a source of water nearby, too, but Grace was too tired, and her feet hurt too much, to look for it. Grateful for what she'd found, she lay down on the mound of hay and burrowed into the sweet-smelling mass like a small wounded animal. No one back in Boston would ever believe that persnickety Grace Livingston could so appreciate such primitive comfort, but she could not recall enjoying her big luxurious bed in Boston half so well. She closed her eyes.

The next thing she knew, someone was shaking her shoulder. "Miss Livingston, wake up. What in hell are you doing in my lean-to at this time of night?"

Grace sat up and blinked against the light from a lantern. Holding it aloft over her head, Matthew Stone didn't look happy to see her. "I thought I heard the horses a while ago. Before going to bed, I decided to come out and check on things. I didn't expect to find *you* here."

A surge of annoyance restored Grace's strength. Brushing hay from her neck and shoulders, she scrambled to her feet and gave him a long withering look, but he didn't exactly wither. "I regret I couldn't make it all the way back to the fort on foot tonight, Mr. Stone. So I returned here to await the morning. Don't worry. Come sunrise I'll be gone."

Lifting the lantern so its light nearly blinded her, he growled: "Why didn't you come to the house? All you had to do was knock on the door, and I would have invited you to spend the night inside, where it's warmer."

Grace bit down hard and chomped on her tongue. The man should have come after her. He hadn't. He'd left her to face possible ravishment and death alone on the prairie. Now he was scolding her as if it were all *her* fault.

"I am not in the habit of imposing on people who have made it clear they don't like me. However, this has been a terrible night, and when morning comes I should like to borrow a gun, if you have one. If you'd be willing to sell a weapon, that would be even better."

"I'm not in the habit of selling my guns, Miss Livingston. And why would you need one tomorrow—today, rather—when you didn't think you needed one yesterday? Has something happened to make you regret dashing about the countryside like a panicked chicken about to lose its head?"

She longed to smack his arrogant face. "No, of course not. It's merely that I . . . well, since everyone has been warning me about the rebel Comanches in the area, I'd like to be able to defend myself if I should encounter one."

"Really? *Have* you encountered one? Is that why you came crawling back here after you stomped off in a fit of childish stubbornness?"

"If I *had* encountered a rebel Comanche, would I be standing here having this distasteful conversation with you?" Grace gave her skirts an angry shake. "I'd probably be lying scalped and dead somewhere, never to be seen again."

He cocked his head, studying her. "Probably. However, I can see by your eyes that *some*thing happened to you, tonight."

"All right! It did. Painted Horse found me."

"Painted Horse?" He arched a brow skeptically. "What do you know about Painted Horse?"

"I heard about him at the fort. He's a vicious criminal who should be caught and locked up in a prison for the rest of his life."

Matt Stone grinned and shook his head. "He's a myth, Miss Livingston, a legend. He doesn't exist."

"He *does* exist! I saw him. He took me up on his horse. I thought he was going to kill me, but he only . . . only . . ."

"Only what?"

"Nothing. When he was ready, he let me go."

"That's *all?* The fierce savage, Painted Horse, took you for a ride on his horse and then let you go, just like that?"

"It wasn't just like that!" Grace spat. "He . . . he took liberties with me first."

"Liberties!"

The way he said it made Grace realize he was thinking the worst. "I don't mean he . . . he ravished me. He didn't exactly. But he did kiss me—and very savagely."

Mr. Stone frowned. "How does a savage kiss . . . *savagely?* Do you mean he hurt you? You don't look hurt."

His impudent gaze traveled from her face down the front of her bosom to her toes. "Except for your feet. Why are you barefoot, Miss Livingston? What happened to your shoes? Your feet are bleeding! Did he hurt your feet when he kissed you—stomped on them, perhaps?"

"Don't you dare mock me! I've endured enough for one night. He kissed me as if he meant to do far worse. I feared for my life, as well as my virtue. I could hardly breathe, and my knees went weak. My heart pounded so hard I thought I might die on the spot."

"Sounds to me as if you *enjoyed* it. I'd like to think I could have that kind of effect on a woman."

Grace drew back her hand and slapped him. Hard. Right across his arrogant face. He never so much as blinked. What he did was grin. He actually grinned!

"Did you slap the poor Indian, too?" he had the nerve to ask. "Is that why he let you go?"

"No, but I should have! I wish I had. I did *not* enjoy kissing him—rather, being kissed *by* him. I was terrified. Certain I'd be killed. That's why I want a gun—so if I ever meet him again I can shoot him before he touches me."

Matthew Stone leaned closer, his eyes mocking. "Do you know how to shoot, Miss Livingston? Have you ever in your life handled a gun?"

"No, but I'm ready to learn."

"I'm happy to hear that. Because it's one of the skills you're going to have to master if you expect me to guide you into Comancheria."

This surprised and excited her. "You're taking me into Comancheria? You accept my offer of employment?"

He rocked back on his heels. "Only on my terms."

"Which are . . ."

"You must agree to obey orders. Every one of them, whether you understand them or not. And you must learn to ride a horse astride, load and shoot both a rifle and a pistol, care for your own horse, and master other survival skills I intend to teach you."

In her moment of triumph, she hardly listened. "You've reconsidered because you want—*need*—my money."

Men were so easy to handle, she thought smugly. All one had to do was make the right offer. It worked as well here as it did in Boston.

His face darkened. Such a dangerous look came into his eyes that she stopped smiling and sidled backward. In the shadowy lantern-light he looked almost evil.

"I have my own reasons for going, Miss Livingston. If you refuse to obey orders or prove incapable of learning everything you should know, I won't take you with me, no matter if you offer me twice what you've agreed. You'll be no good to anyone if you're dead, and that's what you'll be if you don't change your stupid, spoiled behavior."

She lifted her chin. Tonight had taught her a great deal. She realized she had a few things to learn, but that didn't mean she intended to accept insults from a mere employee. "My behavior is *my* business, Mr. Stone. I forbid you to lecture me about it. However, I accept your terms. When do we leave for Comancheria? I'd like to set out as soon as possible, but I need to retrieve my belongings from the fort first."

"No, first you need to learn to shoot and ride. We aren't going anywhere until you master those basic skills."

"Can't I learn while we're en route? I'm sure it will take a long time to find the Comanches."

"I'm sure it will, too. But as soon as we ride away from this ranch we're courting disaster. You have to know how to ride and shoot. Besides, I need to take care of a few matters myself. While you practice sticking on a horse at a walk, jog, and gallop—and shooting a gun and hitting a target, while mounted—I have got to finish training a bunch of mustangs and then deliver them to the fort."

"Fine. Excellent. You can get my things while you're there."

He gave her another challenging look. "Actually . . . if your *things* resemble what you're wearing now, they're too impractical for where we're going. You'll need new things. I'll see to that. You take nothing I don't approve of. We'll be traveling as light as possible."

She started to open her mouth in protest, then clamped it shut again. Now wasn't the time to argue; he might change his mind. She wasn't sure what had made him decide to accept the job. At first she had thought it was the cattle and the big house. Now she wasn't so certain. Matthew Stone *wasn't* like any man she had met in Boston. He resembled Painted Horse more than he did Roger Clairmont. When she was with him, she had the same unsettled frightened feeling. The fact that Mr. Stone spoke perfect English, almost *too* perfect, hardly reassured her. He was now dressed in a normal shirt, trousers, and boots. Gone were the buckskins he'd been wearing when she'd first seen him, but he still exuded an aura of danger and primitive masculinity.

"Let's go to the house," he growled. "Unless you're afraid to be inside four walls alone with me."

"We have just agreed to a business deal, Mr. Stone, so we had better learn to trust one another, hadn't we?"

She walked past him with her nose in the air. If she *couldn't* trust him, better to discover it now than later. He'd be foolish to try anything, of course, and risk losing the cattle and the new house. Once he taught her to shoot, she'd never again have to worry about a man's intentions; until her return to Boston, she'd keep a gun handy at all times.

Matthew Stone's house had two rooms: one for living and one for sleeping. It was worse than she had thought—a shack with no amenities save a roof, some walls, and a soot-blackened fireplace. It had a table but only one chair, a few crude shelves and wooden pegs to hold things, and an odd assortment of barrels and crates. The sleeping room had a bed, but instead of offering it to her, he gave her two blankets and a big heavy saddle to pillow her head. She never said a word, but her expression must have revealed her thoughts.

"This is the way you're going to have to sleep out on the prairie, so you might as well get used to it. At least you'll have an oilskin between you and the ground, which some folks consider a luxury."

"You obviously consider *this* a luxury." She nodded toward the makeshift bed on the hard-packed, dirt floor.

"It is if you have no blankets, no saddle, it's raining or snowing, and the wind is blowing. Enjoy it, Miss Livingston, and welcome to Indian Territory."

He strode into the sleeping room and pulled a piece of hide—*hide*—across the door opening. The room didn't have an actual door. His boots clanked as he kicked them off, the bed creaked, and then . . . nothing. She was left alone with the lantern and her bed on the dirt floor.

She removed her bonnet and set it on the chair. Then she spread out one blanket, gingerly lay down on it, rested her head on the saddle, and covered herself with the second blanket. The blankets smelled musty and were nearly threadbare. They didn't provide much warmth. She was still hungry and thirsty, and wished she could wash her feet. Most of all she wished she were in her bed in Boston.

"Put out the lantern, Miss Livingston This isn't *your* house, and lamp oil isn't cheap."

Grace rose on one elbow, lifted the tin lid of the lantern, and blew out the flame, plunging the shack into darkness. Squirming around on the floor, she tried to get comfortable. It was impossible. The mound of hay out in the lean-to had been kinder to her weary bones. The floor was like rock, the saddle no help. Using it as a pillow would put a crick in her neck by morning. She fell asleep in the midst of listing her discomforts.

When she awoke, it was morning. A square of sunlight lit a patch of floor right next to her nose. Next to the patch of light stood a battered old pair of boots. Apparently Mr. Stone had left them to replace the shoes she had lost on the prairie. That was thoughtful—though it didn't make up for the fact that *he* had taken the bed and given her the floor.

Suddenly she smelled coffee. Turning her head, she saw a blackened coffeepot on a grate over a banked fire in the fireplace. Matt Stone didn't even have a cookstove. Nor was he in the cabin. The hide was drawn back, revealing an empty bed.

She quickly rose. On a crate nearby was a basin of water, but no towel or soap. The table held a tin plate containing three dingy biscuits and a few strips of hard dried . . . something. There was also an empty tin mug, a spoon, and a mug filled with sugar. Breakfast. This was meant to be breakfast.

Her stomach growled from emptiness, so Grace reached for the coffeepot first. She burned her hand before she thought to use a fold of her skirt to protect her fingers, and then burnt her tongue on the coffee itself. It resembled thick, black, boiled ink—drinkable only after she'd mixed it half and half with sugar—but it revived her.

Next she sampled the hard-as-rock biscuits, but she lacked the nerve to try the blackened strips of whatever-it-was. She couldn't believe Mr. Stone had been able to fetch a basin of water, build up the fire, and make the coffee without awakening her. She felt guilty for having slept so long. Still, before she went out to find him—and to locate "the necessary"—she took time to wash her face, hands, and feet, dry them on her skirt, smooth back her hair, put on her bonnet and the old boots which were far too big for her, and shake the worst wrinkles from her garments.

While she was doing all this she resolved to make it clear to Mr. Stone that he must show her more respect as a female. She did indeed have a crick in her neck this morning. He ought to have allowed her the use of his bed last night, while he himself took the bedroll on the floor. Any gentleman would have offered a lady the more comfortable accommodation. Had she been herself last night, she would have demanded it.

Being alone in the wilderness and about to embark on a difficult, hazardous journey, did not mean they shouldn't observe social amenities. She realized she'd have to "make-do" on the trail, but here in Mr. Stone's house, she ought to be afforded whatever small comforts were available. She appreciated the boots, of course, but it was hard to believe he didn't have soap or towels and apparently thought that a person should start the day with no more nourishment than leftover biscuits and dried leather.

Fortunately her luggage held several useful items that would serve them well, both here and when they were traveling— sweet-scented soap, soft towels, a few tins of Ellie's favorite tea biscuits as well as tea, and a crock of honey, which both she and Ellie preferred over sugar. Grace didn't mind if Mr. Stone provided more practical clothing, but surely he wouldn't mind fetching the particular trunk that contained the tea biscuits, honey, and marmalade Mrs. Hugg had thoughtfully provided.

As she tried to think of all she had agreed to last night, when her brain hadn't been functioning properly, Grace grew nervous. She hadn't actually said she didn't mind if he *didn't* fetch her things from the fort, had she? If so, she must tell him immediately that she had minded very much, and that he must be sure to bring everything.

What if Ellie or one of the children should require doctoring on the homeward journey? Grace had packed a small cloth bag with a number of medicinal remedies, and she herself needed personal items, such as a brush, comb, hairpins, and a hand mirror. She couldn't do without a certain face cream, nor an assortment of undergarments, stockings, gloves, and spare clothing for Ellie and the children. Mr. Stone *couldn't* mean to deprive them of everything necessary to comfort and well-being, could he?

Before confronting him on these important issues, Grace stepped outside and slipped around to the back of the shanty in search of the necessary, only to discover there wasn't one. Mr. Stone apparently didn't think he needed one. Somehow she wasn't surprised, nor terribly dismayed. In her short time in Indian Territory, she had already discovered the benefits of a large, full skirt. In it, a woman could squat and relieve herself without baring her backside to the elements—or anyone's interested gaze.

Even so, she didn't want Mr. Stone to see her. Peeking around the side of the house she discovered that he was once again in the corral working one of his beloved horses, so she was able to put the shanty between them while she tended to personal business. Out on the plain alone with him, she would probably have to hide behind her horse or arise and retire before he did, while it was still dark enough to provide concealment—an unpleasant prospect. No sooner had she finished when Mr. Stone called out for her. At least she thought he was addressing her.

"If you're finally up, Boston, it's time you got your butt out here and went to work."

Grace marched around the side of the house and approached the pen, where he was busy saddling a horse. "My name isn't Boston, Mr. Stone, and you have no business mentioning my . . . *derriere.* Such familiarity indicates an appalling lack of respect. While we're on the subject of your disrespect, I must tell you I did not appreciate sleeping on the floor last night while you claimed the bed."

He paused and pushed back the cattleman's hat he was wearing this morning. "You're asking to share my bed?"

"I most certainly am *not* asking to share your bed! How dare you suggest such a thing?"

He narrowed his eyes at her. "If not that, then what?"

He was being deliberately obtuse—damn him! "I think *you* should take the floor and give *me* the bed. Any gentleman would gladly offer a lady the superior accommodations."

He frowned. "Sorry, Boston, but out here we're not ladies and gentlemen, just plain old male and female. You're *welcome* to the bed as long as you don't mind sharing. All your protests to the contrary, that's what you're really after, isn't it? Someone to keep you warm at night?"

"Mr. Stone! I resent your assumptions, sir. If you have any wicked ideas regarding my person, you had best get them out of your head. Our relationship is strictly business. Before we proceed further, do I have your sworn word you will remember this at all times and conduct yourself accordingly?"

"I hardly need to swear it, Boston," he drawled, coating each word with sarcasm. "So far I haven't seen anything to *give* me wicked ideas about your person. You keep yourself buttoned up tighter than a missionary. We could sleep for a week in the same bed, and you wouldn't have to worry about me touching you."

Grace was insulted. She knew she wasn't a raving beauty like Ellie, but Roger—and other men—had found her attractive, buttoned up or not. Roger had wanted to marry her, and before him she had often had to discourage men from trying to get too familiar. Several fortune hunters had tried to put their hands on her, and received good whacks from her parasol for their trouble.

"Forget the bed," she said icily. "I'm sorry I mentioned it. But I *insist* you call me Miss Livingston."

His slow, mocking grin returned. "It's too much of a mouthful, Boston. I can't be saying Miss Livingston this, and Miss Livingston that, for the next few months."

"Then call me Grace, if you must!"

His grin widened. "Boston suits you better."

"Shall I call you Snake? I think the name suits *you*. Or Devil. Come to think of it, Devil is even better than Snake."

"All right . . . Grace. I'm not promising anything, but I'll try it for a while and see if I can stomach it. Here . . ." He held out reins of the horse he had just saddled. "Get in here. This will be your mount."

"This?" Grace climbed between two railings to enter the pen, then eyed the animal with misgivings. It was rather small, a nondescript brown, and somewhat mousey looking.

"You don't like him? He's a nice quiet gelding, but he has lots of stamina."

"He's not very pretty." Grace sniffed. "Why can't I have one like . . . like that black one over there in the corral?"

She nodded toward a fine-looking horse she could envision riding through a park at home. Wearing the right clothing, with the horse groomed to perfection, she'd be the envy of all who saw her.

"That one is only green-broke, and crazy besides. Never judge a horse by its appearance, Boston. They're like women. The pretty ones don't always ride the best. You want a horse you can trust, and this little dun gelding will do just fine. Don't worry that he can't move fast enough, either. He'll be able to outrun anything we meet."

Grace didn't find the information—or his humor—reassuring. She was rather hoping for a horse who liked to go slow. But she supposed that if Indians were pursuing them, the horse had to be able to get away and take her with him. Timidly, she accepted the reins.

"Aren't you going to show me what to do?"

"Do?"

"How to ride. I thought you were going to teach me."

"Oh. Right. I forgot." He took the reins back from her. "All right. Watch closely. I'm only going to show you once."

Tugging his hat down low on his forehead, he turned toward the horse and mounted in one graceful easy motion. Facing her, he said: "It's all a matter of balance, Boston, and learning when and how to shift your weight. I trained this horse myself, and he knows where I want to go and how fast I want to get there almost as soon as I know it myself. Watch me a minute, and you'll see."

Using invisible signals, he made the horse roll back on its haunches and walk across the corral. Near the rail he did something to make it trot, but she couldn't see what it was. As the horse trotted around the pen, Mr. Stone sat perfectly still. He didn't even bounce. *His* butt was glued to the saddle. After a few moments the horse went faster—not a gallop, but not a trot, either.

"This is the lope," Mr. Stone called out to her. "This horse has a wonderful lope. You'll like it."

Grace wasn't at all sure she would like it. She still couldn't discern his signals, and he wasn't wearing spurs like most men did. She assumed a horse went faster because its rider kicked its sides with spurs or smacked it with a whip. She had never bothered with the details; in Boston, she never rode because . . . horses intimidated her. Anyway, the carriage took her everywhere she wanted to go.

"Any questions?" He stopped the horse near her, with*out* pulling on the reins, and Grace could only gape at him.

She might not have ridden, but she'd seen lots of people, particularly men, ride horses. Matthew Stone was the only one who looked more at home on horseback than he did on the ground. He seemed completely at ease, as if he'd learned to ride before learning to walk.

"If you have no questions, I guess you're ready to ride." He swung down from the horse with that same fluid motion she found so graceful and incredible.

"Wait! I didn't see what you did to make the horse obey."

Mr. Stone studied her with some surprise. "I didn't 81 him do anything. He *wants* to obey me. All I did was tell what I wanted him to do."

"But what if he doesn't want to obey me? He doesn't even know me."

"Then he has no way of knowing you don't know how to ride. Just get on him, sit up straight, and turn slightly in the direction you want him to go. Give him a little nudge or squeeze, and he'll go. That's all there is to it."

"Shouldn't I pull on the reins or something?" Grace had pulled hard on the reins of the horse she had borrowed. She'd pulled them first one way, then the other, seeking to influence the animal's direction. When she wanted to stop, she'd pulled both of them together and gripped with her legs to keep from falling off. The dumb horse had gone faster, not slower, as if he were trying to get away from her.

"Get on," he said. "Do as little as possible. With every motion you make, the horse is trying to figure out what you're telling him to do. If you don't know what you're telling him, don't do it."

Grace was confused. As usual, her skirts got in her way. The horse jumped when she landed heavily on its back, and Mr. Stone had to grab the reins to keep it from bolting. He breathed a sigh of disgust. "Softly, Boston. Everything you do with a horse should be soft. Never do more than necessary to persuade him to listen to you. Otherwise, you'll only scare him, or encourage him to fight you."

"Scare him!" Grace mumbled through clenched teeth. She herself was petrified. She struggled with skirt and petticoats, trying to make them smaller but keep her legs covered at the same time.

"Wait a minute." Matt Stone reached beneath her skirt, grabbed a handful of petticoat, and yanked so hard he almost pulled her off the horse. A loud ripping sound signaled the parting of fabric.

Grace smacked at his hands. "What are you doing? Have you gone mad?"

His eyes nailed her. "Relax. I'm making it easier for you to ride." He glanced down at the large section of flaming red petticoat he was holding. "Red, huh? I never would have figured you for wearing red."

"Red p-petticoats are—were—all the rage in Boston a few years back. This is an o-old one."

"Well, they aren't yet the rage in Comancheria. Might be if a few squaws ever got hold of them." He tossed the torn fabric aside. "Go on, Boston. What are you waiting for? Walk him around a bit. Try a trot. Save the lope for tomorrow. I can see I need to teach you a few things before I can trust you to go faster without killing yourself."

Six

Grace spent a half hour on the horse, trying to get him to walk where she wanted him to go. He never once went there, and she couldn't work up enough nerve to ask him for a trot. Looking disgusted, Mr. Stone called her over to the rail.

"You can practice more later, Boston. Right now I want to give you a shooting lesson so you can practice that, too, while I'm gone."

"Where are you going? How soon will you be leaving?"

"Sounds like you can't wait to get rid of me." His lips curved mockingly. "How soon I go depends on how long it takes you to get down from that horse and learn how to shoot. As for where I'm going, I have to deliver a couple horses to the army. If I don't get moving I'll never make it to Fort Sill and back before dark."

Grace attempted to dismount gracefully, but her foot caught in the stirrup and she toppled backwards and landed hard on her backside in the dust. Snorting, the horse sidestepped, trailing the reins she had dropped.

"Tomorrow I expect you to do better." Mr. Stone caught the horse, but didn't offer his assistance or ask whether or not she had hurt herself. "Do that out on the prairie and you can lose your mount, and very likely your life."

Grace jumped to her feet. "I'm just learning! Maybe if I knew the horse's name he'd listen to me when I ask him to do something—like stand still when I'm getting off."

"Or you could just say 'whoa'." Mr. Stone draped the horse's reins over the railing.

"But what's his name?" Grace insisted, resisting the impulse to rub her aching rear.

"He hasn't got one yet. Unless I'm keeping a horse for myself, I don't bother to name it. I leave that for the soldiers at the fort."

"Then you weren't planning to keep this one?"

"Not until you came along. Call him whatever you like. It's your choice."

"I . . . I'll have to think about it." The idea of naming her own horse pleased her. It was just too bad the little dun, as Mr. Stone referred to him, wasn't a flashier looking animal; his name would have to be plain to suit him.

Mr. Stone took her arm and steered her toward the far side of the corral. "Come on. I've got a Colt I want you to try."

"A colt? But I thought you said I was going to ride *this* horse. And you were going to teach me how to shoot a gun."

He heaved another deep sigh and climbed through the railing. "A Colt *is* a gun, Boston. A six-shooter revolver—large bore, long-barreled, easily loaded, and solidly built. In skilled hands it's a deadly accurate weapon, which is why I want you to learn how to use it."

For the next half hour he gave her lessons on loading and firing the Colt. When she couldn't hit anything, he agreed to save the .50 caliber Sharps rifle for another day. Grace was relieved. She didn't think she could lift the heavy rifle, much less load and fire it. Mr. Stone claimed it could bring down a buffalo with ease, but she had no intention of shooting a buffalo. If she could master the Colt he would have to be satisfied.

After her shooting lesson Mr. Stone left. With a mixture of relief and apprehension, Grace watched him ride off, herding several horses ahead of him. She didn't know which disturbed her the most—his departure, or the man himself. Matthew Stone couldn't open his mouth without challenging or belittling her.

She wished there was someone else available to help he...
...llie and the children.

...there wasn't anybody, and she knew she had to become
se... in riding and shooting if she hoped to survive this
...m... Sighing at the magnitude of the tasks ahead
to stroke his ...gain approached her horse. The little dun
...look at her, as wary of her as she
"I think I'll call you ...es were kind, and his muzzle as
benefit. ...palm when she reached out
...liked him.

The name seemed to fit. She knew a man n... ...unston.
A baldheaded, plain looking fellow with spectacles, he possessed hidden talents; he had amassed a fortune in the tea trade.
Livingston ships carried his teas around the globe. So Dunston
it would be. Avery Dunston would never know she had bestowed
his name on a little dun horse with big brown eyes.

"Now, behave yourself, Dunston." She led him out to the
center of the pen, hiked up her skirts, and climbed aboard.

By late afternoon she had fallen off Dunston eleven times.
Not because he was naughty, but because she couldn't get the
hang of riding him at any gait faster than a walk. Whenever she
kicked him with her oversized boots, he instantly obliged with
a trot. She tried her best to sit up straight, as Mr. Stone had
advised, but it was hard to hang onto his mane, the reins, and
the saddle horn all at the same time. She bump-bump-bumped
along, and Dunston didn't like the abuse any more than she did.

He tried to go faster yet, and the only way she could get him
to slow down was to holler "Whoa!" Then he would stop dead,
and she would go flying over his head. It was a wonder she
didn't break her neck. His small size proved advantageous, for
at least she didn't have to go far to reach the ground.

Twice, in order to give them both a respite, she took a turn
with the Colt. As long as she remembered to first check the
seating of the red copper percussion cap on the nipple of the

Colt, she found loading and firing the gun to ʟ was
However, the retort deafened her, and she...
pistol steady, much less aim it properly ...er working
the old barrel Mr. Stone had set up ᶠement. Every mus-
She had hoped to master both ri... cle grumbled. At sunset
Mr. Stone returned, but she...ach ... with a sense of deep frustration,
weeks—possibly months...
hard all day, she could b...
cle in her body ach...
Mr. Stone still ha...
Grace quit f...ed Dunston, who looked every bit as tired and
As she...as she felt, she wanted to weep. Dunston had every
hung...reason to bite her; instead he stood patiently, head lowered,
while she fumbled with the saddle fastenings. She flung the
saddle over a railing and removed Dunston's bridle. He nuzzled
her hand as if to comfort her, and Grace abandoned dignity and
threw her arms around his sweaty neck.

"Oh, Dunston! I know I did miserably today and made you
feel miserable, too. But I promise I'll do better tomorrow. . . .
Are you hungry? I'll fetch some of that nice hay from the lean-to
for your supper, and get you some water, too."

Mr. Stone had left a dozen horses behind. They whinnied
forlornly when they saw Grace feeding Dunston, so she fed
them, too, and hauled buckets of water from the pump at the
side of the house to dump in the horse trough in the corral. By
the time she was finished, night had fallen. Grace felt faint from
hunger, and her head ached.

Entering the house, she faced another unfamiliar task: preparing her own meal. From start to finish. From unknown in-
gredients. Over a nonexistent fire.

She managed to light the lantern, but making a fire wasn't
so easy. For starters, there was no wood, and no coal. All she
could find was a bin full of something that looked and smelled
suspiciously like . . . dried animal dung?

Grace couldn't imagine that Mr. Stone cooked his food over

that. Yet, as sh...
...tire vicinity, she ...ht about it, she realized he must. ...
who'd brought he spotted a single tree, nor had the sol-
here se...ff in the bin. ...o what they'd used, but it re-
through crate...wanted a hot ...l, but an army of servants
sugar, salt, beans, ba...eeds at hom... and even on the trip out
large quantity of the dis... done the ...oking. Rummaging
from the morning still remaine...lves, she found coffee, flour,
hard biscuits. She gnawed at the biscui... yellow grain, and a rather
starting a fire. like strips. The ones
along with two
...worked at

An hour and a half later she had a fire, but her biscuits were harder and flatter than the ones she had already eaten, the beans never did soften, and her coffee looked and smelled like tar. No amount of sugar could make it palatable.

Obviously, to succeed in Indian Territory she had to learn more than just how to shoot and ride. Cooking soared to the top of her list of priorities. By now she was too tired to hazard another attempt. Cleaning up after this one was also beyond her. The coffeepot, heavy skillet, and two pans were burnt black. Flour dusted the floor, and sugar littered the table. Whatever she paid Mrs. Hugg and the kitchen maids at home, it wasn't enough. Negotiating complicated business deals didn't begin to compare with assembling a simple meal, much less an entire banquet.

Tripping over the old saddle that served as her pillow, Grace rebelled against the notion of sleeping on the floor again. If Mr. Stone weren't coming home tonight, she might as well enjoy *his* bed. He'd never know.

Kicking her blankets aside she blew out the lantern, walked into his room in the dark, and collapsed on the bed. It sagged in the middle, but Grace didn't care. In a heartbeat she fell asleep.

Panic awoke her: Someone was crawling i... ...n't
Grace sprang into action. Kicking, claw... head, the
meling the intruder, she shrieked a...ed ...gs crushed her
lively scuffle soon ended. Lying ...
weight of the hard-breathing...
move. He had pinned her h...ds t...
length of his body held ... imp...
legs.

"Settle down, Bosto... ...e? Get off me! I can't breathe."

"*You!* What are ... side but maintained a grip on her
Mr. Stone ea... g firmly over her legs, as if he didn't trust
hands and ...re, remember? A better question would be, 'what
her. "I... are you doing in my bed?'"

Grace was mortified. Mr. Stone's nose was only inches from her nose. His breath fanned her face. "When you didn't appear by sunset I thought you weren't coming tonight."

He stirred—sliding his leg along hers and settling an arm across her waist. "Well, I'm here now—scratched, battered, and bleeding. My compliments, Boston. A Comanche squaw couldn't have fought any better."

"I . . . I didn't mean to hurt you."

"Really? I thought you meant to kill me . . . or ravish me. For a minute there, I couldn't decide which."

"Let me up, Mr. Stone. This is most unseemly."

The warmth and weight of his body, along with the seductive timber of his voice, overwhelmed Grace. They were close as man and wife, and her heart was thumping like a drum.

"*Unseemly?* What in hell does *that* mean?"

"It means you shouldn't be in this bed on top of me! Release me at once, or . . . or—"

"Or what? Just what will you do?" His leg rubbed against her. "If someone else had burst in here instead of me, how would you have defended yourself? You put up a good show, but it wasn't enough, was it? A woman can't beat a determined man. That's why you need a gun. By the way, where's my Colt?"

...just as well be a e...
...ne on the warpath, and then where would y...
now, if I hadn't slit your throat I'd have stripped you naked, and
I'd be humping you like a bull in rut. . . . Without the gun, there
wouldn't be a damn thing you could do to stop me. Do you
understand what I'm saying?"

"Y-yes. I . . . I understand perfectly."

"Good. Then there's no need for me to describe what a
drunken buffalo hunter or a Comanche is likely to do with a
white woman when he's done with her. In your worst nightmares
you couldn't imagine the ways he might make you suffer before
he finally let you die, whimpering in shame and agony. I heard
of one who tied a naked woman spread-eagled, then took a
knife, heated the blade over hot coals, and—"

"I said I understand! The next time you crawl in bed with
me I'll shoot you! I won't even look first to identify you."

"I'm the only one you'd better not shoot—and you'd better
not take my bed again, either. The next time I find you in my
blankets, I'll assume you're here for only one reason. It's been
a long time since I had a woman, and I'll most certainly oblige
you."

Grace gulped. Yesterday he'd told her he could sleep beside
her for a week without touching her. Today he had apparently
changed his mind. The mere thought of him touching her intimately made her stomach knot and her thighs quiver.

Grace straightened and clenched her fists at her sides. "I take it you'd like me to prepare the meal and wake you when it's ready."

"It's what I'd like, but I doubt you'll be up before me. Just make it when you get up and call me. I'll be outside tending the horses."

Grace groaned at the prospect of making breakfast and revealing just how inept she really was. "Certainly, Mr. Stone. I'd be *delighted* to prepare breakfast." *And cram it down your throat, too.*

As she had the previous night, she heard his boots fall to the floor, then all was silent. She groped her way to her own bed, lay down, and wrapped herself in a musty-smelling blanket. She couldn't bear to think about the morning; she still had to make it through the night.

By now she wasn't sleepy. No one—with the possible exception of Painted Horse—had ever made her feel as angry, nervous, and flustered as Matthew Stone did. Because of her wealth and education she had always considered herself superior to most men. But here in Indian Territory her past accomplishments didn't matter; she saw herself as she really was—weak, vulnerable, and shockingly incompetent.

Men like Matt Stone and Painted Horse made her feel exces-

Grace thanked heaven for the darkness which hid her flaming face. The gun was still outside, lying atop the barrel. It had never occurred to her to bring it in the house in case she needed it. How could she have been so stupid and careless? It was probably rusting out there.

"Mighty quiet all of a sudden, aren't we?" His deep caressing tone prickled her flesh and made her hair stand on end. "Look, Boston . . ." He leaned over her, letting her take his full weight, impressing upon her the extent of her helplessness. "You'd better start thinking ahead and *planning* for occasions like this, when you risk losing everything. You're lucky it's me lying on top of you. I could just as well be a drunken buffalo hunter or a Comanche on the warpath, and then where would you be? By now, if I hadn't slit your throat I'd have stripped you naked, and I'd be humping you like a bull in rut. . . . Without the gun, there wouldn't be a damn thing you could do to stop me. Do you understand what I'm saying?"

"Y-yes. I . . . I understand perfectly."

"Good. Then there's no need for me to describe what a drunken buffalo hunter or a Comanche is likely to do with a white woman when he's done with her. In your worst nightmares you couldn't imagine the ways he might make you suffer before he finally let you die, whimpering in shame and agony. I heard of one who tied a naked woman spread-eagled, then took a knife, heated the blade over hot coals, and—"

"I said I understand! The next time you crawl in bed with me I'll shoot you! I won't even look first to identify you."

"I'm the only one you'd better not shoot—and you'd better not take my bed again, either. The next time I find you in my blankets, I'll assume you're here for only one reason. It's been a long time since I had a woman, and I'll most certainly oblige you."

Grace gulped. Yesterday he'd told her he could sleep beside her for a week without touching her. Today he had apparently changed his mind. The mere thought of him touching her intimately made her stomach knot and her thighs quiver.

"If you'll just let me up, I'll be happy to leave," she informed him.

He rolled over, releasing her. She vaulted from the bed, raced into the other room, slipped on the spilled flour, and had to grab the table to keep from falling on her face.

"Boston?"

Clinging to the table's edge, she yelped: "What do you want *now,* Mr. Stone?"

"Since I made the coffee this morning, it's your turn tomorrow . . . and it wouldn't hurt you to fry up some bacon, either. I brought eggs back with me from the fort. If you haven't broken them by now, they're on the table. Fresh biscuits would go well with them."

Grace straightened and clenched her fists at her sides. "I take it you'd like me to prepare the meal and wake you when it's ready."

"It's what I'd like, but I doubt you'll be up before me. Just make it when you get up and call me. I'll be outside tending the horses."

Grace groaned at the prospect of making breakfast and revealing just how inept she really was. "Certainly, Mr. Stone. I'd be *delighted* to prepare breakfast." *And cram it down your throat, too.*

As she had the previous night, she heard his boots fall to the floor, then all was silent. She groped her way to her own bed, lay down, and wrapped herself in a musty-smelling blanket. She couldn't bear to think about the morning; she still had to make it through the night.

By now she wasn't sleepy. No one—with the possible exception of Painted Horse—had ever made her feel as angry, nervous, and flustered as Matthew Stone did. Because of her wealth and education she had always considered herself superior to most men. But here in Indian Territory her past accomplishments didn't matter; she saw herself as she really was—weak, vulnerable, and shockingly incompetent.

Men like Matt Stone and Painted Horse made her feel exces-

sively inferior. Even more odd and disturbing, she felt strangely excited. Mr. Stone and Painted Horse were primitive untamed men who did what they wanted, when they wanted to do it, and didn't care in the least about consequences. They had mastered their savage surroundings, and judged everyone else by their own unique standards. She didn't want to admire them, but in some surprising insidious way, she did. She admired them very much, the same way she had once admired a caged tiger brought back from a far-off jungle and displayed on the streets of Boston. The tiger's strength and cunning had aroused her fascination, as well as her fear.

Tossing and turning, trying to ease her sore muscles, Grace suspected that money didn't mean much to Mr. Stone and probably meant nothing to Painted Horse and Quanah Parker. If the Comanches refused to accept money for the return of Ellie and the children, what could she offer them? Would she have to supply them with guns and horses, so they could continue making war on innocent white people?

It was a sobering thought, one that kept her awake for several hours. By the time she drifted off from sheer exhaustion, it was getting light. She heard Mr. Stone roll out of bed and leave the cabin, but she refused to jump up and start making breakfast. Breakfast—and Mr. Stone—could wait.

When Grace awoke, it was late morning—maybe close to noon. She couldn't jump up fast enough. The last thing she wanted was for Mr. Stone to show up for breakfast and give her one of his mocking looks. She rushed about like a madwoman, making a fire, cracking eggs, cleaning pots and pans with nothing but a spoon to scrape off the burnt parts, boiling coffee, mixing biscuits.

From start to finish, the whole thing was a disaster. The coffee boiled over and put out the fire. She rebuilt the fire and burnt everything, including her fingers. Her biscuits stuck to the skillet, and the bacon burst into flames. Holding the skillet between the folds of her skirt, she carried the blazing pan outside—and met Mr. Stone, coming toward the house.

"That had better not be my breakfast." He nodded toward the flaming skillet.

"It's your bacon!" she screamed at him. "If you want eggs and biscuits, you'll have to cook them yourself—or else starve! I hope you do starve. I'll be starving right along with you!"

Setting the pan in the dust, she lifted her skirts and ran toward the lean-to. She couldn't bear to shed tears in front of Matthew Stone. Plopping down in the hay, she wrapped her arms around her knees and took deep breaths. All she needed was a few moments alone, and she could calmly return to the house and try to salvage the biscuits, if not her pride.

She hadn't yet ruined the eggs. However, since she'd never fixed eggs before, it was entirely probable that she would ruin them, too. She didn't know if Mr. Stone preferred his yolks whole or mixed in with the whites, but she'd already broken the yolks and had no choice now but to stir them all together and hope for the best.

How did Mrs. Hugg *do* it? Her biscuits were so light they almost floated off the table. Her bacon was crisp, not charred, and her eggs *never* ran together or contained broken shells, while her coffee drew exclamations of rapture.

Grace managed not to bawl her eyes out, but she did have to wipe her nose on her skirt, which by now was looking pretty bad, anyway. Regaining her composure took longer; she simply could not go out and face Mr. Stone over that debacle of a breakfast. Soon he'd find out that she hadn't mastered riding and shooting, either.

After a while her eyes began to feel heavy. She leaned back in the hay to rest them a moment. That was all she remembered until someone nudged her foot.

"Boston, take this before I drop it."

She opened her eyes to discover Mr. Stone holding two tin plates full of food, forks, and mugs of steaming coffee. Careful not to spill the coffee, he handed one to her, then sat down beside her. "Eat. Maybe food will revive you. You look like you just crawled out of a grave."

Just what she needed to hear—especially from him.

Grace glanced down at the food: fluffy, yellow scrambled eggs, perfect bacon, and fresh puffed-up biscuits slathered with honey. He must have brought back her trunk, opened it, and found the crock of honey lying right on top. She wondered where he'd put the trunk, then promptly forgot all about it as the food enticed her with its steamy fragrance.

"Oh, my!" she breathed, enchanted.

Two tears rolled down her cheeks and dripped onto the biscuits to mingle with the honey. Picking up her fork, Grace dug into the eggs. They were wonderful, with just the right seasoning. The meal was the best she had ever eaten. She would have to revise her opinion of Mr. Stone, she thought, savoring the honey-drenched biscuits. Maybe he wasn't a savage, after all—oh, could *he* cook! His biscuits rivaled Mrs. Hugg's and surpassed the army's.

When she finished devouring the last crumb she set down her plate, cradled the tin mug of coffee in her hands, and beamed at him. "Thank you, Mr. Stone. I feel so much better . . . and . . . and I apologize for not knowing how to cook. I never had to cook before, you see, but I intend to learn. Next time you prepare something, I'll watch you. I learn fast. I always did. Show me something once and I've got it. Usually," she added, thinking of riding and shooting.

He smiled back, for once without mockery. "I'm glad to hear that. Ready to show me what you learned yesterday?"

"Well, I . . . I practiced all day, but I'm still not very good at riding. Or shooting. Can't you give me another day or two before I have to . . . *perform?*"

Tilting his head, he studied her. She returned his intent regard. Today he was smooth-shaven, and she wondered when—and where—he had shaved. He was also bareheaded. His hair gleamed with copper highlights, the sun-burnished locks pro-

viding a very nice contrast for his eyes, which suddenly reminded her of a green sea on a sunny day.

"Part of the problem is the way you're dressed," he observed.
"But don't worry. I brought some clothes back from the fort
for you. They should help you ride better. Come on. While I
work on the mess you left on the table and floor, you can try
them on for size."

Picking up her plate, Grace followed him back to the house.
Once there, he handed her a tied bundle she hadn't noticed that
morning. As she untied it a stench rose, almost making her gag.
Filthy garments fell out—shirt, trousers, vest, chaps such as
cowboys wore, and some sort of overcoat.

Tossing her an old beat-up hat that had been hanging from
a peg, he said: "There. That should complete your disguise. All
you have to do now is cut your hair, dirty your face, bind
your . . . uh . . . chest, and you'll look like a buffalo hunter. No
one will ever guess you're a woman. And you'll find britches
a lot more comfortable than petticoats and hoops."

Grace held up the offending garments as if they might bite.
She expected vermin to crawl out of them at any moment. "I
can't wear these! The smell alone will kill me. I bet they have
lice. Or fleas."

His features hardened. "That's what you're wearing, Boston.
Don't bother arguing. You have to look like a man, and the only
kind of white men likely to be crossing Comancheria are soldiers or buffalo hunters . . . There may be a cow man or two,
but they avoid that route if they can. They tend to lose too many
cattle."

He lifted a pair of long-blade scissors down from a shelf.
"Want to cut your own hair, or do I have to do it?"

Dropping the garments, Grace's hands flew to her head. Lacking a brush or comb, she hadn't unpinned it since her arrival.
It was disheveled, but still secured in her usual, no-nonsense
style—parted down the center and coiled into two thick rolls
on either side of her neck.

"I will *not* cut my hair. And neither will you. I don't see why that's necessary."

"Because white men don't have hair as long as yours." He sneered, placing the scissors on the table. "Either do it, or forget the whole venture. I want you shorn, dressed, and outside in half an hour to show me what you accomplished yesterday while I was gone."

"B-but I thought you were going to give me a couple more days . . ."

"You must have made *some* progress, Miss Livingston. If you haven't, it doesn't bode well for the future, does it?"

The way he said her name made her actually prefer "Boston." She hated the way he was looking at her, as if no one could be so inept. "B-but those clothes you brought are filthy! They'll give me a rash. And I've never in my life cut my hair. You can't expect me to chop it off just because you say so!"

His face and eyes were implacable. "Then forget it. We aren't going anywhere. You said you'd follow orders, and the first time I give you one, you refuse to obey it. I knew you weren't cut out for this, and now you're proving it."

"Oh, all right! I'll do it. Just leave, will you? I'm certainly not going to cut my hair or strip in front of you."

He grinned. "That's better. Hurry up, Boston. I want to see how you look as a buffalo hunter. Maybe the disguise will improve your riding. It can hardly make it worse."

With that parting shot he left the house. As soon as the door swung shut behind him, Grace picked up the scissors. Trembling, she set them down again. Her hair might not be the color of Ellie's, but it was long and silky and made her feel feminine and desirable when she brushed it. It symbolized the womanhood she had fought so hard to subdue. Without her long hair, she truly would be . . . sexless—robbed of some essential part of herself, a part she secretly cherished.

If Mr. Stone couldn't understand that, too bad. She couldn't possibly explain it to him. What she would do was pin up her hair in a different manner—stuffed up under the hat—so he couldn't tell she hadn't cut it. Once he realized she could adequately conceal her gender, he'd have to relent on the issue.

Picking up the shirt, a dirty blue one of indeterminate fabric, she sniffed it, wrinkled her nose, and resolved to wash the thing at the first opportunity. For now she would humor Mr. Stone, but no matter what he said, she refused to stink like a buffalo hunter.

Twenty minutes later, she marched out of the house. When she saw Dunston already saddled and waiting for her, she forgot her squeamishness and the way her skin was trying to crawl away from her clothes. As she approached him, the poor horse sighed; he knew what lay in store for him. Grace sighed, too. She was *not* looking forward to another day of bumps and bruises.

One glimpse of Miss Livingston's face beneath the beat-up hat, and Matt wanted to laugh. She looked as if Comanches were waiting to torture her. But she never said a word as she untied her horse, awkwardly scrambled into the saddle, and kicked the little dun in the ribs. The horse lurched into a trot, almost unseating her. She hollered "Whoa!" and grabbed the saddle horn. Obviously, she hadn't learned much yesterday.

"Gently!" he admonished. "That horse can feel a fly landing on its skin. You don't have to break its ribs to get a response. Just squeeze him a little—*gently.*"

"I told you I needed another day or two." She glared at him.

Matt bit back a grin. Grace Livingston amazed him. He didn't know how she had managed to survive for so long—the woman couldn't even cook—but he had to give her credit for trying. She was the most stubborn, ignorant, gutsy female he had ever met. So far, she'd passed all his tests. Complaining didn't count against her. It showed she had spirit—and where they were headed she'd need all the spirit she could muster.

He just hoped he could teach her enough over the next few weeks so that she wouldn't come to grief—and take him with her—in Comancheria. She needed *at least* a few weeks before they dared travel. He didn't want to leave before May, anyway. Aside from the horses he had to train, the additional time would ensure decent weather and enough good grass on the plains to sustain their mounts on the journey.

By May the horses would have recovered from the sparsity of winter. Before attempting such a long trek, they needed more flesh on their bones. Starting tomorrow he would hobble them and turn them out to graze every day. With his hay almost gone it was time they started fending for themselves again.

He headed for the corral to saddle a horse, but a shriek waylaid him. He turned in time to watch Miss Livingston soar over her horse's head and land sprawling in the dust. Her hat flew off, and a thick mass of hair tumbled around her face, neck, and shoulders. Not only had she *not* cut it, but she had enough hair for *two* women. The Comanches would be lusting after her scalp the moment they spotted those shiny tresses.

Swearing under his breath, Matt strode to the pen, vaulted over the railing, grabbed Miss Livingston by the hair, and hauled her upright. Pushing her ahead of him, he marched her out of the pen and across the yard toward the house. He couldn't see her face for her hair, but he could *hear* her, sputtering like a coffeepot about to boil over.

"Take your hands off me, Mr. Stone! What do you think you're doing?"

He dragged her inside the house and seized the scissors lying on the table. "I'm doing what you should have done and said you would—I'm cutting your damn hair!"

"Oh, no, you're not!" She flipped an armful of hair back from her face, and her expression gave him pause. She looked as if rape would be preferable to a haircut. Her eyes shone a brilliant gold-green, and sparkled with tears and anger. Furious and fiery cheeked, she silently dared him to lay a hand on her. She intended to fight him tooth and nail, he realized. Her hair meant that much to her.

He lifted a long, glistening strand of the hair in question. It

felt like silk and was a lovely intriguing color—the exact shade
of honey from the comb. He had raided a bee's nest last autumn
and hoarded the honey all through the winter, using the remainder of it only this morning over the biscuits. He'd been looking
to please her . . . and look what it had gotten him: pure defi-
ance.

Still, hair like this shouldn't be cut; it would be a sinful waste.
It should be saved for a man to wrap around his neck and shoulders and bury his nose in while he made love to its owner. It
should be gathered up in handfuls and used to frame her face
before kissing her.

Matt studied Miss Livingston's flaming face. Why did she so
often make him think of kissing? She was so damn prim and
proper! Most of the time he didn't even *see* her as a woman.
But then he'd suddenly spot something in her eyes or in her
face—or as, in this case, her hair—and he suddenly wanted to
grab her and kiss some sense into her. Or kiss her senseless.
Maybe he just wanted to see if he could rouse a passionate
response. She *dared* him to prove to her she was female; didn't
she already *know* it? Maybe not, since she didn't accept the
limitations of her gender.

She shied away from intimacy, but she wasn't sexless—not
with this hair. Or her pink cheeks. Or those flashing eyes. Her
figure seemed to have all the proper curves, he noticed, now
that she had discarded those useless layers of fabric.

He moved the scissors closer to the strand of hair in his hand.
She flinched and looked at him with great pleading eyes. Tears
trembled on her lashes—extraordinarily long lashes, the longest
he'd ever seen on a woman. Oh, hell! She made him feel as if
he were poised to disfigure her face or cut out her heart.

He tossed the scissors onto the table. "You win, Boston. I
won't cut your hair."

Her face brightened.

"However," he continued, forestalling any comments. "You're
gonna have to hide it somehow. Try braiding it first. *Then* pin
it up. If that doesn't work we'll *have* to cut it."

"Oh, I know how to braid!"

"Do you?" He snorted. He wouldn't have been surprised if she hadn't; there was so much else she didn't know that she should have. "If you can't do it tightly enough I can show you the Comanche method. It will hold any hair in place."

He seized a large handful of hair and began separating it into three strands, but her hands flew up to cover his. "This I can do," she said softly. "I don't need your help."

He gazed down into her radiant upturned face. Doing so was dangerous; it made him think about kissing her again. Stepping back, he examined her new clothing. The shirt was too big; she had knotted it at the waist, accentuating the size of her bosom. The trousers hugged her slim shapely hips like wet buckskin. She hadn't donned the vest or chaps yet, and he could only hope they would do more to conceal her now rampant femininity.

This wasn't working out as he had anticipated. She did smell like a buffalo hunter, though. At least, he'd accomplished that much. As long as no man stuck his nose in her hair, from which wafted a floral fragrance, she should be all right. He'd have to keep men far away from her. Only distance would ensure her disguise.

"If you don't need my help braiding your hair, I guess I'll go back to work," he muttered.

"I . . . I guess I will, too." Blushing, she turned away.

He had a chance to study her butt as she retreated. It would *never* pass for a man's butt—not in a million years.

Seven

Over the next several weeks Matt ceaselessly drilled his honey-haired charge in riding, shooting, caring for horses, and cooking over an open fire. Gradually she learned to keep her balance while her horse trotted and loped. She didn't steer too well at the faster paces—she was too busy clutching the saddle horn—but she stopped falling off every time the horse increased his speed.

She learned to hit the barrel at thirty paces when she fired the Colt, but still couldn't manage the Sharps rifle. Every time she tried it, the retort knocked her flat on her . . . *derriere.* Her cooking also improved. Her biscuits were palatable if not perfect, and she learned to soak beans before boiling them. Matt taught her how to carry the day's supply in a water-filled calf's bladder while on the trail. She thought this disgusting, but conceded that it did solve the problem of how to soften beans before cooking them.

Last but not least, she learned how to groom and care for her own horse. To his surprise she took to grooming with enthusiasm, and soon had Dunston, as she'd named her horse, shining like a new copper kettle. However, when she started working on *his* horses, Matt became alarmed. He returned from riding one of his trainees out on the prairie to find her climbing into Renegade's pen with grooming brush in hand.

"Hey, Boston!" he yelled. "Get the hell out of there before you get yourself killed!"

Renegade didn't look at all unfriendly—only curious—but Matt wasn't taking any chances. He was the only person the stallion knew and trusted.

"What?" She turned to look at him. "What did you say?"

"I said, get your butt out of that stallion's pen!"

Quickly, she obeyed, then stomped over to him in her big, ungainly boots. "Why don't you groom that horse? He's filthy. I never see you brush him like you do the others. He might be nice-looking under all that grime. He has sweet blue eyes."

"He's a vicious man-killer. Stay away from him."

"If he's so vicious, why do you keep him?"

"Because he has his uses. I don't want you anywhere near him. The only one who's ever been able to handle him is me."

"Then you should at least keep him clean. Apparently you don't practice what you preach, do you, Mr. Stone?"

"He hates being groomed, that's why," Matt lied. Actually, Renegade *loved* being brushed and curried, but grooming would reveal his markings. "I don't relish being kicked or bitten, so I haven't made an issue of it."

She studied him as if she didn't believe it. Today she wore no hat. Her sun-kissed braids gleamed like dark gold fire, and wind and sun had heightened her color. Her vivid beauty was like a sudden punch in the gut—unexpected, and therefore doubly effective. He hadn't thought of her as beautiful before, but she was; either that, or sexual deprivation had altered his eyesight.

"From what I've seen, you can do anything with a horse. I bet you could train him to accept grooming."

"Probably," he coolly agreed, masking his intense physical response to her with a dismissive shrug of his shoulders. "I'm too busy to bother. I have to finish training the rest of these mustangs and deliver them to the fort before we can leave for Comancheria."

As if to prove his point, the mustang he was riding started prancing and pulling at the reins. He soothed the mare with a gentle "Whoa," and stroked her neck in a manner resembling a mare's nuzzling of her newborn foal. The touch almost always calmed a nervous young horse.

"When *are* we going to leave for Comancheria?" She lifted a slender hand to shade her eyes from the bright sunlight. "I'm ready. Haven't I learned everything you said I must?"

He snorted. "You've done well, Boston, but you're still likely to panic and forget things in time of danger."

"I won't forget things! I'm extremely reliable. Anyone in Boston can tell you that."

"I'm not talking about your good intentions or even your knowledge and common sense. I'm talking about behavior that should be second nature to you—like keeping your seat when your horse jumps out from under you. Or pumping off a shot without having to worry about hitting the target and hitting it, anyway . . . Hell, you still can't handle the Sharps. If something happened to me, how would you survive alone on the prairie? You turn up your nose at pemmican, but it may be all we have to eat at times."

"Those revolting strips of dried deer meat taste like leather! Why should I eat them when I don't have to? I can survive perfectly well on beans and biscuits. You can keep your petrified venison—or whatever—to yourself."

"Pemmican. And it's not just venison, it's also crushed choke cherries. Very nutritious. Keeps you going for weeks. We may not always have beans and biscuits—or be able to light a fire to cook or boil water for coffee. That's what I mean. You still think this trip will be some big, entertaining picnic. It won't be, Boston. When are you gonna realize that?"

"I do realize it." Her eyes blazed. "But I think we should leave before summer comes. You yourself claim it will take half the summer—or all of it—to find Quanah Parker and his band. The longer we delay the more likely it is that Colonel Mackenzie will find them first. And when he does, he'll shoot everybody in sight and identify the bodies later, including my sister's and her children's."

Matt suppressed a sigh. She was right, of course. Normally

he tried to keep Miss Livingston too busy to think or ask questions. Neither of them had the time to indulge in idle conversation. He spent the greater part of the day away from her, out on the plain working with horses. At night they were both so tired that they no longer found it awkward to sleep under the same roof. She rarely even complained any more or challenged his judgement. She just did what she was told, tried her hardest to succeed, and ignored her bumps and bruises.

Considering all that, he supposed she was entitled to ask how soon they were leaving. "Two weeks. Give me two more weeks."

"Two weeks!"

"I promised Grierson at the fort I'd have these horses well-trained. The last ones I delivered were only green-broke. One of them threw a man and fractured his arm. So he's asked me to take particular care with this bunch. . . . Don't look so put out, Boston. You need the time as much as I do."

"Oh, all right," she huffed. "I suppose I do. But the next time you go to the fort, could you please bring back my trunk? There are some things in it I really want to take along . . . and don't *you* look so put out! I've been wearing your stinky old clothes, haven't I? Every single day. If you could possibly locate a . . . a spare set of garments, I'd be delighted to pay for them. And I'd appreciate having my own brush and comb, instead of having to borrow yours."

Suddenly suspicious, Matt leaned over and sniffed. She no longer smelled like a buffalo hunter. She smelled like a woman with sun-warmed skin and hair. Her oversized shirt and under-sized trousers were definitely less filthy. She had apparently done her "woman thing" and washed them behind his back, using the soap he had produced at her insistence.

"Boston," he said menacingly, and her chin lifted a notch higher. "You're supposed to be a buffalo hunter. I can pass you off as a young one, if you'd just cooperate."

"I am cooperating! But . . . well, I need another set of clothes and smaller boots, too. I wrap my feet in strips of my old petticoat to protect them, but my boots still give me blisters. They aren't much better than the shoes I was wearing when I met you."

"What?" He sat up straighter. "Take them off."

"Here . . . ? Now?"

"Yes, here and now! Let me see your feet."

She sat down on the ground and tugged off her boots. Blood-stained strips of cloth bound her feet. Incensed, he swung down from his horse. Unaccustomed to quick movements on his part, the horse pulled backward, but this time he ignored the temperamental filly. "Why in hell didn't you tell me those boots were rubbing your feet raw?"

She thrust one foot back into a boot so he couldn't see it anymore. "Because I didn't want to complain—and the boots do protect my feet from rocks and stones and . . . snakes."

He wanted to shake her, but refrained from touching her. "You should have told me they were hurting you."

"I did tell you. Just now."

"After weeks of misery! Were you planning to wait to mention it until we were a month's ride away from civilization and a *different* pair of boots?"

She shoved her other foot in its boot. "Actually, I wasn't planning on mentioning it at all. I can endure discomfort, Mr. Stone. What I cannot endure is your assumption that I am very nearly an idiot."

"Only an idiot would behave the way *you* do! You should hear the things they're saying about you at Fort Sill."

Her head came up, and her eyes flashed golden. "Just what are they saying? They don't even know me—except for Mr. Tatum and the soldiers who brought me to the agency from Dodge. All of them seemed nice enough . . . and sympathetic to my cause, though they didn't agree with my plans."

"You're living out here alone with me," he grated, not caring if he hurt her feelings. Maybe she needed to have her feelings hurt in order to see reason. "You stole an army horse and rode out here all by yourself. Now you're staying out here, planning to be alone with me for the next several months. So what do *you* think they're saying about you?"

She looked stunned, as if the idea of a ruined reputation had never occurred to her. "Are they . . . maligning my virtue?"

He snorted. "Not Tatum. He's gone. There's a new agent now. His name is Haworth. He heard about you from Tatum, and the last time I visited the fort he demanded I return you—as if I were holding you against your will and ravishing you every night. I can only imagine what the few ladies at the fort are saying, because of course I don't speak to *them*. Rather, they don't speak to me. Then there's the soldiers. I returned the horse you stole, but the man who owns him is still outraged. And the soldiers who brought you to the agency are trying to figure out how they ever let you talk them into bringing you here from Dodge."

Miss Livingston jumped to her sore feet. "Because I paid them well, that's why! I imagine they didn't tell anyone just how much, either. At the time I suggested it should be 'our little secret'. But if they're gossiping about me, I'm sorry I paid them what I did. They might have done it for nothing."

"Undoubtedly. They'd hate to say no to a lady. The point is, anyone who's met you—or only heard about you—considers you witless. No white woman in her right mind would consider going into Comancheria. And if she values her reputation, she'd never take up with Matt Stone. What I forgot to mention when you first came here is that no one in these parts trusts me. I lived a long time among the Comanches and adopted their ways, and my brother *still* lives among them, so my loyalties are somewhat divided."

"I already know that. What I haven't observed for myself, Mr. Tatum told me. And the reason I 'took up' with you is because you're the only man around who can find the Comanches and help me rescue my sister. What people think of me doesn't matter. Once I find Ellie and the children, I'm taking them home with me to Boston, and I'll never see these people again, including you."

"As usual, when I try to reason with you the conversation goes nowhere. I don't know why I keep trying. Guess it's because I don't want to see those pretty braids dangling from somebody's war lance."

She briefly touched her hair, as if trying to reassure herself it was still safe on her head, but her face remained mutinous. "If it happens I should lose my hair, Mr. Stone, you won't be around to see it. Your own scalp will be hanging next to mine."

"That's what scares me, Boston. There's no guarantee the Comanches will be glad to see me. In their eyes I've betrayed them—walked out in a time of crisis when they needed every available warrior to defend the tribe."

"Oh!" she exclaimed. "I . . . I never thought about that."

"That's what I've been trying to tell you. There's one hell of a lot you've never thought about. Knowing how to ride a horse, shoot a gun, and cook over an open fire is just the beginning. What you still don't know could be the death of us, and there isn't time to teach you."

He remounted his skittish mare and left Miss Livingston sitting in the grass with a thoughtful expression on her elegant features.

On his next trip to Fort Sill he took the buckboard, so he could bring back her trunk. He also found a spare set of clothing and prevailed upon the army quartermaster to produce a new pair of boots—slightly smaller than the ones he had first given her. He then bought her a pair of soft, knee-high moccasins, beautifully beaded and decorated with quills; they were handmade by a Comanche woman. He didn't know if Grace would agree to wear them, but they would last like iron and pamper her feet.

By the time he got home, he had decided he was a fool to think she would appreciate them. So he hid them away, planning to give them to her only in an emergency, if something happened to her boots. The new boots thrilled her, and she thanked him profusely, then infuriated him by offering to pay for them. He told her he didn't want her damn money, but she wouldn't back off until he agreed to settle up later, when the trip was over.

Even then, she didn't look happy. He didn't care if she was happy or not; the idea of taking her money rankled him like a thorn digging into his flesh. Whether she realized it or not, Grace Livingston needed him in ways money could never buy. Her insistence on putting a price on everything was the one thing about her he couldn't abide.

By the second week of May, they were finally ready to search for Comanches. Grace watched Mr. Stone examine—for the third time—everything they were taking on three spare horses. He planned to ride the blue-eyed stallion he called Renegade, she would ride Dunston, and the three extra animals were supposed to carry supplies and give their main mounts a rest from time to time.

Grace named the extras Texas, or Tex, for the state they'd be entering, Oklahoma, or Okie, for the land they were leaving, and Lucy, because she liked the name. Mr. Stone neither approved nor disapproved of her choices; he was too busy debating what could possibly be left behind. He insisted they take only the essentials, so that if they found themselves in need of speed, the horses could deliver it. Besides, the more weight each horse carried the more time it would take to load and unload it each time they made camp. Grace had stuffed all her personal possessions into one small hide container called a *parfleche,* which was fastened to the back of her saddle atop her bedroll.

He had consented to take her tea and one tin of biscuits, but balked at the honey, and she'd had to jam the crock into the *parfleche* on top of her spare set of clothes. He hadn't been too excited about soap, either, so she had hidden a few cakes of scented French soap among her belongings, as well as two soft towels she *wasn't* going to leave behind.

She had never imagined that everything necessary to her comfort and well-being could fit in a space no larger than a

large cat might occupy when taking a nap. But that was about
the size of her *parfleche,* and she'd had to give almost as much
thought to packing it as Mr. Stone had given to the larger containers he was loading on the spare horses.

He was taking an inordinate amount of pemmican and ammunition, she had noticed. Since she didn't intend to eat the
pemmican or shoot anyone, he was looking after his own needs
at the expense of hers. About the only thing he hadn't argued
about was her medicine bag; apparently even *he* regarded medicine as a necessary and valuable commodity. Fortunately she
had secured her 'remedies' in a handy little drawstring bag—the
crockery and tin vials all carefully wrapped in their own indi-
vidual pieces of flannel.

Just as she was beginning to despair that they would ever
actually depart, Mr. Stone lifted his head and drawled: "Well,
what are you waiting for? Let's mount up."

"Christmas. Naturally, I was waiting for Christmas."

Her sarcasm had no visible effect. He never so much as
glanced over his shoulder as he went to get Renegade. Dirty as
ever, the stallion stood saddled and ready, with nothing but a
trailing rein to keep him from walking off. Mr. Stone had
brushed only the area where the saddle rested; the rest of the
horse's body was still an ugly muddy color. Her hands itched
with the desire to groom him. Was he really gray-brown? Or
dun-colored like Dunston? Only removing the grime would tell.

Mr. Stone fetched Lucy at the same time that he retrieved
the stallion. Leading the mare over to her, he handed her Lucy's
reins. "You'll be in charge of this one. If anything happens to
your gelding, she'll take his place."

"Nothing had better happen to Dunston." She accepted
Lucy's reins and wound them tightly around one hand.

"Don't do that!" He scowled at her.

"Do what? You said I was in charge of her."

"Don't wrap her reins around your hand like that. If she bolts
she'll take you with her. Hold the reins so all you have to do
is open your fingers to release her."

Grace sighed. She should have thought of that herself; why hadn't she? "Is there anything else I should know before we ride out?"

He gave her a look that made her toes curl. "There's plenty. Your lessons aren't over yet, Boston. Just try to think for yourself, will you? I may not notice all the stupid things you're likely to do."

His answer didn't please her. She was tired of trying to measure up to his impossible standards. He had far too high an opinion of himself, anyway. Looking more like an Indian than a white man, he was once again dressed in buckskins for the journey and had even tied a thong around his forehead to keep his shoulder-length hair out of his eyes. In Boston he'd be considered a crude backwoodsman. Well read or not, well spoken or not, Mr. Stone *appeared* illiterate. Most men who dressed and behaved as he did could barely read or write their own names.

"I'll try to warn you before I do something stupid," she told him. "That way, you can stop me before it's too late."

"First sensible idea you've had since you left Boston," he retorted, but this time, he grinned. "Wish I could hold you to that promise."

He flashed her another charming grin that was impossible not to return. After that he fetched the other two horses and mounted Renegade with that grace and ease she kept trying without success to emulate. She watched how he gathered the reins of the two packhorses in one hand and his own reins in the other, and then imitated him as best she could. Without a backward glance at either her or the ranch, he urged Renegade into a trot. Trying desperately not to thump up and down on poor Dunston's back, she followed.

They rode all day without speaking. Grace didn't mind, because she had enough to do mastering the art of managing two horses. Fortunately her horses followed the other three as if they feared being left behind. Mr. Stone alternated between walking and trotting. It irritated her immensely that he was able to do both as if Renegade's legs belonged to him.

By the time they stopped to make camp in the middle of a treeless plain, both her legs and her bottom were numb. She had no sensation below her waist—until she dismounted. Daggers shot up her limbs, and she nearly fell on her face. Her legs refused to carry her, but she still had to unpack her two charges, rub them down, and prepare for the night. She was hungry enough to eat a live buffalo, but didn't want to *think* about cooking. She couldn't see how Mr. Stone would have enough energy to manage, either.

"Which job do you want?" he asked, coming up to her. "Caring for horses or collecting buffalo chips for a fire?"

The last thing she wanted to do was go looking for buffalo chips in the waning light—and picking them up in her bare hands. "I'll care for the horses," she volunteered, thinking that now she had *five* to worry about, not just two.

"Don't touch Renegade. I'll get him ready for the night myself. Think you can safely hobble the others?"

"Of course. I'll be done before you get back."

By the time he returned she was half asleep—sitting on her bedroll and longing to lie down and rest her head on her saddle.

"Are the beans in the pot?" he snapped. "Are the biscuits ready for the skillet? Is the coffee set to boil?"

She had hoped all she had to do was care for the horses. That had been trouble enough. Tex had tried to kick her when she put on his hobbles, and Lucy had pulled away and led her a merry chase before finally standing still long enough to allow Grace to fasten her two front feet together, so she could walk about and graze, but not escape.

"No . . . I . . . I'm sorry. I thought you were going to do those things. You do them better, anyway."

"Look, Boston. Out here we each have to do our fair share and help out if we should finish first. There haven't been too many buffalo through here recently, and I had a hard time finding enough fuel for a fire. Now that I've got fuel I still have to get the fire going. By the time we're ready to cook it'll be dark, and cooking will be twice as difficult if nothing's been prepared. Don't you feel guilty sitting there like the Queen of England while I do all the work?"

No one had ever spoken to her the way Matthew Stone did all the time. By now she should be used to it, but she wasn't. Not in the least. "I've agreed to pay you enough money so that you *should* be doing all the work. Don't try to make me feel guilty for sitting down to rest for two seconds."

Rising, she dusted off her rear with the flat of her hand and stomped off to get the coffeepot and make biscuits.

"Forget it!" he hollered after her. "Tonight, we'll eat pemmican. If that doesn't please Your Majesty it's too damn bad, 'cause it pleases me!"

She stopped in her tracks. *Pemmican.* She'd vomit if she had to eat pemmican on an empty stomach, but she'd willingly starve before she apologized or asked him to reconsider. If she had to do the cooking by herself, she *would* starve. It was already getting dark, and she was so exhausted from the long hours in the saddle that her head was spinning.

Trembling, she walked back to her bedroll. "Have all the pemmican you want, you big, bossy savage. I'm going to bed."

"What did you say?" Kneeling next to his pile of buffalo chips, he gave her a look that would shrivel a grizzly bear. "What did you just call me?"

"A big, bossy savage! That's exactly what you are, so don't bother denying it." Refusing to look at him, she lay down on her bedroll and pulled a blanket up over her shoulder.

"Well," he drawled after a long moment. "At least we've finally gotten past Mr. Stone. I was beginning to think you were always going to call me *Mister* Stone."

"I am no longer going to call you *any*thing. Not tonight, anyway. Goodnight . . . Savage." She lowered her voice before adding the last, but knew he heard it because he chuckled under his breath.

"Sleep well, Boston."

On her first night under the stars she slept amazingly well and awoke to the glorious sound and smell of sizzling bacon. It was barely light, but a soft glow lit the eastern horizon. The bossy savage was hunkered down near the fire, preparing breakfast.

Hoping he wouldn't see her, Grace rose from her bedroll and headed toward the horses.

"Don't be long, Boston. Breakfast's almost ready."

So much for privacy. Still, she put Lucy between them, and by the time she returned to the fire he was kicking dirt over it to smother it.

"Why are you doing that?" In the chilly air she would have welcomed the fire's warmth.

"So no one will spot our smoke and come to investigate. Dawn and dusk are the only two times we can risk lighting a fire."

"But the Comanches might see it, and finding them is why we're here."

"We're here to find *them*—not for *them* to find *us*. There's a big difference. Sit down. Here's your plate."

Reminded of that other day when he'd kept her from starving, he handed her a plateful of heaven and strength for another day. She devoured everything on it and never once questioned the wisdom of eating beans, biscuits, and bacon for breakfast. If she were lucky, she'd have the same thing for supper. If she weren't, she'd have pemmican.

Over her second cup of coffee she watched the sun rise, and the bossy savage sat still long enough to enjoy it with her. First there was only a soft orange glow, then a bar of golden light, and, finally, *magic*. A huge shining ball inched its way above the horizon, revealing rolling plain and gilded grass stretching as far away as the eye could see.

Only the mountains in the west and an escarpment rising like a table in the far south suggested any other sort of terrain on earth. The immensity of the land gave Grace a sense of deep humility and insignificance, as if she and Mr. Stone were the only two people in the whole empty universe.

Except that it wasn't empty. Antelope gamboled in the distance, prairie dogs barked, and jackrabbits hopped about their daily business. Overhead, huge predatory birds soared through the blue expanse. The wildflowers of spring were fast fading, but the buffalo grass was so green it made her heart hurt to look at it. For the first time, she had some notion of why the Indians wanted to hold onto land she had at first thought barren and depressing, hardly worth battling over.

"This country is much prettier than I first thought it was," she said.

His brows arched in surprise. "Have you seen prettier? I've always thought this land the most beautiful on earth. Despite the storms of winter, it's the most friendly to human and animal life. If you like it now you should have seen it years ago, when I was a boy. The buffalo and antelope herds were so big they covered the plain for as far as you could see."

"They were that big?" She couldn't imagine such a thing. "What happened to them all?"

His features darkened. A moment later, he rose to his feet, abruptly ending the conversation.

"Mr. Stone, wait! Aren't you going to answer me?"

His bitterness had never been more apparent. "The white man came."

Grace longed to challenge the remark; buffalo hunters couldn't possibly be responsible for the destruction of herds so big they had once covered the entire plain. Her bossy savage didn't give her the chance to argue. Without another word he headed for the horses, leaving her to clean up the breakfast mess and ponder his hostility toward his own race.

Eight

The first week of their journey flew past, and Grace gradually adjusted to the awkwardness of spending all day, every day, and every night in the company of The Savage, as she had mentally labeled Mr. Stone. To her great delight, her body ceased to protest spending the entire day in the saddle. After the fourth day she was only stiff—not numb—when night came. Surprisingly she also developed a craving for fresh meat, which The Savage provided with enough regularity to keep her appetite constantly whetted.

At first she hated to see a brown-eyed, fleet-footed antelope or deer tumble to the earth in response to a shot fired at a great distance from the heavy Sharps rifle. But after she tasted venison steaks grilled over a hot fire, she managed to overcome her sympathy for the victim and keep a vigilant lookout for distant movement on the horizon. The Savage always bemoaned leaving the carcass and hide behind, but they couldn't stop long enough to dry the meat, much less the hide, and after a couple days it spoiled. *He* was still willing to eat it, but she regarded the reeking flesh with more loathing than she did pemmican. For her, meat had to be fresh; even then she couldn't gorge herself on it as he did.

"You'll learn," he told her the first night they dined on steaks and he offered her a third one, which she declined. "When you live off the land like the Indians do, you feast when food's

available. That's how you store up enough fat on your body to
see you through times of famine."

"I'm not an Indian. I'll get sick if I eat too much."

"You'll get sick—and possibly starve—if we run out of food
and can't find more right away," he scoffed.

She conceded that he might be right. By the end of that
first week, *despite* stuffing herself almost every night, her
snug-fitting trousers fit loosely, and her shirt was bigger than
ever. Even more amazing, she was sleeping more soundly than
she had ever slept in her life. She lay down on her bedroll,
her head pillowed on her saddle, and—poof!—she'd be gone,
and didn't awaken until morning. Mr. Stone usually had to
awaken her. It was more like dying than sleeping; in Boston
she had never slept like that. She was the sort to lie awake
for hours debating a business move or mentally counting her
money. On the prairie she thought of such things maybe once
during a single day, and often not at all.

At the end of their first week of travel, though, Grace lay
down to sleep and couldn't dose off immediately. She blamed
it on the fact that The Savage had been unusually quiet all day.
Never one to waste words, he could be quite charming and
talkative on occasion—pointing out items of interest on the
plain, teaching her how to distinguish between buffalo, bunch-
flower, and needle grasses, or explaining how best to skin an
antelope, but today he silently brooded.

They were nearing the Staked Plain, or *Llano Estacado,* as
the Spaniards had called it. It walled off Comancheria from the
south and the west, rising in what was now the Texas Panhandle,
south of the Canadian River, and running north and east. To her
eyes the Staked Plain looked like a gigantic walled fortress rising from the prairie. To his eyes, apparently, it looked like . . .
home.

That morning he had explained that Comancheria extended
through half of Oklahoma and part of Kansas, along the Santa
Fe Trail. In recent years, as more and more whites moved into
Indian Territory, Comancheria had been shrinking. The *Llano*

Estacado was now the last bastion of freedom for the beleaguered Comanches, and the closer they got to it, the more distant and introspective Mr. Stone became.

If he still thought of the Staked Plain as home, that home could not have been a happy one. How could anyone be happy among the bloodthirsty Comanches? He never discussed his childhood or life with the Indians; whenever the subject arose, he avoided mentioning his brother, what had happened to his white family, his friendship with Quanah Parker, or any of the other people he must have known, white or Indian.

As she gazed up at the stars Grace indulged in her favorite pastime—trying to figure out Matthew Stone. His past was a mystery and his present filled with contradictions. If he hated whites so much and deplored what they had done to the Indians, why had he returned to the white world?

Since he thought so little of buffalo hunters why did he carry a Sharps rifle and shoot game, as they did? He hadn't shot any buffalo, because they still hadn't seen any—and he wasn't happy about that. Only yesterday he'd told her that by now they should have spotted several small herds, at least. At this time of year what remained of the once countless animals should be headed for the northern grasslands, and crossing through this same territory. The total absence of the bison deeply angered him. His fury was almost a physical thing, giving off vibrations noticeable from fifty feet away.

Grace wished she understood him better. She had always prided herself on being a good judge of character, but The Savage confounded her. He exhibited so much gentleness and sensitivity, along with callousness and cold-heartedness. He defied being labeled as good or bad, moral or immoral, gentle or cruel. He killed animals with great efficiency, but afterwards he always paused a moment and knelt on one knee beside them. Sometimes he gently stroked them, as if apologizing for taking their lives. Was this a habit he had learned from the Comanches?

His way of dealing with horses was similar; she had never witnessed such patient silent communication between man and beast. He never lost his temper with them, and horses responded in kind. Lucy never ran away when he approached with hobbles, and Tex never threatened to kick him.

Once, when she had yanked too hard on Dunston's reins, he had ridden up to her, scowling like a thundercloud, and asked if she would fancy having a piece of iron in her mouth for the rest of the day. He had threatened to put a bit between her teeth and make her carry it, attached to two thongs, so he could tug on them whenever he wanted—and teach her what it felt like to be yanked on unexpectedly.

After that she tried to be more careful of Dunston's mouth and simply "sat deeper" to make him slow down. And these days she always remembered to say "Whoa" when she wanted to stop. She still couldn't ride as if she and Dunston were dancing partners; that might take years to perfect.

Yawning, Grace closed her eyes and willed her brain to relax. Maybe on the Staked Plain The Savage would reveal new insights. Maybe he would do or say something to betray who he truly was—white man or Indian. Perhaps he was just a tormented creature trapped between the two.

Just before she drifted off, she heard a man's voice muttering in the darkness. Making no sound, she strained to listen. The muttering came from Mr. Stone's bedroll. He was saying something—but not in English. It sounded like gibberish. Then his voice rose sharply. As he released an anguished cry she sat up, huddling in her blankets and debating whether or not to wake him.

"No!" he hollered, switching to English. "No, Thad, you didn't have to do that! She was only a child, for God's sake!"

She could hear him thrashing about, twisting and turning in his bedroll. Darkness hid his face, his distress no less compelling for being half-concealed. She scrambled out of her blankets, rushed to his side, and dropped to her knees in the dewy grass next to him.

"Mr. Stone . . ." She touched his sweat-dampened shoulder. He was shaking. She smoothed the tousled hair back from his forehead. He made a sound like a harsh sob. He couldn't be weeping! Not this proud, strong man. Not this man who was so fierce she thought of him as The Savage.

Without hesitation, responding to her own need, she wrapped her arms around his shoulders, offering wordless comfort. His arms slid around her waist and pulled her closer. Trembling in the grip of his nightmare, he clung to her and murmured in her ear. Once again, he spoke gibberish.

Twice he called sharply, "Thad!" and once he muttered something that sounded like "stalking wolf" and another time, "sweet water".

"It's all right. You're safe. It's only a bad dream."

He gave no indication of having heard or being aware of her embrace, other than clinging to her. For Grace, hugging him was a devastating experience. Her breasts were crushed to his chest, her cheek pressed to his jaw, and her hips molded to his torso. The intimate position reminded her of the night he had crawled into bed with her, only this time the contact of their bodies proved more disturbing. She had lost her inclination to fight it. Now she relished learning his contours, and enjoyed every single one of their physical differences.

The Savage wasn't just male, but *blatantly* male—his body harder, stronger, leaner, and more fit than the body of any man she'd ever encountered. He possessed a suppleness and grace that made other men seem brutish by comparison. He was, she thought, *unique*. Whatever battle he fought in his dreams had to be one of great magnitude, for a lesser conflict could not have affected him so. He despised weakness and would *not* be pleased to discover that *his* tears were wetting *her* cheeks.

For a quarter of an hour she stayed locked in his arms. Finally his breathing slowed, he stopped mumbling, and his grip relaxed. She wished she could remain where she was and enjoy the warmth and comfort he unwittingly offered, but when she thought of him awakening suddenly to find her there, she knew she had to leave and return to her own bedroll.

Gently, she extricated herself from his embrace. Before she escaped, he drew a deep breath. "Boston? . . . What's wrong?"

He sat up, and she blessed the darkness of the moonless night for hiding her face. "N-nothing."

"Nothing? Then what are you doing over here?" His hands closed around her upper arms. His heat burned through the fabric of her oversized shirt to sear her sensitized skin.

"I heard . . . something." She *couldn't* tell him she'd heard him sobbing in his sleep. "I . . . I was going to wake you."

He bolted to his feet and reached for his gun, always close at hand. "Stay here. Don't move or make a sound."

Silent as a shadow, he left her and made a circuit of the camp. Moments later, he returned. "Nothing's out of the ordinary. Renegade didn't whinny, did he?"

"No." She shook her head. "That wasn't what I heard."

"Good." He knelt beside her. "At night he's my eyes and ears. If any living thing approaches, he warns me. No one can sneak up on Renegade. He thinks he's guarding his herd."

"That's reassuring. I wondered about the wisdom of both of us sleeping at the same time. Now, I know why you weren't worried."

"Nor should *you* worry." He cupped her face in one hand. "You needn't be afraid at night, Boston. Renegade and I are both looking after you when you sleep. So long as we don't leave a fire lit to mark our camp, it's unlikely anyone will accidentally stumble across us. This prairie is too damn big."

"I . . . I should go back to bed then."

He didn't answer immediately. His hand slid down to rest on her shoulder. Gently, he kneaded it. When he did speak, his voice had the texture of velvet. "I guess you should—but maybe you'd prefer to stay here, where I can keep an eye on you. My bedroll is big enough for two."

She wanted to stay, wrapped in his arms as she had been a few moments ago, but they were moving too fast—rather like a horse bolting from fear and galloping across the prairie out of control. She needed more time to think about this. It wasn't what she had planned; *he* wasn't the right man for her, possibly for any woman. She was a Boston blue blood, and he was . . . The Savage. A woman of her social class and strict moral up-bringing didn't agree to share a man's bedroll, simply because he had asked her. The idea was appalling. But for just a moment, she wished her name weren't Livingston.

"No," she said. "Thank you, but I'm fine now. Really."

She *was* fine—but the only way she could retain her dignity was to pretend he hadn't been suggesting something improper and that she hadn't been ready to accept the offer.

With a deep sigh he removed his hand from her neck, leaving her feeling cold and vulnerable. "Too bad you won't stay, Boston. I guarantee you'd find the night memorable. I'd give you something to think about besides fear."

"I'm not afraid! And I didn't come over here hoping to share your bedroll. I came because I heard you. You were talking in your sleep—having a nightmare, I think."

"You heard me? What was I saying?"

"I couldn't understand a word, but I think it was . . . Co-manche talk."

After she said it she was sorry. His mood shifted and he moved away from her. "If I talked in my sleep tonight, it had nothing to do with you, Boston. If you ever hear me again, ignore it. My dreams are *my* business. Don't butt in where you're not wanted."

She almost blurted that he'd been weeping. For a man as hard and proud as Matthew Stone, such knowledge would be devas-tating. So she said nothing.

"Believe me, in the future I won't bother you. Goodnight, Mr. Stone." She rose and headed for her bedroll.

His mocking voice followed. "I'd rather you call me Savage than Mr. Stone. Coming from you, it sounds kinder."

She didn't respond. He *was* a savage. What else could a woman call a man who weakened her moral fiber? First he made her feel things she didn't want to feel. Then he mocked her when she acted on those feelings. She never should have gone over there. She had learned her lesson; comfort a wild injured animal, and it was likely to turn on you and bite.

The following morning began in agony. Grace *never* got cramps during her monthly, but today they were severe and disabling. She had packed clean cloths in her *parfleche* in preparation; still, it was humiliating to have to deal with the issue in the middle of an open plain.

Luckily Mr. Stone never glanced her way as she went out among the horses. However, when she returned and started rummaging through Lucy's packs, he shouted at her.

"What are you doing? Don't change anything, or the pack won't be evenly loaded. The mare could develop sores from carrying it."

"I'm looking for my medicine bag. I need it."

She had intended to save her remedies for dire emergencies; the pain relieving elixir she had brought might not even work on cramps, but she had to do something; she could never mount Dunston and ride all day otherwise. And she certainly couldn't tell The Savage what was wrong with her.

He stalked over to her. "Leave everything alone. I'll look for your medicine bag."

She stepped back, but not before he got a good look at her face. "Are you ill? Are you in pain? Why are you clenching your teeth like that?"

She hadn't realized she was clenching her teeth. "I'm not sick. I just need my medicine bag."

"Go sit down before you fall down. Your face is the color of clay. I'll get your damn medicine bag."

She stumbled over to her saddle and sat down on it sideways, drawing her knees close to her body. When she and Ellie were younger, Ellie had always been the one to get cramps. Grace had never had much sympathy. She had suspected her sister was exaggerating her discomfort to gain attention. Their mother and Mrs. Hugg made a big fuss over Ellie, preparing special teas and providing hot compresses. No one ever mentioned the cause of her mysterious ailment; they told everyone Ellie suffered from "a female indisposition."

Now Grace wished she had paid more attention to cures for the problem. She had never felt such pain; what if it wasn't due to her monthly? What if she were dying of some grave sudden illness?

Mr. Stone's moccasin-clad feet stepped into her line of vision. "Here's your bag." He knelt in front of her. "What do you want from it? I'll get it. Your hands are shaking."

Her hands *were* shaking. "H-how should I know? I don't know what will help. A couple of things are intended to relieve pain, but. . . . oh, just give me the bag."

She snatched it from him and promptly dropped it. He grabbed the bag in one hand and her elbow in the other. "Tell me what's wrong with you. Maybe I can help."

"I don't want you to help! Just give me the bag and leave me alone." A wave of nausea hit her, and she groaned and fought to keep from vomiting.

"Get up. No, lie down. Where does it hurt?"

"Here," she moaned, clasping her lower abdomen. "I don't know what's wrong. I've never had pains like this before. Usually, I hardly know it's happening."

"What's happening? Do you mean you're bleeding?"

To admit such a thing to this man of all men was something Grace couldn't do. So she ignored the question.

"Get on your hands and knees." He pulled her up and turned her around. "That's right. Kneel here in front of me."

Straddling her from behind, he reached around her front and started kneading her belly. She was too miserable to care about the shocking impropriety of the position or what he was doing. Incredibly, as his hands manipulated her she began to feel relief. He stroked deeply and rhythmically, loosening and relaxing her. The cramps ebbed and finally disappeared.

She drew a deep breath, lay down on her stomach, and rested her head on her crossed hands. Still straddling her, he asked: "Feel better?"

"Much better, thank you." She rolled over. He moved to one side and sat down casually near her. "Where did you learn to do that? How did you know it would help?"

He shrugged. "Once, when I was still a youth living among the Comanches, I saw two women in the woods near our encampment. They'd been sent away, but I didn't know why. Curious, I spied on them. One woman seemed to be in pain, and the other did that to her to stop it. It worked. That's all I knew. When the women saw me, they started screaming, warning me to leave them alone. It was forbidden for me to be there. I sprinted all the way back to the tipi, where my Comanche father, Night Hawk, told me I must never spy on women, or even look at a woman during her time of bleeding. If I did, I would lose my male power. The women had been sent away to protect the men from losing their powers during the time of female uncleanliness."

"Female uncleanliness!" Grace didn't appreciate the notion that women were unclean during their monthlies. Still, she was fascinated. The Savage was relating an actual incident of his life among the Indians. "And did you? Lose your power, I mean. After all, you looked at those women."

He grinned. "Not that I noticed. That's how I knew he was wrong. Oh, I worried about it for several days, but about a week later I had my first sexual encounter. All my male powers seemed to be perfectly intact."

Oh, how he did love to shock!

"With whom did you have your first . . . um . . . sexual encounter?" She blushed while she asked the question.

"Can't remember her name." He studied her until her cheeks flushed even more from embarrassment. "Among the Comanches, sex outside of marriage isn't such a big deal, Boston, unless it's a matter of a brave taking someone's wife without the husband's permission. I think she was an aunt."

"An aunt!"

"An older female relative. It was her duty to initiate me, so I wouldn't bother the younger prettier girls, who almost always went to men old enough to be their fathers. Comanche warriors buy their wives with horses, and it takes a long time to collect a herd big enough for a bride price, especially for the most desirable maidens."

"Men *buy* their wives with horses?"

"The system has worked well for centuries. Don't condemn a custom you know nothing about, Boston. Whites do things that seem strange to the Indian, too."

"But I want to learn about their customs! They sound so interesting. And they must have *some* merit, because what you just did worked wonders. I don't understand why or how, but my cramps have disappeared."

"Glad to hear it, because we have a long hard ride ahead of us. Today, we'll meet rough terrain—hard on humans and even harder on horses."

He ended the discussion, leaving Grace with much to think about. She had made a small dent in the wall he had built around his past. In terms of pride and dignity it had cost plenty, but the price was worth it. She wanted to learn more about the people who had captured her sister. Suddenly, the savages appeared more human; Comanche women suffered cramps the same as she did! What other similarities did they share?

"So tell me what it was like growing up in Boston, Boston."

The horses were climbing a steep narrow trail leading to the high plain, and Grace was fearful. If Dunston made a mistake in where he placed his feet, they would plunge to the earth far below. She almost welcomed the question; it took her mind off her potentially imminent demise.

"I grew up surrounded in comfort and what most people would call luxury. Servants did all the work. My father owned a prosperous shipping business, and Ellie and I wanted for nothing—except perhaps a brother. My parents were disappointed that they never produced a son, someone to carry on the family tradition."

"So why didn't they find a rich husband for you when you came of age and let *him* take over the business?"

"Both my parents died before my future was secure. They perished in a carriage accident on the wharf. Something frightened the horses, the carriage overturned in a crowded area, and . . . well, my parents and the driver were all killed. The story hit the papers, and half of Boston turned out for their funerals."

She could see The Savage shaking his head as he urged Renegade up the rocky incline. "And everyone says it's dangerous out here in the wilderness. Sounds to me like a big city is worse. Was that what soured you on horses?"

"It didn't sour me on horses. Well, yes, maybe it did. City life *can* be dangerous, but one gets used to it." *As you have grown accustomed to dangers on the prairie.*

"Was your sister married by then?"

"Oh, yes!" Grace scraped her boot against the wall side of the incline, but was too afraid to make Dunston move closer to the precipice. "Ellie had eloped the year before with her husband, William. He took her west to find their fortune."

"But she's younger than you."

"Yes, by two years. Her elopement broke my parents' hearts. At the time, they were concerned about *my* future, and parading young men before me at every opportunity. I hadn't yet seen one I liked. After Ellie's desertion I stopped looking and devoted myself to becoming the perfect attentive daughter. Guess I was hoping I could atone for her mistake. I was always interested in my father's business, and after Ellie left, we spent many long hours together in his office. He allowed me to help keep his books. I learned so much during that year. As it turned out, I was fortunate to have had that time alone with him. It prepared me for my future."

"You took over after your parents died?"

"Not immediately—no. At least, not entirely. During the mourning period I simply tried to keep things operating. Our clients were accustomed to seeing me with my father, and they didn't withdraw their business after his death. They knew we had a very competent solicitor who handled many arrangements while my father was still alive. His name is Bartholomew Gumby, and he continued to handle things after my father died. He is still managing my affairs. I put him in complete charge before I left Boston."

"When did you decide to devote your whole life to running the family business?"

She hadn't actually said she had done that, so Grace glanced at him in surprise. Intent on guiding Tex and Okie up the steep trail, he never looked back at her.

"A couple years *after* the deaths of my parents. By then I was quite enjoying the challenge of the business. It consumed me totally and alleviated my grief. By then I had discovered I could make things happen—you know, put together my own deals and arrangements. People didn't always take me seriously, but Mr. Gumby helped me, and I managed to make some handsome profits for myself and the company's investors."

"No man came along with a marriage proposal?"

"Oh, I've received a proposal, Mr. Stone. You needn't sound as if you doubt it."

"Have you? Tell me about it."

"No. That's rather personal, and can hardly be of any interest to you." She wasn't going to tell him about Roger, his exact opposite in every way. "It did not work out."

"You scared him off. He wanted someone sweet, shy, and manageable—not a female who knows her own mind and does exactly as she pleases."

"*I* was the one who ended it, not he!" Grace bristled. "He . . . he disappointed me."

"Disappointed you? How?"

"I don't wish to discuss this any further."

"Never mind. I can guess."

"Guess *what?*"

"How he disappointed you."

She waited for him to elaborate. When he didn't, she burst

out: "You shouldn't make judgements about things you know nothing about, Mr. Stone!"

"Why not? You do," he shot back.

"Such as?"

"Everything, Boston. You have an opinion about everything, whether or not you have firsthand experience. Take Comanches, for example. You've admitted you'd like to learn more about them, but you still think they're terrible people. If I tried to change your mind about them, it wouldn't be easy."

"No, it wouldn't. But I have a dead brother-in-law to consider."

"We all have our dead, Boston. And we all mourn."

"For whom do you mourn?" she asked, trying not to betray her eagerness to learn more about him.

"That's rather personal," came the dry reply.

"If I won't talk, you won't—is that it? How many of the sordid little details of my life must I reveal before you tell me *any*thing about your life?"

"I've already told you some things."

"Not enough." *Not nearly enough.* "I still feel as if I hardly know you."

"You'd get to know me a lot better if you consented to share my bedroll."

The audacity of the man! Did he think he was dealing with a common strumpet? Why did he keep hounding her?

"Humph!" she responded, at a loss for words to put him in his place.

He glanced back over his shoulder at her, his eyes dancing. "I've promised not to disappoint. Don't you believe me?"

"Do keep a civil tongue in your head! And watch the trail. We could plunge to our deaths at any moment."

"How sad if you die without ever knowing a man, Boston. A waste, I'd say."

"If you mean *know* in the biblical sense, I disagree. You are exceptionally conceited if you think a woman hasn't lived unless she's been intimate with you."

He snorted derisively. "I can tell you haven't been long in the wilderness. After a while out here you start to understand that life is so precarious and uncertain you ought to grab whatever pleasure you can, *while* you can. When death stares you in the face, it doesn't ask if you're ready. Have you done everything you wanted—lived life to the fullest, and seized every possible scrap of pleasure? It just takes you, sometimes violently and painfully."

"And have *you* savored life's pleasures, Mr. Stone?" She was thinking of the poverty in which he lived—the bare little shack and the plain fare he ate—but he, apparently, was thinking of something else.

"I've tried, Boston. In my own small way, I've tried."

She yearned to ask him if he had ever felt velvet next to his skin or drunk champagne or sat down to a lace-draped table laden with delicacies. Had he ever tasted fruit or rum from a tropical island, smelled the fragrance of a rare perfume, or viewed a magnificent theatrical performance?

She didn't think so. She had experienced all of the finer things, yet he presumed to lecture her on her failure to enjoy life! What gall. What irony! The man was so profoundly ignorant that he didn't know what he was missing.

Yet, as she thought about it, she realized she *had* been denied certain things most women took for granted: marriage, family, children, her own home lovingly created by her own two hands and those of a husband she loved with all her heart and deeply respected.

She had been willing to settle for less with Roger, simply to gain a business partner and ward off loneliness. What might it be like to love a man passionately, with no reserve either physically or emotionally? What would it be like to yearn for his embrace and go willingly and joyously to the marriage bed?

Until she'd met Matthew Stone she had never asked herself these disturbing questions. He pricked her as few people in her life had managed to do. Ellie had always been the emotional one, given to tears and laughter in equal measure. Ellie had viewed life with the eyes of an idealistic dreamer. She—Amazing Grace—had been the practical, no-nonsense one, the level-headed, dutiful daughter in love with the workings of business and finance, immune to the charms of the male species.

She mustn't dwell on those thoughts or be distracted from her goals. She had a fine life in Boston—an enviable life—and she intended to return there as soon as possible and take up where she had left off.

Marriage to Roger was no longer an option; she had destroyed that possibility. By the time she returned home, Roger would have found himself another over-ripe heiress, anyway. It didn't matter; she could no longer be satisfied marrying a man to whom she was not personally attracted. Now that she knew she was capable of *intense* physical attraction, she couldn't be satisfied with anything less.

However, Matthew Stone would never fit into her world, and she would never fit into his. It was senseless to spend so much time thinking about him. But as the long hours of hard riding continued, Matthew Stone, The Wicked Savage, was almost *all* she could think about.

Nine

The high plain of the *Llano Estacado* stood between the eastern timberlands and the blue-shadowed western mountains. For centuries the climate had been cyclical, alternating wet years with dry. Spring brought the rains that produced a riot of wildflowers glowing in the dark green, matted grasses. Under the summer sun, the grass turned sere and brown, and the plain more closely resembled a barren desert.

Even then, Mr. Stone told Grace, grass grew in certain places, and water could be found. Despite the harshness of winter storms, the earth rarely froze, which was what made the plain so perfect for wildlife and those humans who respected the land's dictates and abided by them.

Rivers abounded: There were nine major ones—the Arkansas, Cimarron, Canadian, Washita, Red, Pease, Brazos, Colorado, and Pecos, as well as many smaller tributaries. They had cut canyons and arroyos that provided shelter from the constant wind. Their sandy banks supported stands of cottonwoods, wild plums, and mustang grapevines. To the east, pecan, walnut, elm, chinaberry, ash, *bois d'arc,* hackberry, Osage orange, willow, redbud, haw, persimmon, and oak trees proved this was no desert. Even in the dry west, mesquite flourished.

Everything man needed to survive was here—or had been, before the white man came. For all Mr. Stone's talk of the destruction of the vast herds who made the plain their home, Grace still didn't believe so many animals could have existed; on the fourth day after they had entered the *Llano Estacado* her eyes were opened.

They were riding across a vast treeless region, flat as a tabletop, when she noticed a strange, noxious scent on the wind. The further they rode the stronger the stench became. Becoming nauseated, Grace broke the silence of their ride to ask what it could possibly be.

Mr. Stone halted and waited for her to catch up with him. Normally he rode ahead, leading Tex and Okie, while she brought up the rear with Lucy. She hadn't seen his face since that morning, and now wished she hadn't bothered to ask the question. His ferocious expression struck a chord of fear in her heart; more than ever he looked like a savage. His mouth was a grim slash, and his eyes smoldered. His glance could have burnt holes in leather. She could not detect a hint of the humor or gentleness he displayed on other occasions. He seemed to be plotting violence.

"You'll see soon enough what you've been smelling for the last hour," he growled.

"But what is it? Tell me. I want to know."

"Buffalo," he snapped, then rode ahead, as if words cost money and he dared not waste them.

If buffalo smelled as bad as this, she was glad they hadn't encountered any so far. They must be filthy beasts indeed, to emit such a terrible odor. The horses didn't like the smell any better than she did. As they drew closer to its source, Dunston and Lucy started tossing their heads and snorting, only reluctantly proceeding in the direction Mr. Stone was taking them.

Expecting at any moment to see the huge beasts at long last, Grace anxiously studied the horizon. All she could see was a glistening, yellowish body of water lying in the distance, a remnant of the spring rains Mr. Stone had described. Overhead, numerous big birds—vultures—circled . . . and then she saw the buffalo.

Hundreds lay on the ground—perhaps thousands. Their huge bloated bodies dotted the plain for almost as far as she could see. They were all dead, every last one of them. Someone had stripped away their hides to expose dark rotting muscles, flesh, and bones with gristle still clinging to them.

At first Grace couldn't assimilate the carnage. She thought some of the beasts were still alive. They moved. Closer inspection revealed wolves and coyotes roaming among the carcasses, burying their heads in the spoiled meat and emerging with dripping jaws and eyes glazed with gluttony. Flies hovered in clouds, their buzzing incessant, as Mr. Stone passed the first of the fallen victims.

"Can't we go around this?" Grace gagged on the stench.

"No. It would take too long. The smell will only follow us, anyway. We'd have to go miles out of our way to avoid it. Pull your kerchief over your nose. It'll help."

At the start of their journey, he had provided her with a blue kerchief to knot around her neck and cover her mouth and nose in case of dust storms. Grace followed his advice and tugged the cloth up over her mouth and nose, but the barrier didn't help. The stench was too strong. Swallowing hard, she tried not to breathe deeply. Still, her stomach churned, and she feared she would be sick.

Everywhere she looked she saw dead bison, recognizable only by their huge size. How could there be so many? How could anyone have killed them without all the others fleeing?

Apparently they *had* fled, for the bodies extended for miles. The trampled, darkly-stained grass indicated that many of the beasts had tried to escape even after they'd been shot. Only some of the smallest, the babies, hadn't been stripped of their hides. Grace wondered why they'd been shot at all, if the hides had so little value. It was wanton, savage destruction: heartless and cruel, ugly and shocking. She could not imagine what sort of men would do this, and she felt a clear echo of the rage stamped on Mr. Stone's face.

By late afternoon, they had passed through the worst of it. Grace dreaded making camp and trying to eat. She doubted she'd be able to keep food down. Mr. Stone stopped long before she was ready. Suddenly he halted, slid down from Renegade, and dropped to one knee to examine the ground. Riding up to him, she saw the remnants of a campfire and the imprint of horses' hooves.

"Who's been here—the men who killed the buffalo?"

"Looks like it. They camped here not long ago—couple of nights, at most. My guess is they're taking their time, killing and skinning buffalo as they go. Did you see the stack of hides back there?"

Somehow she had missed it. She was glad. She didn't need to see any more horrible sights today. He remounted in his usual effortless manner.

"Come on. We'll head west to make camp. They're up ahead of us, and I don't want to catch up to them unexpectedly. Tomorrow I'll ride out early, check their trail, and figure out how best to avoid them and still get where we're going."

"Where exactly are we going?"

"To find the Comanches."

"I know that. But I thought you were looking for Indian signs. Have you seen any?"

"We're still too far away from the region where I think they're hiding. I haven't seen a single hint of their presence, or proof that they've passed through the area."

"Were you expecting to find dead buffalo?"

He shook his head. "Not to this extent. Every year the hunters start earlier in the season. It just goes to show how stupid and greedy they are. At this time of year, the hides aren't prime. Indians hunt buffalo mostly in the fall, when the animals have grown their winter coats. The whites don't even wait for the calves to mature. They kill 'em before their hides are worth anything."

"I saw all the calves." Grace sighed. "I know nothing about buffalo, but still, I was saddened. It's all so wrong . . . all that spoiled meat. All those wasted lives."

"Indians kill only what they need to feed and clothe their

families. They use everything. Only *your* people make waste like this."

Your people, too, Grace thought.

They rode until long after sunset. Supper was pemmican. Mr. Stone didn't want to light a fire. That was fine with Grace; she still couldn't eat anything. She could not have tolerated even coffee and biscuits. By now they had gone far enough into the wind that the stench no longer followed them, but she fancied it had seeped into her hair, clothing, and bedroll. Before she lay down to sleep, she shook out all her belongings and prayed the wind would remove the lingering taint. Mr. Stone ate silently and spread out his bedroll without a word. Tonight he didn't tease as he sometimes did, or give her long, sensual looks that invited her to change her mind about sharing his bedroll.

A new moon rose, and it was colder than usual, with a strong wind. Wispy white clouds sped across the star-filled sky, wolves howled in the distance, and Grace shivered in her blankets. The altitude was higher on the Staked Plain than elsewhere, and summer hadn't yet arrived. Sometimes, the night air stung. Tonight, Grace suffered from the bone-deep chill of having ridden so many miles through death and decay. . . . How harsh the land seemed! No wonder it produced harsh men. Men like The Savage. Men like the buffalo hunters who spent their days killing and stripping off skins. Men like Painted Horse.

Grace hadn't thought of Painted Horse for a while. Somehow she could easily imagine him galloping across the high plain beneath the new moon. This was his sort of land and his sort of night. Hugging herself, she tried to block out the image of his white horse emblazoned with handprints. Even more frightening was the man himself—face gleaming with war paint beneath the curved buffalo horns. She *never* wanted to meet him again. But she fell asleep dreaming of him and, knew she would never forget him no matter how hard she tried.

When Grace awoke it was morning, and Mr. Stone and Renegade were gone. A wave of panic swept her when she sat up and realized she was completely alone. Miles of rough country lay between her and any sort of civilization. If The Savage failed to return, she would have to rely on herself—a terrifying thought. She'd rather face an angry stockholder or investor in a failed business scheme than have to cope with staying alive in this harsh wilderness.

She recalled Mr. Stone telling her he intended to ride out this morning to check the trail of the buffalo hunters. She wished he had awakened her before leaving. Or better yet, taken her with him. Being alone frightened her more now than it had when she had first come to Indian Territory. Now, she had a better understanding of the dangers she faced.

Atop her *parfleche,* she found the Colt he had left her; it was loaded and ready to use. Still, nervousness gnawed at her. What if something happened, and he didn't return?

Afraid to make a fire, Grace ate some pemmican to still the rumblings in her stomach. She brushed out her hair, rebraided it, and turned her attention to grooming the hobbled horses. When that was done, she loaded the horses so they'd be ready to leave when Mr. Stone returned . . . *if* he returned. Having done everything she could, she sat down on the ground and waited.

By the time he finally came, the sun had nearly reached its zenith in the burning blue sky. Driving several horses ahead of him, he rode right up to her. Renegade was covered with lather and breathing hard, and Mr. Stone himself looked drawn and weary.

"Where have you been?" She didn't care how strident she sounded; she was furious. "Where did you get those horses? Are we taking them with us?"

He posed his own surly question. "Are you ready to leave?"

"Of course, I'm ready. I've *been* ready."

"Then take the hobbles off the horses, mount up, and let's go. We've already wasted half the day."

He made it sound as if the delay were all *her* fault. "Just how do you intend to lead all these extra horses? I have all I can do managing Lucy and Dunston."

"These extra horses will make good spares if we should need them. If we don't need them, the Indians will be glad to get them. Don't worry, Boston, you don't have to do a thing. Renegade and I will handle it."

"From the looks of Renegade, you're working him too hard. He could use a good grooming and a long rest."

"None of us can rest right now, so quit whining and get moving."

"I'm *not* whining! But if you aren't going to tell me where you were and what you were doing all this time, you can go straight to perdition!"

For the remainder of the day, Grace didn't speak to him. Nor did he speak to her. Charming as a boulder, The Savage rode ahead of her, herding Tex and Okie along with the newcomers. Seething inside, she followed. His refusal to explain his long absence or the presence of the new horses sorely rankled; he had no right to keep secrets or ride off and do as he pleased.

They both tended to forget it at times, but he was her employee—a man she had *hired* and promised to pay generously. Some might say *too* generously. How dare he treat her with such callous disregard for her feelings! Well, she would give him a dose of his own medicine. She would behave as if he didn't exist, either.

Late in the afternoon, lulled by the heat and the steady pace, Grace half-dozed in the saddle. Luckily, there were no more dead bison or other unpleasant distractions. The terrain was flat and uninteresting, consisting of nothing but buffalo grass rippling in the ever-present wind. Occasionally they passed a clump of mesquite.

When Dunston suddenly halted, Grace roused herself to determine why. Ahead of her Mr. Stone had also halted, and his charges had dropped their heads to graze. The Savage's peculiar posture alerted Grace that something was wrong. Usually he sat straight as a lance, with a bearing that could only be described as arrogant. Now he slouched, and actually seemed to be . . . swaying.

At the very moment that she called his name, he toppled from the saddle and fell heavily to the ground, catching one foot in the heavy leather stirrup. Renegade never moved a muscle; he only swung his head around as if he, too, were amazed by his master's odd behavior.

Grace leapt from her horse in a manner that would have done credit to a Comanche. Leaving Dunston and Lucy to graze, she sprinted toward Mr. Stone, released his foot from the stirrup, and turned him over to lie flat on his back. His buckskins were drenched in blood, the source of which was some sort of shoulder wound. Until she removed his shirt, she couldn't gauge the seriousness of the injury, but the sight of the blood stunned and frightened her.

"Mr. Stone! Can you hear me?" Gently, she shook his arm.

He didn't answer, other than to groan. All day he had ridden in what must have been agonizing pain. Now, apparently, he had reached the end of his strength; that meant *she* was in charge, responsible for both of them.

She sprang into action. With an efficiency that shocked her, she tied a clean cloth around Mr. Stone's shoulder to stanch the bleeding, unloaded the horses and hobbled as many as possible, spread out Mr. Stone's bedroll, dumped out the *parfleche* containing her medicine bag, assembled all their canteens of water, and tore strips from a spare flannel shirt to provide additional cloths. Then she gathered enough buffalo chips to make a fire, got one going, and started heating water in the coffeepot.

She'd never done it before, but she figured that nursing was all common sense, anyway. Even if she made a few mistakes, it was better that letting Mr. Stone lie there and bleed to death on the plain. When everything was ready, she took off his shirt. The sight of his bare chest, sprinkled with crisp, curling, copper-colored hair, gave her a moment's pause. But she quelled her misgivings about touching a half-naked man, especially *this* man, and gently cleansed the nasty looking crease in his shoulder. A fragment of blackened metal stuck to his raw flesh. In her anxiety over removing it, she forgot all about the awkwardness of the situation.

When finished, she sprinkled a yellow powder from her medicine bag over the wound before bandaging it. The powder supposedly prevented infections, and she desperately hoped it would work. Mr. Stone had been shot, but rather than penetrating or remaining in his flesh, the ball had forged a deep path across his collarbone and disappeared, causing blood loss but no critical damage—none she could see.

She maneuvered him to lie atop his bedroll and then covered him with one of her blankets. He never stirred. Confident she had done all she could, she tackled supper. By now it was twilight. She knew she had to hurry and put out the fire before darkness revealed the burning embers. A simple meal of biscuits, bacon, and coffee revived her flagging energies. However, she couldn't get Mr. Stone to eat anything. Setting his food aside for later, she smothered the fire, retrieved her pistol, wrapped herself in her remaining blanket, and sat next to his prone figure, where she could keep an eye on him during the night.

With nothing left to do but think, she finally allowed herself to speculate on what had happened when Mr. Stone left her that morning. He must have run afoul of the buffalo hunters. The extra horses he had brought back with him suggested that he had exchanged gunfire with the hunters, perhaps killing them, and then had stolen their horses. She had heard no gunfire, but the wind might have scattered the sound before it reached her. She had to face the shocking truth: *Her savage might well be a cold-blooded murderer.*

Sitting there beside him, Grace grimly considered the possibility. Had his anger against the buffalo hunters been great enough to drive him to murder? She wanted to give him the benefit of the doubt, but if he *hadn't* killed them, why had he hidden the fact that he was wounded? Did he think she would never notice he was bleeding to death?

Had she not been so angry with him she would have noticed

much sooner. Tomorrow, no matter what he said, she would insist that he rest a couple of days before continuing their journey—assuming, of course, that he didn't die during the night. The wound itself wasn't enough to kill him, but the loss of blood and any resultant infection could prove fatal; she'd heard of people dying from what had started out as simple cuts and lacerations.

Stubborn idiot. No doubt he considered it unmanly to complain of so slight a thing as getting shot. When he was better she'd give him a good scolding—one he wouldn't soon forget. He had foolishly endangered his own life and hers. Without him she didn't stand a chance of surviving this trip and finding the Comanches on her own. If she did find them, or they found her, how could she ever explain what she wanted? It was Mr. Stone's job to do all the explaining. But here he was—seriously hurt, helpless, and unconscious—with nothing to show for it but a few extra horses.

Maybe he had stolen the horses and left the buffalo hunters on foot to teach them a lesson. . . . No, he'd done something much more wicked and shameful, something he didn't want her to know—such as killing the men outright. *That's* why he'd failed to mention that he'd been shot in the process.

Her savage probably deserved what he'd gotten; but then she thought of the slaughtered buffalo, and recalled her own anger. She couldn't kill anybody over it, but she had never experienced the same suffering as her savage. *Her savage.* What a mystery he was! Since he was so unwilling to explain himself, she might never understand him. And he wasn't her savage; he was *The* Savage, and she'd better remember that.

Curling up next to him, Grace succumbed to weariness. Barely had she closed her eyes when the heat of his body awakened her. He wasn't just warm; he was feverish! And muttering to himself again.

Fumbling for a canteen in the darkness, she dribbled water down his throat, spilling most of it on his chin. Anxious to cool him somehow, she took off her kerchief, wet it, and dabbed his face and mouth. Thrashing and moaning, he brushed aside her ministrations and babbled nonsense. He didn't recognize her or even seem to realize she was there. Suddenly he grabbed her wrist and with surprising strength pulled her over on top of him.

"Sweet Water, honey, is that you?"

"Mr. Stone, it's me—Grace Livingston . . . who's Sweet Water?"

"Don't go, sweetheart. Don't leave me," he mumbled. "Don't listen to what they're saying. You know I'm no coward. Hell, I've taken more white scalps than Quanah. . . . Please. Stay with me. I know you love me. . . . Don't go."

Mesmerized, Grace devoured every word. "I won't go. I'll stay. Just tell me about . . . Sweet Water."

"Weren't we good together, at least at first?" he pleaded. "I tried to make you proud. I know what you want and need. You deserve a great warrior, someone totally committed to The People. That's me—*was* me, until . . . until . . ."

"What?" she urged. "Tell me."

"But it's no good anymore. Don't you see? I can't keep living a lie. I only did it this long for you . . . and for Quanah and my brother. For Thad. No, I mean Stalking Wolf. For him. He's one of you, more than I've ever been. He's never known any other life but this. He can't remember, not like I can. I remember everything . . . *everything*. Do you know what that's like? Have you any idea? . . . No, of course not. How could you? You were born a Comanche. You only know the Comanche side of it. I should never have married you, but you were so beautiful. Don't leave me. Stay with me. You're all I've got. We'll make a new life together—not white, not Indian. We can do it—Sweet Water, don't go!"

He resumed thrashing, and Grace rolled to one side to avoid being struck. Throwing off his blankets and flailing his arms and legs, he struggled in the grip of his fantasies. Afraid he would start bleeding anew, Grace summoned all her strength, threw herself across his body, and held him down.

"Mr. Stone, stop it! Can you hear me? You've got to stop this thrashing about, or you'll harm yourself."

As quickly as his agitation had erupted, it subsided. "C-cold," he stammered. "S-so c-cold."

His teeth were chattering. Grace gathered every available blanket, including their two saddle blankets, covered him, and again stretched out beside him, trying to share her warmth.

Gradually, he quieted. As sleep reclaimed him, his breathing became deep and even. Grace stayed at his side, but sleep now eluded her. Her savage belonged to another woman: *a Comanche named Sweet Water.* He himself had killed and scalped whites. Enough to impress his beautiful wife. Grace no longer had the slightest doubt he had killed the buffalo hunters. Worst of all, she was half in love with him! Even knowing he was a murderer, she couldn't stop herself from caring. *His* pain was *her* pain—and if that wasn't love, what was?

Did his Comanche wife still live? Would seeing Sweet Water again make Mr. Stone want to return to the Comanches? Rejoining his brother and Quanah Parker was bound to affect him, too. Any fool could see that it wouldn't take much to drive him into the opposite camp.

Grace acknowledged her own jealousy. She abhorred the idea of Mr. Stone being married, especially to an *Indian.* She didn't want to care for him, but she did. She wished he had called out for "Boston" instead of Sweet Water. What had happened to her pride?

Now, at last, she understood how her sister had been able to abandon her own family and run off with a man she barely knew. Love was a sickness, a mental and emotional disorder that produced eccentric, out-of-character behavior.

However, she refused to accept the situation like some helpless ninny. She would fight her ridiculous inappropriate feelings with every breath she took. *She would not yield to them.* Grace Livingston would *never* waste herself on a tormented killer with a violent past and an uncertain future. Only because he was ill would she cradle him in her arms. Once he recovered, she would never get this close to him again.

Several times during the night he awoke thrashing and mumbling. Grace was able to calm him only by holding him tightly and murmuring in his ear. Near dawn he broke into a sweat. She used the remnants of the torn shirt to wipe him dry, so that he wouldn't catch a chill. After that he slept deeply, and she was able to relax without checking on him every few minutes. She must have slept, too, for when she awoke, his hand was cupping her breast.

Light flooded the sky, but the sun's rays had not yet reached them. Lying still, she tried to decide if he had regained consciousness and knew what he was doing or was still delirious and unaware of his actions. Then his fingers began to move, gently exploring, and she knew he had regained his senses. She grabbed his hand and held it still.

"Boston?" he murmured, his tone questioning.

"You . . . you must be feeling better." She started to get up but he pulled her back down, his strength surprising.

"Don't go yet. Please don't go. Just let me hold you."

"But . . . your shoulder."

"A flesh wound. That's all it is—nothing serious."

"But you lost consciousness! And you bled so much . . . and you . . ." She was going to mention his ramblings about his wife, but the words stuck in her throat.

"I dreamed. I had strange dreams. I have those even when I'm *not* wounded. They mean nothing."

Nothing?

"Please," he whispered. "I just need to hold you."

She couldn't say no. She had thought he was dying, and now he wasn't. It was a miracle. What harm would it do if he simply held her? They lay still together for several long moments. Gradually, the tension left her. She released his hand, and he moved it slightly until it was once again near her breast. This time when he fondled her, she allowed it. A curious languor claimed her, rendering her incapable of objection.

Heedless of his injury, he curled around her, hugging her as he caressed her breast. If she made any sudden movements, she might hurt him—or so she excused her reluctance to stop him. As he snuggled a little closer, the lower half of his body pressed against her *derriere*. Desire exploded in a dizzying rush.

Mortified by her own responses, she hardly dared breathe. In the past, she had rarely thought about her sexuality. Now, as he awakened long dormant feelings, she wanted to revel in it. Temptation burned hotly inside her. Perhaps she was a secret Jezebel, titillated by the dangerous and forbidden!

As she wrestled with a lifetime's training in self-denial, Mr. Stone's other hand insinuated itself around her body, so that he now held both breasts. Oh my! His fingers were so agile and clever. Within moments her whole body was quivering with need. She couldn't subdue her own purr of pleasure. Hearing it, he gently turned her toward him, leaned over her, and kissed her.

The simple act evoked vivid exciting images of naked flesh pressed to naked flesh. Drowning in sensation, she clung to him—being careful not to touch his shoulder—and swam through dark scented waters toward some shimmering promise of rapture. Matthew Stone could teach her everything she wanted to know and deliver her from eternal loneliness.

"Gracious!" She sighed when the kiss ended. "Are you sure you—?"

"Yes, I'm sure. This is the best medicine a wounded man could ever have."

He resumed kissing her, and his tongue silently taught her about mating. When he combined kissing with stroking her breasts, she feared she might truly expire. A moan started in her throat. As she released it, he moved his mouth to her left breast. Boldly, he nuzzled her through her shirt, then tugged the shirt free from her trousers, eased it up, and pulled *down* the lacy edge of her chemise.

Her chemise, the type called a *jaconet,* was made of cambric, trimmed with lace, and buttoned down the center. Mr. Stone jerked impatiently at the front of the garment and sent all the buttons flying. Before she could formulate a protest, his mouth descended on her bare breast, and his hand slid inside her trousers and across the taut fabric of her drawers to cup her between her legs.

Grace bucked in astonishment.

"Let me, Boston," he growled in a voice so low she didn't recognize it. "Let me."

While he waited for her answer, he held her possessively, as if he *owned* her femininity. In a blinding burst of treachery, her body responded with a deep pulsing ache that shuddered through her like the long roll of thunder preceding a violent storm. She wanted nothing more of life than to shamelessly spread her legs and let him have his way with her.

Too soon, her mind shouted rejection: *No matter what he said, the man was gravely injured. Worse, he was a murderer. She couldn't trust him. He'd take what he wanted and leave her devastated and brokenhearted. She could conceive a child and be left to bear it alone while he returned to his Comanche wife and dazzled her with his expert lovemaking.*

Ten

"Mr. Stone!" It wasn't easy to summon enough authority to let him know she truly meant for him to stop.

He nuzzled her neck. "Boston, don't tell me you don't want this as much as I do. I've no taste for forcing a woman, something your white soldiers have been known to do to squaws when they find them alone and vulnerable."

"And something Comanches have been known to do to white women every chance they get."

He withdrew his hand from her lower body. "Not every chance. And not every Comanche. Do you want this or not, Boston? Your body tells me you do. However, you keep pretending you have no feelings for me, so I'm giving you the opportunity to back off while you still can."

Grace was suddenly so embarrassed she couldn't utter a coherent sentence. Acknowledging the intimacy of their position and the truth of what he was saying, she flushed with shame. "I . . . I . . ." she nervously stammered.

"You *what?* Make up your mind, Boston. . . ." He sounded bossy and business-like, but his throaty growl betrayed his own inner turmoil. "Ah, but your breasts are magnificent!" he sighed. "They're all rosy and swollen—proof that you want me. I could make it so good for you, Boston. I could make you feel better than you've ever felt in your life."

She pulled her shirt down with a jerk. "Don't look at me!"

"Why not? Has someone told you you're not beautiful? If

so, they were wrong—or they never saw you flushed with desire, your eyes sparkling, your hair shining in the sun. . . .
You're a prime piece of womanflesh, Boston—a lovely ripe female crying out for a man's loving."

By now the sun's rays *had* reached them. Mr. Stone's hair
gleamed with coppery highlights, and his eyes were as green
as the buffalo grass. They were devil eyes. And he had a devil's
grin. His rugged male beauty robbed her of breath. She pawed
his bandaged shoulder in a halfhearted attempt to push him
away. He winced when she touched him, reminding her that he
was badly injured.

"You . . . had better let me up," she croaked, sounding more
like a frog than a woman. "In your condition you shouldn't be
doing this. Deny it all you like, but you *are* hurt. Besides, I . . .
I *don't* want you. N-not like this."

"Not like what?" His smile faded. "You mean not lying under
God's blue sky on a bed of thick grass perfectly fashioned for
men and women to share while they pleasure one another? . . . .
Ah, I see. This isn't good enough for you. You fancy more
luxurious surroundings. A big four-poster bed covered with a
fluffy quilt. A two-story, fancy house. And you want a man with
pale white hands, soft as a woman's because they've never done
a day's lick of work."

Or killed anybody.

"Is that so terrible?" Squirming away from him, Grace
clutched her shirt together over her naked bosom and sat up.
"When I lie down with a man, I want one who has given me
his name, along with his body and all his worldly possessions.
One who's committed to me for the rest of our lives and will
always be there for me and my children. I am not some loose
immoral female, Mr. Stone, who never thinks of the consequences of her actions. So stop sniffing after my skirts like
some . . . some pushy, male dog."

"You aren't wearing a skirt. And you didn't bind your breasts
like I told you to, either," he added accusingly.

"I didn't think my—they—were big enough to worry about."

"They're plenty big enough. And so are your hips. I can tell you're pure female from two miles away."

"Then I should have worn a skirt, after all."

"You can't ride as well wearing a skirt." He, too, sat up. Grimacing, he clutched his head in both hands.

"What is it? Does your head hurt? I *knew* we shouldn't—"

"My head and my shoulder hurt like hell! Since you don't intend to alleviate my pain, let's not discuss it, shall we?"

"D-doing what we were doing kept you from feeling pain?"

He lifted his head and gave her a wry mocking glance. "I didn't feel a thing a few moments ago . . . pain, I mean. I was too busy savoring other sensations—the ones you won't permit yourself to feel."

"I'm not made of stone. Whatever you may think. And I felt plenty while you were . . . while we were—"

"So you admit it, at least."

"I admit to nothing! I'm just not in the habit of trading intimacies with near strangers."

"Too bad, Boston. I'd give nearly anything I own to have you touch me the way I was touching you. I've dreamed of you caressing me like that."

He wanted her to . . . ?

Her cheeks flamed at the notion, and she couldn't return his mocking gaze. She couldn't even face him, so she turned her back to him. He laughed—the scoundrel!

"Believe me, Boston, if you suddenly grabbed hold of my crotch, I can promise you it would take my mind off a bum shoulder and a headache."

"I have a headache powder in my medicine bag. Would you care for some?" she murmured, red-faced but trying to hide it.

"I'm a man, Boston, in case you haven't noticed. Men don't take headache powders."

"Oh, and I suppose they don't explain how they happened to get shot, either."

"No, they don't. At least, I don't. What happened yesterday

doesn't concern you. So there's no need for you to know about it."

She jumped to her feet and faced him. "Doesn't concern me! It certainly *does* concern me. If you had been killed, what would have happened to me?"

He rose and towered over her, exuding all the male strength she found so challenging and irresistible. He shrugged, then winced again. "If I should die unexpectedly, reverse your direction and travel northeast. Eventually you'll encounter civilization. . . . Either that, or you can light a fire and keep it burning day and night. Someone will be sure to spot it."

"And rape or kill me! Or make me a slave."

"Probably. But this trip was *your* decision. I tried to talk you out of it. So don't blame me if what I warned you against actually happens."

She narrowed her eyes and glowered at him. "Sometimes I hate you, Mr. Stone. Do you know that? Or if I don't, I could *learn* to hate you very easily."

"Or love me," he drawled. "You could also learn to love me. All you have to do is take off your clothes and come to me without shame or embarrassment. As explosive as things are between us it's gonna wind up bein' one or the other—love or hate. Take your pick, Boston."

"Love isn't only about taking off one's clothes!"

"Maybe not, but it makes a hell of a good start. Considering who you are and who I am, what does the rest of it matter? We're hardly a good longterm match, Boston—except in passion. You're every bit as passionate as I am only you hide it better, while I don't try to hide it at all."

"Naturally not, since men aren't the ones who have babies," she sneered.

"Worried about babies, are we? If you had my baby, I'd stand by you. Of course, it might not be in the manner to which you're accustomed. Therein lies the source of your hesitation."

"It does not! Only don't worry about it, because I'm never going to have your baby!"

"Where's my shirt?" he asked, looking around. "What did you do with my buckskin shirt?"

Grace stalked over to the spot where she had left it spread out on the grass to dry after she'd sponged off the worst of the bloodstains. Snatching it up, she threw it at him. "Here's your bloody damn shirt!"

"My, my, Boston, such language," he tsk-tsked. Glancing down at the shirt, he exclaimed: "Whoa! Dirtied it up a little, didn't I?"

"You almost bled to death all over it!"

"Guess I'll have to be more careful in the future. Maybe tonight or tomorrow, I can find a river when we camp. I need to bathe—and wash this shirt. You can bathe, too." He gave her a sly look. "We can bathe together."

"Go to hell, Mr. Stone." She stomped off to look after the horses, realizing only after she'd left him that her language was definitely worsening. This time she hadn't sent him to perdition, but to hell. He was having a terrible effect on her language.

Two nights later, they did indeed camp beside a river. Grace was still ignoring him, so she didn't ask him the name of it. Broad and shallow, with sandy banks and a smattering of scrubby brush along its banks, the river glittered in the early evening light as if diamonds had been scattered across its placid surface.

As she unloaded Dunston and Lucy, Grace looked up to find Mr. Stone stripping off his clothing. Except for a fringed pouch hiding the bulge between his legs, he was naked as the day he was born, and every bit as magnificent as she had imagined— broad-shouldered, slim-hipped, muscular, and beautifully proportioned. If ever there was a perfect specimen of the human male he was it—the ideal model. Except for his bandaged shoulder, of course.

Grinning at her shocked expression, he beckoned to her. "Come join me, Boston. This will help take the stiffness out of my shoulder. Besides, I bet you could use a bath, too."

"Not with you watching me. And I refuse to watch *you!*"

Grabbing a towel and a bar of her scented soap, she stomped further downriver and found a small indentation along the river-bank, screened from view by a thicket of thorny, green-leafed bushes leaning out over the brownish water.

Stripping down to her chemise and drawers, Grace waded into the sun-warmed shallows. If Mr. Stone came after her, hoping for a peek at her nakedness, he wouldn't see nearly as much as he hoped. She intended to use this opportunity to wash her undergarments, along with her body. She immersed herself, came up sputtering, and began soaping her hair and skin. The fragrance of the soap tickled her nostrils, and she inhaled it with greedy delight.

She had so missed bathing! Out here on the plain, cleanliness was a luxury. In the past she had always taken it for granted. Never again would she fail to appreciate squeaky-clean hair and grime-free clothing. So lost did she become in her bath that she forgot to keep watch for Mr. Stone. Instead of rushing through her ablutions, she took her time and savored the glide of water on slippery skin. Finger-combing her hair, she suddenly felt a hand close around her ankle.

"Don't!" she shrieked, only to have her mouth and nose fill with water as Mr. Stone pulled her under the surface and thoroughly dunked her.

She came up gasping. "Stop! I can't swim! I'll drown."

"You can't swim?" His eyes were mischievous, his tone teasing. "Guess I'd better teach you, hadn't I?"

He hooked an arm around her waist and pulled her off her feet, dragging her outward, where the water was deeper.

"Oh, please, no! I beg you! Don't take me out in water over my head."

"It isn't over mine," he said. "Hold onto me. I'll keep you from drowning."

She clung to him tightly, which was surely his intent. In no time at all they were in water deep enough to ensure that she keep both her arms and legs locked around his torso. Eyes dancing, he grinned with satisfaction.

"Better not let go of me, Boston. The water is deep. I myself can barely touch bottom."

"You're doing this on purpose—you despicable savage!"

"Have to live up to my reputation, don't I?" He pressed his pelvis against her, and she didn't dare pull back. . . . My goodness, but he was huge! And wearing nothing at all. Wide-eyed and open-mouthed, she gaped like a fish as he allowed her to feel the full-length of his . . . unmentionable.

"Like that?" he asked, sliding back and forth between her clenched thighs. "I took the liberty of removing my breechclout. Wouldn't you like to remove your drawers?"

"No, I would not! What kind of man are you, to take advantage of me like this?"

"A man who's been too long without a woman, Boston— more specifically, too long without *you*." His hands wrapped around her buttocks and held her still. "Mmmmm, you smell good." He sighed.

"It's the soap you said I shouldn't bring. And I thought you were going to teach me to swim!"

"I am . . . in a minute. First I just want to smell you—and feel you. Too bad you didn't remove everything. I want to feel you skin to skin."

At the thought of being skin to skin with him, Grace nearly swooned. She inhaled a mouthful of water and began to choke. Mr. Stone regretfully pulled her toward shore, where he gave her a hard thump on the back between her shoulder blades.

"You'd do anything to avoid the inevitable, wouldn't you, Boston? Even drown."

Now that her feet touched bottom and the water was only waist deep, she seized the opportunity to put more space between herself and him. His size frightened her. He was much too big—or she was much too small. How on earth would he ever fit inside her, if—by some remote chance—she changed her mind about sharing his bedroll?

"Go away." She sniffed. "I want to get out now."

"But I want to stay and watch you get out. Wet cloth has a

way of clinging, and I'm sure I'll be able to see almost every luscious inch of you. If you'd like, you can take a look at every not so luscious inch of me."

"You are truly wicked, aren't you? I keep telling you no, and you keep trying to change my mind. I don't want to be intimate with you! Why do you hound me so?"

"Boston, don't cry. You aren't going to cry, are you?"

She hadn't meant to cry, but now she felt like it. She was just so confused! Just because they were male and female and alone together didn't mean they had to allow nature to take its course. He couldn't know how fearful she was—not only of his size and of the act itself—but of all the possible consequences. Childbirth was only one of them. If he touched her—if she let him—she would never be the same again. She *knew* it. She would be forever changed. But she didn't think *he* would change. The next time he was alone with a woman for days on end, he'd be every bit as eager to bed *her*. Sweet Water was the woman he loved, not Grace Livingston.

"I am not going to cry," she said stiffly. "I will not permit you to make me cry. You only want me because you can't have your Comanche wife."

He looked thunderstruck. "How in hell do you know about her?"

"I know. In your delirium you raved about her."

"I raved about her?"

Grace nodded.

"When was I delirious?"

"You don't remember?"

He shook his head.

"I held you that first night after you were wounded. You thrashed about and called her name."

"I never did! I wouldn't do that. What we had is over. It's been over for a long, long time."

"It's not as over as you think it is. Deep down you still care for her."

"And that's why you won't let me near you? Because of Sweet Water?"

She dashed away a tear, hoping he wouldn't see it. "Not just because of her—no. You fail to see I'm not the sort of woman who can toss aside her virtue and think nothing of it."

"Do you think I chase after every woman I meet? That I'm the sort of man who wants just *any* woman? I want *you,* Boston, because I know—I sense—we'd be special together. When we first met, I didn't even find you attractive. But the more time we spent together, the more I found myself wanting you. Now, it's as if I'm possessed. I think about you all the time. I imagine making love to you—touching you all over. Giving you pleasure. Kissing and caressing you. When I close my eyes at night, all I can see are your milk-white thighs—"

"Good heavens. When did you ever see my thighs?"

"Oh, hell! Didn't you ever see—or want to see—mine?"

Gracious. Could he read her mind? She *had* thought about his thighs—how muscular they were in his buckskins, how they might look with*out* buckskins. Even now, she wanted to look down in the water and *see* him—and not just his thighs.

Obviously they'd been alone together too long. This ravenous mutual hunger was a consequence she had not expected. Now she knew why society considered it improper for young ladies and gentlemen to spend time alone together before they were wed. No wonder parents insisted upon chaperones! People who didn't even like each other were capable of the most primitive animal desires.

"I admit to a certain . . . prurient curiosity, Mr. Stone. That doesn't mean I need to indulge it. We are *not* animals."

"I am," he growled. "When I see you standing there, so wet you might as well be naked for all the protection your garments provide, I want to take you in my arms and teach you what it means to be female. We may be human, but we have the same basic instincts as every other animal on earth—only *we* complicate everything a hundredfold. If we were two cats or dogs or horses, we sure as hell wouldn't be standing here *discussing* our feelings—we'd be acting on them."

"Oh, leave me alone, will you?" She marched out of the water. "Stop watching me and . . . and lusting after me!"

She snatched up the towel and wrapped it around her body.

"I can leave you alone, and I can stop watching you, but I doubt very much that I can stop lusting after you. A man doesn't choose to lust or not to lust. He can only choose what he does *because* of his lust."

"Well, you'd better choose to control yourself, because I fully intend to control myself."

"Control is what you're good at, isn't it, Boston? Matter of fact, it may be the thing you're *best* at. As for me, I need a good long swim in some very cold water."

He's right, she thought, watching him as he turned, dove into the water, and swam out deeper. She was famous for her control. Over the years she had learned to mask nearly all of her feelings, to the extent that she almost *never* acted on pure instinct. The one exception had been when she'd heard about Ellie's capture. She had made up her mind in an instant that she was going to rescue her sister, and she'd been willing to spend every dollar she had and endure any suffering or discomfort to achieve that goal.

Though unexpected, this conflict with Mr. Stone was hardly insurmountable. The fact that she wished he had pressed a little harder—taken her in his arms and kissed away all her objections—meant nothing in the overall scheme of things. Eventually they would find the Comanches, and the entire circumstances of their relationship would change, affording relief from all this togetherness.

They only wanted each other because they had no one else to talk to or think about. Forced to share one another's company day and night, they had become obsessed with the idea of sex. In any other setting they wouldn't have spared a second look at each other, let alone have sunk to *this*.

Grace took advantage of Mr. Stone's absence to hurry and

dress in her spare set of clothing and then wash her dirty garments and hang them to dry on the bushes. There wasn't time to brush out her wet hair until much later that evening, following a silent, awkward meal consisting of roasted fowl and biscuits, which she barely tasted.

Leaning over the dying fire, she brushed out her hair as quickly as possible. She was counting on the fading warmth to eliminate the last lingering dampness before night fell, and Mr. Stone smothered the embers. Mr. Stone sat across from her, saying nothing but watching her as intently as he'd earlier watched and ensnared the prairie chicken for their dinner. His eyes glowed as hotly as buffalo chip coals, but he'd said not a single word to her since his return from his swim. She wondered if this was how it was going to be from now on—utter silence between them, filled only with unspoken thoughts.

Pretending to ignore him, she struggled to work the brush through a snarl at the back of her head, where she couldn't see it. She wished she had a pair of scissors to cut it out, instead of struggling like this. While she muttered to herself and yanked at her hair, Mr. Stone rose from his bedroll like some sleek, supple feline and strolled over to her. One would never guess he even *had* an injury. His recovery astounded her.

Taking the brush from her hand, he said: "Hold still. I'll do it—unless you're afraid to have me touch you."

"I'm not afraid of you!" That was partially true. She was more afraid of herself and what *she* might do if he touched her. Drawing her knees up in front of her, she hugged them while he knelt behind her and brushed her hair.

He didn't yank or pull on it, but set down the brush for a moment and patiently worked on the snarl with his fingers. When he was finished, he resumed brushing her long hair—using gentle thorough strokes that made her shiver, close her eyes, and tilt her head back, reveling in the sensation.

He brushed her hair until it was crackling, but he never touched her otherwise. Then he silently handed her the brush, kicked sand over the fire, and lay down on his bedroll. Within moments he fell asleep. Only after she was sure he was sleeping could Grace find the strength to seek her own bed.

All he had done was brush her hair, but she felt as if he'd made love to her. His hands had been so gentle, teaching her what she was missing by refusing his other ministrations. This was going to be hard, the hardest thing she'd ever done. But how could she just give into him? She couldn't. As he had been quick to point out, they were hardly a good, long-term match for each other. He'd be as out of place in Boston as she already was in Indian Territory. What sort of future could they possibly have?

Lying on her bedroll she braided her hair in the dark and made the braids so tight they would never come undone until she herself undid them. Satisfied that every single hair was restrained, she closed her eyes and wished she could restrain her desires as easily as she did her hair. She could hear Mr. Stone breathing, and remembered how nice it had been to sleep next to him and awaken to find his arms around her.

All by herself, she was lonely.

Behave yourself, Grace, she firmly lectured, but she knew it was going to be a long frustrating night.

Matt listened to Grace toss and turn, and he had to fight every instinct he possessed to keep from getting up and joining her. Brushing her hair had been an exquisite torture, one worthy of a vengeful Comanche squaw, who could keep her victim writhing in agony for hours before she finally took pity on him and killed him. . . . Did Grace Livingston have any idea how much he was suffering?

He doubted it. Virgins rarely realized the effect they had on men. Despite her age—she had to be almost as old as he was— she was still a virgin. Of that he had no doubt. Every day he had to watch her brushing her beautiful hair, bending over in her tight britches, oblivious to the view she was affording him, kicking off her boots to reveal slender, white ankles and feet.

and making all those unconscious feminine gestures men always noticed but women never did.

When she was angry, he had to watch a blush climb up from her bosom to redden her throat and slowly consume her cheeks. When she was happy or content, he had to watch her teeth flash in a smile, the dart of a pink tongue as she moistened her lips, and the glint of gold promise in her lovely hazel eyes. Somehow, some way—she wasn't sure when or how it had happened—she had managed to worm her way into his affections, so that he found himself enthralled by her, wanting to watch her all the time, make her laugh, impress her, or simply make her look at him.

His desire was getting out of hand. Weak as he still was—with his shoulder hurting like hell—he wanted her, and knew he wouldn't be able to get a good night's sleep again until he had her. Not when she was lying only ten feet away from him every night. The only remedy for his pitiful condition would be to hurry and find the Comanches, but he had yet to discover a single clue to their whereabouts. The presence of the buffalo hunters must have driven them further south.

That was another thing: the buffalo hunters. He hadn't meant to kill any of them. He had only intended to steal their horses and leave them on foot. But they'd caught him in the act, grabbed some of the horses, and come after him. To keep them from trailing him and finding Grace at the camp, he'd had to double back and ambush them from a clump of mesquite. Even then he had only meant to slow them down by wounding a couple. One of the men had gotten off a lucky shot, hitting him, and he'd retaliated, instinctively—killing him cleanly. He had winged two of the remaining, but the third was unscathed and probably plotting vengeance.

He'd paid little attention to his own wound. Flesh wounds bled a lot and could make a man dizzy and feverish, but they didn't usually kill him. So he had ignored it. Collecting as many horses as he could round up, he had returned to fetch Grace and flee the area. It was too bad he hadn't had time to disguise

himself as Painted Horse, but he didn't think any of the men
had gotten a good look at him—though they might have noticed
Renegade's blue eyes. Fortunately the stallion's distinctive
markings remained hidden beneath a layer of dirt and old dye.
Matt intended to be long gone from the area by the time the
three men made it on foot to the nearest fort to tell their story.
If it hadn't been for Grace he wouldn't have bothered with the
ambush. As it was, he regretted killing someone. When he left
the Comanches to rejoin the world of white men, he had vowed
never to kill again.

In more ways than one, Grace's presence was a damned in-
convenience. Everything he'd worried about had happened: Because of her, he was forced into doing things he didn't want to
do. Because of her, he couldn't sleep at night. Because of her,
his stomach was tied in knots all day, and he was about to
explode from sexual tension. She probably didn't feel much
better. If she would just consent to sleep with him, they could
both get it out of their systems and concentrate on the formidable task still facing them.

But Grace Livingston had remarkable control over her sexual
urges. *Most* women demanded declarations of love before they
consented to sleep with a man, but he had hoped Miss Livingston was different. She differed in other ways from most
women; why couldn't she be unique in this one?

Instead, in spite of her prickly independent exterior, she demanded even more from a man than most women. He could
never measure up to her standards. She was a wealthy, high
society queen, while he was a . . . nobody . . . not in his own
mind, perhaps, but in the minds of everyone he knew.

He captured and broke horses for a living. She managed a
far-flung shipping empire and rubbed shoulders with rich and
powerful people all day long, back home in her precious Boston.
She thought of him as her hired hand—*not* as prime husband
material, and certainly not as a lover. Yet, he was fairly certain
he could satisfy her in the role of a lover and provide a brand
new dimension to her narrow view of life.

What galled him the most about their entire relationship was her lack of respect. Everything in which he took pride and had spent half his lifetime perfecting—his riding and shooting skills, his ability to survive and flourish in a harsh environment—didn't seem to impress her all that much. Like most whites she placed little value on those things that mattered most to an Indian. When she finished using him for her own purposes, she would toss him aside and forget him as easily as the white man scorned the red man, who had taught him how to live on the open plain.

He had known he shouldn't take her with him, so he shouldn't be too surprised by his present predicament. He deserved this hell of his own making. . . . Damn, but he wished the trip were over!

Tomorrow he'd make sure they got an early start and didn't quit until long after sundown—and if Miss High and Mighty Boston didn't like eating pemmican for the next week or two, that was too damn bad. From now on he intended to set a faster pace and press on relentlessly until they finally found the Comanches.

Eleven

"What does it mean?"

Flushed with excitement, Grace stood up in her stirrups and leaned forward in the saddle. After a grueling week of physical privation and hard riding, her muscles and nerve endings now quivered—not from fatigue or hunger but sheer exhilaration. They had found their first Indian sign, and Mr. Stone had stopped his horse and jumped down to investigate. He was now on one knee, studying it in the long grass.

To Grace the sign said nothing, nor would she have recognized it as a sign. It consisted only of a couple of stones, a bent twig, and a handful of dried horse dung, but the objects were arranged in a fashion that apparently provided information to Mr. Stone.

"The sign's old," he muttered in disgust. "Several families passed through here in early spring. Headed west, they left this marker to tell the rest of the tribe where they were going."

"Were they Comanches?"

He shook his head. "Nope. Apaches, most likely. They don't mark their signs the way we do. But there were four warriors among them and a small herd of horses. See? It's all right here."

"Where?" She rode Dunston a little closer.

"Watch it! You'll destroy it." He spread his hands protectively over the little collection of items. "Indians from the same tribe may be looking for this sign. We don't want to disturb it."

Grace peered at the emptiness of grass and sky in all four

directions. She didn't see any Indians. She was starting to think she and Mr. Stone were the only two humans alive on the whole of the Staked Plain. Her attention returned to the sign. "Explain it to me. I want to understand."

He pointed at each of the dried balls of horse dung. "Four warriors. That's important information, so each warrior gets his own marker. Three families." His hand moved over the stones. "Going west." He touched the twig. "See where it's pointing? . . . . A small herd of horses." He indicated a pile of horse-hair tangled in the long grass so it wouldn't blow away.

"But how do you know that these things didn't just get here by coincidence? How can you be sure it was early spring when they were placed here?"

Picking up the twig, he used it to probe a horse apple. "The dung is dry as dust. So is this twig. The fresher the objects, the more recent the sign. Also, the twig couldn't have gotten here by accident. Do you see any trees nearby? No. Someone carried it here. Same with the stones. They're small, almost unnotice-able—unless you're specifically searching for them. Sometimes twigs are used to indicate the number of horses or warriors, but when you see only *one* twig, it usually means direction."

"Amazing. We've ridden mile after mile, and all this time you were watching for a little pile of stones, twigs, and horse manure."

He glanced up at her with a glint in his eye. "What were you watching for—a painted sign that said Comanches, Straight Ahead?"

"I wasn't sure what to watch for. You never told me. Why don't you share your knowledge of the Comanches? I really would like to know more about them. At least describe Quanah Parker, if you don't want to discuss your *private* life."

"Quanah Parker," he repeated, remounting Renegade. "All right, I will tell you about him."

Quanah Parker was the son of a white woman named Cynthia Ann Parker who was stolen by the Indians when she was nine years old, he told her. Quanah's Indian name was actually

Kwahnah, or Sweet Odor, and his father was a much respected chief named Nawkohnee.

"Nawkohnee and Nadua, as Quanah's mother was called by the Indians, loved each other. Their tipi was a happy place. I enjoyed going there with my younger brother to play with Quanah because we were always made to feel welcome. Nadua had blond hair and stood out from the Indians, just as *I* did with my reddish-colored hair. She showed me how to darken my hair and skin with plant dye so I looked more Indian. Of course, neither of us could do much about our eyes. Hers were bright blue, while mine . . . well, you can see for yourself what color my eyes are."

She knew without looking that his eyes were hazel. They turned bright green in some lights, or if he was angry or experiencing some other deep emotion. His eyes were her main clue to his otherwise zealously guarded feelings.

"You dyed your hair?" she prompted.

"I'm telling you about Quanah, not me."

"Of course. Go on. I want to hear more about Nadua, too, since her situation resembles my sister's."

Mr. Stone frowned. "I'm afraid that's not a happy tale. Nadua, or Cynthia Ann, was first taken captive by the Comanches in an ugly incident along the Navasota River, a tributary of the Brazos in Texas. Her family, the Parkers of Virginia, had put up a log stockade and settled there with about thirty other pioneers. One day a party of a hundred warriors, most of them Comanches, showed up to parley. Hungry, they demanded beef. As they saw it, the Parkers were occupying *their* land, and had killed or driven off the local game. When the Parkers refused, the Indians attacked." He gave her a sidelong glance. "Are you sure you want to hear this story?"

When she nodded he continued. "There were lots of Parkers—I get them mixed up. All I know for certain is that Cynthia's mother, a woman named Lucy, fled with her four children along the river. The Indians caught up with her and made off with Cynthia and her younger brother, John, along with some other women and children. At first they were all badly treated."

Grace watched him closely as he related this, but his face remained impassive. She sensed that he, too, had been badly treated when first captured, but had long ago forgiven the Indians responsible.

"Eventually Cynthia Ann and her brother were adopted by the Comanches—different families. In time all but Cynthia were traded back to the whites. John didn't want to be white, and kept returning to the Indians, while Cynthia Ann—Nadua—grew up, married Nawkohnee, and bore him children, one of whom was Quanah. She had no desire to find her white family, either, but the Parkers kept trying to locate her. They told their sad tale to anyone who would listen, and over the years stirred up a lot of hatred against the Indians."

"I imagine they did," Grace cut in. "Can you blame them? I feel the same bitterness and determination to regain little Emily. I certainly don't intend to forget about her and leave her to the Comanches."

"Do you want to hear the rest of this or not?" Mr. Stone's eyes flashed emerald, betraying his irritation.

"I'm sorry. I won't interrupt again."

"Well, they finally *did* get her back. It happened like this. Nawkohnee, Nadua's husband, was leading raids against the whites in retaliation for army raids against the Indians. He ventured too close to Parker's fort, and the Texas rangers picked up his trail. A ranger captain named Sul Ross pursued Nawkohnee's tribe across the Staked Plain and stumbled across their unarmed camp on the Pease River. It was December of 1860, in the middle of a howling, west Texas norther. Believing their camp secure because of the storm, Nawkohnee and his braves had gone hunting. Ross ravaged the camp, killing women, children, and a Mexican slave, the only grown male in camp. One of his men took aim at a fleeing squaw, spotted her blond hair, and realized she was a white woman. Turned out to be Nadua, Quanah's mother, carrying his eighteen-month-old little sister

Topsannah, or Flower. The rangers forced Nadua to return with
them to the whites. She couldn't remember any English, but the
Parker family eagerly reclaimed her. In their jubilation at re-
claiming one of their own, the Texas legislature awarded Nadua
a league of land and a pension of a hundred dollars a year for
life to make up for her hardship."

"Why is that so sad?" Grace burst out. "She was reunited
with loving relatives. The government only did what they could
to ease her situation."

"It was sad because she was torn away from her Comanche
family, and never did recover from the shock and sorrow of it.
Shortly thereafter, a white man's disease killed Topsannah, and
Nadua mourned in the Comanche fashion, mutilating herself
and howling like an animal. Believing she had nothing more to
live for, she starved herself to death, while her 'loving relatives'
stood around wringing their hands and wondering why they'd
bothered to rescue her."

"How tragic!" Grace murmured. "A sad tale indeed."

"That's not all of it. Nawkohnee grieved so hard for his beloved wife that he never recovered from an infected wound.
That winter he also died. Pecos, or Peanut as we called him,
Quanah's younger brother, fell ill shortly thereafter—also from
a disease unknown to the Indians before the white man came.
Quanah, my friend, who was only thirteen years old at the time,
lost his mother, father, sister, and brother within a few short
months. . . . My brother and I grieved with him, for they were
our second family. Overnight Quanah became a man. Older than
he by several years, I was already riding with the warriors, but
in no time his courage and daring outshone everyone else's,
including mine. We all looked to him for leadership. We wanted
revenge for what the rangers had done to our village on the
Pease River, for we had all lost someone. My Comanche mother
managed to escape, but one of her sisters was slain . . . and I
was as vengeful as anyone, riding, raiding, and killing any white
man who dared cross my path."

Grace shivered to hear this cold recitation, delivered in mea-

sured tones that gave no hint of regret. As he relived these violent events, Mr. Stone appeared to have forgotten her. "Quanah's
twenty-six or twenty-seven now, but he's packed more living
into his years than men who are far older. In all the time I've
known him, he's never broken his word, signed any treaties, or
ceded any lands. If he *had* made agreements, he would abide
by them. He's that kind of man—which you'd never know if
you listened only to the lies the whites have spread about him."

"Sounds like a paragon of virtue," Grace said dryly. "Though
I wonder if the families of his victims think so."

Almost the moment it left her mouth, she regretted the sar-
castic comment. Mr. Stone's face darkened.

"I knew you wouldn't understand. I don't know why I bothered telling you about him. Like most whites you don't want
to hear the truth about the man. You prefer to believe he's a
fire-breathing monster warring on innocent settlers. Well, those
settlers are not so innocent, and Quanah Parker has more honor
in his little finger than most white men have in their whole
bodies."

Nudging Renegade ahead of Dunston, Mr. Stone put distance
between them. This wasn't the first time he had fervently defended the Comanche leader. Even knowing his sympathies, she
had thoughtlessly baited him. Biting her tongue in exasperation
at her own thoughtlessness, Grace urged Dunston to a faster
pace and hurried after him.

"Forgive me! I shouldn't have said that. It's just that I keep
thinking of Ellie and the children—and her poor husband, dead
because of the Comanches. Quanah Parker could have been the
one who killed him."

"Quanah's been driven to violence. Can't you understand
that? I saw both my parents and my little sister die at the hands
of the Comanches, but over the years I came to realize why the
Indians had done it. They face annihilation. They have no choice
but to fight for what they're losing. If the whites have their way,
the Indians will disappear from the face of the earth."

"You saw your own parents and your sister killed?" Grace gaped at him.

"Forget it! I don't want to talk about it. It happened a long time ago. The point is, I myself once hated the Comanches, but I wound up fighting for their cause. For every Indian atrocity you throw in my face, I can throw a white one back at you. Neither side is totally right, and neither is totally wrong."

"I might agree with you—except I've heard about more Indian atrocities than I have about white ones."

"And just how many *Indians* have you talked to?" He sneered. "Except for what I've told you, you don't know a damn thing about it."

"Not a single one. I admit that. But I'm still entitled to have an opinion."

"From now on you can keep your damn opinions to yourself. As will I."

They didn't speak for the remainder of the day. The evening, too, passed in silence. They avoided speaking to each other all through the night and even during breakfast the next morning. By now each knew what had to be done and they did it, without question or comment. For her part, Grace vowed not to say another word to Mr. Stone unless he apologized. She intended to apologize, also. However, she thought he should do it *first,* since he was most at fault. Why did he have to take exception to any opinion that didn't agree with *his?*

He must have made a similar resolution, because he never so much as opened his mouth. Nor would he look at her. Half the morning passed in gloomy silence—until they came to the remnants of what had once been a small Indian encampment.

They were riding beside a small stream cutting across the grasslands. Grace spotted the skeletons of blackened lodge poles ahead of them, standing stark against the blue sky.

Questions trembled on her lips. Instead of asking them, she watched Mr. Stone for his reaction. The closer they got, the bleaker he looked. The tipis had all been burnt, and charred belongings lay scattered across the prairie.

Grimly, she wondered what had happened to the inhabitants of the encampment. As they rode closer and saw scattered bones and human skulls, that question was answered. Fleeing men, women, and children had been shot down and fallen in their tracks. Their bodies had never been buried. Their garments were tattered and torn, their flesh eaten away by scavengers or destroyed by the elements. Only their bones and occasional clumps of tangled black hair now remained to tell their story.

The skeletons reminded her of the dead buffalo, except that these people had died a long time ago, leaving behind half-burned baskets, *parfleches,* and disabled weapons. A lingering odor of decay hung over the area, but the wind had scoured the landscape, scattering the lighter objects.

Mr. Stone rode into the center of the worst destruction, while Grace paused at the perimeter—too dismayed to go further. She watched as he dismounted and dropped Renegade's reins to ground-tie him. The horses he'd been herding promptly began grazing among the bleached bones and discarded household effects.

Grace would have preferred riding quickly through the area and leaving it far behind, but Mr. Stone had other ideas. Slowly, he walked among the refuse and skeletons. When he found a large piece of hide intact, he dragged it to the center of the encampment and stretched it out. Then he began collecting the bones of the fallen. Unable to contain herself, she rode up to him as he was picking up the bones of what could only have been a child.

"What are you doing?"

He straightened, his expression ferocious. "Isn't it obvious?"

Without waiting for her answer, he deposited the bones in the center of the stretched out hide, then walked to the next skeleton. By now it was obvious; he meant to collect all the bones and dispose of them.

Grace debated with herself for a full minute before dismounting to help. She didn't want to touch the bones, didn't want to be this close to them. But she couldn't allow him to perform the distasteful task all by himself. As she reached down to pick up the first bone, he grabbed her hand.

She straightened and eyed him impassively.

"You don't have to do this," he growled. "These aren't your people. This isn't your problem. I can handle what needs to be done by myself."

She lifted her chin. "I want to help. These were human beings. If we should die violently out here on the plain, I hope someone has the decency to do the same for us. Were these people Comanches?"

"Yes, but not the Antelope Band—Quanah's people. By the design of their clothing and moccasins I'd say they were Honey Eaters, what the Comanche call *Pehnahterkuh.*" He held her gaze a long moment, his fierce gaze softening. "Thank you, Boston."

A lump rose in her throat. "You're welcome," she managed to whisper.

They gazed into each other's eyes for a long poignant moment. Then Mr. Stone turned away to resume his grisly task.

When all the bones had been collected, Mr. Stone built a scaffold from blackened lodge poles. Atop the scaffold he laid out all the bones facing east, and below it he heaped the belongings of the massacre victims. He didn't explain his actions, but Grace surmised he was following Indian burial customs. She had expected him to actually *bury* the bones, but at least the scaffold would deter wolves and coyotes. When he finished he surprised her by asking her to take the horses and retreat a short distance while he performed a brief ceremonial ritual.

"May I watch? I promise not to interrupt."

A muscle worked in his jaw, and his brow furrowed in disapproval. "I'd rather you didn't. You won't understand."

"After you finish, you can explain it to me . . . Please let me stay."

"All right, stay. But don't say a word or protest anything I do. Agreed?"

"Agreed."

She mounted Dunston and led Lucy about thirty feet away from the scaffold, then watched as Mr. Stone chanted and circled the structure. Bending at the waist, he performed an odd heathen sort of dance. He was right. She didn't understand what he was doing, or why. It made her feel uncomfortable, and she had to clench her teeth together to keep from protesting when he suddenly whipped out a knife and cut off a lock of his copper-colored hair.

He scattered the shorn hair in four directions, allowing the wind to carry it away. Wielding the knife with sudden deadly intent, he gashed his own upper arm on the same side as the bandage he still wore to protect his injured shoulder.

This was too much, and Grace screamed his name. "Mr. Stone!"

He raised his head, and his glance froze her in place. "You said you wouldn't interrupt."

"I . . . I . . ."

"If you can't stand to watch, leave me!"

"No! No, I'll stay."

With his gaze fastened upon her, he raised his arm aloft and allowed blood to dribble down it unheeded. Then he tilted back his head, closed his eyes, and chanted gibberish in a singsong voice.

The back of Grace's neck prickled. Her heart raced. She wanted to look away, but couldn't. She reminded herself that he was only mimicking some mysterious ritual of the Comanches and not enacting his own personal beliefs. If he still believed in such primitive customs, he would be living among the Comanches, not among the whites.

At last he finished. After smearing ashes on his knife wound, he calmly collected Renegade and the other horses. Without saying a word or inviting her to follow, he mounted and rode off as if he'd forgotten her. Grace urged Dunston into a lope. "Mr. Stone—wait!"

Slowing down, he glanced at her in surprise; he *had* forgotten her. "Why did you cut your hair and gash your arm?" she demanded. "Among the Comanches, is that a customary act for mourning the dead?"

"For the women it is. They cut their hair, chop off fingers, and otherwise mutilate themselves when they mourn, especially if the loss involves a husband or great warrior. Men don't usually do these things. However, since there are no women around to mourn the dead in the traditional fashion, I wanted to express grief on behalf of everyone who died here. That's why I cut a lock of my hair and gashed my arm. If the rituals aren't performed in some manner, even an imperfect one, the spirits of the dead may never reach the land beyond the sun."

"The land beyond the sun?"

"The happy hunting grounds. All the Plains' tribes believe in it. It's a place where no one ever goes hungry or suffers from heat, cold, old age, injury . . . or attack."

"Like our heaven. Do the Indians also believe in a hell?"

"Not that I've heard. As far as I can tell hell was invented by white missionaries. Indians who fail to reach the happy hunting ground are trapped here on earth and wander aimlessly. That's a kind of hell, I suppose, but there's no fire involved. I just wanted to ensure they got safely to the other side and weren't stuck here forever."

"But you . . . you don't actually believe these things yourself . . . do you?"

"I don't know what I believe anymore, Boston. If there's a Heavenly Being who truly cares for us, He shouldn't allow things like this to happen." He jerked his head in the direction of the blackened lodge poles.

"God isn't to blame. *People* are! The question is, who did it?"

He sent her a scathing glance. "Come now, Boston. Who do you think attacked and killed those Indians?"

"All right, I imagine it was white men—the army, perhaps, or buffalo hunters. But it *could* have been other Indians. Don't they go around attacking each other—one tribe hating another?"

"In the old days, yes. Nowadays, rarely. If it had been Indians attacking Indians, we wouldn't have seen any hair. Indians always take scalps. It's a way of expressing triumph over their enemies, a manner of degrading them and stealing their power and strength. These people all had their hair—which tells me they were *definitely* killed by white men."

"Children, too," Grace murmured, still distressed about the presence of so many small skeletons.

"Of course. Haven't you heard the expression, 'Nits only grow into lice?' "

She hadn't heard it and was appalled. After that there was nothing more to say. They rode onward, each lost in thought and unwilling to share their musings. With every step their horses took, Mr. Stone seemed to withdraw more into himself, and Grace didn't know how to bridge the growing gap. The blood-soaked, ash-encrusted sleeve of his buckskins only served to remind her of how very different and far apart they were. Matthew Stone might have left the savages, but savagery had not left him. The Comanches had imprinted his soul, as surely as if they'd branded his body.

For the next two days and nights, silence reigned between them. In the past, Grace had often sensed Mr. Stone watching her, assessing every move as she did chores or brushed out her hair. Now she sensed only coldness and distance. Gone was the sexual tension of the previous weeks. For all he took note of her she might have been alone on the Staked Plain—or have disappeared into thin air.

On the morning of the third day, she lost her temper. Before she had finished loading Dunston and Lucy, he mounted Renegade and casually rode away, herding his charges ahead of him. This was the second time he'd ridden off without her, seemingly unaware of her existence.

"Wait a minute!" she screamed at his retreating back. "I've had quite enough of this! I'm not to blame for what happened to your friends, the Honey Eaters. Yet you treat me as if I planned the whole attack."

He spun Renegade on his haunches and leveled his gaze on her for the first time since they'd left the site of the attack. "I never said *you* were responsible. As I recall I was blaming God, whom you valiantly defended."

Tiny details of his appearance shafted her heart: he sat so straight and tall on his stallion, his long legs hugging the horse's sides as if they grew there. Every inch an arrogant powerful male, he gazed at her with pure disdain, even hatred, condemning her not only for her race but for her sex. She knew he hated weakness, and she, unfortunately, exemplified it. She still couldn't ride, shoot, hunt, or cook as well as he could. Moreover, she had this ridiculous need for comfort and companionship. She couldn't stand to be ignored. Couldn't bear to never see him smile or look at her. She longed for closeness, and all she got was rejection.

"Forget God. You and God will have to work out your own relationship. Right now I'm talking about me. You treat me as if I'm your worst enemy. I'm sick of it. I won't stand for it any longer."

"What are you going to do—fire me?" A spark of humor flared in his eyes.

"If I could, I would! I helped you gather those bones back there, and you thanked me. For a moment we connected and shared something. After that you shut me out and ignored for me two solid days."

"And you can't stand being ignored, can you?" His scornful look cut her to shreds. "You want my full attention? All right, Boston, you've got it."

He rode back to her, leaned down, and slid a hand behind her neck to pull her to him. Then he kissed her—a bruising, punishing, searing kiss that ignited a fire in her veins and made the fine hairs on the back of her neck stand on end. When he finally released her, he growled: "Now, you've got my undivided attention. Still want it, Boston? There's plenty more where that came from. Just say the word."

"Savage!" She drew back her hand to slap him.

He grabbed it and prevented her. "You're damn right I'm a savage—and proud of it. Sometimes I wonder why I ever left the Comanches. I don't know why I shouldn't stay with them when we find them and help them fight for what little freedom they still have left. Coddling a spoiled white woman somehow doesn't appeal to me—not when I have more important matters on my mind."

"Oh, Matt! You aren't really thinking of returning to the Comanches, are you? You wouldn't!"

"Why in hell wouldn't I? At least I could die proud and free, fighting for a way of life I understand. What does *your* world have to offer me? What can *you* offer— cattle?" He gave a harsh bark of laughter.

"When I was a Comanche I had enough buffalo to meet my needs and everyone else's. They were free for the taking. Horses? I had more horses than I could ride or train. A fancy house? I had the mountains for my walls, the grass for my carpet, the sky for my roof, and the sun and moon for my light. I didn't need a damn thing. I had it all—friends, family, and a reason for living. Now that I'm a white man, what do I have? A god-forsaken little ranch that's little more than a hovel. Cattle I have to buy, and horses I have to guard . . . and not a damn soul to love. No one to greet me when I come home, to snuggle with me under a buffalo skin or hold me during the cold night. I haven't a damn thing, Boston. I live with silence every day of my life. I gave up a life I cherished to return to my so-called people, and I loathe and despise every damn one of them, you included!"

Grace trembled. She fought the urge to sob. His facade had finally crumbled, revealing a misery she had dimly suspected but never really understood. Until now. She reached out to him, but he didn't see her hand. Already he was turning away . . . riding off . . . his back straight as a Comanche war lance. How he must hate revealing his pain to her! She was the enemy . . . *his* enemy, a symbol of every white person who had ever killed Indians or scorned his overtures of friendship.

Had he made many overtures? She didn't think so. He was hurting too much inside to seek friends among those he condemned. It wasn't fair that he condemn her! In his heart he must know that. She couldn't help it that she had it all—everything money could buy. What he didn't understand was that even with all her money she could never buy love, the only thing truly worth having.

How he must resent her offer of cash, cattle, and a big house! And fencing. If any man would hate fencing, it would be Matthew Stone. . . . Why had she tried to tempt him with all those necessities useless to an Indian? Only white men cared about such things, and in his heart he was still Comanche. No wonder he hated her, ignored her, and scoffed at her. He couldn't be bought with material objects.

All she had to give him was love, but if she offered it now, he would never accept it. He was far too proud; he would see it as pity. . . . Could she even offer him the kind of love he needed? They had *nothing* in common, except a desire to find the Comanches . . . and desire itself.

Twelve

That same afternoon they discovered a burned-out army supply wagon surrounded by the ravaged, half-decayed bodies of four white soldiers. Despite the stench, which was every bit as bad if not worse than that of the dead buffalo, Grace insisted they accord the same respect to the victims of this attack as they had to the Indians.

"Did you expect me to pass by without stopping?" Mr. Stone's mouth was carved from granite, his eyes from flint.

"Would you have stopped to bury them if I hadn't made an issue of it?" she retorted, doubtful that he would have.

"You'll never know, will you, since you didn't give me the chance. Given your self-righteousness, I expect you to help me." He slid down from the saddle. "You'd better hope I can find a shovel in this mess, or we'll be digging graves with our fingernails."

They did find a shovel, but in the end dug only one large grave, and Mr. Stone performed all the work. It grew dark before they were finished. They decided to do the actual burying in the morning and retreated a couple miles upwind of the tragedy to spend the night.

As they made camp, Grace resolved to think of some appropriate words to say over the grave by way of a funeral service. She tried not to think about the awful sights she'd seen that day, but she couldn't eat any pemmican and feared she'd be unable to sleep. Mr. Stone had dragged the bodies together and thrown a discarded canvas tarpaulin over them, so they wouldn't have to look at them as he worked, but Grace knew she'd never forget them.

All of the soldiers had been scalped and most had been mutilated, either by humans or wolves and vultures. One man had still been alive when overwhelmed by his attackers; he'd been tied spread-eagle and upside down to a wagon wheel. Not much was left of his body. Fire had charred it, along with the wagon.

Nothing of value remained in the vicinity. Even the boots and uniforms of the dead men had disappeared. Grace had prowled among the ashes, searching for clues to the soldiers' identities, but she hadn't found a thing to tell her who they were or where they'd come from.

As she spread out her bedroll by the light of the stars and an almost full moon, she finally mentioned the problem uppermost in her mind. "Mr. Stone, what should we do about . . . about what we found today?"

"Do?" The question came from the midst of the horses where Mr. Stone was checking hobbles to make certain none of the animals strayed during the night.

"What do you mean, *do?*" He came toward her, a dark silhouette carrying a saddle under one arm. "We'll bury them tomorrow. That's all we *can* do and probably more than the poor bastards deserve. I'm sure they were carrying supplies to MacKenzie, who's somewhere out here killing Indians, who in turn are trying to kill him."

"That's what I mean. Shouldn't we inform the authorities of what happened? How far are we from the nearest fort?"

"Farther than I want to detour. Whoever sent them and whoever was waiting for the supplies have probably already guessed what happened. Sooner or later the army will find the wagon. We'll mark the grave, too—with a cross made from half-burned timbers."

"It's all so terrible!" she wailed, overcome by the horror of it. "One man had his . . . his . . ."

He'd had his genitals cut off, and his heart ripped out. Mr.

Stone had tried to cover the body before she got a good look at it, but he hadn't moved fast enough. Despite the decay, she'd seen evidence of the worst possible abuse.

Turning away, unable to contain herself any longer, she lowered her face to her hands and silently wept. Sobs racked her, but she sought to conceal them from Mr. Stone. She didn't even know the names of the dead soldiers, or the names of the dead Indians. How would their relatives ever know what had happened to them? . . . It was such a terrible senseless waste!

She'd witnessed the aftermath of the worst the two races could inflict upon each other and inhaled the poisoned air wrought by violent death and destruction. She could no longer pretend she was unaffected by it all. She mourned the deaths of everyone on both sides and grieved for the relatives, who would forever wonder about the fate of their loved ones.

"Boston," Mr. Stone murmured, his voice gentle as his arms suddenly slid around her.

She bit her lip to subdue her sobs, but they rolled out of her, anyway. Turning and clinging to him, she allowed her feelings to pour forth in an outburst of emotion and delayed reaction.

"How can human beings do such terrible things to each other? Are we nothing but animals, after all? Why can't we solve our differences in ways other than murder, torture, and bloodshed?"

He didn't try to answer; he simply held her, molding her to him, offering his warmth and the haven of his strong body.

"How could those soldiers have gunned down defenseless women and little children?" she continued, knowing she was babbling but unable to stop herself. "How could the Indians have tortured and scalped the poor soldiers? I never knew people could be so cruel and heartless! I mean, I've heard tales—read in the newspapers—but I never actually *saw* such things or smelled them, or encountered them firsthand. I didn't really believe they could happen until now."

"I know . . ." he said. "I know. I've lived with this ugliness for most of my life, and I still can't get used to it."

"I'll never be able to sleep again! If I do, I'll have nightmares."

"At first, yes . . ."

"Not just at first! *You* still have them! I know you do."

"Yes," he conceded. "I'm afraid I do."

Burrowing into him, she bawled on his chest. "We're all monsters! We're all doomed! If we can do such terrible things to each other, what hope is there for any of us? How can we ever find joy or peace or happiness?"

He tilted her face up, cradled it in his hands, and brushed the tears from her cheeks with his thumbs. "We have to make our own happiness, Boston. No matter what's going on around us, somehow we have to make our own."

"I can't!" she wailed.

"Yes, you can. You're strong and courageous. You're the most stubborn determined woman I've ever met. If anyone can do it, you can."

"I don't think I'll ever be happy again! Not after all we've seen on this journey. And it isn't over yet. We might see even worse, if that's possible."

"Anything's possible. We have to seize happiness where we find it and conquer fear as best we can."

"I don't know how you've endured all you've suffered! I've never met anyone who's been through as much as you have but still manages to go on . . . to keep fighting . . . keep trying . . ."

"Ah, Boston, what choice do I have? I've narrowly escaped death more times than I can count, yet somehow I manage to keep living. Each time I survive another ugly incident, it heightens my appreciation for life. I don't mean for just the big things, but for the little things you barely notice otherwise. Did you know breathing can be a pure pleasure?" He laughed softly, in a self-deprecating manner. "I try to remember that when I'm sad and lonely . . . and feeling sorry for myself like I've been doing lately."

"I get lonely, too," she admitted. "Sometimes I think I've always been lonely . . . and I always will be."

"Does it have to be that way for us, Boston? Is there a chance . . . even the slightest chance . . . ?"

"Yes," she whispered without a moment's hesitation. She leaned into him, revealing her need and her enormous want.

He enfolded her so tightly in his arms that she could barely breathe. Their mouths met in a dizzying kiss, and their bodies forged together as he embraced her with stunning eagerness. The taste, scent, and feel of him swamped her senses, revealing possibilities she hadn't allowed herself to consider. Now she considered them, and discovered that she wanted him more than she had known it was possible to want a man. She wanted him on top of her, under her . . . any way she could get him.

They sank to their knees on her bedroll. He leaned over her, bending her backward, and she clung to him and pulled him closer. She couldn't get enough of him. He was air, light, warmth, and wonder—everything she had ever desired—a potent, pulsating force filling all the lonely, empty, aching places in her heart.

His hands tugged at her clothing, and she clawed at his garments. Overhead the moon smiled down on them, silvering his profile and painting his hair with liquid light. The stars illuminated the heavens, shining pure and bright, as if they'd never borne witness to man's inhumanity to man.

It's beautiful, she thought. *It's all so beautiful!*

The wind blew across their nakedness, and she cupped his face in her hands and drew him down to her. With exquisite tenderness he nibbled her mouth and kissed his way down the arch of her throat. He teased her breasts with tiny bites and long licks. She moaned and squirmed beneath him, but he refused to hurry.

"Lie still, Boston. Let me love you. You're so sweet . . . so tender. Your skin is like silk . . . or the hide of a newborn fawn. Never have I touched anything softer."

She ran her fingers across the muscles and planes of his chest, marveling at his contours and the texture of the fine curly hair there. He epitomized everything masculine, and she thrilled to her own explorations. He alternated stroking and caressing her with deep drugging kisses, until her head spun and her need spiraled.

His caresses became more intimate—and more demanding. She refused him nothing, spreading her thighs when he gently nudged them apart, taking hold of him when he showed her how he wanted to be held, kissing him as he had taught her, and mating with their tongues.

Gently and patiently he prepared her for union. She was ready long before he seemed to think so. She trembled with frantic urgency—eager for the release only he could give her. "Mr. Stone!" she pleaded.

"Mr. Stone?" he mocked, pausing. "Couldn't you bring yourself to call me by my first name—Matt, or even Matthew?"

"Matthew," she breathed. "Matt . . ."

He didn't look satisfied.

"Someday, I will teach you to say my Comanche name," he whispered. "That's what I want to hear you moan before I come into you. Only then will I know you're truly mine, and I am yours."

She thought she might die if he didn't take her soon. "Matt . . . please," she whispered.

He rose up over her, positioning himself.

Before he could enter her, though, Renegade whinnied. They heard him clearly. It was a whinny she'd never heard the stallion make before. Commanding. Warning. Telling them something was wrong.

Mr. Stone levered himself off her. Grace grabbed for her clothing and scrambled into it faster than she had ever dressed in her life. When she stood up, Mr. Stone seized her hand and pulled her back down again.

"Shhh," he whispered. "Don't make a sound. Don't move."

Crouching beside her, he pointed. She peered into the far distance. Out on the moonlit plain she saw movement. Shadowy figures riding horses. They were too far away for her to tell if they were white men or Indians.

"Who is it?"

He shrugged. "Can't see clearly enough. Indians, I suspect. They often travel at night when there's a Comanche Moon. Whoever they are, let's hope they don't spot *our* horses. If they do, they'll assume we're the enemy, and attack."

That was all the prompting Grace needed to lose the last vestige of arousal.

They watched until the figures disappeared from sight, and only then did Mr. Stone—Matt—don his clothing. When he had finished he kissed her distractedly. "Try to get some sleep. I'll stand guard for the rest of the night, just in case they saw us and double back."

She shivered. "Do you think they did?"

"Wouldn't surprise me. If I spot any movement out on the plain, I'll wake you, and we'll make a run for it. Better still, if you hear Renegade whinny again, run to Dunston as fast as you can. I'll have him saddled. Don't wait for me. Get on him and ride for your life."

"I won't leave without you!"

"Yes, you will," he sternly insisted. "I'll provide a diversion, and then join you. Renegade can outrun anything on four legs. Dunston can't. He needs a head start."

"I don't want to lose you! Not now—when I've only just found you!"

He grinned and lightly grazed her chin with his knuckles. "Believe me, Boston, I won't be so hard to lose. Trust me a little, won't you?"

"I trust you with my life," she told him, meaning every word. Tonight she had given him her heart, soul, and very nearly her body. She had never believed in half measures; once she made up her mind about something, that was it, she was committed . . . and she'd made up her mind about Matthew Stone.

He smiled again, and her heart shuddered in reaction. "You

don't believe in holding back, do you? Once you've decided on something, you've *decided*."

She nodded. "Yes. That's exactly how I am. What about you?"

He eyed her thoughtfully. "I guess I'm the same way, Boston. That makes us quite a pair, I'd say."

She returned his smile, smiling from the inside out and feeling happier than she could ever remember. It wasn't the proper time for declarations, not with the possibility of being attacked. But she wished she could shout it for all the universe to hear: *I love you, Matthew Stone.*

What an amazing, miraculous fact!

Less than an hour ago she'd been miserable, alone, and afraid. Sunk in despair. Now, she owned the world and all the good things in it. She refused to think of complications or difficulties. She simply wouldn't admit to them. Surely, if they both tried hard enough, there wouldn't be any.

Knowing Matt was watching over her made it possible for Grace to sleep. She slept like a baby. In the morning, he woke her and served a fine breakfast of light as air biscuits made from the last of their flour, along with bacon, beans, and coffee. She was so happy she could scarcely eat, and could only sit watching him over the rim of her coffee mug.

"If you keep looking at me like that, we'll never get those bodies buried and resume our journey," he warned with a glint in his eye.

That sobered her. How could she have forgotten the distasteful task that still awaited them? They hurried and packed the horses, then returned to the site of the wagon massacre. The grisly job of burying the bodies subdued Grace's newfound joy, and when it came time to say a prayer over the mass grave she had no trouble summoning a few tears. On behalf of the wives, mothers, and possible descendants of the slain soldiers, she cried while she recited the Twenty-third Psalm.

"Yea, though I walk through the valley of the shadow of death, Thy rod and Thy staff comfort me," she said and thought about her own situation. The *Llano Estacado* wasn't a valley but a plain. On it, she had found life, love, and purpose, which helped cancel out the sorrows. Now, if only she could rescue Ellie and her children, she would count herself truly blessed.

After they finished they continued riding in a southerly direction, and that afternoon found them in an area of high, stony cliffs, where Matt discovered another Indian sign. He dismounted to examine it, then walked over to Grace and spoke quietly.

"I think we're nearing a stronghold of Indians. I can't tell if it's Quanah's band or not. They're not identifying themselves. I'd like to ride ahead to investigate, but first I need to take a few precautions."

"Of course. Whatever you think best. Will there be time enough to see much before it gets dark?"

"By the time I'm ready to leave, I hope it is dark. Night will be the best time to spy on them and find out who they are. In this rough country they'll feel safe and may risk building a fire. Even without a fire the moon is bright enough for me to see them. All I have to do is keep *them* from seeing *me*—or make them see only what I want them to see."

Grace didn't understand what he meant by that, but she was disinclined to ask questions. She'd been looking forward to nightfall, and had hoped they might finish what they'd started the previous night. She hid her disappointment. After all, they had come here to find the Comanches, and it appeared they might have found them. She should be excited and glad, not resentful and worried.

"Can I help with anything?" she asked, dismounting.

"No, I've got it all planned. All you have to do is wait here and look after things until I return."

She waited for him to say more, and when he didn't, she set up camp and cared for the horses. Taking Renegade and one of the packhorses, Matt disappeared among the rocky crevices of the high cliffs.

The shadows grew long and golden, indicating only an hour

or so until sunset, but Matt still hadn't returned. Feeling abandoned and out of sorts, Grace gloomily laid out the bedrolls—next to each other, just in case—gathered materials for a small fire she doubted she was going to be allowed to light, and filled the coffeepot with water from their canteens.

"Boston," said a familiar voice. She looked up eagerly, expecting to see Matt.

Her heart missed a beat. The man who'd called her name wasn't Matthew Stone—nor did his horse look like Renegade. Before her stood a half-naked Comanche warrior wearing only a bison headdress, tall, fringed moccasins, and barely enough hide to cover his private parts. Beneath the curved horns of the headdress, war paint slashed his face. Streaks of vivid color splashed his magnificent body in a distinctive pattern she immediately recognized.

Renegade had been transformed from a scruffy dirty beast of indeterminate color into a gleaming white stallion with patches of tan on his head, chest, and underbelly. Blue handprints stamped his coat, leaving no doubt he was the bold steed ridden by the Comanche warrior known as Painted Horse.

Grace opened her mouth in a soundless shriek. Robbed of speech, she could only stare while the world crumbled around her and her own inner foundations collapsed.

Matthew Stone was Painted Horse. The man she loved was a hunted criminal . . . a heartless murderer . . . a thief and despoiler of women and children . . . a Comanche hero.

Calmly, he led Renegade toward her. "The Comanches will be far more likely to accept me with open arms instead of a hail of arrows if they think I'm one of them. That's why I'm dressed like this. It's my disguise, what I wear when I'm scaring buffalo hunters or stealing cattle and horses to help keep the Indians alive."

"I know who you are," she said. "You're Painted Horse. Have you forgotten? You were wearing your *disguise* the first time you kissed me."

He had the audacity to grin!

"Comes in handy for scaring spoiled white women, too, only I failed to convince you to return immediately to the east. That's when I knew you were tough enough to survive out here, and I could risk bringing you with me."

"You deliberately deceived me! You knowingly lied to me. You're nothing but an outlaw, a cold-blooded killer . . ."

As he realized how furious she was, his grin disappeared. "I deceived you, yes. I couldn't very well admit I was Painted Horse right from the beginning, could I? As for being a killer, I'm that, too—but hardly cold-blooded. I don't kill anyone unless they're trying to kill me. At least, I haven't done so since I decided to leave the Comanches. It was the constant killing that finally convinced me to go. I couldn't take any more raiding and warring. My Comanche wife thought I'd lost my courage. . . . Maybe she was right. I don't know. But after I returned to the whites I needed a way to help the reservation Indians and keep them from starving. This was all I could think of, and it's worked pretty well. . . . You're the only one I trust enough to tell my secret. Even now I'm only revealing it because it's necessary. If I ride into a Comanche camp dressed like this, they won't be as likely to shoot me. Or you, either. My brother—if he's still alive—and Quanah will know who I am. I hope they will have heard what I've been doing to aid the Comanches and won't draw their guns on me. . . . That's my plan, anyway."

"And what a fine plan it is! The only drawback is that you had to let me in on it. Had you intended to tell me in the beginning?"

"No, I hadn't. But after last night, after we . . . well, I thought maybe you could handle it now. I *want* you to know who I am. It'll be no good between us if you don't know."

"You want me to call you Painted Horse when we . . . when we're . . . ?"

"Yes! I want you to call me Painted Horse." Dropping Renegade's reins, he strode over to her, his eyes blazing. "Look at me, Boston. This is who I am. This is my reality. I can no more deny it than you can stop being a white woman. Maybe someday

I won't have to do this anymore. The whites will stop slaying the buffalo and starving the Indians. But right now, I'm needed. Painted Horse has to exist. . . . Hell, the whites won't even permit our horses to live! Do you know what the army does to horses like Renegade? They shoot 'em. They round 'em up and shoot 'em. Just because the Indians love them. Actually the Comanches revere them. Painted horses represent everything a warrior cherishes."

"I don't care about all that! You can try to justify yourself all you want, but the plain truth is you're a liar, a thief, and a murderer. I hate you! I'll never forgive you. You've caused too much grief and sorrow—not only for me, but for lots of other people!"

"So you've chosen hate. I warned you it would be one or the other. I should have known it wouldn't be love."

"You expect me to love a painted savage? You honestly expect to walk up to me—dressed like that—and have me fall into your arms and embrace you? . . . What about my sister and her children? I don't even know if they're still alive. Her husband most certainly isn't. I can't possibly love you—you stupid fool!"

He stood there and took it. Saying nothing. Doing nothing. In his eyes she read agreement. He knew he was a fool, and everything else she had called him.

"I'll be back for you after I find them," he muttered.

"I'm going with you."

"Then I'm not going."

"You have to go!"

"I don't have to do a damn thing. With all this shouting we can just wait until they find us. I'll be surprised if they don't."

Grace eyed the high cliffs. Fear gushed through her like a geyser. "Are we really that close to them?"

"I don't know. That's what I need to find out. Up there in the cliffs I discovered a cave. You should be safe enough there. I can cover the entrance with brush."

"It's too late in the day for you to go looking for Indians. We'll both go tomorrow. We'll go in the daylight."

He said nothing for a moment. Then—surprisingly—he agreed. "All right. If you insist. You're the boss, the one who's paying me."

"And don't you forget it!"

His head lifted slightly. His nostrils flared. "How proud you are to be white. How arrogant. Don't worry, Miss Livingston. I'll never forget."

For a brief fleeting moment her heart cried out for him to call her Boston, to say the name he'd given her, and to use the wry teasing tone she had come to expect and appreciate.

No, she thought. It was better this way. Better to remain Miss Livingston—a rich, lonely spinster. It hurt too much to be Boston.

Thirteen

Matt waited until he was sure Grace had fallen asleep. Then he left the cave and went to get Renegade. When she woke she would be furious, but he couldn't possibly take her with him until he knew for certain what lay in wait for them: welcoming friends or bitter enemies.

He regretted having revealed himself to her, but she would have discovered that he was Painted Horse sooner or later. At least now she had no illusions, and neither did he. She could never love the man he truly was. Knowing how she felt about him, he would somehow have to submerge his own feelings for her. They were lucky they *hadn't* made love last night. If they had, the scorn with which she viewed him today would have been unbearable; as it was, he could hardly bear it.

Fortunately he had no time to waste on self-pity. He had to discover what they were up against and return to the cave before Grace did something stupid—like come after him. As frightened as she was of Indians, she would probably stay put for a while, waiting for him, but with Grace he could never be certain. If she thought she had a good reason, she'd march into hell itself in pursuit of her goals.

Her persistence was a nuisance, but also one of the reasons why he admired her. He had begun to hope—foolishly—that they stood a chance together. But her reaction to the discovery that he was Painted Horse had proved otherwise. He was a fool.

Her hatred of Indians ran too deep to allow for any exceptions; she hated Painted Horse most of all.

Trying to concentrate on the task at hand, Matt rode higher along the rocky trail hugging the side of the steep cliff. He needed all of his concentration to keep Renegade from taking a wrong step or becoming nervous due to the slippery shale underfoot and the close quarters. Had there not been a full moon to light his way, he would have had to abandon the effort.

Reaching a small flat plateau, he dismounted, ground-tied Renegade behind a thicket of wind-battered greasewood, and cautiously walked along the rim, searching for the dim glow of a dying fire or the telltale wisp of smoke rising from the dark void below him. A light breeze carried the murmur of men's voices. Matt dropped to a crouch and moved toward the sound. It was elusive, but after a few moments he discovered its source.

The opposite side of the plateau appeared to be a sheer drop too steep to climb, but voices drifted upward, proving that a trail existed. Stretching out on his belly he inched his way toward the precipice and peered over.

Below was a wide shelf of rock big enough to accommodate the four men camped there, along with their tired-looking mounts. The men lounged around a small dying fire which emitted hardly any light or smoke. In the moonlight Matt could see they were Apaches, not Comanches. One man lay on his side, either asleep or unconscious, while the other three nursed various wounds and injuries.

Nose twitching like a dog's, Matt detected the sweet, metallic odor of congealed blood combined with the sooty smell of burnt flesh—a scent he immediately recognized. In an effort to tend their injuries, the Apaches had apparently dug out the bullets and cauterized the worst wounds. They were now discussing the battle in which they'd received them. Matt crawled as close as he dared and practically hung over the precipice, eavesdropping on their conversation.

Comanches and Apaches were historic enemies, but Matt had a good ear for languages and could decipher the speech of nearly any Indian he was likely to meet. Twenty minutes later he knew what had happened: Mackenzie had crossed the border of the Rio Grande, forayed deeply into Mexico, and destroyed both the Kickapoo and Apache settlements at Santa Rosa. Many had died, women and children among them, and others had been taken captive. Only a few had managed to escape, including these four.

Wounded, exhausted, and hungry, they didn't know what to do next or where to go. Apaches and Comanches alike considered themselves protected from the U.S. Army in Mexico. After conducting raids on white settlements in Texas, they often fled there and found a haven from pursuing soldiers. Now the rules had changed, and Mexico could no longer be considered safe. This incident would fuel a new level of alarm for all Indians.

Careful to make no sound, Matt retreated, remounted Renegade, and started back toward the cave where he'd left Grace. As he once again negotiated the rocky trail in the moonlight, his mind buzzed with questions. What were Mackenzie's plans? Did the army have permission to cross the U. S. border to attack the Indians?

The gossip Grace had overheard at Fort Sill suggested they *did* have permission—which raised an even more important question: Had the United States and Mexico adopted a *joint* policy of annihilation?

Matt needed answers. If he hoped to convince the Comanches to surrender while there was still an opportunity for them to negotiate their futures, he must take time out from their search for the Indians to detour to the nearest fort. He had to hear for himself where things stood. Without the latest information he would have a hard time convincing Quanah Parker to listen. *This* could be the tool he needed to persuade the Comanches to surrender—a statement from the army detailing their relationship with Mexico. With no place left to hide, Quanah would have to face the inevitable.

Fort Griffin was the nearest outpost. Mackenzie operated out of three major forts: Forts Richardson, Griffin, and Concho, a relatively new outpost built at the headwaters of the Concho River. Only occasionally did the colonel travel as far north as Fort Sill. Tales of his successful operations didn't usually reach there until months after the actual incidents. Matt hadn't heard of Mackenzie's September attack on the *Kuhtsooehkuh* band of the Comanches until last January. Over fifty Comanches had been slain, and one hundred and thirty taken captive in a raid on an encampment along McClellan Creek, high in the Texas Panhandle.

This Mexican attack rivaled it. What impressed Matt the most was that the Indian villages in Mexico were some eighty miles from the border, across a waterless, alkali desert. The average army recruit mounted on the average army horse could never make it; Mackenzie's Buffalo Soldiers must be using Indian ponies and becoming very tough, indeed.

Matt wasn't completely surprised by this: Mackenzie was reportedly a hard taskmaster. Grierson at Fort Sill had told him that Mackenzie had taken dirty, illiterate mercenaries—black and white men alike, the dregs of the army—and through his willingness to spread-eagle every slacker against a wagon wheel, won their respect and taught them how to fight Indians, using the Indians' own methods. Quanah needed to hear exactly what he was up against.

What should he do about Grace? Matt wondered. Taking Grace to Fort Griffin in her present frame of mind could mean imprisonment. If she even *hinted* that he was Painted Horse, they'd clap him in irons. Yet he couldn't leave her out on the plain alone. She would never consent to it, nor would it be safe. He must persuade her to protect *his* identity and her own, because Fort Griffin attracted all sorts of scoundrels.

The buffalo hunters had set up camp outside its walls in a wild, lawless settlement called The Flats. The only white women in residence were whores, saloonkeepers, or both. Matt hadn't been there in a long time, but he doubted it had improved much. He dreaded the thought of taking Grace into such a hellhole. Before he did so, he *had* to win her cooperation.

Hard on the heels of this thought came another: Too bad he
couldn't just leave her *inside* the fort and continue the search
for the Comanches on his own. Considering the dangers facing
them—and the deterioration of their relationship—the idea appealed to him. So long as she stayed in the fort, kept her mouth
shut, and behaved herself, no one would discover she was a
woman. She would be all right. But of course he could do nothing until their present rift was mended, and they reached an
understanding regarding her behavior.

By the time Matt arrived at the cave, the eastern sky had
lightened. Leaving Renegade among the horses to graze for a
few hours, he climbed up to the enclosure and entered it. In the
dark he removed his headdress and war paint. By then it was
light enough to see Grace curled up fast asleep in her bedroll,
as oblivious to his presence as she had been to his absence.

Before retiring she had unbraided her hair, and it swirled
around her slender frame like a shawl, half-concealing her. He
sighed deeply. Things couldn't continue as they were. She was
further away from him now than she had ever been. Coldness
now replaced the all too brief warmth so recently kindled between them, and he hated it.

In the weeks they had spent together, his desire had become
almost uncontrollable. Never had he wanted a woman this
much! He wanted her physically, but also yearned to see her
eyes glow with happiness, her mouth curve in a smile when she
spoke his name, and to be able to touch her, tease her, and sleep
with her locked in his arms through the night.

She had become as necessary as breathing. He didn't dare
call his feelings for her *love;* he wasn't sure what love was. A
constant ache in a man's gut? A tightening in his chest whenever
their gazes met? A feeling of helpless rage and frustration when
she lost her temper and shouted at him or ignored him? He
hadn't had such intense physical reactions to Sweet Water, and
he had thought he loved her. Maybe he hadn't cared for his
Comanche wife as much as he believed. He really couldn't recall his feelings toward her, except that he knew he had once

desired her tender young body and been jealous when she abandoned him and turned to another.

He didn't know what he'd do if he ever saw another man holding or kissing Grace—kill him, probably. He hadn't yet possessed Grace, yet she possessed *him* in ways he couldn't begin to fathom . . . and it scared the hell out of him.

For several long moments he stood looking down at her, studying the fall of honey-colored hair, the fine, regal features, and the slender grace of her recumbent figure. Just watching her he became aroused, his body aching with repressed desire. If only they hadn't been interrupted the other night . . . if only . . .

She might claim to hate him, but she wanted him, too. Maybe passion was the one way he could reach her . . . and teach her how foolish it was to fight the attraction between them.

Moving his bedroll next to hers, he lay down beside her and fitted his body around her. Burying his nose in her soft hair, he greedily inhaled the scent of flowers that always clung to her. The floral overtones came from the fancy soap she used, but to him the fragrance seemed uniquely Grace. Whenever the wildflowers of spring lent their sweetness to the prairie wind, he would think of Grace Livingston . . . his wonderful, infuriating Boston

Grace dreamed she was in Matthew Stone's arms. Or Painted Horse's. They were one and the same, she remembered, and sorrow made her heart bleed and her soul tremble. . . . Why did he have to be Painted Horse? She could never love a Comanche! But she could never *stop* loving Matthew Stone.

She didn't want to think about her predicament. At the moment she wanted only to savor the feel of him as he held her cocooned in a warm embrace. His nuzzlings made her skin prickle in anticipation. Within moments arousal flooded her. Her body throbbed in its secret places, and she knew she couldn't deny him—even if he *was* Painted Horse, a hated, feared Comanche . . . a renegade, like his stallion.

"I don't want to want you," she murmured as his hand found her breast.

"Nor I you," he responded. "But I do. I want you so damn much."

His fingers found ways to torture her with temptation, and his voice soothed and cajoled her, obliterating all her objections. "I'm sorry," he murmured. "Sorry for the way I've treated you—sorry for the life I've led. I wish we could meet again and start over. Most of all I wish I could be the man you want me to be."

"I wish you could, too." She sighed.

She tried to picture him dressed like Roger—in fashionably cut clothing complete with the proper embellishments—and almost laughed out loud. It would never work. Matthew Stone *belonged* in his molded buckskins, or a breechclout and high moccasins. No matter how other men dressed, they paled in comparison. She didn't really want to change him; she loved him the way he was.

"Can you forgive me—accept me—as I am?" The question reflected her own inner debate. As his hot breath stirred her hair, she turned in his arms to see his face in the dim morning light.

"I don't know," she answered honestly. "But you're not a fool, and I'm sorry I called you one. Can you forgive me?"

"I'm not sure you were wrong!" he said, laughing softly. "Sometimes I think I'm the biggest fool who ever lived. Despite our differences—maybe *because* of them—I can't stay away from you."

"And I can't stay away from you," she whispered. "God help us both."

His eyes branded her and his mouth hovered near hers. Breathlessly she awaited his next move. It came quickly. "Maybe *this* will help us make up our minds."

He kissed her deeply and possessively. Drowning in his arms, she wanted him with every fiber of her being. The kissing led to sweet, heart-stopping caresses and the shedding of garments. When they were naked, Grace impatiently tugged at the leather thong around his forehead which held back his long hair. The thong was a small reminder of his Comanche heritage, and she sought to destroy their hold on him so she could make him completely her own.

Entwining her fingers in his hair, she again drew him down to her. He parted her legs with one hand, and this time she didn't fear their joining; it seemed natural and inevitable. Waiting for it to happen, she held her breath and rocked against him.

He laughed deep in his throat. "Don't be too eager, Boston. In lovemaking, patience yields a rich reward."

The sound of her name on his lips—the name he had given her—brought an explosion of joy. No longer was she Grace Livingston, with all the fears, inhibitions, and worries the name implied. She was Boston, a new person, and if *she* could change, why couldn't he?

"Take me, Matt. Please take me."

"Gladly," he whispered, moving over her.

Still he didn't enter her. With hands and mouth he stoked the flames of her passion higher and higher. He teased and tormented her. He stroked and caressed her until she grew frantic. Only then did he plunge inside her in one long smooth thrust that tore her asunder, momentarily blunting her pleasure. She gasped and trembled beneath him. He held her still and kissed away the tears that trickled down her cheeks.

Gradually the pain ebbed, and her body adjusted to the newness of his possession. She thought it was over then, but it was only beginning. She sensed it when he renewed his kisses. Never unsheathing himself, he thrust slowly and deeply within her. After a moment she found his rhythm and yielded to the tremors rising inside her.

Caught in the grip of rapture, she cried out her ecstasy at the very moment he balanced himself on his hands and stiffened above her. His buttocks shuddered as he pumped his life force into her, and she received his seed with a strangled cry of elation and wonder.

Afterward, she lay limply, unable to move. He lowered his body onto hers again and kissed her hair and damp brow as if in apology. "I didn't hurt you, did I?" he murmured, contritely but with a hint of male triumph.

"Yes . . . you did a little. But it was worth it. In the end, it was well worth it."

Now there was no mistaking his pride and possessiveness. "I'm glad! I wanted it to be good for you, Boston. I knew it was your first time, and the first time can be painful for a woman."

How had he known that? She herself had never learned much beyond the bare basics of what occurred between men and women. She had never discussed the subject—not even with Ellie, the most likely candidate for exchanging such confidences. Oh, they had speculated, giggled, and laughed over it a couple of times, but only romantic Ellie had actually run off with a man to find out for herself what it was all about, and she'd never shared what she'd learned with Grace.

To Grace, the experience was earth-shaking. She belonged to Matt now, and he to her. Wherever she went, whatever she did, she would think of the circle of his arms as home.

"Listen, Boston." He moved to lie alongside her instead of on top of her. "We need to talk."

"Not yet! Oh, please not yet!" She couldn't bear any more painful discussions that might tear them apart. The peace they had found was still too fragile. The least little disagreement might shatter it.

Leaning on his elbow, he kissed her forehead. "I don't mean about us personally. While you were sleeping, I found the Indians who left that sign we saw yesterday."

Already, she felt threatened. "You went looking for them without me?"

"Hush," he said, "or they're liable to hear you."

"Hear me! How close are they?"

"They're on the other side of this mountain. Well, they probably can't hear you, but it's never wise to take chances."

"Then they aren't Comanches. If they were and you had spoken with them, you wouldn't be so cautious."

"You're right. They aren't Comanches. They're Apaches—ancient enemies of the Comanches. I spied on them. They were tired and wounded, and never saw me."

He told her how Mackenzie had gone into Mexico and destroyed the Indians' villages there—and what he wanted to do now.

"You think Quanah Parker will surrender and return with us to the reservation once he finally realizes how slim his chances are of hiding out on the Staked Plain forever," Grace summarized when he had finished.

"More or less," Matt agreed.

"You didn't accept this job because of the money, the cattle, or the big house I promised you, did you?" Grace had to confirm her own suspicions. "You did it solely so you'd have the opportunity to convince the Indians to give up the battle to keep their freedom."

He slowly nodded. "You yourself warned me that Mackenzie had been given free rein to hunt down the Indians. I was afraid it might be my last chance to make Quanah and my brother see reason. That's what decided me . . . but you already knew that, didn't you?"

"Yes, but I wasn't entirely sure what it was I said that persuaded you. For most people money holds *some* appeal."

"Not for me." Moving away from her, he sat up. "But I also disliked the idea of handling a disturbed woman and two rebellious children by myself. I haven't had much experience in that sort of thing."

He brushed her cheek with his fingertips. "None of that matters now, Boston. Right now we have to find out what's happening—what the army's plans are for the future. If Mexico and the United States *have* joined together to destroy the Comanches, Quanah will be forced to accept the fact that defeat is imminent. If he doesn't surrender, he and his rebels face certain death."

"And so do their captives."

"The captives will die first," Matt soberly agreed. "Without weapons they can't defend themselves. Often they're the *first* ones shot in the heat of battle."

"Then we'd better head for Fort Griffin." Grace sat up and touched her palm to Matt's face. "You needn't worry that I'll expose you to the authorities. I can just imagine what they would do to Painted Horse if they ever got their hands on him."

"Save some concern for yourself, Boston. When I tell you about The Flats, you'll understand why I'm worried about you, too. It'll be just as dangerous for your identity to be discovered as it will be for mine. There are no 'gentlemen' in The Flats."

"I'm not afraid. *You* will be with me."

He shook his head and sighed. "Yes, but I'll be far outnumbered."

"I don't care. You're all the protection I need."

"If only you didn't look so damn female!"

"I've never looked *less* female in my life. When I'm dressed, I mean," she amended as his mocking gaze swept her nakedness.

"Well, you've never looked *more* female than you do right now." He leaned closer, as if he meant to steal a kiss.

Winding her arms around his neck, she nuzzled his neck. "How long will it take us to get to Fort Griffin?"

"If we leave right away, two or possibly three days of hard riding."

She burrowed into him. "But only two nights?"

"If we leave right away."

"Three nights. I *must* have three nights alone with you. That—and finding Ellie and the children—is all I'll ever ask. I promise."

"Three nights," he agreed. "We'll be sure and give ourselves three nights."

* * *

Those three days and nights were the happiest, most fulfilling, of Grace's entire life. All day long they rode without stopping, pushing the horses to their limits to cross plateaus, grasslands, and rivers that Grace barely noticed. Matt occupied all her thoughts and daydreams. They needed no words between them to know exactly what the other was thinking—and their mutual thoughts made Grace blush.

She counted the hours until they could dismount, make camp, and fall into each other's arms. Whenever she recalled what they did during the night, her body responded with flushed cheeks, heaviness in her breasts, and aching desire in her loins. Embarrassment alternated with sheer delight. She had never dreamed she could feel this way! It was a glorious sickness. It *couldn't* last . . . could it?

On their last night together, after a hot, dusty day, they camped near a nameless river, played naked in the shallows, made passionate love on the bank, and returned to the river for a swimming lesson before dark.

Grace didn't want to swim; she just wanted Matt to hold her. She would use any excuse to keep his arms around her. Tomorrow they must rejoin civilization, if The Flats could be called that. She had no idea what the future held, but she had the strong premonition that this brief time together was precious and sacred . . . and she wished it would never end.

They avoided all discussion of the future; how could they discuss it when they didn't know if they were going to have one? Matt never said he loved her, and marriage was never mentioned. Grace knew she could solve all their financial problems, but that in itself was a problem—a big one. She couldn't picture Matt in Boston, nor herself living in a shack for the rest of her life. If they were to have children, she would want the best for them. And if they *did* manage to rescue Ellie and the children, she would *have* to return east. It was where they belonged, and so did she.

She pretended to pay close attention while Matt lectured her on the fine art of staying afloat in water over her head, but all the while her mind was elsewhere—and Matt finally realized it. "Are you ready to try swimming on your own? Have you heard a word I've been saying?"

"I admit I haven't heard a word. Don't let go of me yet, Matt. I'm not ready." *In more ways than one she wasn't ready for him to let her go.*

"Let's get out." Cradling her in his arms, he carried her from the river.

She snuggled against him, and her wet hair streamed water down his side as he headed toward their bedrolls. When he reached them, he buried his nose in her neck and murmured: "I want you to know, Boston. These last few days have been wonderful, the best I can remember."

"For me, too!" she cried, hugging him.

He set her down and they embraced.

"Whatever happens I'll always remember this part of our journey."

Was he saying good-bye?

"It isn't over yet," she reminded him. "And I don't want to stay long at the fort. Only as long as it takes for you to find out what you need to know. Then we'll leave."

"Yes, if all goes well . . ."

"Stop worrying. It *will* go well."

"Boston . . ." He took her face in his hands. "I want you to consider remaining at the fort afterward. No!" He clapped his hand over her mouth. "Hear me out. From here I want to go by myself to find the Comanches. If your sister and her children are still alive, I'll bring them back to the fort to collect you. By myself I can travel faster, and it'll be safer for you here, especially if the army has teamed up with the Mexicans to wipe out the Indians. I don't want you in the way of any crossfire or . . ."

Grace removed his hand from her mouth. "Absolutely not! I won't hear of it! Besides, you already told me what a wild terrible place The Flats is. So how can you even think of leaving me there?"

"I said I wanted to leave you at the fort, not at The Flats.

The fort won't be so bad. Now that I've had time to think about it, I . . ."

"Stop thinking! I won't be left behind—and don't sneak off while I'm asleep, either. If you do, I'll steal a horse and come after you. If I can't find you, I'll search for the Comanches on my own. But I won't be left behind. Do you understand that?"

"All right. . . . It was worth a chance. I had to try. I care too much not to try, Boston."

He cared for her. He wouldn't use the word 'love,' but at least he cared.

She pressed against him. "I care for you, Matt."

Not just *care.* I *love* you.

Since he wouldn't admit it, she wouldn't, either. The thought pierced her with sorrow. She refused to acknowledge it. They still had tonight, and she didn't want to ruin it. Tomorrow would come soon enough.

Fourteen

In the morning Grace watched as Matt led Renegade into the river and carefully washed away the last remnants of war paint from the stallion's white coat. Most of the paint had come off in previous river crossings, but a few stubborn stains remained. When they, too, disappeared, he led the horse out of the river and rubbed ashes, dirt, and the crushed leaves of a mysterious plant into his coat again.

"I'll bet you wish you could leave him clean," Grace commented as Renegade's markings blended with the grime.

"One day his markings won't count against him, and I'll be able to ride him proudly and brag about all his good qualities. You should see this horse around cattle. His instincts, speed, and agility are just what you need in a ranch horse. He cuts cattle as if he were born to it, and I'm hoping he'll pass all that along to his foals."

"I'd like to see his foals some day—and maybe ride one."

To her own ears she sounded wistful. Grace wondered if she'd be around long enough to see Renegade's foals. Very likely she'd be back in Boston. Matt started to say something, but just then Renegade snorted, buckled at the knees, hit the ground, and started rolling on the sandy embankment. Laughing, he stepped away from the flailing hooves.

"You see? He likes being dirty. Rolling is a horse's way of grooming himself and getting rid of itchy spots."

"I know that," she told him. "Dunston and Lucy like to roll as soon as I remove the saddle or pack from their backs."

"You've grown fond of the horses, haven't you, Boston?"

The question was innocent enough, but she suspected he was fishing for her intentions. Little did he know how confused and uncertain she felt when it came to her future. Today he had traded his buckskins for clothing more typical of a white man. She thought him marvelously handsome and not in the least Indian-looking. Did different clothing make him *feel* different? . . . How would *she* feel when she had to go back to wearing a skirt instead of britches?

"When I . . . when I have to leave the horses, I'll be very sorry." *Tell me not to leave. Ask me to marry you. Beg me to stay . . . or offer to follow me wherever I go.*

"Dunston and Lucy wouldn't do well in Boston," he pointed out. "But I guess you already know that. They like the wide open spaces too much. If they had to be cooped up in a barn for the rest of their lives, their spirits would shrivel and die. They need their freedom."

Was he talking about the horses or himself? He needed freedom even more than they did.

"Our carriage horses are stabled all the time," she confessed. "They only go out when they're harnessed. In the city there are no wide open spaces full of tasty green grass where they can graze."

"And no big sky. No mountains. No plains. No wind blowing in your face. No sunsets to take your breath away or sunrises to make you feel humbly grateful for a brand new day. No nights of endless, shining stars . . ." Trailing off, he watched her intently. "I don't know how people can live in cities, crowded close together, stuck inside four walls, breathing foul air when they do manage to get outside."

"It isn't as bad as you think. There's lots to do in a city—so much happening all the time that you never notice what you're missing."

"Forget it, Boston. You'll never convince *me* that a city is a good place to live. . . . Get ready to ride, will you? It's time we got out of here."

Annoyed, she lingered. "I'm not trying to convince you of anything. I'm just *educating* you. Have you ever seen a really big city?"

"No, and I have no desire to see one. I'd feel . . . dead or imprisoned away from the plains and prairies. I thought *you* were beginning to love the wilderness. Guess I was wrong."

"The wilderness is great! It's just grand. But what's it like in the middle of a bad winter? And in high summer? Already it's hot and dry. I shudder to think of August."

"August can be a trial," he conceded. "But even in August there are compensations."

"Such as?"

"Knowing autumn is on the way . . . and solitude. We have all the solitude you could possibly want out here—regardless of the season. And room to roam. That more than makes up for the heat and dust of August, the occasional violent thunderstorm, and the hardships of winter."

"So you say." She sniffed, heading for her horses. "For myself, I rather doubt it."

By noon they were nearing The Flats. Even from a distance the place looked worse than Matt had described it. Headed in the same direction, competing for the trail, were teams of mules, horses, and oxen pulling wagons piled high with stiffened buffalo hides.

Grace fought to keep from gagging on the familiar odor. She was sure the buffalo hunters themselves added to the awful smell; never had she seen a rougher, dirtier, more violent-looking breed of men. To do this kind of work and live this sort of life they must be making good money—or be desperate.

"How much does a buffalo hide bring back east?" she asked Matt as a wagon piled high with skins rumbled past them, its driver cussing loudly and snapping a whip over the backs of the poor straining horses.

"Last I heard, three dollars and seventy-five cents apiece. From here the hides go to Dodge City and are shipped east by rail, like cattle. It's a big business, but it won't last long—not the way the buffalo hunters are operating. If they don't stop the killing soon—or someone doesn't stop them—the herds are finished. They'll be gone in our lifetime."

He rode ahead of her toward the main thoroughfare of the sprawling settlement, his grim expression reminding her of the previous discussions they'd had about buffalo. It must be hard for him to watch this activity without being able to prevent it. The tragedy of the situation didn't excuse his actions toward the hunters, but Grace sympathized with his cause. She couldn't imagine a worse industry than buffalo hunting.

As they approached The Flats, Grace studied the motley collection of unpainted frame buildings slapped together out of lumber that must have been hauled in over hundreds of miles. Dance halls, hotels, and saloons predominated. Night was a long way off, but raucous, tinny music, loud voices, and the occasional pop-pop-pop of pistol fire poured from open doorways. Men and horses jostled one another on the crowded streets, and the few women Grace spotted were dressed in low-cut, brightly colored gowns, and huge, feathered hats.

When Matt saw Grace eyeing the women with interest and a little surprise at their attire he leaned over and whispered: "Whirlago girls."

Never having heard the term, she raised her eyebrows in question.

"You know—hookers." He snorted in exasperation when she shrugged her shoulders and shook her head, indicating she still didn't understand. "They're called hookers for 'Fighting Joe Hooker', the Union general in the War Between the States. He had a regular penchant for ladies whose services he could buy."

"Oh!" Grace exclaimed, feeling foolish. She turned around in the saddle to peer at a female in a peacock-blue gown cut so low that her bosom threatened to spill out of her bodice. The woman flashed a big smile, revealing a single, solid gold front tooth.

"Stop gawking. She'll think you want to do business."

"Goodness gracious!" Grace jerked around to face forward.

"And stop saying things like 'goodness gracious'. You're supposed to be a buffalo hunter or a skinner."

"A skinner?"

"The men who go behind the hunters and skin the animals they've killed."

Grace shuddered, suddenly unsure she could pull this off. She tugged her hat down low over her face and tried to look unapproachable. Already she couldn't wait to leave this place. It reeked of sin, unwashed bodies, and strong spirits. Half the men on the street were intoxicated, and all of them looked dangerous. Most were buffalo hunters, dressed like her and Matt, but a few wore suits and fancy vests. She suspected they were cardsharps or saloonkeepers, the men who ran the town's booming businesses.

"Stay close to me," Matt warned. "We're going to the livery stable to put up the horses. Then I'll find a place for us to stay. At the stable they should be able to recommend a hotel with a spare room."

Grace put Dunston's nose to Renegade's tail. She knew it was dangerous and invited a kick, but the two horses behaved themselves, and they found the stable without incident. There, Matt ordered her to remain mounted while he secured Renegade, Lucy, and the other packhorses plus the three extras inside a couple of empty corrals behind the stable.

"I'm gonna look for the owner. Sit here and pretend you're waiting for someone. Don't invite conversation," were his last words to her.

She would have laughed at the notion except that she was too petrified. She had no intention of opening her mouth. Dunston whinnied forlornly when he saw the other horses leaving, so Grace allowed him to crowd as close to the first corral as he could get. He clearly found the town as unnerving as she did.

Matt winked at her and entered the stable in search of the owner. Several minutes later he returned in company with a tall bewhiskered man wearing baggy trousers held up by suspenders.

"Those are our horses." Matt nodded toward the corrals. "And this here is the partner I told you about—the fellow whose tongue was cut out by the Comanches."

In her surprise at that announcement, Grace's jaw dropped, but she quickly shut her mouth and glared at Matt. He hadn't mentioned how he intended to explain her silence. His excuse was a good one, but she still didn't like it. Keeping her opinions to herself wasn't one of her strong points, and Matt's grin—behind the stable owner's back—indicated how well he knew that.

"Ran afoul of them murderin' savages, did ya', young fellah?" the man asked. "Well, don't worry. There's plenty of poor sods right here in The Flats who bear the mark of run-ins with the Indians." He turned to Matt. "Yer friend speaks sign language, don't he?"

"Uh, no," Matt said, "Not yet. He didn't spend enough time among the Indians to learn it. And he was fresh from the east when they attacked and killed everyone else on his wagon train."

"That a fact," the man said, stroking his whiskers and looking impressed. "He's damn lucky t' be alive, ain't he? Waal, the Comanches are gonna get whut's comin' to 'em any day now. You wait an' see. Colonel Mackenzie is after 'em, an' he's the first army officer I've seen who has the balls t' keep searchin' 'til he finds that rascal Quanah Parker an' brings 'im t' justice."

"What's the latest news on Mackenzie?"

Grace could tell Matt was trying to be casual and not reveal the extent of his interest, but a muscle twitched in his jaw, and she could only hope the stable owner didn't see it.

The man leaned toward Matt and lowered his voice. "Ain't nobody s'posed t' know, but the news has spread faster than an outbreak of cholera. Mackenzie rode clear inta Mexico t' rout them red devils. We ain't heard yet whether or not he succeeded, but knowin' him he probably did."

"Into Mexico!" Matt looked properly shocked. "How'd he get permission? Did he cut some kind of deal with the Mexican government?"

"Damned if I know. And nobody else knows, either. 'Cept maybe over t' the fort. If yer really curious, you'll have t' ask there. We don't want the army pokin' their noses inta our business, so we don't poke our noses inta their's. Live an' let live, I always say. But I can tell ya' we're real proud of Colonel Ranald S. Mackenzie, especially if he drove them rascals outa their hidey holes in Mexico."

"Maybe I will ask at the fort." Matt idly scratched his chin. "We were thinking of headin' down to Mexico, and I'd like to know first what's goin' on."

"You're welcome t' go ask, stranger. Me, I stay away from the fort—and so does nearly everybody else in The Flats."

"So where can we get a place to stay while we're here? What's the best hotel?"

"Hotel? Yer lookin' t' stay in a hotel?" The man laughed so hard his whiskers shook. "Good luck, stranger. The hotels are most always full. Men shoot each other over rooms. They come in off the range lookin' an' smellin' worse'n dead buffalo, an' they wanna be treated *right* when they get here. So they all crowd inta the hotels. . . . Only rooms you can get anymore are the ones in the gamblin' halls. 'Course, they don't come cheap. They're worse'n the hotels by far, but then most of 'em have extry added attractions."

"I don't care what it costs," Matt said. "Who's got the best rooms?"

"Lottie Deno," the man said without hesitation. "Ever hear of her?"

Matt shook his head, and the man continued. "Why, that redheaded poker queen is damn near a legend all over Texas. She keeps a few fancy rooms, but she's mighty partic'lar about who she rents 'em out to. She either hasta know the fellah an' already like him, or it's gotta be someone she meets an' takes a special shine to. Your friend there is kinda puny for her tastes, but *you* might fit the bill. All you gotta do is trot over an' see. She'll take one look at ya' and make up her mind on the spot. . . . That's our Lottie. Mighty opinionated. Runs a clean game, though, an' if anybody gives her trouble, her hired gunmen chase 'em right outa town. Oh, her girls are right toothsome, too."

Oh, we don't want to stay there! Grace sent a silent, pleading message to Matt, but he wasn't looking in her direction.

"Thanks. We'll give Lottie a try." He motioned for Grace to dismount. "Come on, Shorty. Give the man your horse, and let's go see Miss Deno."

"Shorty, huh?" The stable owner gave Grace the once-over as she climbed down from the saddle. "Good name fer ya', kid, I'll say that. Hell, you look like you jus' let go of yer Mama's apron strings. Why, you ain't got whiskers yet! At least, none I can see."

"Don't let looks fool you," Matt interjected. "This lad is real handy with a Colt. His experience among the Comanches taught him he had to learn to defend himself."

Grace patted the butt of the pistol Matt had insisted she carry at all times in the waistband of her trousers while they were in The Flats. Hoping she looked convincing as a young man, she swaggered past the stable owner.

"We'll be back later to check on the horses," Matt called over his shoulder, putting himself between her and the fellow.

"Don't worry about yer horses. I'll see they're well cared for—an' I'll warn the help t' steer clear of yer stallion. He looks a mean 'un."

"Just have them toss the feed over the rails, an' stick a bucket of water inside with caution. As long as nobody touches him, the stallion shouldn't give you any trouble."

"We won't touch him," the man promised. "I ain't anxious to lose no fingers."

Grace could only guess what Matt must have told the man. How easy lying came to him! Was that a legacy from the Comanches? They started back down the dusty street they had just traversed on horseback. Twice they had to dodge men fighting on the boardwalk, and several times step over bodies lying in drunken stupors.

Once, Grace forgot herself and clutched Matt's arm for protection, but Matt only shrugged her off. "Easy, Boston. Keep your distance. I won't let anything happen to you."

"This place reeks of wickedness! I've never seen so many inebriated fools."

"Hush! I think we're almost there."

Matt led her inside a pair of swinging doors into a two-story building crammed with men, gaudy women, and small wooden tables ringed by chairs. Sawdust littered the floor, and Grace glimpsed a shocking painting of a naked lady lying on a crimson velvet coverlet. The place also held a long wooden bar with a big mirror behind it, several large brass spittoons, and a huge chandelier hanging down overhead.

She couldn't believe her eyes; it was a den of luxury and iniquity worthy of Boston or some other big city! Someone had gone to great trouble and expense to create such extravagance in the middle of a desolate plain.

A shapely female who looked as if she'd been poured into her scarlet silk gown suddenly materialized in front of them. Trimmed with black lace, satin bows, and ostrich feathers, her gown epitomized poor taste, but it somehow suited this hard-eyed woman, with her fiery-red hair, red cheeks, and heart-shaped, pouty mouth.

"Poker, gentlemen?" she purred, swinging her hips as she descended upon them. "Or did you merely want somethin' to burn the trail dust from your throats?"

"Neither." Matt stepped in front of Grace. "We want a room."

The woman's lashes fluttered as she looked Matt over from head to foot. "For *each* of you, or *both* of you? I might be able to find somethin' for *you,* honey—but your little friend will have to look elsewhere."

Grace had the sudden irrational desire to throw herself at the woman and claw out her eyes. She almost said something, but Matt shot her a warning glance. "We can sleep in the same room. If it's only got one bed, one of us will take the floor."

"Now that would be inconvenient, wouldn't it? Especially if one or the other of you should decide you want comp'ny for the night."

"We're not interested in whirlago girls. We just need a place to sleep."

"How long will you be stayin', handsome?" The woman sauntered closer to Matt and leaned into him, revealing more of her voluptuous bosom. Grace caught a whiff of her sultry perfume. Up close she looked older than Grace had thought at first, but still she was pure female—and as predatory as a cat stalking a mouse.

"Don't know yet. It all depends. We've got some business over at the fort. Soon as it's finished we'll be leaving."

"Too bad. I wouldn't want ya'll to rush off before we get to know each other a little better."

Matt persisted despite the woman's blatant efforts to seduce him. "Have you got a room or not?"

"For *you,* honey, I'll throw someone else out," she promised. "Though I wish you'd let your little friend find his own lodgin's."

"My little friend is my partner. Got his tongue cut out by Comanches, but he can say plenty with a revolver."

"My, my! Guess I shouldn't be so quick to dismiss him then, should I? I'll ask one of my girls to make him feel right at home."

"No girls," Matt repeated. "And we want the room right away."

"Patience, honey. You jus' let ole Lottie see what she can do or you. In the meantime ya'll can wet your whistles at the bar.

If you just rode in you must be mighty thirsty. First drink is on me. . . . Sam!"

A baldheaded man behind the wooden bar raised his head. "Yeah, Lottie?"

"Fetch these two tired travelers a couple shots of my best bourbon. They'll be stayin' with us while they're in town, and I want 'em to feel welcome."

"Sure thing. Gentleman, step right up!"

Keeping her head down, Grace followed Matt to the long wooden bar. There was no place to sit; everyone stood leaning against the bar, one boot resting on the low brass railing, and downed their drinks in a single long swallow.

"Hope you boys can hold your liquor." The bartender set two glasses half-filled with an amber liquid down in front of them. "Especially you, young feller. This is Lottie's finest. It'll grow enough hair on your chest to make you look like a buffalo."

Grace turned to Matt, but he never so much as glanced her way. Instead he picked up his glass and tossed down the contents. Realizing she had no choice but to do likewise, she grabbed the glass, lifted it to her lips, and drank quickly, draining it as she'd seen Matt and the other men do with their drinks. For a split second, she thought everything was going to be fine. Then she tried to breathe.

Her throat had closed, and no air could get past the obstruction. All she could feel was a fiery burning sensation, starting in her mouth, sliding down her throat, and coagulating into a ball of flame in her stomach. Her eyes watered. Her ears buzzed. She choked and gasped and bit her own tongue. Still, she couldn't breathe . . . couldn't even signal her distress to Matt.

Fortunately he guessed what was the matter and clapped her hard on the back. She wheezed and sputtered, gulping air like a drowning person. Around her the onlookers broke into cheers—all laughing and talking at the same time, enjoying the spectacle she'd made of herself.

"That's Lottie's finest!" one man chortled. "Why, I've seen fellahs pass out afore they could catch their breath again. You done right good, young fellah! Sam, fetch him another. This one's on me!"

"One is plenty," Matt growled, shouldering the man aside. "My partner's not used to strong drink."

"Well, here in The Flats he better *git* used to it. The water ain't hardly fit t' drink. One more, an' we'll leave him alone."

Matt's hand went for his gun. Grace reached out to stop him. She nodded vigorously, remembering not to lick her lips or otherwise betray herself. The matter wasn't worth fighting over. Surely she could survive another whiskey.

"All right, drink it, but you might pass out," Matt warned, angry at her interference. "If you do I'll just let you lie there. That whiskey is about four times as strong as any I've ever drunk."

"You bet it is," Sam, the bartender, agreed. "Lottie won't even sell it to most folks—only to those she especially likes. Can't say as I see what she sees in you, stranger, but your partner looks game enough. Appears to me Lottie took a shine to the wrong feller."

"I never asked for her approval," Matt said, bristling. "All I wanted was a room."

Sudden tension vibrated between the two men. A deadly calm had come over Matt, like the calm preceding a storm. Grace's heart pounded in alarm. If Matt picked a fight in here, he'd be greatly outnumbered. She spotted Lottie Deno standing halfway up a wooden staircase, watching. A little half smile curved the woman's lips, as if she relished the confrontation—and wanted to see exactly what Matt would do when challenged.

Taking a deep breath for courage, Grace grabbed her refilled glass and once again downed it. This time the whiskey went up her nose as well as down her throat, and caused a fit of coughing. Through it all she could hear clapping and cheering, but she couldn't *see* anything for her tears. She had the oddest sensation that her head was floating off her shoulders, and her feet refused to stay on the floor.

After that she wasn't sure what happened. The room spun

too fast. A wall of laughter surrounded her. Someone—Matt?—picked her up, tossed her over his shoulder, and marched up a flight of stairs with her to the accompaniment of loud booing, hissing, and more laughter. A door closed and all was suddenly, blissfully, quiet and as black as a moonless night.

Grace's next conscious thought was one of anguish. Someone had cracked her head open or tried to scalp her! She had never experienced such blinding pain. If she so much as blinked, pain seized her, blotting out everything. Moaning, she tried to guess where she was, apparently not in her bedroll. Softness cushioned part of her body and reminded her of her bed in Boston. Too bad she couldn't enjoy it,

A voice floated above her, disembodied and slightly mocking. "Not feeling too well, are we, Boston? Serves you right. You didn't have to take that second drink. I wouldn't have let anyone force it on you."

"No, you'd have killed them over it and gotten shot yourself." She gritted her teeth; talking only made things worse. She didn't dare open her eyes.

"Stay here and sleep. I don't think anyone will bother you. It's early morning and no one's stirring yet. I'll hurry back as soon as I can."

Early morning? Did he mean the morning of the day after *their arrival in The Flats?*

"Where are you going?" opening her eyes, she tried to rise on one elbow, but the pounding in her head only intensified.

"To the livery stable and then to the fort. On the table beside you, you'll find a glass of water I got from one of our canteens. Drink it when you feel up to it. When I return I'll try to bring back coffee."

"No coffee," she moaned, sinking back down. "No water. If I drink anything I'll only be sick."

"It'll pass. It always does. Do you think you can get up and lock the door behind me? That way if anyone knocks or tries to come in, you can just ignore them."

"Sure. I'll jump right up. Just go. I'll be fine."

I'm dying, and he expects me to get up and lock the door!

"Don't go anywhere. Don't even stick your head outside the door. Enjoy the fancy accommodations. They're just your style. Everything you need is here—except food. And I'll bring some of that, too, when I return."

"Oh, do bring me some pemmican."

"Pemmican? You want pemmican?"

What was wrong with the man? Didn't he understand sarcasm when he heard it?

"I adore pemmican! Or bring me buffalo tongue. I'll eat it raw. Can't think of anything I'd like better."

"Buffalo tongue *is* a great delicacy, Boston. A Comanche wouldn't hesitate to eat it raw. They eat the livers raw, too, smeared with the salty juices from the gall bladder, and raw brains from the cracked skull, and fresh bone marrow. When they're done with that, they strip the warm guts with their teeth . . ."

Grace turned over and shoved her fist in her mouth. "Get out of here! Just go."

Laughing, he retreated. "Don't forget. Lock the door after me."

But she did forget—or more accurately, she refused to get out of bed to do it. To escape the pain and dizziness she slept, and the next voice to awaken her was female.

"I *knew* you weren't a boy."

Grace opened her eyes to discover Lottie Deno standing in the open doorway, one hand on her shapely hip and a knowing gleam in her eye.

Fifteen

"You are the reason that handsome hunter won't look at me. I figured as much."

Grace didn't know what to say to that, so she didn't say anything. She pulled the covers a little higher and wished she could stick her head under them and hide. It was too late now. She wasn't wearing her hat, and her disheveled braids had fallen down around her shoulders.

Lottie Deno entered the room and closed the door behind her as if she owned the place—which of course, she did. She walked over to a dainty little chair with a stuffed seat covered in embroidered cabbage roses and sat down on it. Grace simply stared at her; this morning—or was it afternoon already?—the woman was wearing a frothy, lacy, peach-colored garment that could only be called indecent. Grace could see the contours of her body right through the sheer fabric.

"How do you like the accommodations?" Lottie indicated the room with a nod.

For the first time, Grace noticed it. The furnishings were all of a shiny, dark wood, lace hung at the windows and covered the tables and backs of some of the chairs, and the floor boasted a thick, flowered rug. Mirrors, glass lamps, ornate hairbrushes, tiny bottles and jars, and miniature oval paintings all proclaimed it a feminine boudoir . . . and the taste of its owner wasn't bad. Not bad at all.

"Oh, I forgot!" Lottie chortled. "You can't answer—the Comanches got your tongue!"

"Not really," Grace admitted. "Obviously, you've guessed by now that Matt only said that so I wouldn't have to speak."

"Obviously. So what's a la-de-da lady like you doin' in a place like this?"

"How do you know I'm a lady?" Grace moved her head slightly to see if the pain had subsided. It was still there, but was less intense.

"Oh, puh-leeze!" Lottie waved a heavily be-ringed hand. "I'm an expert at sizing up other females. I knew you was a lady from the way you walk, and now the way you talk, and certainly in the way you looked at that handsome hunter of yours. And the way *he* looked at you. Whirlago girls never give—or get—such looks."

"Oh," Grace said. "I didn't know that."

"Well, it's true. I can read you like a Montgomery Ward Merchandise Sheet. You think you're better'n me, don't ya'? Maybe you are, honey. You've likely never had to work a day in your life, while me, I'm a workin' woman who don't eat if she don't work."

Grace thought it ironic that she was lying there in a gambling queen's bed being lectured on not working, when she'd worked every day of her life. How could the woman make all those assumptions just by looking at her or listening to her?

"I work," she said. "Would I be dressed the way I am if I *didn't?*"

She lifted the cover and peeked beneath it; she *was* still dressed in her buffalo hunter's clothes, so the question was a fair one.

"That's what I wanna know," Lottie said. "What are you doin' in The Flats, and why are you dressed like a man?"

Grace debated how much to tell her. She finally decided she had nothing to lose by confessing her purpose in being there.

"My hunter, as you call him—Mr. Stone—is my employee. I hired him to bring me out here to find the Comanches."

"Good heavens, girl! Why would you wanna find them murderin' Comanches? They'll kill you as soon as look at you."

"They've got my sister and her two children." Wincing, Grace sat up. "I came out west to rescue them and take them home with me to Boston."

A fleeting look of sympathy crossed Lottie's painted features. "Hasn't anybody told you they're probably dead by now? You're wastin' your time, honey, and riskin' your life for nothin'."

"That's what everyone keeps telling me. But I can't be sure of that until I find the Indians. Mr. Stone—Matt—thought I'd be safer if I posed as a man."

Lottie snorted. "Sounds like a man's way of thinkin'. The only problem is maintainin' the disguise. If everybody in The Flats wasn't half-drunk all the time you'd never have pulled it off this long."

"Will you keep my secret?" Grace bluntly demanded. "By the way, my name is Grace Livingston."

Lottie cocked her head, studying Grace. "I don't know, Miss Grace Livingston from Boston. That depends. Exactly what are yer feelin's toward Mr. Stone?"

"That's none of your business."

"I'm makin' it my business. He's the best lookin' critter to walk into my gamblin' hall in two—maybe three—years. Truth is, I was beginnin' to despair I'd ever again see a man I liked. Most of the ones who come t' The Flats stink of buffalo an' failure. Not your man, though. He looks like he's got plans, dreams, and goals. Seems t' me the right gal could be a part of 'em. What I'm tryin' t' say is, if you don't want him I do."

Grace had never expected to hear a woman speak so boldly and plainly. Or to meet one who wanted a man so crassly and openly. But then, Lottie Deno had to be one tough female to have set up a gambling hall in a place like this.

"I want him," she responded, afraid to say she didn't or hadn't made up her mind. "And he wants me."

"I was afraid of that." Lottie sighed, standing. "Can't blame me for tryin'. You just better keep an eye on him, 'cause my girls ain't stopped talkin' about him since the two of you walked through the door. Watch Glory, especially. She's desperate to get out of The Flats. She swore t' fight me for him if you didn't want him, and t' fight *you,* if you did."

Grace gasped. "They *all* know I'm a woman?"

"Honey, we may come from different backgrounds, but we can always smell each other. Every female in the place knew you was a woman right off. You didn't fool one of us."

Leaving Grace to ponder that disturbing piece of information, Lottie strolled toward the door. "If ya'll want a bath I'll have some hot water sent up. There's a tub over there behind that screen in the corner. You're welcome to use the soap, but I'll have to charge extry for it."

"I've got my own soap, but I'd love the bath. Send one up as soon as you can."

"Delilah will bring the water. She grew up bein' a slave, like her mama and papa, but soon as she could she fled the south and come out here lookin' t' finally be her own woman. I hired her quick, and I ain't never been sorry."

"That's . . . nice." Again, Grace didn't know what to say. Lots of people had apparently come west searching for freedom and opportunity—and found both. But oh, what a price they sometimes had to pay!

"I s'pose you'd like somethin' to eat, too."

"Ah . . . maybe later. Food doesn't appeal to me just now. I'm still recovering from your bourbon."

"You sure looked funny! I enjoyed that, I did. . . . Be careful, honey. And watch your back. In The Flats, you can't trust no one."

With that last bit of advice, Lottie Deno left.

After his talk with the fort commander—the officer in charge until Colonel Mackenzie's return—Matt returned to the livery stable to check on the horses. The stable owner engaged him in conversation, and Matt spent a half hour telling the man not much of anything. What he had learned at the fort was his own business, no one else's, and he didn't intend to discuss it with a single soul, except perhaps Grace.

How much to tell Grace was the problem: at the fort he'd learned that Mackenzie had *not* had official orders to cross the border. The commander had even denied that Mackenzie had done it. However, he confirmed that the colonel had approval to do whatever it took to force the Comanches to surrender. This included shooting all the Indians' horses, killing all the buffalo and/or game that sustained the holdouts, destroying any villages he found, and taking no prisoners. The commander had naturally assumed that Matt would wholeheartedly approve of such tough measures. He'd even boasted about them.

In view of all this Matt had reached the conclusion that Grace *must* stay at the fort, where she would be safe from the bloodbath he knew was coming. He suspected she'd want to leave immediately to continue the search for the Comanches in the hopes of finding them before the army did. For a little while, at least, he could delay arguing over what they should do. The last thing the commander had mentioned was that a scout had arrived earlier that morning to relay the information that Mackenzie was en route to the fort to pick up more supplies. The freight wagon they had sent out to him had apparently never reached him. No one knew what had happened to it.

At this point Matt had described the burnt wagon and the bodies he and Grace had found. The commander had then invited him to return to the fort to speak directly with Mackenzie, an invitation he had eagerly accepted. This would be his chance to discover more about the colonel's plans, such as where he intended to search next for the Comanches. Matt could then warn Quanah to avoid those areas. He still had hopes of reaching the Indians first. Renegade could travel faster than any army detail. But if Matt had to take Grace along and match his pace to hers . . .

Well, he wasn't going to take her, and that was that. Mackenzie would surely agree to allow her to stay at the fort and to guarantee her safety. Until then she'd have to maintain her disguise, and he'd have to think of a way to convince her to stay behind.

Planning his strategy, he threaded his way through the late afternoon crowd jamming Lottie's gambling hall, mounted the staircase, and walked down the hall to the room Lottie had assigned them. He was about to knock. Then he decided to try the door and make sure Grace had followed his instructions to lock it. The door opened easily. Shaking his head, Matt stepped inside and closed the door behind him.

The bed was empty! Matt's heart hammered in his chest. Just as he was about to race from the room in search of Grace, he heard a sound. It came from behind the screen set up in one corner. Stalking over to it, he shoved the screen aside. There sat Grace in a huge copper tub, up to her ears in bubbles. She smiled at him, and he forgot what he was going to say to her. With her face scrubbed clean and shiny, her damp hair piled on top of her head, and her hazel eyes glowing like lamps, all he wanted to do was climb into the tub with her, not deliver a lecture.

"Now, this is a real bath," she chirped, perky as a little bird. "Not cold, like a river, and not too deep or shallow. There are no rocks on the bottom, no sand to make you itchy, and you won't get sunburned in places the sun should never see, anyway. . . . Want to try it?"

He couldn't refuse such an invitation. "Is there room enough in there for two?"

"I'll *make* room," she promised.

He stripped off half his clothes before he thought to ask the obvious. "How in hell did you manage this, when you've supposedly lost your tongue? . . . And bubbles, yet! You didn't let anyone know you're a female, did you? Damn it, Boston, you must have!"

"Lottie came to visit me, and she already knows. So do *all* the women. Apparently they're more observant than the buffalo hunters who saw us yesterday."

"Ha! More likely, they were just more sober. Later we'll have

to decide what to do about that." Matt finished stripping and
eased into the tub facing Grace. He hardly fit, and his knees
stuck out of the water. "Turn around," he ordered.

"No, this is *my* bath. *You* turn around."

"I want you to sit here," he explained. "Between my legs."

"Between your legs?" She smiled impishly. "In that case,
maybe I'll humor you."

"Humor me! Turn around, Boston, or you'll be sorry."

"Goodness, you scare me to death!" She rolled her eyes and
shivered delicately, then turned around, sloshing water over the
side of the tub onto the floor.

He pulled her into the circle of his arms where she belonged,
and where he had access to every soapy, slippery inch of her.
She leaned her head back on his shoulder and sighed. "Don't
expect me to do anything too strenuous, because I still have a
terrible headache."

"I'll make your headache go away," he promised.

"No, first I want to hear what you've been up to. Did you
go to the fort?"

*How like Grace to grill him when there was so much else
he'd rather be doing!* Answering questions wasn't high on his
present list of priorities.

"I'll tell you about it later. This isn't the time for conversation."

"Matt! You have to tell me now." She started to turn around
again, but he held her in place, her slick, bare bottom wedged
tightly against him, driving him wild with desire.

"I didn't hear anything I didn't already know," he soothed.
"And anyway, Mackenzie wasn't there. But he's on his way to
the fort and should arrive any day now. I think we should wait
until I can talk to him before we do anything further."

"You mean wait until *we* can talk to him," she corrected.

Matt had already decided he didn't want Grace along when
he spoke to the colonel. Handling Mackenzie was *his* job. Besides, he couldn't discuss her if she were present. Actually he
was hoping to keep her confined to this room until he could

safely move her to the fort. Now that Lottie and her whirlago girls knew she was a woman, it wouldn't be long before everyone in town discovered the fact. When that happened there would likely be trouble.

"Naturally, *we* . . ." he lied, not about to argue at the moment.

"If Mackenzie won't be here for a couple days yet, I guess we have plenty of time for *this,* haven't we?"

She rubbed her bottom against him, and he groaned and tightened his hold on her. "Plenty of time," he assured her, lowering his mouth to the enticing spot between her neck and shoulder.

He lost himself in the pleasure of the moment and found great joy in soaping Grace and scrubbing—caressing—her. She, in turn, scrubbed him all over, touching places that sparked his passion to the level of an inferno. When he tired of the game he rose from the water, lifted her in his arms, and stepped out of the tub. Drying her—and being dried—provided another delightful diversion.

At last he couldn't stand it any longer and swept her into his arms to carry her to the bed. "Hurry, Matt," she whispered, her head rolling back on his shoulder. "Hurry! I can't wait much longer."

Neither could he. They fell on the rumpled bed, but just as he mounted her and slid home to their mutual reward, a drunken shout sounded outside the door.

"Where is she? Where's that new gal Glory told me arrived yestidy? By damn, I got my money, and if nobody tells me where she is I'll break down every damn door 'til I find her!"

Glory? Who was Glory? And who was the new girl the lout was trying to find? Not Grace, surely!

The door flew open, a man charged through it like a wounded buffalo, and all hell exploded.

One minute Matt was on top of Grace—*in* her—and the next minute he was standing up stark naked and pummeling a short heavy man Grace had never before seen.

"Glory told me I could be first to have her!" The man bellowed.

"This isn't the one!" Matt bellowed back, grabbing the man in a headlock.

"Waal, if she ain't the one who in hell is she? I ain't never seed her before."

"She's my *wife,* damn you!"

His wife?

The man ceased struggling and turned his pinned head to look at her. "That true, lady?"

Grace snatched the covers to her naked bosom and nodded.

"Waal, I'll be damned," the man said. "Glory didn't say nuthin' 'bout the new gal bein' married."

"Well, she is, and I'm her husband. So get out and leave us alone." Matt released him and the man straightened, rubbing his neck.

"I'm a-goin'. But you better tell all the fellahs downstairs, 'cause there's line of 'em waitin' their turn. Whenever a new whirlago girl shows up, she's got more business than she can handle. Until the newness wears off, she's in big demand."

"Soon as I dress I'll come down and make it clear to them," Matt growled, and Grace had never seen him look more ferocious, not even when he was Painted Horse.

"Yes, sir!" the man said. "This should be good. I'm gonna go place my bet on *you.* Y'all look like you can fight off any man who offers a challenge."

"Do that," Matt snarled. "You'll get rich."

"Matt, you can't!" Grace wailed as the man ran out. "Someone's liable to shoot you the minute you walk down the stairs. Those men are animals."

Matt was already pulling on his pants. "Shut up, Boston. Don't interfere. I fight for what's mine."

The contrast between him and Roger was never more apparent. But for once Grace heartily wished that Matt were more like her old fiance, a coward afraid of his own shadow.

"Please don't fight, Matt . . . please! I'll get dressed, and we'll find another way out of here. We'll leave without saying good-bye. We can put money on the table to cover our bill. Please, Matt—you'll get hurt!"

"You don't have much faith in me, do you?" His gaze raked her. "What kind of man would I be if I *weren't* willing to fight for my woman?"

His woman. His wife. She loved the sound of both words and the sentiments they expressed. Roger would never have faced a roomful of dangerous men for her sake.

"I don't want you to fight," she repeated. "Let's just leave."

"We can't leave yet. Stay here. Lock the door and wait for me."

With that, he left her.

As soon as the door slammed shut, Grace scrambled into her clothes and found her pistol. Checking to see that it was loaded, she jammed her feet into her boots, opened the door, and raced for the stairway. The sounds of fighting drifted up to her. Glass shattered, women screamed, men roared, and Lottie Deno's shouting voice soared over the melee. "Stop it! All of you. Yer breakin' my stuff, and before too long someone's gonna get killed."

Grace stood at the top of the steps, pointed her pistol at the heavy brass chandelier, and fired. She hit two round glass globes and snuffed the flickering oil wicks inside them. The chandelier rocked and swayed above everyone's heads, and the noise startled them. Hot oil rained down onto upturned faces, and the victims cursed and shook their fists at her. At least she had everyone's attention.

Six men held Matt pinned to the floor, yet Grace saw that *they* bore the brunt of the damage while Matt himself looked barely winded. He had only a small cut above one eye, while they were bruised and battered. Warily, they all gazed up at her.

"Let him up—*now.*" Grace somehow managed to keep her voice from cracking. "I'm not a whirlago girl, and I'm not for sale."

"You ever change yer mind, sweetheart, you let me know,"

one man called out to her. "I like a gal who's willin' t' fight fer a man."

"You sure he's worth it, honey?" another man added "We just about had 'im licked. 'Course, it took six of us. The bastard fights like a Comanche."

Grace noted the bloody noses, swelling eyes, and split lips. "He's worth it . . . Where's Glory?"

A tall, thin woman with ebony-black hair stepped out of the gathering. Wearing an emerald green gown with matching green feathers in her piled-up curls, she exuded the essence of a true harlot. "I'm Glory." She lifted one foot to a chair, yanked up her skirt, and boldly adjusted an emerald-green garter. "What do you want with me?"

The men cheered, and one hollered: "I'll be glad t' tell ya' what *I* want with ya', Glory, sweetie."

Grace pointed the pistol at her. A collective murmur of protest rose. Shoving down her skirt, Glory jumped behind a burly buffalo hunter. "Don't shoot!" she screamed.

"Then don't spread any more lies about me. And don't let me see you anywhere near Matt Stone."

"I don't know nobody named Matt Stone!"

"Him." Grace motioned to Matt with the pistol. He had gotten to his feet, but she could see now that he was hurt. A line of white rimmed his mouth, and he held his arms close to his chest.

"Oh—*him,*" Glory said.

Matt staggered toward the steps and mounted them, then reached for the pistol. "Give me that, Boston, before you hurt someone."

"Not until you're safe inside our room. Get going. I'll cover you."

"Damn stubborn woman." Matt eyed her as if *she* had done something wrong—not him.

"You tell her, fellah! Don't take no backtalk from yer wife!" an onlooker shouted.

A murmur of agreement and argument rose, until Lottie Den

drowned it out with her booming voice. "Show's over, gentlemen! Leave them be now. Step up to the bar or a gamblin' table. If ya' ain't got no money t' spend, you might as well go elsewhere."

Grace followed Matt back up the stairs and down the hall to their room. Once inside, Matt went to the bed and gingerly sat down on it, then stretched out on his back.

"What's wrong?" Grace demanded. "You're hurt, aren't you?"

"Only my ribs," he grunted. "And my pride."

"Was I supposed to let them kill you?" She leaned over him and probed his chest with her fingers until he winced.

"Watch it. I was winning the fight. I just needed more time."

"Of course you were winning. The odds were only six to one."

"Fair odds for a Comanche."

"You are *not* a Comanche! You're a white man, and it's time you acted like one."

"Can't, Boston." He grinned ruefully as she tore up a sheet to bind his bruised or broken ribs. "Once a Comanche, always a Comanche. I'll have better luck turning you into an Indian than you'll have turning *me* into a white man."

"I don't think so. I abhor violence. Why, I'm shaking so hard that if I took a drink of milk it would turn to butter in a matter of minutes. You are the most exasperating man I've ever met, Matthew Stone! Sit up, now, so I can bind your ribs."

He sat up, perching on the edge of the bed, while she wound strips of sheeting around his upper chest. "Do you know what the hell you're doing?" he grunted.

"No, but if I don't do it right, I'm sure you'll tell me."

He did tell her—twice—how to do it better and provide support to the spots that hurt. When they were done he tried to take her in his arms again, but she pushed him back down on the bed. "You're in no shape for games, and neither am I. I'm going to lock the door, and then we're going to sleep."

"If you had locked the door in the first place, this never would have happened."

"It won't happen again. Believe me, I've learned my lesson."

"Boston, Boston. . . . what am I going to do with you?"

Marry me! Make me your wife in real life, and never, ever let me go.

When she had seen him pinned to the floor, only a few seconds away from death or serious injury, something had snapped inside her. She *would* have killed anyone who touched him, and gladly died trying to protect him. When it came to Matt Stone she had no control over her emotions. It was a frightening feeling, all the more so because of the uncertainty of the future. How could she bear to part from him when the time came?

They stayed in the room alone together for three days, waiting for Mackenzie. Several times they went out to a hotel for meals, but the outings were tense and miserable. The buffalo hunters clearly resented Matt and silently ogled Grace. She could hardly eat for fear someone would pick a fight with Matt. As for Matt, he was so busy sizing up every man who looked at her that he never even noticed what was set in front of him.

Lots of men looked. They liked to stand back as she walked by and then bend over to stare at her bottom. She knew her trousers were tight, but she didn't think her bottom merited *that* much scrutiny. Whenever they stared at her so blatantly—some even whistled—Matt grew livid.

"What did I tell you?" he hissed at one point. "I warned you this would happen."

"You said I'd be *safer* in a man's clothing. If I'd worn a skirt they wouldn't look twice."

"They'd look twice if you were dressed in a gunny sack. Most of these men are too poor to afford whirlago girls, and they haven't laid eyes on any other females in months."

"Well, I'm sorry I'm a female, but it's not my fault men are so bestial!"

Late in the afternoon of the third day Lottie came to tell them that Mackenzie had ridden into the fort. She'd heard it from couple of half-breed scouts who had come to town to have a good time before riding out again.

"Thanks for telling us, Lottie," Matt said at the door.

Naked under the covers as she waited for Matt to return to her, Grace could hear Lottie's voice. "Don't thank me! I'm only tellin' you 'cause I want my room back. You've stirred up a hornet's nest 'cause you got your own woman when everybody else has t' share. I can't wait 'til the two of you leave here. The sooner yer gone, the better."

"Now that Mackenzie's come we should be clearing out soon."

"Good. I'm glad t' hear it."

As Lottie's footsteps retreated Grace jumped out of bed and began dressing.

"Where do you think you're going?" Matt snapped, blocking her way.

"To the fort with you to see Mackenzie."

"I'd rather you wait here." When Lottie had first knocked at the door, Matt had donned his pants. Now, he pulled on his shirt.

"Why?"

"He'll talk to me more freely if you aren't there"

"But I want to hear what he has to say!"

"I'll tell you when I get back. In the meantime why don't you gather our things together, so we can leave as soon as possible?"

"Do you want me to go to the livery stable and load the horses?"

"No!" He paused in the act of tugging on his boots. "I don't want you to set foot outside this room without me. I mean it, Boston. If some drunken hunter catches you alone—"

"All right! I'll stay here, hiding away like a good little girl."

"See that you do."

He didn't even kiss her before he departed.

Gnawing her lower lip in frustration, Grace sat on the side of the bed. She should have gone with him. She didn't want to be *told* what the colonel said; she wanted to hear it for herself. Perhaps he had information about Ellie and the children! If he had been out fighting Indians, he might already have found Quanah's band and brought back their white captives.

Grace couldn't sit there and wait. Matt wasn't the boss of this outfit; *she* was. If she were careful no one would spot her, let alone stop her. If someone did she had her trusty Colt, and she wouldn't hesitate to use it. Never mind what Matt had to say about it; she was going to the fort to meet Mackenzie!

Sixteen

In his efforts to supply horses for the army, Matt had met
many officers, but Ranald S. Mackenzie outranked them all,
whatever their rank. He'd heard countless stories about the man,
most of them probably exaggerated, and his first meeting confirmed his half-formed opinion: Mackenzie was hard on men,
hard on horses, hard on other officers, but hardest of all, perhaps, on himself.

As the colonel ushered Matt into his quarters at the fort and
motioned for the door to be closed behind them, he didn't smile,
didn't make conversation, and didn't relax his military bearing
for a single moment. He took his seat behind a plain wooden
table that served as a desk, but didn't invite Matt to sit down,
or welcome him. Matt fetched his own chair and made a point
of seating himself before explaining the purpose of his visit. If
the colonel could be cold and remote, so could he. Mackenzie
had no reason to be rude, while Matt had *every* reason to hate
the man. Considering the colonel's single-minded devotion to
killing Indians, Matt certainly didn't want to admire him, but
in some strange way he did. In this hard-eyed, professional soldier the Comanches had found a worthy opponent.

"I'm told you discovered the remnants of a burned-out, army
supply wagon and buried the unfortunate victims," Mackenzie
finally said, with a hint of impatience. He made a steeple with
his fingers and rested his elbows on the desk in front of him,

then eyed Matt with all the emotion of a rock in uniform. "Tell me what you found, please, Mr. Stone."

Matt told him. He then attempted to shift the conversation to the more interesting topic of the colonel's efforts to locate the Comanches, but Mackenzie cut him off.

"Exactly what is your interest in the Comanches, sir? Why are you here?"

Matt suddenly realized that Mackenzie knew nothing about him; he didn't recognize him as the man who'd been supplying his horses for the last several years, nor had he been told the details of Matt's conversation with the fort commander.

"I've been hired by the sister of a woman who was captured, along with her two children, by the Comanches late last summer," he began.

Twenty minutes later Matt knew no more about Mackenzie's plans than he had known when he entered the fort. He had gleaned only one new nugget of information: In those cases where white captives were found among the Indians, Mackenzie rigidly adhered to the policy of "taking no prisoners." Everyone in the band, including women and children, paid the price. That was how he made his decision to slay or spare the rebels—and it explained all those small skeletons out on the plain.

As for his plans, the colonel avoided revealing specifics, such as where he intended to concentrate his search efforts over the next few months. Matt knew only that the 4th Cavalry would be maintained in the field, vigorously patrolling for Indians, in order to prevent the remaining rebels from hunting or storing meat to see them through next winter. If Mackenzie couldn't *catch* the Indians he intended to starve them.

"If you're good with a gun," the colonel concluded, "you may join our campaign and ride along with us. When we find Quanah Parker's band you can determine for yourself if there are any whites among them fitting the description of those you're searching for. Otherwise, leave the Comanches to us, Mr. Stone. I cannot guarantee the safety of whites foolish enough to roam the Staked Plain. At the very least you risk being caught in the crossfire between my forces and the Indians."

Matt hadn't yet revealed that Grace was with him, awaiting his return in a gambling hall in The Flats. He had decided to save that information until *after* he'd had a chance to assess which way the wind was blowing. The moment had come to petition the colonel to grant her safekeeping. He didn't plan to join the colonel's forces, but after all he'd heard today he was even more determined to leave Grace behind at the fort.

He was just about to say something when a fresh-faced young soldier burst into the colonel's quarters. "Sir! I'm sorry to interrupt, but there's an excited female outside who says she must see you at once."

"An excited female?" The colonel frowned. "Tell her I'm occupied. She'll have to wait her turn."

"But sir, she says she's with this gentleman here—claims to be his employer. Says the two of 'em have been searching all over Comancheria for her sister."

The colonel's cold-eyed gaze fastened on Matt. "You brought the sister of the victim *with* you?"

Since he shared the colonel's disapproving view on the matter, Matt squirmed inside. "She wasn't easy to leave behind, Colonel. Believe me, I tried, but she insisted on coming. That's another reason why I'm here. I was hoping she might remain at the fort while I . . ."

"Mr. Stone! A genteel white woman doesn't belong in the heart of dangerous Indian territory or anywhere near The Flats. You should never have brought her this far. If you place any value on her life or virtue, you must get her out of here at once. Take her back to Fort Sill. I can't imagine a worse place for a gently-bred easterner, particularly a female, than here."

"I agree. However, when you meet her, you'll understand why . . ."

"I have no intention of meeting her!" In his agitation, the colonel stood. "Ensign, tell the woman I shall *not* see her!"

"Yes, sir!" The young soldier saluted, snapped his heels together, and started to leave—only to have Grace herself barge into the room, almost knocking him down.

"Colonel Mackenzie!" she cried. Then, seeing *him,* she added with much less enthusiasm: "Matt . . ."

"Colonel Mackenzie, meet Grace Livingston." Matt tilted back his chair and lifted his feet to rest on the desk. Crossing his arms, he settled back to watch the fireworks between bossy Grace in her too-tight britches and baggy shirt, and the over-disciplined colonel. *This* should be interesting: a determined she-wolf confronting a buffalo bull in his prime.

Ten minutes later Grace was still battling, but Mackenzie had lost all patience. "No, madam, you cannot accompany us into the field! Nor can you remain at the fort, as your employee, Mr. Stone, suggested. If the two of you do not depart this area immediately, I'll have you escorted twenty miles from here and left. After that, I will assume no responsibility for your continued good health. I am *ordering* you to cease your efforts to find the Comanches, and to leave this matter entirely to the United States Army."

Matt might have found amusement in Grace's obvious annoyance, but by now he was too furious with her to muster a grin. She had *begged* the colonel to allow them to accompany him on his continued search to find the Indians. She knew very well why *he*—Matt—wanted to find them, and that his purpose was completely at odds with the colonel's. That hadn't deterred Grace. She had placed her own concerns above his, despite Mackenzie's allusion to the fact that if he *did* find her sister and her children among the Comanches, he would use it as an excuse for executing every last member of Quanah's band, including Quanah, and—unbeknownst to *him,* but fully known to Grace—Matt's brother.

As long as Grace got her precious relatives back, she didn't care what happened to the Indians, and she never *would* care, no matter how much he might wish otherwise. Apparently she put more faith in Mackenzie's tracking skills than she did in his. After all they'd been through together, this was bitter medicine to swallow.

Matt had known her views about the Comanches all along, but he still felt betrayed—and wildly jealous. There could be no doubt: Grace had taken one look at Mackenzie's uniform, noted his impressive air of efficiency, and decided to make *him* her new champion. Matt himself meant nothing to her; the hours of sweet lovemaking they'd spent together hadn't bound her to him, or even boosted her opinion of him. Once again a woman had measured him and found him wanting . . . had decided that another man suited her better . . . had trampled his pride and wounded him to the quick . . . had discovered all his weaknesses and strengths and firmly rejected him.

"But Colonel," Grace started in again.

Matt had had enough. He rose to his feet, tipping over the chair as he did so. "Give it up, Grace. It's done. Come on, we're leaving."

She argued all the way out of the fort. "I think we *should* join forces with Mackenzie. It may be the only way we'll find the Comanches. He's got hundreds of scouts and trackers at his disposal. If we *don't* accompany him he'll get to the Indians first, before we do. When he does, if there are no witnesses present to deter him he won't exercise a single ounce of restraint. I'm sure of it! Ellie and the children will be killed, right along with the Indians. You should have taken *my* side, Matt, and helped me to convince him. Instead you plotted to leave me behind at the fort!"

Matt stopped walking and grabbed her arm, so angry he couldn't see straight. He didn't know where to start when it came to listing his own complaints. Her betrayal had left him devastated. "What's inside your head, Boston? Better still, what's inside your chest? Have you even *got* a heart? Or are you so blinded by a fancy blue uniform that you can't see what you're doing to me—to *us?*"

"What are you talking about? You were going to abandon me and continue on by yourself!"

"I should have left you behind long ago!" he shouted. "Actually, I never should have brought you. Bringing you was the worst mistake of my life!"

"And coming was mine! I put my trust in you! And I don't know why, because all you've ever done is lie to me!"

"I trusted *you,* and what did I get for it? First time you meet someone else who can possibly advance your cause, you forget what's between *us* and flutter your long lashes at *him.* Next thing I know you'll be jumping into a bedroll with him."

"Flutter my lashes! Jump into a bedroll with him! I don't know what you're talking about, you big stupid savage!"

"We're back to that again, are we? I'm a savage, while you're Miss Perfect. Well, that's exactly what I am—a savage—but you, Miss Livingston, are nothing but a whirlago girl masquerading as a lady! Too bad you didn't get a chance to *kiss* Colonel Mackenzie. Maybe then you could have persuaded him to take you with him."

"Oh, you are despicable! Absolutely despicable."

As they tramped through the open gate of the fort they encountered a trail-weary bunch of soldiers herding some bedraggled, color-splashed horses ahead of them. *Painted* horses. Indian horses.

"Soldier!" Matt cried. "Where are you taking those animals?"

The soldier eyed him belligerently. "We caught 'em on the plain, and we're bringin' 'em inta the fort to keep the Injuns from havin' 'em."

"But what'll happen to them now?" There were a couple of nice mares in the bunch, the kind he would one day like to breed to Renegade.

"Colonel Mackenzie will give the order t' shoot 'em. That's what he usually does. We can only use so many ourselves, and some soldiers refuse to ride Injun ponies."

"They're going to shoot all those horses?" Grace was incredulous.

"Don't worry, Miss Livingston," Matt retorted. "They're only horses. What do *they* matter?"

"What do you mean, what do they matter? I don't approve of killing horses—or buffalo, either."

"Well, how do you feel about human beings? If Mackenzie finds your sister and her children in Quanah's band he'll kill every last Indian in the camp. That's his new policy. You heard him say it."

"What? I *didn't* hear him say that! I never knew that's what he *intends!* My fear is—was—that he might shoot Ellie and the children by accident. You know, in the excitement of battle!"

"Well, now you know the truth," Matt snapped and strode ahead of her.

Lying little bitch. Not for a minute did he believe she hadn't known that. Mackenzie had said it right in front of her . . . hadn't he?

But as Matt walked away, rigid with fury, he couldn't remember everything the colonel had said to Grace; he'd been too busy focusing on the notion that she wanted to accompany the colonel instead of searching for the Comanches alone with him. He distinctly remembered the colonel saying it before Grace arrived, but afterward . . .

He told himself it didn't matter when or if Mackenzie had said it. The point was: Grace had chosen the colonel as her new hero. She hadn't even hesitated. For that, Matt would never forgive her.

Grace couldn't understand what she'd done wrong; Matt was the villain. Once again he had lied to her and attempted to leave her behind at the fort. If she hadn't rushed over there to talk to Mackenzie herself, she might never have known about his perfidy. For him to turn around and accuse *her* of betrayal was unbelievable. This time he had gone too far.

She followed him back to the hotel in silence. It was over between them—completely over. She'd hold him to his bargain to help her find the Comanches, but never again would she trust him. Never again would she allow herself to hope they might find a way to resolve all their differences and learn to live together in peace and happiness. That was impossible now; he had *made* it impossible.

When they got to the hotel they marched upstairs and gathered their things. Neither of them discussed the fact that it would soon be dark and not a good idea to set out so late. When they were finished she said: "I'm going to find Lottie and settle our bill. Do you want to just meet me at the livery stable? You can go there now and start packing the horses."

He stood in the center of the flowered carpet and looked at her, really looked, as if he'd never seen her before. "I'm not taking you with me," he announced with chilling resolve.

"You intend to leave me here in The Flats to be raped? Now that you no longer want me, you don't care *who* gets your leavings, is that it?"

It hurt to say such things to him, but his eagerness broke her heart.

"Stop it. Once I'm gone Mackenzie will have to let you stay at the fort. He won't have any choice. In the morning you can tell him I ran off and left you during the night. Play on his sympathies. You're good at that."

She fought to keep from weeping or screaming useless denials. He'd never believe them, anyway. "And where are *you* going?"

"To find the Comanches. If your sister and her kids are with them, I'll bring them back here to the fort. If not, you'll never see me again."

"And how long am I supposed to wait? *Hoping* I see you."

"Until you do, or until Mackenzie himself finds the Comanches. He will eventually. As you so graciously pointed out, he has a better chance than I do, what with all his scouts and trackers."

"I meant no criticism of you when I said that! However, it's true. When I was trying to convince that young soldier at the fort to let me see the colonel, trying to explain that you and I were together—or *used* to be together—he told me, 'Now, don't worry your pretty little head about your relatives, ma'am. Colonel Mackenzie's Buffalo Soldiers an' scouts outnumber the Indians ten to one. He has the best trackers in Comancheria—in the whole world, if the truth be known.' "

"He doesn't have a Comanche-trained tracker like the one standing in front you," Matt said bitterly, and Grace knew she'd pricked him again when she hadn't meant to do any such thing. She couldn't tell her side of it without angering him.

"I can find them before he does," he muttered in a low vengeful voice that tore at her heart.

"If you do you'll still need *me.* It makes no sense for you to leave me behind."

"Nothing makes sense to you except what *you* want. After this we can't stay together, Boston. You know it as well as I do."

That was the trouble; she *did* know it. This rift had driven them so far apart that traveling together would be agony, more difficult than either of them could handle.

"Then I guess this is good-bye, Matt. . . . Wait! I should pay you something for all your trouble. After all, you did get me this far."

His nostrils flared and his eyes darkened. A muscle leapt in his jaw. "You don't realize when you're insulting me, do you? Insulting people comes naturally to you."

"We had a business deal . . . and I always honor my agreements."

"But I haven't delivered on *my* end of the bargain—yet. And I don't want your damn money. Keep it to reward Mackenzie, in case *he* finds your sister before I do." Picking up his things, Matt turned on his heel and stalked from the room without another word.

Grace's first impulse was to rush to the door and close it behind him—shut him out of her life forever. She couldn't find the will to move. Her feet and her heart were frozen. The noises of the gambling hall drifted up to her: men laughing, cussing, and talking . . . the clink of glassware . . . the shuffle of cards . . . the murmur of women's voices.

A loud shout sounded from below: "That's *him!* There's the fellah who brought in them hosses belongin' to our partners! He took 'em to the livery stable, sayin' they was *his*. Grab him. Don't let him git away!"

"Hell, it's the same fellah who's got himself a wife while the rest of us hafta make do with whirlago gals!"

Grace didn't wait to hear more. She grabbed the Colt Matt had left her and raced for the staircase. This time, she'd bring down the whole chandelier if necessary!

By the time she got there, several burly buffalo hunters had flattened Matt against the wall. One had the butt of his big Sharps rifle pressed across Matt's throat, cutting off his air. Matt's face was already turning blue; he couldn't even struggle. His hands were held fast—each by a different man. But he was kicking, trying to disable his opponents with his feet.

"Let him go!" Grace shouted. "I can explain where we got those horses."

"Go ahead, then. If yer his wife, you oughta know!" The man holding the rifle looked like a buffalo. Big, shaggy, and twice as mean, he didn't release the pressure on Matt's throat for even a second

A smaller man turned to the crowd. "We jus' rode in this afternoon, and reco'nized them hosses right off," he told the onlookers. "We was s'posed t' meet our partners here at The Flats, but when we described our boys t' the feller at the livery stable, he said the hosses b'longed t' someone who didn't sound like our partners at all. Someone musta *stole* them hosses and done away with ole Gus, Hank, Clyde, an' Harold. This here is the hoss thief and murderer. The stable owner described him good, and it couldn't be no other."

"We found those horses wandering alone out on the plain," Grace shouted over the din. "Release my husband. He can tell you how it happened."

The burly man pressed the barrel of the rifle even harder against Matt's windpipe. "I don't b'lieve ya'. Keep talkin', lady, or yer man's gonna wind up dead."

Grace started down the staircase but stopped halfway. If she had to shoot the chandelier to prove she meant business, she needed distance. "It's true! Let go of him. He didn't steal those horses. We couldn't understand why they were wandering the plain alone, so we rounded them up and brought them with us. If they belong to you, you can have them back."

"But where's Gus, Hank, Clyde, and Harold? What happened t' *them*, huh? Jus' answer me that!" The buffalo man punctuated his questions with little grunts as he shoved against the rifle barrel.

Grace feared he would break Matt's neck. Matt had ceased struggling and gone deathly still. He was losing consciousness. "The Comanches must have killed them! You're blaming the wrong person. How could one man—and a mere female—take on four big buffalo hunters, anyway?"

"She's got a point there," Lottie said from behind the bar. "Let him go now, gen'leman, before you kill him. Let him go, or I'll have to sic my guards on ya'."

"If it was Comanches that done it, they'd have taken the hosses with 'em," the burly fellow disputed. "No, I think it was *this* guy."

Grace raised her pistol. Instead of pointing it at the chandelier, she pointed it at him. "Release him this minute or I'll shoot you. He's dying from lack of air."

Suddenly Matt braced himself against the wall, lifted both feet against his opponent's belly, and shoved hard. Bellowing, the man flew backward into the onlookers. To provide diversion, Grace fired at the chandelier. She hit whatever was holding it up, and the whole thing came crashing down. Women screamed. Men fumbled for their pistols. Shots rang out, and a drunken brawl ensued.

"Run!" Matt mouthed at her.

Grace bolted down the remaining stairs. At the bottom he

grabbed her hand, and they ran out of the gambling hall. Down the street they sped—traveling as fast as Grace could manage. When they reached the stable they dashed through it to reach the horses in the corral out back. They didn't see the stable owner; except for a few horses, the stable was deserted.

"Throw a couple packs on Lucy while I get the horses saddled," Matt croaked.

Grace couldn't take time to decide which packs were the most important. The stable owner had allowed them to store their gear in a lean-to out back, and she seized whatever was handy. She got the bedrolls and canteens along with a few *parfleches,* hastily packed them on Lucy, and tied them down as quickly as possible.

By then Matt had Renegade and Dunston saddled. "Hurry! They've discovered we're gone. A mob's approaching. Hear 'em?"

With one foot already in the stirrup, Grace paused a moment before climbing into the saddle. She did hear them now—men shouting about not letting the horse thieves and murderers get away. They were firing guns into the air as they racketed down the street in the gathering darkness. Voices screamed for justice and called for both of them to be strung up in the middle of town as a warning to others.

"Let's ride!" Matt urged, and she bolted into Dunston's saddle.

He took Lucy's lead rope and galloped ahead. Tex and Okie, whom they hadn't had time to pack, kept pace beside them, running free. Grace turned Dunston loose to follow Renegade. Concentrating hard on keeping her seat, she clung to the saddle horn and prayed they had made good their escape.

A couple of hours later, when Matt was sure no one had bothered to follow, they slowed to a walk and permitted the exhausted horses to rest. All of the animals were winded, and Okie had fallen far behind. Tex had kept up with them, but he was limping, and only Renegade displayed any energy. Prancing at the walk, he let them know that he had relished the wild gallop and was ready for more, if needed.

"I see now why you want to breed him," Grace murmured with a nod toward the stallion. "He's still eager to go."

"Maybe he is, but I'm not." Matt lifted an arm to wipe the sweat from his brow, his voice hoarse and gravelly.

"Are you all right?" Grace rode closer and peered at him in the starlight.

He nodded. "For a while there, I thought I was finished. That guy was strong as a bull."

"For a while there, I thought you were, too."

"Thanks, Boston."

She didn't bother protesting she hadn't done anything. She had, and she took a quiet pride in it, even though Matt was the one who had finally broken free of the fellow. "You're welcome."

They rode a bit farther. "I suppose this doesn't change anything between us, does it?" he finally asked.

"No . . . it doesn't."

How could it? Nothing had changed; they were pretty much back where they had started.

They didn't speak after that. They just rode—putting distance between themselves and The Flats.

Over the next several weeks the weather grew unbearably hot. High summer now enveloped the plain. Deep cracks appeared in the dry earth, and the grasslands became sere and golden. Twice they spotted soldiers on the horizon, and twice eluded them. It wasn't all that difficult; the land lent itself to hiding. Ancient rivers had cut deep canyons and arroyos in the land. Within them, safe from prying eyes, anyone could hide. Sometimes, at the bottom, there was even water and green grass for the horses.

No wonder it was so hard to find the Comanches, Grace thought as she swayed in time to Dunston's ground-covering walk. It was hard to stay awake. By the time they carefully made their way down a steep rocky trail to the bottom of one of the canyons, anyone else in it had departed by some other uncharted trail.

She could understand the army's frustration; she herself was terribly frustrated. But Matt never displayed anything but patience as he led her from one arroyo or canyon to another, doggedly searching for some sign of Quanah's band. Occasionally, he dismounted, knelt on one knee, and spent an absurdly long time studying a clump of grass, a pile of stones, or some other natural phenomenon. She could see no message, but Matt seemed to think that if he stared at it long enough it would yield some hidden wisdom. Maybe he would even hear an Indian whispering where all the other Indians had gone.

They had left over half their belongings behind at The Flats, including their extra canteens, so they often went hungry and thirsty. Matt always knew where to find water, but great distances lay between rivers, streams, and watering holes. Even with careful rationing, they never had enough water to last until they found the next source. Often, they watered the horses but denied themselves barely more than a taste. They did the same with food, and Grace's britches now fit so loosely they were in danger of sliding off her hips.

Not that Matt appeared to notice. These days he zealously guarded his emotions, no longer watching her as he once had. Nor did she watch him, except covertly. Grace pretended that her desire for him had died, along with her love and loyalty. If he still felt anything for her, she could not discern it from his behavior. At night they slept apart. Too tired to move but too tense to sleep, Grace would lie on her back and look up at the stars. She was afraid they would never find any more signs of Indians; maybe the Indians were all dead by now.

On one hot, dusty afternoon, Matt suddenly halted, slid down from Renegade, and knelt in the windblown, golden grass. Grace watched him with only marginal interest; she'd seen him do this a hundred times, and had no reason to hope that this time he'd discover anything worthwhile.

"Well?" she inquired after several moments, when he neither moved or announced his disappointment.

"This is it," he murmured almost too low for her to hear.

But she did hear him. "This is it? You've found something?"

His eyes were bright green in the dark tan of his face. "You wouldn't call it much, but to me it's plenty. Now I know exactly where the Comanches are hiding."

Seventeen

"Where are they?" Grace trotted Dunston up to him. For the first time since they'd left The Flats the world looked brighter, and she felt alive and excited.

Matt stood and wiped his hands on his dust-laden trousers. "In the Palo Duro Canyon. The Mexicans probably know of the place since it has a Spanish name, but I doubt the army is familiar with it. Mackenzie has supposedly been mapping the Staked Plain as he searches, but I doubt he's ever found it or he'd be checking it frequently. It's a natural hiding place and not easily spotted from a distance. Unless you rode right up to it you'd never know it was there. . . . I had a hunch we might find them in that particular canyon, and now I've got proof that's where they're hiding."

Grace studied the ground at his feet. She saw nothing out of the ordinary—no unusual markers that couldn't have gotten there by chance. "How can you be so sure?"

His eyes locked with hers. "Would you insist on Mackenzie defending his hunches—or would you simply accept that he knew what he was doing?"

Grace bit her lip and looked away. She wished this enmity between them would cease. They couldn't go back to the way they'd been before The Flats, but she kept hoping they might become more tolerant of each other and able to conduct a normal conversation without undertones of blame and hostility.

"Will we get there today?" She stared at the level plateau

around them. It didn't suggest a nearby encampment of Comanches, or anyone else. The only sign of life was a huge bird of prey wheeling through the blue arc overhead.

He nodded. "We'll be there by tonight, but can't enter the canyon itself until daybreak. It's a hard ride down to the canyon floor and I don't want to risk darkness overtaking me while I negotiate the trail."

Me. I.

He didn't intend to take her along. She didn't even consider arguing. What good would it do?

He remounted Renegade, and they set out. By evening they had reached the lip of a vast crevasse cutting deeply into the high plateau. As Matt had said, until you rode up to it you didn't know it was there. He got down from his horse, dropped to his hands and knees, crawled to the rim, and peered over the edge. When he looked back at her he was grinning, the first grin she'd seen on his face since their fight.

Silently, he motioned for her to join him. She dismounted and did as he had, crawled to the edge of the crevasse and looked down. A gasp of surprise escaped her. Far below, a glistening stream wound through the canyon, and along its narrow banks were hundreds—thousands?—of horses grazing on the rich green grass. Among them stood tipis, scattered for a length of at least three miles.

What an idyllic scene! Tiny figures moved among the horses and tipis—a group of children chasing a pack of dogs, some women clustered near the stream, several men lassoing a horse. Pinpricks of fire emitted wisps of smoke that rose and faded against the canyon walls before they could reach the upper rim to alert passersby to the presence of humans.

"Comanches. My people," Matt whispered, though no one below could possibly have heard them.

"Quanah's band?" Grace wanted to be sure.

He nodded. "I recognize some of the horses . . . and I'd know their lodges anywhere by the distinctive symbols painted on them. My Comanche parents are here, and Quanah and my brother."

This far away Grace could scarcely see the symbols, but she noticed racks of drying meat and people of both sexes engaged in various tasks outside their homes. It hardly seemed possible that the encampment could be so serene and peaceful. She didn't know what she had expected. Screaming captives in the throes of torture? Painted savages waving bloody scalps?

They retreated and made their own camp, and Grace asked Matt how long he intended to be gone investigating the encampment.

"It'll take me several hours to find my way down to the canyon floor. Once I do, it won't be long before I know if they're glad to see me or anxious to rip out my heart. If I don't return by tomorrow night, I want you to ride like hell away from here the following morning."

By tomorrow night she might be alone in this endeavor. If they killed Matt outright—Please, God, no!—could she muster the nerve to go down there by herself in search of Ellie? The issue had never before arisen. The Indians *had* to welcome him. They *must*. If they didn't, if they killed him, she didn't know what she would do.

"If I don't come back, head for Fort Griffin. Don't go barreling down there like a wide-eyed idealist. When Mackenzie comes in from the field, you can describe the canyon and its approximate location, and let *him* worry about rescuing your sister."

The suggestion shocked her. "You want me to reveal the Comanches' hiding place to Mackenzie?"

"They won't be able to hide in the Palo Duro forever. Sooner or later someone besides us will find it. I'd prefer you *didn't* tell him, naturally, but knowing you . . . well, you might as well tell him as go riding down there. I'm sure you'll do one or the other, and I'd rather you run to the colonel and live a long life than ride down there and die immediately."

He would rather spare her *than his precious Comanches.
Telling Mackenzie was as good as destroying them.*

"Matt . . ." she said softly.

Heading for Renegade, he appeared not to have heard her.
"Get some sleep. I've got a lot to do yet tonight."

By morning he had transformed himself and Renegade into
Painted Horse.

In spite of all the things of value they had left behind at The
Flats, the elements of his disguise were among the few items
to survive the incident. They had been hidden deep inside one
of the *parfleches* she had managed to take with them. This time
she couldn't find it in her heart to hate his fierce appearance,
perhaps because he didn't look quite as fierce as usual. He
hadn't applied any war paint, nor fastened long braids to his
already long hair. Still, he was pure Indian—and more beautiful
to her eyes now than he had ever been in the past.

Since they'd left The Flats his splendid body had remained
hidden inside his clothing, but now his skimpy breechclout revealed precisely what she'd been missing all these lonely weeks.

As he strode toward her she couldn't utter a word; she could
only stand there, helplessly devouring him with her gaze. He
wore an embroidered band around his forehead and had darkened his coppery hair so that it gleamed almost black in the
early morning sunlight. The necklace of animal teeth and silver
ornaments shone starkly against the dark expanse of his chest,
but the smooth, rippling muscles *beneath* the adornments were
what caused her mouth to go dry with longing. By now his
shoulder wound was only a pink crease, she noticed.

"What? No war paint?" she gently mocked, to cover her intense reaction to the sight of him.

"I'm not going to war. I'm arriving home after a long absence."

Her heart twisted painfully. Of course, he wouldn't wear war
paint to what he hoped was a warm reunion with friends and
family. Avoiding his gaze, she turned her attention to Renegade.
Like his master, the stallion was beautiful—gleaming white

again, the patches of rich tan on his head, chest, and underbelly shining like fresh paint.

Matt saw where she was looking and commented: "They'll welcome the horse, if not the rider. Because of Renegade they might spare me, no matter how angry they might still feel about my defection."

Grace turned back to him. "What do you mean?"

"Renegade is the type of painted horse known as a Medicine Hat. To the Comanches he's sacred. The fact that I return riding him will mean something, especially since the People know me as Painted Horse. When I lived among them, I always rode a colorful horse, but none equaled Renegade. When they see us together, they should realize I'm the one who's been supplying the reservation Indians with beef and running off buffalo hunters."

"I hope so," Grace said, and meant it. If they instead regarded him as a returning traitor, her worst fears would be realized. She'd lose him for good.

"Good-bye again, Boston. . . . How many more times must we go through this? Not too many more, I hope."

Before the final time, you mean.

"Good-bye, Matt. Or should I say, Painted Horse?"

As he mounted Renegade and started riding away, she couldn't bear to let him go so casually, not when she might never see him again. Choking back a sob, she ran after him. Seeing her, he stopped and waited.

"What is it?"

The question vibrated in the air between them. She shook her head, unable to answer. When he saw her tears, his face softened. Bending down, he cupped her chin in one hand, and kissed her—quickly, as if he didn't dare linger. Then, without looking back, he rode away.

The trail to the canyon floor was steep, narrow, and rocky. At one point Matt had to dismount and lead Renegade behind him. He watched for signs of another trail, but didn't see one, nor could he recall any from his previous visits to the Palo Duro. It had been a long time since he'd been here. On several occasions, when he and Thad were growing up among the Comanches, the tribe had wintered in the canyon. The high steep walls offered shelter from the winter winds, the tribe's horses had plenty of room to wander in their search for grass, and everyone had water to spare.

Each family had always chosen its own particular spot to camp, often alongside relatives or close friends. The length of the canyon ensured that no one felt crowded, and as long as the fall hunting had been good, no one went hungry. The canyon had always offered peace, fellowship, and safety during the coldest, most threatening time of year, so Matt wasn't too surprised that the Comanches had returned here in time of danger. It might be high summer, but the same features that provided a haven in winter did so now, when the enemy was Mackenzie and not the weather.

Yet, as Matt reached the canyon floor and remounted Renegade, he tried to view the Palo Duro from the standpoint of a stronghold in case of attack. It could prove to be a death trap instead of a fortress. He recalled some of the older Indians boasting that all one had to do to escape from invading enemies was scale the walls and disappear into the surrounding plain. . . . But the horses couldn't escape. They would have to leave the same way they had come, on the twisted torturous trail he had just descended.

The old, the very young, and women with infants would have a hard time getting out, too. If Mackenzie discovered the place, he'd destroy all the food supplies and ammunition the Indians had assembled, along with the lodges and everything else that sustained the tribe. There'd be no way to move things quickly.

Matt rode some distance toward the tipis before anyone noticed him. Quanah apparently felt so secure in the Palo Duro that he hadn't even posted guards. A round-faced little boy suddenly looked up from the bow he was trying to string, and his dark eyes widened beneath the spill of black hair across his broad forehead.

Calling upon his rusty but not forgotten Comanche, Matt calmly asked: "Do you need help? I can show you how to string that bow quickly and easily."

Hollering at the top of his lungs, the boy jumped up and raced toward the tipis. People poured through open doorways and converged on Matt, surrounding him in the space of a few heartbeats. Having done his duty, the boy fell silent and waited to see what his elders would do. An eerie silence ensued, indicating uncertainty on the part of the onlookers.

To show his good intentions and also his bravery, Matt had left all his weapons with Grace. Saying nothing, he now rode through the village, heading for the tipi belonging to Quanah. Until Quanah acknowledged him there was no sense greeting anyone. Quanah's greeting—or lack of one—would shape the responses of everyone else, even his brother.

Matt could feel the People's eyes on him and Renegade. He knew many recognized him. He could tell by the slight flaring of their nostrils or narrowing of their eyes. Whites so often thought that Indians showed no emotion, but to one who had lived among them, they revealed their feelings in a hundred silent but eloquent ways.

A tiny, familiar, white-haired old woman approached. Frail and hunched over, she could barely totter in his direction. Supported on either side by two young girls, she hobbled toward him as fast as her old legs could carry her. It was his Comanche mother, Gray Owl, her black eyes alight with joy at his return, her face radiant with pride that he came riding such a fine horse.

His Comanche father, Night Hawk, trailed her. Night Hawk had disowned him when he announced his intention of returning to the whites. Now he looked right through Matt, as if he weren't there. Night Hawk, too, had greatly aged. Both his Comanche parents had been old when Matt left them; he hadn't expected to find them still alive. He wondered how long the tribe had been living in the canyon. The very old and the very young could not have withstood the rigors of running constantly across the plains.

Quanah had done an admirable job of caring for the People. They were all lean-looking, even those who tended toward stockiness, but they were alive, while most of the other bands had perished or surrendered.

Halfway to Quanah's tipi, a woman screamed and flung herself on the ground at Renegade's feet. Her black hair concealed her identity, and not until two braves—one of them Matt's brother—lifted her and dragged her aside, did Matt recognize her. Wailing, sobbing, and screaming his name, Sweet Water struggled to free herself, but the two men held her tightly between them.

As he passed Matt exchanged a long look with Thad, the man known among the Comanches as Stalking Wolf. His brother did not greet him or show any reaction upon seeing him again. Matt knew he would withhold his approval or disapproval until *after* Quanah had expressed his. Thad had always been more Indian than the Indians. He no longer retained even a hint of his white heritage. His eyes were brown and his hair a naturally darker shade than Matt's. His bearing and demeanor proclaimed him pure Comanche.

Matt did not acknowledge his brother, either, but rode straight past him and the struggling weeping woman. Sweet Water's behavior mystified him; he couldn't understand it. From the way she was acting one would think he was a dearly beloved husband returning home from war. He felt nothing at seeing her again. Whatever affection he had once nurtured had died a long time ago.

Arriving at Quanah's lodge, Matt halted Renegade and waited. Quanah would appear when he was good and ready. His friend had always had a keen sense of drama; he invested even simple occasions with an air of excitement and mystery. He knew instinctively how to manipulate emotion. These qualities set him apart from other men and made him a charismatic leader.

Minutes passed, and still Matt waited. No one moved or ventured a word. Except for Sweet Water's sobs, the only sound was the thin wail of the hot summer wind keening down the canyon. At last a figure crawled out of the low entrance to the tipi and stood. Now Matt could see what had taken so long. Quanah had donned his ceremonial clothing—the garments he wore to celebrate solemn or religious occasions. The intricately beaded and long-fringed buckskins were made of the finest hides, and scraped, pounded, and chewed by his wives until they were butter-yellow and as soft as the skin of a newborn baby.

Quanah's hair—never cut, in the fashion of all Comanche males—was parted down the middle, carefully braided and greased, and sported a single yellow feather. Quanah had the typical high cheekbones of his race, and his mouth and chin looked Indian, but his eyes and nose suggested his white heritage.

For a long moment Quanah studied him. Matt silently returned his perusal. Then the Indian leader gave a shout of welcome and rushed forward, pulling Matt from his horse and wrestling him to the ground. Pandemonium erupted as everyone surrounded the two men, all of them shouting, cheering, and hollering.

The fight was a friendly one—two comrades pitting their strength against each other as they had done as boys. Matt held his own, but he could not pin Quanah to the ground. Neither could Quanah pin him. Once they had wrestled ceaselessly, each trying to prove who was mightier. Now, as then, no winner emerged, and at last Quanah called a halt to the game and extended his hand to Matt to pull him upright.

Only then did Stalking Wolf approach. "Welcome, my brother." His tone was formal. He never cracked a smile. "Where are your weapons? Surely, you came to join our fight."

"Later," Quanah interjected, his face wreathed in welcoming smiles. "Business must wait. First, we will sit down together and pass the pipe. No matter the reason, the return of my friend, Painted Horse, gives us cause for great rejoicing."

"My horse . . ." Matt began, accustomed to putting Renegade's needs ahead of his own.

"Will be treated like the sacred treasure he is," Quanah assured him. "Come . . ."

Two hours later, with the feasting, pipe smoking, and small talk behind them, Matt was still seated in a ring of warriors, flanked on one side by his brother and on the other by Quanah. The ceremonial ritual for the return of an esteemed friend had been conducted in a secluded area above the stream, on a shelf of rock shaded by stunted, windblown trees. Already they had discussed Mackenzie's pursuit of the band, their successful methods of eluding the army, the births, deaths, marriages, injuries, diseases, and triumphs of mutual acquaintances, and how Matt had been so fortunate to attain a horse as fine as Renegade. There remained only one important topic of discussion: why Matt had returned to the Comanches.

No one except his brother had been tactless enough to ask; a lull simply occurred, affording Matt the opportunity to introduce the subject. His brother had hardly spoken a word during the past two hours, but now he watched Matt expectantly, almost angrily, as if he'd already made up his mind that he wasn't going to like Matt's explanation.

Matt knew each and every man in this circle of distinguished warriors. His Comanche father was too old to join it any longer. These were the current leaders of the tribe, its lifeblood, the men who made the decisions in battle and conducted the raids and hunts. They were the men closest to Quanah—as *he* had once been close.

Some faces were missing. Either the men had fallen in battle or lost their lives in pursuit of buffalo. Those who remained were still an impressive bunch. Small in number, no more than thirty, they excelled in pride, courage, and valor. They were the last of the True Human Beings, as the Comanches had once called themselves.

How could he convince them to surrender? From the size of the camp he could see that the tribe could still mount a decent sized force of warriors. Most of these men represented others who would ride at their beck and call. Matt dreaded telling these battle-scarred fighters that he didn't think they could win or continue hiding forever. He couldn't picture them cooped up on a reservation without horses or weapons, dependent on whites for even the simple comforts of food and water. These men were living legends who'd spent their lives roaming the plains; he knew what it meant to lose that kind of freedom. He, at least, could still mount a beautiful Paint horse and gallop over the horizon, pretending he was still one of them.

"I know you are wondering why I have returned," he said by way of introduction.

"If you are ready now, tell us," Quanah answered. "If not, we will wait."

"Waiting won't make it any easier."

As Matt stated his case for the surrender of all the Comanches, mouths thinned, bodies stiffened, angry glances were exchanged, and his own brother gazed at him with open contempt.

"Why did you even bother to come?" Stalking Wolf demanded. "Do you think we fear Mackenzie? Our medicine is stronger, our hearts braver, our weapons more deadly, our courage unflagging—"

"I *know* all that," Matt said. "No one can possibly question your courage, determination, or bravery. But there are too few of you, and too many of the whites. And Mackenzie is different from those who have gone before him. He's not afraid of you and he's no longer willing to negotiate. He talks of extermination—of killing Indians as the whites kill buffalo. Without mercy, hesitation, or regard to the future. If he finds you he'll spare no one—not even the children."

"Pah!" his brother spat. "He will never find us. We know the plain too well. The army knows it not at all. Have they found this canyon yet—or a dozen others? We are the People. We will survive."

Quanah said nothing, only listened, as others added to the

argument. In the canyon the band had managed to store food, ammunition, and nearly everything else they needed for the near future. Their horses numbered almost fifteen hundred, and women were once again giving birth and rearing children, new warriors to replace those who had died in battle.

"Have you seen all the dead buffalo?" Matt persisted. "When the buffalo are gone, how will you live?"

This brought laughter. The Indians had seen many dead buffalo, but no one believed that all the buffalo would one day disappear. The herds were too big; they were hiding up north. When the killing stopped, they would return and produce more buffalo. The buffalo had always returned. Even in times of drought and famine, when the People despaired they would ever see them again, the herds had eventually returned. No one—not even the whites—could kill all the great, powerful animals. The Great Spirit and the spirits of all those who had once hunted them now watched over them; they would roam the plains forever.

Matt's arguments fell on deaf ears. Yes, the warriors conceded, life had been hard for them these last few years, but since they'd come to the Palo Duro, it had improved. When they conducted raids, they were careful now to avoid leading the soldiers back to their hiding places. Mackenzie's Buffalo Soldiers—so called because they, too, wore buffalo robes in winter and resembled shaggy buffalo with their dark faces and kinky hair—had been looking for them for months without success. They doubted the army would ever find them, but if they did the tribe would simply flee to some other canyon, and eventually Mackenzie would give up and go away, as so many others had done before him.

Matt saw he was making no headway and it was growing late in the day, so he finally told them about Grace and asked about her sister and her sister's children. No one had seen or heard of them. No white captives lived among the Indians currently sheltering within the canyon, but Quanah expected more Indians to join them before winter. Whenever he had the chance to send up smoke signals without alerting the army to his whereabouts, he let the remaining Comanches know where they could find him.

Those already in the canyon had been hunting and gathering food in anticipation of the arrival of battle-weary friends and relatives who would be coming from long distances and dodging soldiers along the way. They wouldn't have had time to dry meat or hides for winter.

"We need every warrior, every hunter," Stalking Wolf said, watching Matt intently. "Those who reach the canyon safely will be weak and exhausted from running and fighting. We who are still strong must help keep the others alive. You are needed, my brother. If you stay a while and assist us, you can ask those who come if they know anything about the white captives you are seeking."

"They may be dead already," Matt pointed out. "And winter is still far off."

Quanah laughed. "Never fear, my friend! Winter will be here before you know it. Go and fetch your white woman and bring her to us. Stay a while. When the heat of summer wanes, our far-flung brothers and sisters will come looking for us, hoping to put up their tipis and join the fall hunt before the snow flies."

"Yes, stay," Stalking Wolf urged. "Think of Sweet Water. Your pretty wife is lonely for you." He grinned slyly.

"Sweet Water is not my wife! She left me for another long before I departed the Comanches. Surely, you remember that."

"Yes, but she still belongs to you, and her lover is dead. He was killed many moons ago and she has not yet found another protector. Now that you have returned, she wants you back. Did you not mark how she wept and called your name?"

Stalking Wolf obviously relished Matt's predicament. "She is still beautiful, my brother. It is your right to cut off her nose if you wish, since she committed adultery, but it would be a pity to ruin her good looks. In her gratefulness that you have forgiven her, she will no doubt be eager to please you."

"I haven't forgiven her. And I want nothing more to do with

her. Since none of you will listen to me when I preach surrender, I ought to leave here and never return."

"No!" Quanah entreated, his dark eyes glistening. "Do not be foolish, old friend. You have made a long journey to find us. You said you brought a white woman with you. Bring her to us. She must be brave to have made this journey, and I would like to meet her."

"She's brave," Matt agreed. "She has as much courage as a Comanche warrior."

"Hunh!" his brother grunted. "Too bad we cannot give her to the women to torture. *That* would be a true test of her courage."

Years had passed since the days when Stalking Wolf had competed to outshine his big brother, yet Matt still saw traces of his brother's lack of confidence and desire to put others down in order to make himself look bigger.

"If anyone mistreats her in any way they will answer to *me*," he warned.

"And to me," said Quanah. "Painted Horse is my friend who has finally returned to his family and loved ones. All those he brings with him are welcome."

"I hope so," Matt said. "But I'm sorry, Quanah, I don't intend to stay long. A few days at most."

Eighteen

"But we must stay until the other Indians return!" Grace argued later that night. "What's the point of coming all this way and searching all this time if we leave before we know for certain that my sister and her children *aren't* with the other Indians?"

She couldn't believe Matt was being so stubborn. She didn't care how long they had to wait; she wasn't leaving until she had satisfied herself that Ellie, Jonathan, and Little Emily were lost to her for good.

"The longer we stay the more opportunity you'll have to convince your friends of the error of their ways," she added, trying to convince him.

"They are *never* going to change their ways, Boston, and the chances of your sister being among the Indians on the run is so slim as to be almost nonexistent. *Those* Indians are starving. They'll be coming in sick, exhausted, and hungry. Quanah himself is expecting them to be in bad shape, and when there isn't enough food to go around, white captives go without. Staying here will mean more heartbreak for both of us. If Mackenzie finds the place before we leave it, I'll be forced to choose sides. The Comanches will be expecting me to fight for them, and I'll have a hard time *not* defending them. That means I'll have to kill soldiers. Are you prepared to stand by and watch me do that? I'm a good shot and almost never miss."

Grace sat down on the saddle that served as her pillow at

night. Night had arrived, and the stars had appeared, but the seat was still warm from the sun beating down on it all day.

"All right. I see your point. But you aren't seeing mine. If we leave here in a day or two, as you suggest, I'll spend the rest of my life wondering if Ellie is still alive somewhere, and if my own flesh and blood is doomed to the same sad fate as the Comanches. If *you* want to leave, go ahead. But I'm going to stay—at least until somebody tells me that all the Indians who are likely to show up here to spend the winter have arrived."

"Hah! If you stay too long you'll wind up spending the winter with the Comanches. When high winds and snow shut down the plains you'll be trapped in a tipi, dependent on handouts from people who are starving because of the whites. I can't believe you want that, Boston."

"No, I don't want that." Grace tried to remain calm and reasonable when she felt like screaming. "But I'd at least like to stay long enough to satisfy myself that Ellie isn't coming to the canyon with the Indians who are still out on the plain."

Matt finally sighed. "Then I'll make you a deal. We'll stay—but only through the rest of the summer and into the fall. Before winter sets in we'll leave, whether they've appeared or not. When I say it's time to go, you'll go—with no argument. Certain signs signal the onset of the first major winter storm. When I see them we'll have to leave immediately to reach Fort Sill before it hits us."

"Will we be able to make it in time?" An image of Dunston struggling through snowdrifts as high as his head flashed in Grace's mind.

"If we travel fast and light, leaving everything behind but you, me, Renegade, and Dunston—and we don't stop for anything. In other words, if we travel Comanche fashion."

"Then it's a deal," Grace assented. "I bet the other Indians will come soon, giving us plenty of time to make it back to Fort Sill before winter—and, I hope, to take Ellie and the children with us."

"You mustn't get your hopes up too high, Boston. No one knew a thing about your sister, which tells me they aren't alive—or it wasn't Comanches who took them. The Comanches get blamed for everything, even the crimes committed by Apaches or other tribes passing through Comancheria."

"Oh, it was Comanches! The army investigated the incident."

"Well, we can certainly trust the army," Matt retorted sarcastically. "Get some sleep, Boston. Tomorrow you'll finally get to meet these monsters you've been hearing about for so long."

"I can't wait," Grace said. She meant it. Though disappointed by Matt's news about her sister, she had the feeling she *would* see Ellie again—and soon. If Matt could have hunches so could she, and she felt in her bones that Ellie and the children were still alive and on their way to the canyon this very minute.

In the morning they packed quickly for the descent into the Palo Duro. The journey down to the canyon floor was more arduous that Grace had expected, but the closer they got the more excited she became. The immense herd of horses grazing alongside the stream greatly impressed her. She saw horses of every conceivable color, but the ones that drew her eye were the color-splashed Paint horses. Some were white with dark patches of black, sorrel, or tan on their faces and bodies, while others were mostly black or tan with broad splashes of white. Color patterns varied from large patches of color to small ones, and some even had several colors intermingled in their manes and tails. Grace loved them on sight, especially the spindly-legged, curious youngsters who fearlessly trotted up to them when they reached the canyon floor.

Like the young horses, the Comanche children displayed wide-eyed curiosity. As Matt and Grace rode toward the tipis, black-eyed, black-haired youngsters surrounded them—sometimes sidling close to touch Grace's arm or leg and then leaping away like nimble foals, startling themselves and laughing.

Grace couldn't understand a word of their chatter but they looked friendly, and so did the women crawling out of their tipis and standing to watch them pass. Grace noticed how straight Matt sat on his horse, and how little heed he paid to anyone. He rode ahead of her, as usual, and they didn't stop until they reached a tipi where a tall, distinguished-looking Indian awaited them with folded arms. Grace guessed he was Quanah Parker. Nothing marked him as the fierce warrior and leader accused of so many heinous crimes. To Grace, Matt himself looked more fierce in his Comanche garb—and more handsome. Quanah in no way outshone him.

The Indian standing next to Quanah seemed faintly familiar; as she noticed him Grace's heart jumped a little. This had to be Matt's brother. He resembled Matt around the eyes and nose, and in the stubborn tilt of his chin. He wasn't as compelling as Matt, nor as tall, but he looked every bit as dangerous and opinionated. His glance flicked over her like a whip, and she could tell immediately that he wasn't impressed with what he saw. She didn't even merit a second look.

Matt drew to a halt, dismounted, and began speaking in a low, level tone, apparently introducing her. Both Quanah and Matt's brother—if indeed that was who he was—glanced at her with interest. The men stood together conversing in the Comanche language for several moments, and Grace grew impatient at their rudeness. At the first lull in the conversation she blurted: "Pardon me, but what are you saying? Matt, please tell me."

Everyone stared, as if surprised to learn she had a voice. A flicker of amusement played about Matt's mouth.

"No Comanche woman would dare interrupt a man, even her own husband, much less an important chieftain. I suggest you keep your eyes open and your mouth shut, Boston, until I can tell you later what's being said."

"Forgive me," she apologized. "I didn't know."

She smiled at Quanah and Matt's brother, then shrugged her shoulders to show she meant no disrespect. At that moment a tiny, shriveled woman hobbled toward them, two young girls supporting her on either side. Matt nodded in the old woman's direction.

"This is my Comanche mother, Gray Owl. She's come to take you in hand and welcome you to the tribe. Go with her, Boston. Try to please her and do whatever she says. If she likes you her friendship will go a long way toward ensuring your acceptance by the Comanches."

"Oh!" Grace studied the wizened, little woman. "But where will *you* be?"

"Here, probably. I'll find you later. Don't go looking for me. You're among the Comanches now, and they have their own way of doing things. Try not to offend anyone."

Grace gulped. She hadn't given much thought as to whether or not she might offend anyone; her first impulse had been to judge *them,* to see if they were offending *her.* What Matt said was true; she had entered the Comanche world now, and she was far outnumbered. So she had better try to make friends and avoid stirring up a hornet's nest of potential enemies.

The old woman hobbled up to her and released a torrent of gibberish.

"She wants you to get down from your horse and follow her," Matt translated. "Don't worry about Dunston. No one would dream of harming him, and she's already assigned someone to look after him."

"Yes, of course!" Grace exclaimed, dismounting. "Where is she taking me?"

"To her tipi—or wherever we'll be staying while we are here."

"We . . . ? We'll be staying together?"

"Would you rather be apart?"

"No, but . . . it's just that . . . I don't want anyone to get the wrong idea about us."

Matt grimaced and shook his head. "Go with her. We'll discuss this later."

"All right," Grace agreed. She started to follow the little woman, who looked as if she must be a hundred years old, but was still amazingly spry and spunky. As she did so she had to pass another woman—this one young and beautiful. Indeed, she was so lovely that Grace paused for a second look. The girl had lustrous, long, black hair, dark mysterious eyes, full red lips, and a figure normally only achieved by a tightly laced corset. Grace doubted she was wearing one.

For some reason the woman watched her with equal interest, and a hostility Grace couldn't begin to fathom. The young woman deliberately stepped in front of her, blocking her progress, and glared at her as if daring her to pass.

Grace drew a deep breath and debated what to do. Fortunately, she didn't have to do anything, for Gray Owl saw what was happening and released another torrent of incomprehensible language. The younger woman grudgingly stepped aside, but the look she gave Grace was chilling.

Who could she be? Grace wondered, and why was she so hostile? An answer popped into her head: *She must be Sweet Water, Matt's Comanche wife.*

Swept with a sinking feeling and praying she was wrong, Grace hurried after Gray Owl.

By early evening the Comanche women had installed Grace in her own tipi with a brush arbor nearby, for sleeping in good weather. Gray Owl had supervised the swift construction of the amazingly efficient and comfortable-looking dwellings. The tipi consisted of twenty-two slender poles—roughly twenty feet in length—erected on a four pole base and covered with twenty bison skins, flesh side out. The inside diameter of the conical shelter was about fifteen feet.

The low doorway faced east and had a flap which could be closed in cold weather or for privacy. The tipi also had flaps which could be maneuvered to emit smoke when a cook fire burned in the tipi's center.

The arbor, on the other hand, was nothing more than a raised platform covered with brush to provide shade from the hot sun or a light rain if a person wished for shelter during the day or night but still wanted to enjoy the canyon breezes. During the hot months the arbor must have its advantages, but to Grace the tipi was a true marvel, cool and dark in summer, and probably warm and cozy during the winter.

After the women had erected it they set about furnishing it—with thick buffalo robes for sleeping, stones to ring the fireplace, various utensils for cooking, and numerous *parfleches* and containers. One held a large quantity of pemmican, while another yielded dried fruit. The fruit resembled small, wild plums or large dried cherries, or maybe both, mixed together. One basket contained an ample supply of nuts and seeds, none of which Grace recognized.

The generosity of the Indian women astounded her. Gray Owl showered gift after gift upon her—mostly from the meager store of items in her own tipi, which stood nearby. Some came from women Gray Owl had apparently prevailed upon to supply basic items of necessity. For Grace, it was a humbling experience to receive gifts from people who lived in poverty; their resources couldn't begin to compare with her own.

Granted, she had no access to her wealth at the moment, but she had never thought of herself as needy even though she currently possessed very little. Pawing over everything she had brought, the Indian women had apparently decided it wouldn't sustain her for long. Therefore, they had set about providing whatever they thought she needed to set up proper housekeeping in the canyon.

Gray Owl's final gift brought tears to Grace's eyes. Tottering over to her inside the new tipi, the old woman handed her a hide-wrapped bundle. With suddenly trembling fingers, Grace accepted it, opened it, and gasped at its contents. Inside was a soft, beautifully beaded garment meant for a female. Ten inch long fringe hung from the sleeves and the hem of the dress, and silver conchos had been woven into it. Along the bodice, both front and back, tiny round shells formed a geometrical pattern. It must have taken countless hours of painstaking labor and a great deal of skill to design such a masterpiece.

"This is for me?" Grace temporarily forgot that none of her new friends understood English.

Gray Owl nodded, her black eyes alight with pride in her handiwork. She indicated with gestures that Grace should exchange her grimy shirt and trousers for the soft new dress. The six other women crowded into the tipi all nodded approvingly. All afternoon, the women had used hand signals to communicate; Grace didn't understand half of what they had said, but some of the gestures were beginning to make sense.

"Thank you. I don't know why you're giving me all this, but I truly thank you." Smiling, she ran her fingers appreciatively over the soft, buff-colored garment. "I'll change into it as soon as I've had time to find my soap and wash properly."

Gray Owl clapped her hands together and shooed the younger women from the tipi, leaving Grace alone to contemplate her new accommodations. The afternoon had been so busy she hadn't had time to think of Matt and what he might be doing. When he came—if he came soon—he'd be hungry. She herself was hungry; they'd have to eat pemmican and dried fruit tonight, but maybe he could hunt for fresh meat tomorrow.

Gray Owl had left a stack of buffalo chips for fuel, and Grace considered making biscuits. The women had also supplied her with a small barrel of flour stamped with the words "U.S. Army." She didn't want to think about the supply wagon and the bodies she and Matt had buried, but the flour had to have come from somewhere, and she suspected that the supply wagon was its source. When one of the young girls had first carried the barrel into the tipi, she had found it difficult to conceal her reaction. Mindful of her resolution to avoid making enemies, she had managed to look appreciative instead of outraged.

The idea of making biscuits from stolen flour had scant appeal, and Grace moved restlessly around the tipi, rearranging things to suit her own tastes. Matt's belongings had been brought to the tipi, along with her own. They were definitely going to have to discuss this further.

If they were going to be here for several weeks, possibly even months, Matt would have to sleep elsewhere. On that point she wouldn't yield. There must be no resumption of intimacy; pregnancy was only one of the risks she faced. More damage to her already badly wounded heart was another, more serious possibility. She could always lie to explain the presence of a baby in her life to her friends and acquaintances back home in Boston; but how could she explain losing her will to live, along with her ability to enjoy life ever again? Loving Matt was simply too painful.

She couldn't forget that he had wanted to abandon her at The Flats. Obviously, he didn't love her; he had only used her. And she was so besotted with him that she had allowed it. No more! She must accept that they had no future together and refrain from indulging her own needs and desires, because in the long run the pain would only consume her. Matt must either leave the tipi and find another place to sleep, or she would make her bed elsewhere.

Grace sat down to wait for him and tried out a woven backrest; it was as comfortable as a chair. Leaning back against it, she closed her eyes. No sooner had she done so than his voice intruded upon her anxious thoughts.

"Making yourself right at home, I see," he drawled, entering through the small opening.

She nodded and sat up straight. "Yes, it's my—*our*—tipi Gray Owl supplied it, along with everything else you see here We need to talk about this, Matt. We are not spending the nigh together alone in here."

"You'd prefer sleeping out in the arbor? It'll be cooler out side—but not as private."

"You know what I mean," she said, rising to her feet. " refuse to spend any more nights alone with you."

"Why should it suddenly bother you so much?" He towere over her, forcing her to look up at him. "We haven't done any thing recently to cause such vehemence on your part. You'v slept in your bedroll. I've slept in mine. We can do the sam thing in a tipi as well as out on the plain."

"I don't like it! That's why. People—the Comanches—will consider us a couple, and we're not. They will assume we're intimate, and I can't allow that assumption. It might give *you* ideas, especially if we have to remain here for very long."

"They already consider us a couple, Boston. Actually, they think you're my wife. If we're going to stay here a while, that's exactly what you'll want them to think."

"Why? Is this like The Flats? Do I need to fear ravishment from some of your people, as well as among the lower-class elements of my own people?"

His face darkened with anger. "Why must you make everything so damn difficult? . . . Among the Comanches there's no such thing as a woman without a protector. Every woman needs a man to supply her with meat and hides. Without them, she can't survive on her own. The Comanches assume that you're my wife. That's why Gray Owl gave you this lodge and everything in it—at great sacrifice to herself and many others, I might add."

As if he feared she might turn away and cease listening, he placed his hands on her shoulders. Little did he know she hung on his every word; he just never said the words she most wanted to hear. "If you *aren't* my wife, the only other thing you can possibly be is my slave. Like it or not, that's the only other choice, Boston."

"Why can't I be a free woman, a single woman, like I was back home?"

"Because, as I said, you need a man to look after you! Our relationship must be defined. If I deny you the protection, safety, and esteem of being my wife, you will only be a despised white woman, subject to mistreatment and abuse by everyone else in the tribe."

"L-like Ellie?" Grace forced herself to ask.

Matt nodded. "Yes, like your sister. You'd better hope some brave took a shine to her and made her a wife, because if she isn't a wife she can't be having an easy time of it. Other women will look down on her and force her to do the dirtiest, most disagreeable chores. They may beat or torture her just to amuse themselves, and her owner will look the other way. Men don't protect a woman from other women—unless the woman is someone they cherish. Even then the woman is expected to win her own place in the pecking order of the squaws. That means she handles any challenges that come her way without running and crying to her husband. You're lucky Gray Owl is so happy to have me back—and even happier that I'm married. She wants grandchildren from this union. That's why she's so eager to make you feel welcome."

"G-grandchildren?" Grace wavered.

"Yes, grandchildren. Among the Indians of all tribes, old people live primarily for their grandchildren. In times of war, famine, or danger, grandchildren become a great rarity. I don't know why, exactly, but among the Comanches, women never bear many children, even in times of plenty. I suspect it's because they live most of their lives on horseback, following the buffalo from place to place. It isn't unusual for a pregnant woman to lose a child before it's big enough to survive on its own. When she does carry it to term, she often has to bear it on the trail alone, then mount her horse and catch up with the others. It isn't an easy life for a woman—*any* woman. For a woman without a man, it can be pure hell."

"I see." Grace's hope for her sister's survival flickered a little. Now she had to pray that Ellie had married some savage, or she might not have survived this past winter. At least, now, she had a better understanding of the problems her sister had to face.

"I swear not to touch you, Boston, but for your own safety and well-being, I insist we maintain the pretense that you belong to me and we care deeply for each other."

That's all it was to him—a pretense.

Unable to hide her bitterness, Grace pulled away from him. "All right, if you insist. But you will sleep on that side of the fire ring, and I will sleep on this side. No matter how long we remain here, you will honor and abide by that arrangement."

"I won't come closer unless you invite me," he solemnly agreed.

"I will not invite you!"

"I believe you. You needn't shout. Women who are happy in their marriages *never* shout at their husbands. . . . Now, what is there to eat in all these containers?"

Later that night, after they had eaten, the Comanches held a celebration in honor of Matt's return and his union with Grace. They lit a huge fire in the center of the encampment and danced around it, chanting, singing, and making a joyous clamor with gourds, drums, and other primitive musical instruments. To Grace the dances seemed lewd and suggestive, but Matt explained that they were totally innocent and indicative of good will.

"The whole tribe is wishing us long life and the fertility of rabbits, that's all," he explained with a wink. "They want us to raise up more Comanches to replace those who have died in battle against the whites."

It was all very well for him to joke about it, but Grace's cheeks flamed at the notion. Her children—if she ever had any—would *not* be raised as savages. Even so, she couldn't help noticing how adorable the Comanche children were. Round-cheeked and shy, curious but well-behaved, they surrounded her and Matt, eager to be close to them since they were the center of attention.

As sparks and smoke from the big fire rose in the darkness of the canyon, reddening its high walls, Grace wondered if there were any soldiers in the vicinity to mark the fire's location and hear the noise of the dancers. If there were, these darling youngsters might die . . . an appalling thought!

She had lived among the Comanches for a single day, but already she felt protective of them. It was a strange, alien feeling . . . one that almost frightened her. She didn't want to care about the Comanches any more than she wanted to care about

Matt; somehow, she cared, anyway. How would an old woman like Gray Owl ever survive an attack? Or for that matter, another harsh winter?

These dancing, chanting, happy souls—or others like them—had killed William, Ellie's husband, and hundreds of other whites. She mustn't feel sorry for them; they deserved whatever terrible punishment lay in store. But glancing down at a little girl, exhausted from all the excitement, who had suddenly lain down beside her and fallen asleep with her head pillowed in her lap, Grace could summon no anger or resentment.

She felt only a huge deep sorrow. Whites were supposed to be civilized, far more advanced in every sphere of life than the Indians, yet she had witnessed more violence and cruelty among whites than she had yet to see among the Comanches. Of course, she hadn't witnessed the Indians at their worst yet, but their generosity, kindness, and simple humanity could not be denied.

They were human beings like herself—not animals, as she had thought. This sleeping child was no more savage than any other child of any other race. She was little more than a baby. When she grew up, she'd do only what she had been taught. . . . And what had life taught her so far? To hate and fear white soldiers who made it necessary for her to hide in a canyon.

The child's mother eventually came to claim her, the fire died down, and the Comanches went to bed—either seeking out their arbors and tipis or sleeping curled up beside the dying embers. Matt took Grace's hand and whispered: "Come. We can leave now. The celebration has ended, and I imagine you're tired."

She was. She could hardly keep her eyes open. She allowed Matt to lead her away to their tipi, and once inside she stumbled to her blankets in the darkness, stretched out on them, and closed her eyes. In her mind's eye she pictured the fire—the red, dancing flames, and the crouching, stamping figures silhouetted against it. She could not recall seeing the beautiful young woman she feared was Matt's Comanche wife. . . . Where had she been tonight?

I must ask him about her, tomorrow.

Yes, she decided, tomorrow she would ask him. Tonight she was too sleepy. She could feel herself drifting off, floating in that half-conscious state between awareness and loss of consciousness. . . .

What was that noise?

It was a quiet, stealthy sound that reminded her of fabric tearing—or being torn. Grace lay still, listening. All she could hear now was Matt breathing deeply, snorting just a little as he sometimes did when he slept. After a moment the sawing sound continued; it seemed to be coming from the back wall of the tipi.

She wished Renegade were nearby, ready to warn them if anything were wrong. She could just make out the moonlit entrance to the shelter—a square of darkness several shades brighter than the darkness inside the tipi. The interior of the tipi wasn't completely black; her eyes had adjusted, and she could now see dim shapes and objects along the walls and sides of the tipi.

One of those shapes—a large one—moved. It leapt toward her, landed heavily on top of her, and pinned her to the blankets. The unexpected weight almost knocked the breath from her lungs. Somehow, she still managed to scream.

"Matt . . . help me!"

Nineteen

Grace's cry roused all of Matt's fighting instincts. Bolting to his feet he saw Grace and an unknown assailant rolling about on the floor of the tipi. A stray moonbeam near the entrance momentarily silvered the blade of an upraised knife. Matt seized the hand holding the knife and gave it a savage jerk that dragged the intruder off Grace and tossed him—rather, *her*—across the tipi.

As the knife spun through the air and fell, he clamped his free arm around the attacker's waist. The fullness and softness of her buckskin-clad breasts didn't surprise him. The fall of her black hair had revealed her gender, and now he thought he knew her identity.

Her body felt familiar and her musky scent sparked memories. He hadn't held or smelled Sweet Water in years, but he'd know her anywhere; a man didn't forget the shape or scent of a woman who had once been his wife.

Matt dragged her outside into the moonlight, where he could see her better. Spitting with fury, Sweet Water spun around and tried to claw his face. Grabbing her wrists, he held her away from him. All the fight suddenly left her, and she sagged against him, wailing and sobbing.

"You are mine! How can you take another woman to your blankets—and even worse, a white-eyes! Let me go, and I will kill her!"

"If you lay a hand on her, *you* will be the one to die," Matt threatened. "I can take anyone I please to my blankets. Why are you even here? You left me long ago and fled to another."

"I was wrong, Painted Horse! So wrong. I know I have shamed you. Cut off my nose, if you wish, but don't cast me aside. I will never again mock you or look at another brave."

Weeping copiously, Sweet Water collapsed at his feet. "Punish me! I beg you to punish me. But do not send me away. When winter comes I will starve. I have no man to look after me now. Because of what I did to you, no other warrior will have me."

"That's not my concern. I have taken a new wife. I don't need you to warm my blankets."

"Then keep us both! You are a great hunter. You deserve two women. . . . Providing for both of us should be no problem for *you*."

"Matt, is it Sweet Water?" Grace asked from the entrance to the tipi. "What is she saying? She tried to *kill* me."

He and Sweet Water had been speaking in the Comanche tongue, but now he switched to English. "Go back inside, Boston. I'll handle this."

A torch flared—and then another. The disturbance had awakened half the encampment. Quanah and his brother were coming toward them. Inwardly, Matt groaned. Now he'd have to do something about Sweet Water. Everyone would expect him to kill her on the spot or punish her and take her back. She had made it impossible for him to ignore her; if he did nothing he'd appear weak and cowardly. He'd lose their respect, and they'd never listen to him.

As for Sweet Water, she'd think she had won and attack Grace again, hoping to get rid of her once and for all. The next time the People would applaud her for fighting to reclaim her man. His wily Comanche wife knew exactly what she was doing. Rising, she glared at him triumphantly.

"Do it, Painted Horse. Kill me now—or punish me and keep me. I don't care which. If you kill me, you'll be sparing me the pain of starvation this winter. I'd rather die quickly than starve. However, if you keep me, I'll serve you well. But I shall be your *first* wife, and she will be your second. She will have to serve *me*. That is the Comanche way—and you *are* still a Comanche, aren't you?"

The taunt hung in the air and everyone watched him expectantly, waiting to see what he would do. The entire band had now crowded around them, and their faces told him he had no choice but to decide now what to do about her and live with the consequences.

"Matt?" Grace sounded hesitant, as if she were trying hard not to say or do the wrong thing. "Please . . . I *must* know what she's saying."

"Kill her and finish it," Stalking Wolf advised. He raised his torch, clearly illuminating the two women. "For the sake of your honor you must do as she says, my brother—kill her or take her back again. You can't let this insult pass." He reached for the knife strapped to his thigh. "At least, cut off her nose. The she-wolf deserves that much."

"Painted Horse, I *beg* you! Take me back!" Sweet Water's fingers dug into his arms. "I still care for you . . . and I will be a good wife to you—better than *she* can ever be."

"I don't want two wives." Matt pushed her hand away. He wanted only *one* wife, but she was too good for him. Too rich. Too proud. Too high and mighty. He could never offer her a life to compete with the life she had known, the one awaiting her back in Boston.

"Then set the white-eyes aside and accept *me*. I will fight her for you!" Sweet Water pleaded. "It's the only way to settle it." She eyed him resolutely. "You owe me this, Painted Horse. I would never have left you in the first place if you had not betrayed the People in your thoughts and dreams. Is a white woman a better wife for a Comanche warrior than a Comanche? Why have you returned here if not to fight beside us for our freedom?"

"He came to urge us to surrender," Quanah quietly announced, and a ripple of disapproval ran through the crowd. "That does not make him a coward or prove he has turned his back on us. The army knows him as Painted Horse, the lone Comanche who rides when the moon is full, stealing horses and attacking buffalo hunters. They have put a great price on his head for his crimes against them. Nor is his woman without honor and courage. She came seeking her sister among us, not knowing if we would welcome her as friend or attack her as enemy. For however long they wish to remain, they are welcome."

"My brother must tell his white woman what Sweet Water is saying," Stalking Wolf demanded. "Sweet Water has challenged her, and if Painted Horse has no taste for two wives, he must allow them to fight to prove who will share his tipi while he is here."

"*I*—not they—will decide who shares my tipi," Matt growled.

"You must rid yourself of one or the other," his brother persisted. He offered Matt his knife. "Take it, and do your duty."

"I don't want your knife!" Matt shouted. He couldn't think of a way to settle the matter short of actually stabbing Sweet Water in the heart.

No matter what he did Grace would hate him for it, and if he did nothing, she would be in constant danger. Whenever disagreement arose among squaws with equal claims to the same brave, the women settled it among themselves. The stronger would intimidate the weaker, who became little more than a slave. Matt had never suspected this would happen, or he wouldn't have brought Grace into this mess. He'd known there would be danger, but not a personal vendetta.

"Let your white woman decide for herself if she wants to fight for you," Stalking Wolf urged, and Quanah nodded, supporting his brother.

"It is the proper way to settle the issue, my friend," the Comanche leader declared. "You must settle it now or there will be no peace in the Palo Duro. You will have to take your white woman and leave here at once."

The ultimatum decided Matt. He glanced at Grace, standing now in front of the tipi, watching him intently, and awaiting his explanation. Her honey-colored hair gleamed in the torchlight. Two spots of hectic color stained her cheekbones, and her hazel eyes brimmed with worry. Next to the dark Comanche women and Sweet Water, she looked fragile, pale, and innocent.

Her beauty smote him like a blow. If anything happened to her, if Sweet Water harmed a hair on her head, he'd kill the bitch. He wouldn't think twice about it.

"Give me a moment," he said to Quanah. "I would speak to her alone." He nodded toward Grace.

"I will await your decision in my lodge," Quanah responded. "In the meantime, Sweet Water will go to your brother's lodge, where he can watch over her to see that she does nothing rash."

"My lodge! I don't want that troublemaker in my lodge, speaking to *my* wife!" Stalking Wolf exclaimed.

It was the only satisfaction the incident afforded Matt, watching his brother react to the news that he must assume responsibility for Sweet Water, if only for a little while. Stalking Wolf's wife was a plain-faced, shy, little woman named Summer Moon, whose belly was big with their second child. Earlier in the day Stalking Wolf had confided that their first child had been born dead after a long, arduous labor. Matt knew that his brother cherished Summer Moon and now guarded her like a hawk, trying to keep her safe and healthy to bear this new babe.

He could sympathize with him for not wanting Sweet Water to disturb the tranquility of his lodge—but his brother deserved this small comeuppance.

"Guard her well, my brother." He smirked at Stalking Wolf. "If she escapes from you and returns to press her claim before I am ready to deal with her, I will hold *you* responsible."

Accepting a torch from an onlooker and stepping past all of them, Matt took Grace's arm and steered her inside their tipi.

Grace couldn't believe it. She listened in stunned silence to Matt's explanation of what had occurred outside. For several moments she thought it over, then announced her decision.

"I'll have to fight her for you, won't I?"

"No," Matt said, his green eyes brilliant. "You don't have to fight her. A better solution would be for us to pick up and leave. . Indeed, now that I think about it, it's the *only* solution."

"I refuse to leave. You promised me we could stay until the first signs appear that a winter storm is on the way."

"This changes everything, Boston. Unless you don't mind if I slit Sweet Water's throat, we have to go. She's made it impossible for us to stay."

"Not if I fight her—and win."

"Don't be ridiculous! How are you going to win? She'll kill you, Boston. Either that, or you'll have to kill her."

"The fight must have . . . rules. And you'll have to teach me how to fight so I can beat her."

"Of course. In the next few hours before sunrise, I'll turn you into a Comanche warrior, capable of conquering a woman who was born a Comanche. . . . Oh, that makes sense! Shouldn't be any trouble at all."

There was so much sarcasm in his tone that Grace wondered why he didn't choke on it. "We can do it. I'm taller than she is, though we probably weigh about the same. And I'm tough. My recent style of living has toughened me considerably."

"She's lived like this all her life. Be reasonable, Boston, and start packing our things."

"I am *not* leaving! I refuse to be driven away by a jealous female who didn't stand by you when you needed her most!"

He slanted her a questioning glance. "You're presuming to judge her? She thought I was a coward because I refused to go on any more raids or kill any more whites. Quite a few in this camp share that opinion, especially since I'm now urging surrender."

"If I were your wife—your *real* wife—I would stand by you no matter what. If you did something I couldn't understand, I'd try my best to see your side of it. She didn't. She never gave you a chance. And now, just because the man she ran off with is dead and no one else will have her, she wants you back."

Grace was sure she understood Sweet Water's motivations; the woman *couldn't* have loved Matt or she would never have been able to give him up and seek happiness in another man's arms. Grace herself had long ago decided that no other man could ever again entice her into his bed. Not after Matt.

"Whatever her reasons for issuing this challenge, you can't accept it, Boston. The human body has some vulnerable spots, and if you knew about them it might give you a slight edge over her, but I can't teach you enough in one night to ensure you can beat her."

"Then we won't fight," Grace said. Inspiration suddenly struck. "We'll . . . race! I can run quite fast. I think I can win."

"Not as fast as a Comanche. However, if you were to race horses against each other . . ." He looked thoughtful for a moment. "The Comanches love horse racing even more than a good fight. They'll gamble anything they own on a horse race— horses, weapons, blankets, even their wives and daughters . . ."

"Is *nothing* sacred?"

"Only their medicine bags. No warrior would risk losing his precious medicine bag."

"Medicine bag. You mean like *my* medicine bag?"

"Sort of—only it doesn't contain medicine."

"Then what does it contain?"

"Sacred objects. Items that give a man special strength or power."

Grace wanted to hear more about medicine bags, but there wasn't time at the moment to discuss them. "Who would I ride in a horse race—Renegade? He could outrun anything on four legs, but . . . but I'd be a little afraid to ride him."

"He's your only chance, Boston. I'll fasten a thong around his neck, and all you'll have to do is hang on to it. He'll do the rest."

Grace's heart began to pound. She broke into a sweat. "But who will Sweet Water ride?"

"Someone will have a horse they'd like to pit against Renegade. They'll offer their best, just to prove who's better, and Sweet Water will be able to take her pick. From the fact that I give you permission to ride my sacred horse, everyone will know that I want you to win. It's a good solution, Boston. If you lose, no one gets hurt . . . but we will have to depart immediately. Either that, or Sweet Water gets to be First Wife and you'll have to settle for second, a dangerous, risky position I don't recommend."

"Don't worry, I won't lose." Grace made up her mind to win.

"Then I'd better go and tell them. I may have to talk Quanah into the idea of a race. And Sweet Water will have to agree, of course. If *she* loses, we can't do much more than make her swear to leave you alone and never again come near us as long we're here in the Palo Duro."

"Matt, when you come back, perhaps you'd better show me a few of those vulnerable spots on the human body. Just in case. I'd like to be prepared, you know . . ."

"I know," he hastily agreed. "I'll show you a few. Just in case."

The Comanches loved the idea of a horse race. Matt had only to mention it, and both his brother and Quanah offered horses for Sweet Water to ride. Normally, only warriors raced horses, but in this case they all agreed that a horse race was a good way to solve the problem of who got to be First Wife—Sweet Water, Matt's actual first wife, or Grace, the newcomer.

Quanah himself delivered the news to Sweet Water and gave her no chance to refuse. She must either race or relinquish all claims to Matt. Sweet Water grudgingly agreed. Her choice of mount surprised everyone. She didn't want Quanah's prime stallion, another painted horse though not a Medicine Hat. She wanted a small, swift mare she had long admired.

"This mare can fly like the wind," she announced to all those gathered around Quanah's tipi. "And she is sacred, too. She has one blue eye and one brown."

Matt had never known the Comanches to esteem this particular phenomenon, but several of the older braves shook their heads and murmured among themselves, agreeing that Sweet Water had made a wise choice. They liked the idea of pitting one unusual animal against another, even if one were a mare and the other a stallion.

Here again, Sweet Water demonstrated her cunning: The women promptly began pulling for the mare, hoping the female could outdo the male. They began betting among themselves who would win, and most favored Sweet Water. The race was set for noon of the following day, or rather *that* day; by now, it was close to dawn.

Returning to his tipi Matt found Grace sitting on her blankets and hugging her knees. In the torchlight, she looked wan and worried.

"It's all arranged," he told her. "You race at noon."

"Have you told Renegade?" She tried to smile, but the joke fell flat, for her lips were quivering.

"I'll tell him in the morning. He won't be half as nervous about it as you are."

"I'll probably fall off, and Sweet Water will win."

"No, you won't, Boston." He knelt down beside her and wished he could take her in his arms and hold her. Mindful of the gulf between them, he didn't. "You want to stay here so much that even if Renegade should fall and break a leg in the middle of the race you'll just get up and finish on foot, *still* beating Sweet Water's horse. . . . I *know* you will."

"You don't think he'll actually fall and break a leg, do you?" Terror flared in her eyes.

"No, no. . . . He's much too surefooted. Forget I said that. Let me give you a lesson, now, in 'vulnerable places.' " He yearned to touch all of *her* vulnerable places, the ones he hadn't touched since The Flats.

"I think you'd better. If nothing else, it will take my mind off the race."

"We've got hours until the race. Stop worrying about it."

But he could see, as he started to teach her where and how to deliver disabling blows, that all she could do was worry. He, on the other hand, wasn't worried at all. Renegade could outrun any horse on the plains; only Sweet Water herself merited worry. When she lost, would she be willing to abide by their agreement and leave Grace alone? If she didn't he would *have* to kill her. He could only hope she didn't get to Grace first.

Promptly at noon, with the sun beating down like a hammer striking an anvil, the Comanches led Grace to a spot near the stream at one end of the canyon. Pointing to a feathered lance in the far distance, they indicated that the first rider to reach the lance would win the race.

"Do you understand what they just told you?" Matt asked, and she nodded.

Sign language was beginning to make sense to her. Grace could now recognize the words for horse, buffalo, sun, friend, and child, plus a few others. One particular word puzzled her greatly. The Indians would say it, look at her expectantly, make a sign, and then repeat the word. She had no idea what it meant.

Seeing Quanah Parker make the sign and say the word now, she asked Matt to translate. "It's their word for *you*," he explained. "They've started to call you Honey Hair. They like your hair, you see."

His frown told her he was displeased about something.

"Unless they're planning to scalp me there's nothing wrong with that, is there?" she whispered.

"Only that four different braves have offered to take you off my hands if you lose this race to Sweet Water. Apparently, they so like the body that comes with the hair."

"Oh!" Her face flamed beneath the brim of her hat. She had to don the lovely Comanche dress Gray Owl had given her, because her trousers were better for riding. "What did you tell them?"

"I said I'd think about it. I didn't want to provoke another fight before we'd gotten past this one."

While they waited for Sweet Water's arrival, Grace cast about for a less provocative topic of conversation. "Why were so many horses outside our tipi this morning? They almost trampled me when I first went outside."

Matt's scowl grew even fiercer. "Someone—I don't know who yet—is interested in trading for you. They thought I might be interested in exchanging you for a nice herd of horses."

"Oh!" Grace thought it best to say nothing more, lest she introduce another touchy subject.

"Yes, oh. . . . All I can say, Boston, is that you'd better win this race. If you don't I'm not sure they'll let you out of the canyon. They don't consider you a person, with thoughts and desires of your own. They look at you as an item of barter. Someone to buy and sell."

"Oh." Realizing that she had just repeated herself several times, Grace moved away from Matt and looked around for Renegade.

Matt's brother was leading the stallion toward her, and never had he looked more beautiful. Feathers trailed from his mane and tail, and his coat gleamed like satin in the sunlight. Sensing the excitement in the air, he was prancing, snorting, and tossing his head.

Where was his saddle? She couldn't possibly ride him bareback! He wore only a bridle and didn't even have the thong around his neck that Matt had promised her. "Matt!" She spun around to ask him about the thong, but it was too late.

Sweet Water had arrived—beautifully dressed for the occasion in an elaborately fringed and beaded dress and high moccasins. Her lustrous black braids hung to her waist. Her black eyes sparkled, and she must have painted her lips to achieve such a luscious shade of carmine.

She was stunning, and appeared very confident as seven

men brought up her horse, a small, wiry-looking mare with one brown eye and one blue. The mare's coat was white with reddish-brown patches, and she immediately caught Renegade's interest; he whinnied when he saw her, then began rearing.

Sprinting toward him, Matt grabbed hold of his reins. "Easy, boy. Take it easy now."

For the first time since Grace had known the stallion, he utterly ignored Matt. He rose on his hind legs and pawed the air, scattering the Comanches. Matt had all he could do to hang onto him. The problem suddenly became apparent. Renegade wanted to breed the mare, not race her. Grace didn't know a whole lot about horse breeding, but if ever a mare looked ready to be bred this one did. She swung her hind quarters toward Renegade, squatted, lifted her tail, and relieved herself. Renegade screamed in a manner Grace had never heard him do before and again reared. When he came down, Matt latched onto his ear and twisted it to get the horse's attention.

Unaccustomed to such harsh treatment from his beloved master, Renegade clacked his teeth together mere inches from Matt's jaw. But Matt held on and spoke soothingly, momentarily distracting the stallion from his frenzy.

Matt said something in Comanche, and two braves suddenly swooped down on Grace and lifted her onto Renegade's back, while Sweet Water, refusing help, scrambled effortlessly aboard the mare. Someone thrust Renegade's reins into Grace's hands. "Forget the reins!" Matt cried. "Grab mane and hold tight. Steer with your legs. Make him pass the mare and keep him there. Once he's ahead of her he'll be all right. It's the wrong time of year for it, but the damn mare's in season."

If this were the wrong time, when was the right time? Grace wondered. She had no more time to think because the mare streaked past her, and Renegade followed. Remembering Matt's advice, Grace clutched at the mane whipping in her face, crouched low over the stallion's neck, and urged him to greater speed.

She had never ridden bareback and was amazed to discover

that she could discern the horse's movements beneath her far better without a saddle than with one. Hours of riding had given her a security she hadn't realized she possessed. She found she *could* steer him using only her legs and the slight shift of her weight on his back. It seemed he could detect *her* movements better now, too, but he didn't want to pass the mare. He crowded her hindquarters, almost knocking her over.

Sweet Water pulled a stick from her moccasins, whacked him across the nose, and began flailing on the mare's hip. Renegade veered slightly to the right, giving Grace a chance to redirect his energies. Calling his name, she stuck to him like a burr and urged him to extend himself and really run. He did. His flying hooves clattered briefly on stone, then pounded on dry earth and grass. He passed the mare easily and didn't seem to notice he had done so. The thrill of the race had replaced the need to breed, and Renegade ran as if he and the wind were brothers, capable of leaving the earth far behind.

Grace never saw the marker signaling the stopping point. She stopped because she didn't want Renegade to break a leg on the rocky, uneven ground at the far end of the canyon. Blowing hard, he came to a standstill, and she turned him around and rode back to the marker. Sweet Water awaited her, her face rigid with anger.

At the race's starting point, the Comanches were yelling screaming, and jumping up and down in excitement. Grace sa vored her moment of triumph. Mindful of the possibility tha Renegade might be interested in taking up where he'd left of with the mare, she didn't get too close to Sweet Water. Howeve Sweet Water boldly approached her.

In a sudden, swift motion that caught Grace off-guard, Swee Water flung herself at Grace. She knocked Grace off Renegad and landed on top of her in the grass. A knife appeared in he hand, and once again Grace found herself fighting for her life They rolled over and over. Grace could hear the Comanche shouting, and was sure Matt was trying to reach her, but sh doubted he could do it in time to stop Sweet Water inflicting damage.

Desperately she tried to recall all that Matt had taught her during the night, but her mind refused to function. Sweet Water wielded the knife with taunting, deadly efficiency. Grace managed to avoid being stabbed, but the woman succeeded in nicking her a couple of times. Laughing, she aimed for Grace's face, but Grace scooted out of the way. They both gained their feet, and Sweet Water circled her, lunging and waving the knife under Grace's nose.

Twice the blade cut through the cloth of Grace's shirt and drew blood. Once it sliced her hand. The wounds caused brief, stinging sensations. Grace was too intent on avoiding worse injuries to worry about minor ones.

"Boston!" Matt shouted. "Remember what I taught you."

As Sweet Water maneuvered around her, Grace caught a glimpse of him. Four warriors held him tightly, preventing him from interfering. She was on her own; she had to start concentrating on how to save herself or she would never come out of this alive.

Twenty

The throat. The temple. A hand's width above the navel. Just below the kneecap. The kidneys. . . . Shove the nose straight back into the brain. Gouge the eyes.

Slowly, Grace's mind resumed functioning, and she remembered Matt's list of vulnerable spots and disabling techniques and his general advice on self-defense. The knife made it hard to do anything; she didn't want to get close enough to risk getting cut or stabbed.

Stumbling on an unseen stone as she dodged a knife slash, Grace got an idea. Behind Sweet Water were lots of stones. All she had to do was force her opponent to step back into them and hope that she, too, might stumble. In that split second when the woman was vulnerable, Grace could butt her in the throat or perhaps in the stomach, knock her down, and take the knife.

A brave standing in the ring of onlookers suddenly tossed Grace a knife of her own, but she wasn't quick enough to catch it. It clattered among the stones, and Sweet Water laughed at her clumsiness. Grace seized the opportunity to kick at the woman's weapon. Surprised by this sudden show of aggression, Sweet Water backed up a step. This time Grace launched herself headfirst. As she collided with Sweet Water's mid-section, red-hot pain lanced her shoulder. It didn't matter; she couldn't stop her momentum.

Sweet Water flew backward and hit the ground hard. Grace sprawled on top of her. Forgetting the knife, Grace scrambled to her knees and gouged Sweet Water's eyes, chopped at her throat, kneed her above the navel, and hammered on her chest. Matt hadn't told her to do that, but instinct drove her now. Succumbing to fury, she lost all restraint and pummeled the woman—repaying her for every knife cut, every laugh, every trick, and then some.

She didn't know the fight was over until Matt himself dragged her off Sweet Water.

"Calm down, Boston. Sweet Water's unconscious. There's no need to kill her. You can if you want to, but you'll only hate yourself when you finally come to your senses."

"Kill her?" Grace hadn't realized that's what she'd been doing.

She heard someone gasping and fighting for breath; amazingly, it was her. She stared down at her unmoving opponent. Blood streaked one of Sweet Water's glossy braids. Her eyes were turning black and blue, and her lips were swelling. She looked as if she'd locked horns with a buffalo bull and lost the contest.

The Comanches were cheering as if she had done something truly wonderful, but Grace suddenly felt awful. Guilt and horror racked her. For a few wild, reckless moments she *had* wanted to kill Sweet Water. Something akin to the abandon she felt when she made love with Matt had come over her, rendering her witless, centered totally on attaining release.

What she had done with Matt had been sublime, but this was sordid and ugly—a chilling madness, all the more frightening for being totally unexpected. If Matt hadn't stopped her, she would have killed the woman and relished every minute of it.

"I didn't mean to . . . to hurt her," she protested, swaying dizzily.

Matt slid an arm around her back and one beneath her legs and lifted her, cradling her to his chest. "You didn't, huh? You could have fooled me. The Comanches are greatly impressed. They've never seen a woman fight like that. They're saying that's why I chose you over one of their own—because you're a warrior woman, not a mere squaw."

"Oh, Matt! Will Sweet Water live?" Grace struggled to look back at her victim as Matt carried her away from the jubilant scene. "I don't know what came over me! All I wanted to do was save myself. I didn't intend to actually hurt her."

"Blood lust. That's what came over you. Now you know what it's like in the heat of battle, when men do terrible things they don't want to remember later."

"Men maybe, but not *me!*" Appalled at her own behavior, Grace huddled weeping in his arms.

"Don't cry. At least, wait 'til we get to our tipi. Stop feeling sorry for Sweet Water. She had a knife, and you didn't. She *intended* to kill you. If you doubt it, look at yourself. You're bleeding all over both of us."

Grace didn't care about the blood or her own wounds. She only cared that she had tried—and almost succeeded—to murder someone with her bare hands.

Shortly after they arrived at the tipi Gray Owl appeared with her little retinue of helpers. She elbowed Matt aside and knelt next to Grace, who was lying limply on her blankets. Perhaps it was the loss of blood or simply the realization of what she'd almost done, but Grace could barely summon the strength to raise her head and protest when Matt started to leave the shelter.

"Where are you going?" she managed to ask.

"Gray Owl is sending me away. The women want to dress your wounds, sew up the worst ones, and prepare you for the victory feast. . . . Don't worry, Boston. They know what to do. I'll only be in the way."

"I'm in no shape for another celebration. Why can't they leave me alone? I'd rather you stay."

"They won't leave you alone because you're a Comanche now—not Honey Hair any longer, but Warrior Woman, their new name for you. They want to make a fuss over you." He flashed her a brief but reassuring smile. "You've got some bad cuts, but none are life-threatening. At least they won't be when

Gray Owl gets finished with you. You'll probably live another hundred years."

"This is no time for teasing. . . . Ouch! That hurts!"

Ignoring her outburst, Gray Owl continued probing the deep cut on her shoulder. Grace's wounds suddenly stung, ached, or throbbed, or did all three together. Grimacing, she stifled a groan. Her new name was Warrior Woman. She had better show some courage.

"I'll be back to check on you in a bit."

Grace scarcely heard Matt. As the women went to work, her own pain and misery commanded all her attention.

By nightfall she felt wonderful—pain-free, exhilarated, and better than she ever had in her life. Noticing her suffering, Gray Owl had given her some medicine—the best, most effective remedy Grace had ever had. It had looked like a button—a dried up button—and tasted like a carrot. Whatever it was, it worked wonders.

After the women finished tending her wounds, they insisted on bathing and dressing her and then brushing, braiding, and decorating her hair. Grace no longer cared what they did to her; she *loved* these women and regarded them as her dearest friends. Her sisters. They were all sweet and wonderful, and she was so happy to be there among them.

Rummaging among the *parfleches* she and Matt had brought with them from The Flats, Gray Owl produced a pair of lovely, decorated moccasins to go with the dress she herself had given Grace. Grace was astounded; she hadn't known the moccasins were rolled up and stuffed in the bottom of that particular *parfleche*. She wondered why Matt hadn't offered them to her earlier; her heart swelled with love and gratitude. Obviously he had been saving this fine gift for some special occasion.

When they led her out of the tipi to join the feast already in progress, Grace felt as if she were floating. Once again there were dancers, a huge fire, the smell of roasting meat, and chanting. Grace took her place beside Matt, who was seated on a

beautiful white buffalo robe set back a comfortable distance
from the roaring fire.

Her heart brimmed with joy and the need to tell him how she
felt about him. Smiling, she held out her arms to him. "I love
you, Painted Horse!" she grandly announced.

Matt's first reaction was amazement. Then he frowned at her
and asked: "What in hell's wrong with you? Are you all right?"
His eyes scanned her Indian garb, from her Indian-style braids
to her new footwear. "I see you found the moccasins I brought
in case your boots wore out or gave you trouble. Except for the
color of your hair, skin, and eyes, anyone might think you're a
Comanche. I, however, know better."

"Oh Matt, I love the moccasins, and I have never felt better
in my life! Why do you ask if there's something wrong with
me?"

"You've never said you loved me before—or called me
Painted Horse. You must have suffered a hard knock on the
head. . . . How are your cuts?"

"What cuts?" Grace couldn't remember any cuts. She
couldn't remember anything except how much she loved him.
Never had he looked more handsome: Pure Indian. Pure *man*.
Her man. Her Indian. "Painted Horse, I want you. Right now.
This very minute. I *must* have you."

He didn't move. He simply stared at her. "Boston, what did
Gray Owl give you? She must have given you something, because you're clearly not yourself tonight."

What an odd thing for him to say! She thought she was more
herself than she had ever been in her life. This was the real
Grace Livingston—Warrior Woman—and she wanted her man
Painted Horse, to take her back to the tipi and make love to her
Or make love to her right here and now.

"She gave me some medicine. Such wonderful medicine! You
must ask her what it's called. It relieved my pain and made me
feel . . . perfectly grand!"

"I'll bet it did. And I'll bet I know what it was."

"You do? Tell me. I should like to have some to put in my medicine bag in case I ever need it again."

"Peyote. She gave you peyote . . . and you won't think it's so wonderful or grand tomorrow morning. I've seen what it does to Indians who belong to the Peyote Cult. They get sick and claim to see visions."

"I'd adore seeing visions!"

"Yeah, but first they lose the contents of their stomachs, and when there's nothing left in their stomachs they retch helplessly. It's not a pretty sight."

"If I get to see visions, I won't care."

"Oh, you'll care."

"I *do* care—about *you!* Please. Take me back to the tipi and let me show you how much I love you. Please, my dearest Painted Horse, my one true love." Leaning against him, she brazenly nibbled his ear.

"If we do what you're suggesting you won't like yourself much in the morning."

"Yes, I will! Try me. Oh, I'm so happy! For the first time in my life I know who I am and what I really want—*you!*"

"Boston, the peyote is talking, not Grace Livingston. Don't do this to yourself. Don't do it to me." He sounded wary and anxious, but she knew she could make him happy, as happy as she was.

She ran her hand down the front of his chest—and lower. "I'm your wife. They all think I'm your wife. Haven't I *earned* the right to consider you my husband?"

"Don't joke about that!" He seized her hand. "Are you telling me you're willing to stay here forever in Indian Territory? You want to build a new life with me? You'll *always* want to call me Painted Horse? And you'll *never* want to return to Boston?"

"I want to be wherever *you* are. I love you. That's what I'm telling you."

"Boston—" he began, but she cut him off with an ardent kiss.

She put her whole heart into it and when she was done he

looked as if he, too, had taken peyote, and was ready to join her in this new state of being.

"You shouldn't kiss me like that—not unless you mean it."

"I do mean it." She kissed him again. "Painted Horse, love me. Take me back to the tipi and love me."

She kissed him a third time. This time, he capitulated. Rising, he offered her his hand. She took it, rose to her feet, and stood swaying a moment, trying to maintain her balance. Lightheaded and dizzy, she feared falling down, but her magnificent warrior swept her into his arms, lifting her as he had earlier that day, and carried her away from the fire and back toward their tipi.

No one stopped them; no one said a word. The celebration continued without them. When they arrived at the tipi he carried her inside and set her down, but kept his arms wrapped around her. "Boston, we're both going to regret this tomorrow. I shouldn't let you do it, but—heaven help me—I've missed you so damn much!"

"And I've missed you! I can't live without you, my darling Painted Horse. You're the air and the wind. I need to breathe you inside me every night . . ."

"Inside you," he murmured hoarsely, and pulled her down onto the blankets.

Ravenous for the touch, taste, and feel of him, Grace lost all reserve. She couldn't get enough of him, and with every kiss, caress, and moan he demonstrated that he couldn't get enough of her. They wasted little time in preliminaries and quickly shed their clothes, joined their frantic bodies, and began the dizzying journey to the heights of fulfillment and ecstasy. It was glorious . . . incredible . . . earth-shakingly beautiful. And it couldn't last. Too soon it was over, and Grace lay spent and sighing in Matt's arms.

"I love you so much, my darling Comanche, my Painted Horse," she whispered.

"Hush," he said, pulling her closer. "Lie here with me and enjoy the moment. Don't say anything you'll regret later."

I'll never regret this. As long as I live, I'll never regret this. It's the finest moment of my entire life.

But the next morning she did regret it, just as he had promised. Her wounds were a hot agony. Gray Owl's stitches tugged at her too-tight skin, and over and over she vomited into an iron kettle. Thirst drove her to the brink of insanity. Whenever she succumbed and gulped water, she became violently ill again.

Matt sat nearby, alternately sponging her forehead with a damp cloth and holding the kettle up to her mouth. "I'm sorry, Boston. I warned you this would happen. Next time, refuse the peyote. The first giddy effects aren't worth the consequences you must suffer later."

"Matt! There's a giant lizard in the corner! He has fangs three feet long! Save me. He wants to eat me! . . . . Oh, no! Look at that butterfly. It's as big as an eagle and has a tomahawk for a nose!"

"Visions, Boston. They're only visions. I warned you about them, too. The Comanches try to interpret them. They think the visions have personal meaning."

"They do!" Grace earnestly agreed. "What's Sweet Water doing here? Why did you let her in the tipi? She's brought her knife, and I can't fight her again. I'm much too weak."

"Shhhh . . . don't be afraid." He stroked her forehead, but her headache only worsened. "You're imagining things. Sweet Water's gone. Late yesterday she left the canyon."

"But where did she go? What will happen to her?"

"I don't know. She's now an outcast. She'll probably die—not from what you did to her, but from thirst, hunger, or lack of shelter. She's facing life on the plain alone, and that's what happens to women alone."

"It's all my fault!" Grace erupted into dry, heaving sobs. "If I had never come here this wouldn't have happened."

"That's true, but what happened is *her* fault. She did it all to herself. . . . Try to sleep, Boston. You'll soon feel better."

Grace finally slept, but a full week passed before she felt better She ceased seeing visions much sooner than that, but she couldn't forget how she had behaved while under the influence of the peyote. She had poured out her heart to Matt, admitted her deepest, most hidden feelings—and he hadn't reciprocated. Hadn't said he loved or adored her. Hadn't sworn to cherish her always. Hadn't agreed to marry her, or begged her to stay with him forever. She remembered every word they'd spoken; he had tried to talk her out of making love and warned her that she would regret it. . . . Was this how a man behaved when he truly loved a woman?

It couldn't be. She would always cherish the memory of their night of abandon, and never forget how passionately Matt had responded to her, but if he didn't care enough to offer his heart along with his body, then she mustn't permit intimacy between them ever again.

She didn't have to say anything to Matt; after that one wild night he resumed sleeping on his own side of the tipi, and she needed no further proof that he, too, regretted their indiscretion. Nothing except passion bound them. He didn't share the emotional bond she felt for him, and she was too proud to beg for the crumbs of affection he tossed her way when they made love. She wanted total surrender, not some pale imitation of it such as a man might give to a whirlago girl.

Summer waned and autumn arrived, bringing welcome relief from the merciless heat. Whenever they left the canyon to hunt and prepare for winter, the Comanches had to dodge soldiers. Matt rode with his brother and Quanah as the warriors desperately searched for game, particularly buffalo. They found very few, but the meat and hides they did bring back to the Palo Duro fueled small celebrations.

Grace joined the Indian women in all their activities: drying meat, scraping hides, making buffalo robes, and searching for nuts, roots, and other edibles. The women laughed at her clumsy efforts, but Grace was soon speaking sign language and even understanding a bit of Comanche.

The days flew by—busy, entertaining, and oddly satisfying. The unwritten rules Grace had always chafed against at home did not apply here, and she loved the freedom of being her own person and doing precisely what she pleased. Most of all she loved being busy for a worthy purpose—not to make money, which had brought her little personal fulfillment in her lonely everyday life back home, but to feed and clothe hungry people and guarantee their survival. Everything she had done in Boston now seemed artificial and unimportant. Here in the canyon, among the Comanches, she took great pride in mastering skills that helped people in ways she could measure. Such homely tasks as processing hides and gathering foods gave her a greater thrill than watching figures add up on paper.

Her nights were far less fulfilling than her days, but Matt was often absent, which made them bearable. When he finally appeared she was so tired from the day's labor that controlling her longing for him wasn't all that difficult. . . . And if *he* had longings, which she doubted, he managed to conceal them very well.

Each day she awoke wondering: Would this be the day Ellie would come?

As the days shortened and the nights lengthened Indians trickled into the canyon. Matt interviewed each hungry bedraggled newcomer, while Grace anxiously tried to decipher what was being said. No one had seen or heard any news about a blond white woman and her children who had been captured well over a year ago.

Grace began to lose hope. When the nights grew frosty, Gray Owl provided her and Matt with additional clothing and a single, extra-thick buffalo robe to keep them warm during the long, cold nights. Since they weren't sharing a bed Matt gave the robe to Grace, but all she could think about was how pleasant it would be to snuggle with him under the robe when the winds began to howl outside.

One morning Grace awoke to find a light powdery snow on the ground, and she didn't need Matt to tell her that winter was fast approaching.

He told her, anyway. "Boston, it's time to leave."

She nodded, and two tears rolled down her cheeks. Annoyed with herself, she quickly dashed them away. She had promised not to argue and she wouldn't, not even with silent tears. "I know. I'll pack our things."

She sensed him watching her as she stood at the entrance to the tipi gazing out at the fresh dusting of snow. It had turned the canyon into a silvery dream world, but frozen her heart.

Now that she knew how to work hides, she had deviated from the typical Comanche design for a tipi by enlarging the entrance so people could come and go out without stooping or crawling. Since she'd made the change, several of the younger wives had done the same. Everyone else clung to the old design, even though the new one was obviously better.

Still, it gave her a good feeling to know she'd been instrumental in bringing about change. It was only a small one, but it showed that the Comanches *could* change if they saw the value in it, which fed Grace's certainty that they would surely one day listen to Matt's arguments for surrender. . . . She tried to remember this as she focused on their pending departure.

Matt slid his arms around her waist and gently turned her to face him. "If they were coming, Boston, they would be here by now. We can't wait any longer."

She wouldn't look at him—didn't want him to see her tears. "I said I know. When do you want to leave?"

"The day after tomorrow. Take your time getting ready. I would like one more day to make a last plea to Quanah."

"It's just too bad we have to depart before Summer Moon's baby is born." Grace sniffled. "I'm anxious to see if she has a boy or a girl."

In the last few months Grace had made friends with Quanah Parker's wives and several others, but Stalking Wolf's shy little wife was somehow closer to her than the rest. She had even made friends with Stalking Wolf. Since he was Matt's brother she had wanted to get to know him better.

Not only did Stalking Wolf bear a strong physical resemblance to Matt, but he shared Matt's mocking sense of humor

When the two brothers were together, they continually argued, but Grace sensed a mutual affection and deep fraternal bond beneath their rivalry.

"Whatever the child is, boy or girl, I hope it's healthy and that Summer Moon endures this labor better than the last one, when she almost died," Matt responded. "I'd like to see the baby, too, but if we don't leave soon we'll be stuck here for the winter."

"This morning I'll visit her lodge and tell her we're preparing to return to Fort Sill. After that I'll go see your mother and father. Perhaps we can all share a meal together before we leave."

Gray Owl would be heartbroken, Grace knew. So would Matt's Comanche father, Night Hawk. Only recently had the old man begun to treat her and Matt with any real warmth; during their first weeks in the canyon Night Hawk had all but ignored them.

"When you go to my brother's tipi, wait before you tell them. I'll meet you there and we'll tell them together. Stalking Wolf has been hoping I'd change my mind about returning to the whites again. When he saw how well *you* were getting along with the women, including his own wife, his hopes spiraled. I kept telling him that one day soon we'd have to go, but he refused to believe me. Only a few days ago he told me he always knew I'd return to the Comanches and when I did, I'd realize all I was missing living among the whites. . . . God only knows I *do* realize it. I *have* missed being a Comanche, and savored this time among them."

"I . . . I wish we *could* stay," Grace murmured, and she wasn't saying it because she hated to give up the idea of rescuing her sister. She suddenly wished that she and Matt could somehow live in peace and plenty among the Comanches—and *truly* as man and wife. She had discovered that she didn't need a big house or a shipping business to manage in order to be happy. All she really needed was Matt's commitment to keep working

on their problems until they found a way to solve them. . . .
Most of all, she needed his love.

But she had about as much chance of marrying him as the
Comanches had of living undisturbed on their beloved high
plain. She and Matt would never be able to reconcile their differences, and the Comanches would never achieve either peace
or plenty. It wasn't meant to be. No matter how she tried to
evade the issue she was Grace Livingston, heiress to a shipping
empire, and he was Matthew Stone, otherwise known as Painted
Horse, and a Comanche at heart.

"The sooner we leave, the better," Matt said, resting his chin
on her hair. "The Comanches don't need another couple of
mouths to feed through the winter. They have barely enough
food as it is. We weren't able to find enough buffalo, and if the
winter is long and harsh the Indians won't be able to hunt in
the early spring when food supplies run low. Spring is never a
good time to hunt, anyway. A hard winter kills off the weak
animals, and the strong ones roam long distances looking for
food. This means the Comanches will probably be hungry."

"I hadn't thought of that," Grace admitted. "I thought we
had lots of food. When we were drying meat it seemed as if we
had *more* than enough."

"The stores won't last long. But after we're gone the People
will have more to share among themselves. They won't have to
worry about feeding us, along with the new arrivals."

"Guess I'd better pay my visit to Summer Moon. I want to
spend as much time with her as possible before we go, because
it's unlikely I'll ever see her again." Grace slipped away from
him. "I'll meet you there."

Picking up a water bladder, she stepped out into the snow.
Taking time to enjoy the view that would soon be lost to her
forever, she headed for the stream. Several women were there
fetching water and talking excitedly among themselves. Grace
caught only the words "Summer Moon" and "baby," and she
threw down her water container and ran for her friend's lodge,
which stood a mile or so upstream.

By the time she got there she could see that it was too late; some tragedy had already occurred. Gray Owl met her outside the entrance to the tipi and solemnly shook her head. The women standing nearby started wailing, shrieking, and pulling out handfuls of their long black hair. No one would allow Grace to enter, but she thought she heard chanting and harsh weeping within. Then she saw Matt sprinting toward the tipi, coming from the direction of their lodge.

She met him halfway. "Something terrible has just happened!" she gasped. "Summer Moon is either dying or already dead. I can't understand what the women are saying, and they won't let me go inside!"

"You're right," Matt gravely informed her. "It's Summer Moon and the baby. One of Quanah's wives just came to fetch us. During the night Summer Moon went into labor. The pains were so hard and strong that my brother refused to turn her over to the midwives. He wanted to care for her himself. His efforts did no good. The wailing means Summer Moon has died, and the baby with her."

"Your poor brother! We must go inside the tipi at once and help him prepare the bodies for burial. Everyone's tearing out their hair and . . . and . . . Matt! Look! Gray Owl has a knife and she's slashing herself with it! We must stop her!"

"Boston!" He grabbed her arm, so she couldn't run back and interfere with the old woman. "Let them be. This is how they mourn. Don't you remember? I explained it all to you that day out on the plain when I mourned the deaths of all those people whose bones we found. You can do nothing for them. Besides, you must come with me now."

"Now? But we're needed here! We *can* do something. Your brother must be comforted, and Gray Owl is bleeding. . . . They've all gone mad!" She *did* remember that day out on the plain when Matt had cut his own arm—but this was far worse. Right before her eyes these gentle, friendly people had turned into . . . howling *savages,* running around mutilating themselves.

"Boston, listen to me." He squeezed her arm to get her attention. "I have other news. Some new arrivals have just been spotted. They're descending the trail into the canyon. Among them is a small boy with blond hair and blue eyes."

Twenty-one

Grace was sure that if she lived a thousand years she would never forget her reaction to that announcement. Her mouth went dry, her legs felt wobbly, and her heart skipped several beats.

"Get hold of yourself, Boston. You look as if you're going to faint."

"I don't faint," she mumbled. "Ellie does—but not me."

"Good. There's enough happening around here without you fainting. Quanah's already gone to see who they are. The woman who spotted them said they were in bad shape."

They? How many are there? What do they look like? Maybe Ellie's one of them but is wrapped in a blanket or something, so no one can see her hair."

Matt shook his head. "No. They are all Comanches except for the little boy. He's about four or five years old."

"Jonathan is four. No, he's five now. And he has blond hair and blue eyes—like Ellie."

"It might not be Jonathon, Boston. It could be another little boy. In any case you can't go rushing up the trail to waylay them. You'll have to wait until they get down here and Quanah hears their story. Until then you can't go near them."

"Well, what do you expect me to do? You won't let me go back and help your brother, and now you're forbidding me to greet these newcomers. I can't stand around doing nothing!"

"I want you to walk calmly back to our tipi and gather together everything we can do without—extra food, blankets, cooking pots. . . . Who knows what the new arrivals will need? Probably everything. If you give them gifts, they'll be more likely to allow you to examine the boy and see if he's Jonathan."

"Why shouldn't I be allowed to examine him?"

Matt sighed, as if he thought her strange for asking. "They may not permit you to speak or get close to him. If it *is* your sister's son and they've adopted him, they won't be willing to just hand him over to you. Once Comanches adopt a child it's as binding as a blood relationship. They think the child belongs to them."

"If that child is Jonathan he belongs to Ellie—and to me. I *will* rescue him, Matt. If I have to I'll steal him."

"I understand how you feel, Boston, but you'd better understand how *they* feel. The boy may be a replacement for a son they lost in battle, or a child they never had. His Comanche mother will be as possessive about him as you are—or your sister was. Young males are particularly prized. One day they'll be warriors and hunters, defending their elderly parents and keeping everyone from starving."

Grace clenched her fists and fought to control her anger. She had thought she had put anger behind her. Even now, she wanted to weep for poor Summer Moon and her baby—but her anger at the Comanches had returned in full measure, swamping her with conflicting emotions.

"I'll go to our tipi. I'll do as you say. But you must find Quanah. I want you to be there when he asks about the boy, so you can tell me everything they say."

"I will," he agreed. "But first I'd like a few minutes alone with my brother."

She nodded and watched him head for Stalking Wolf's tipi. Then she hurried to their tipi to do as he had suggested.

In no time the newcomers—three families—were installed in their own tipis. They had brought only four skinny horses, and had no food and very little in the way of winter clothing or blankets. They gratefully accepted everything Grace gave them—but they wouldn't let her near the boy.

She could only watch him from a distance. Apparently warned to steer clear of her, he stayed close to his Comanche mother and father, who never let him out of their sight. Grace had no doubt he was Ellie's son; he resembled his mother.

Even more exciting, she had learned that Ellie herself was en route to the canyon. Quanah and Matt had questioned the boy's Comanche father, Three Toes, so-called because he'd lost two toes in the wild melee of a buffalo hunt. Three Toes had told them that a yellow-haired white woman and her young daughter were coming with another family that had fallen far behind the larger group.

The boy's white mother was ill and confined to a *travois*. Her owner, an old warrior who already had two wives and didn't need another, had foolishly refused to abandon her to die on the plain, as Three Toes had suggested. So Three Toes had left them and gone ahead to find shelter before winter trapped them all out in the open.

Matt had remembered to inquire about Ellie's infant, the child she had supposedly been carrying when she was taken captive. Three Toes claimed to know nothing about an infant; the yellow-haired woman hadn't had a baby when her owner, Buffalo Hump, had first purchased her. Three Toes and Buffalo Hump had traded many fine horses to obtain the woman and her children from a warrior named Spotted Lizard, who had died shortly thereafter in a skirmish with soldiers.

Three Toes had adopted the boy to replace a tiny son lost in an attack, and Buffalo Hump had taken the two females to help his old squaws with their labor. In the opinion of Three Toes, Buffalo Hump had been cheated in the deal, because the yellow-haired woman was sickly. Perhaps when they reached shelter in the canyon, she'd get better and could perform her duties, instead of being a burden to Buffalo Hump and his wives.

The yellow-haired woman and her daughter *had* to be Ellie and Emily; their descriptions matched exactly. The little girl even had hair the color of Grace's, just as Ellie had written her. Now all Grace had to do was wait. Quanah promised to post guards at the top of the canyon trail to watch for them, and Matt himself agreed to ride out on the plain in search of them.

Late that same afternoon the Comanches buried Summer Moon and her stillborn infant in a deep crevasse in the canyon wall. Grace attended the burial but kept her distance, for the mourning rites still shocked her and made her uncomfortable. The howling and hair tearing continued, and Gray Owl chopped off her little finger. Summer Moon had been very dear to her and was, in fact, her niece, which Grace hadn't realized.

She blocked out her own sorrow by thinking about her nephew and anticipating the possible appearance of her sister. She and Matt didn't discuss the issue of their planned departure; until Ellie appeared, they weren't going anywhere.

And she did appear—six days later, in the midst of a blizzard that roared out of nowhere to bury the canyon in wind-driven snow. Two shivering squaws dragging a loaded *travois,* one old man leading a couple of pathetic-looking horses, and a little girl stumbled off the canyon trail and headed toward the line of tipis. Despite the fierce weather Matt had gone out to look for them, and now he brought them to Grace, who was standing at the entrance to the tipi and peering into the storm in search of *him.*

She ushered them all inside the warm shelter and murmured a silent prayer of thanksgiving. While Matt fastened the flap behind the group, Grace bent over the travois and removed the blanket shielding the face of its occupant. The still, silent figure was Ellie—half-dead, lips blue with cold, and looking thirty years older than Grace remembered.

Ellie opened her eyes but didn't recognize Grace. While Grace heaped blankets and buffalo robes on her sister, Matt unwrapped the little girl, who stood quietly, barely able to move almost as unaware of her surroundings as her mother.

Only the two squaws and the old brave had enough energy and presence of mind to make themselves comfortable. Saying little, they squatted around the fire and extended their hands to it, content to let Matt and Grace care for Ellie and Emily. Whe the trio had warmed themselves they dug into the dried venison stew simmering in a pot over the banked fire. Grace served Emily two huge helpings. The girl ate hungrily, but Ellie swallowed only a little broth that Grace spooned into her mouth.

When they had all been fed they fell asleep where they sat. With so many bodies in it the tipi was crowded, and Matt offered to bed down in his brother's tipi, where only the two of them would be competing for floor space.

"No, don't go!" Grace softly begged. "I want you here in case I need you. I don't speak Comanche well enough to make myself understood to Buffalo Hump and his wives if they awaken. It will be awkward explaining who I am, and why I'm here and helping them."

"You don't have to explain anything yet. No one's going anywhere. We're all stuck here until spring. You've got the whole winter to explain things."

He was right. Still, Grace didn't want him to leave. "Please stay, Matt. I may need help with Ellie. She's so frail and ill."

"She's probably just exhausted and half frozen. Give her time to recover before you start worrying . . . but all right, I'll stay. After I see to their horses I'll be right back."

Luckily, everyone passed the night without problems. The blizzard raged for two days and two nights. On the third day after Ellie's arrival the weather cleared, the snow began to melt, and Buffalo Hump's wives set about erecting their own tipi. Some of the other Comanche women pitched in to help, Grace provided some of the items they lacked, and by nightfall they were ready to move into it.

The two wives—both large and unsmiling—came to get Ellie and little Emily, but Grace refused to relinquish them. "No!" Shaking her head emphatically she indicated with sign language that her sister and niece ought to stay in *her* tipi.

Shrugging their shoulders and nodding to each other, the two women bypassed Ellie's pallet but determinedly took hold of Emily's hands, one on each side of her. Grace stood in front of the tipi entrance, blocking it, so they couldn't exit with the little girl, who up until now had said very little and pretended not to know or remember English.

"You can't have her!" Grace announced. "She's staying here with me and her mother. I'm the child's aunt. Ellie is my sister . . . Do you understand? Oh, where's Matt? I need him to explain this to you. I knew I'd have to tell you sooner or later, and now is the time!"

Matt had left several hours ago, without telling her where he was going. Buffalo Hump had gone with him. It was Grace against the two women, who probably *did* understand but had chosen to ignore her.

"Aunt Grace?" the little girl calmly piped up, as if she'd known all along who Grace was. "You'd better let me go. I belong to them, you see. They've been kind to me, but that's because I always do what they say. If I don't, they may beat me. Our first owner beat me, Mama, and Jon almost every day. He didn't hurt Jon and me too bad, but he hurt Mama. And Mama's too sick to take a beating right now."

Stunned by the child's revelations, Grace knelt before her. "You *know* I'm your Aunt Grace? You understand what I'm saying?"

Emily nodded, her small face solemn. "You look like me Mama said you did. I knew who you were right away."

Grace studied the child's honey-colored hair, hazel eyes, per nose, high cheekbones, and stubborn chin; it was like looking at a mirror image of herself at the same age. "If you knew sweetheart, why didn't you say something? Why have you been so quiet all this time?"

Emily never so much as blinked. "It's better not to let the Comanches know what you're thinking. They can be nice, but they can also be mean. Mama and I are slaves. Jon was lucky Because he's a boy he got adopted, but I didn't."

"Jon is here," Grace told her. "Your brother's in this camp Now that the weather's improved you'll get to see him."

Emily shrugged. "He won't talk to me. Comanche boys never

talk to their sisters, and Jon's a Comanche now. He likes being a Comanche, 'cause he gets to do whatever he wants."

"I won't let them take you out of here." Grace nodded toward the two stone-faced squaws. "I'm not a slave, and I can stop them. That's why I'm here, to take you and your mother and your brother back to Boston with me."

Emily shook her head. "They'll never let us leave, Aunt Grace. Buffalo Hump says he won't trade us back to the whites, 'cause his wives are getting old and he needs us to do the work for them. But they won't mind if Mama stays with you until she gets better. . . . Do you want me to ask them if it's all right if she stays here?"

In the absence of Matt to explain things, Grace acceded. "Yes, please. Tell them your mother is too weak to be moved. She won't be able to work for weeks yet, if ever."

Emily's eyes widened. "Oh, I can't tell them that! I'll just tell them Mama should stay for a while until she's stronger."

Looking up at the two women, Emily spoke in what sounded to Grace like flawless Comanche. She was only seven now, yet she behaved as if she had skipped childhood altogether and assumed the role of an adult, a very *wise* adult.

When she finished, one of the women muttered something, and Emily beamed at Grace. "Black Antelope says Mama can stay. She's First Wife so she's the boss, and if she says so it's all right."

"Tell her thank you," Grace said. "I'll let her know when your mother is feeling better—and of course, you must come very day to visit her. That will cheer her up and help her get better quicker than anything."

Emily became sober again. "If I have time. I expect I'll be very busy doing Mama's work, as well as my own."

Not after I explain all this to Matt, Grace thought angrily. She nodded, rose, and stepped out of the way. "Go with them then, Emily, and I'll see you soon."

Matt didn't return all day, and Grace spent the time nursing Ellie, encouraging her to eat, watching over her while she slept, brushing out her hair, and helping her to relieve herself in a spare pot designated for the purpose. She tried to talk to her sister, but Ellie neither listened nor appeared aware of her presence. Her body was there, but her mind was elsewhere.

By the time Matt walked in that night, Ellie was once again sleeping—a deep, unnatural sleep that resembled a coma. Soldiers attacking the tipi would not have awakened Ellie.

"Oh, Matt!" Grace looked up from the fire she had just banked for the night. "I'm so glad you're back."

"Where is everyone?" Matt stamped slush from his feet and peered in all directions. "Where's your sister's little girl?"

"Emily had to go to the tipi Buffalo Hump's wives set up today. They wanted to take Ellie, too, but I wouldn't let them. I tried to keep Emily, but she went willingly. Not only is Emily a slave, but she thinks and acts like one! It's terrible what they've done to her—and to Ellie and Jonathan."

She shared what Emily had told her and added: "I don't care what Buffalo Hump or his wives say. He'll have to give them up, Matt. And we must think of a way to get Jonathan away from Three Toes."

Matt removed his outer garments and sat down on a buffalo robe across from Ellie's silent, blanket-heaped form. "Take it easy, Boston. It's going to be a long winter. I spent time with Quanah, Buffalo Hump, and Three Toes today, and I heard more of the story about Ellie and the children. Three Toes calls Jonathan 'Small Toad', and he and his wives dote on the boy. I don't know how we'll ever get him away from them. Emily's name is Sad Face, and even though she's just a slave Buffalo Hump is fond of her, and so are his wives. I asked Buffalo Hump if he'd be willing to trade for Ellie and Emily, and he said no. Three Toes wasn't willing to trade for Jonathan, either."

"That confirms what Emily said. But Matt, both men are going to have to change their minds. There must be something they want or need."

"Horses. They both need horses. All they had, except for the few they brought here, were killed by the soldiers."

"We could give them some of ours!"

"I've already thought of that. I've even thought of offering . . . Renegade."

"Oh, no, not your stallion! The rest, yes, including Lucy and Dunston—but not Renegade. I couldn't let you do that, Matt. He's irreplaceable. He means too much to you."

"It isn't your decision. It's mine," Matt said evenly, but his eyes held a glint of warning. "He should be enough to buy two females, whom the Comanches consider worthless, anyway, but I'm afraid he won't suffice for a son. Three Toes would want at least a hundred head of horses, among them some prime mares, *and* Renegade, before he'd be willing to cut a deal . . . and whatever Buffalo Hump demands, we haven't got it."

"Who do we know who has horses to spare?"

"My brother. And Quanah. They each have several hundred. Today I counted over fifteen hundred head in the canyon. Quanah and Stalking Wolf are the two richest, most wealthy Comanches here—rich in horses, not money."

"But . . . would they be willing to give you some? Or could offer to *buy* them?"

He gave a snort of disgust. "You still don't get it, do you, Boston? Out here, your money's worth nothing. It can't buy a thing. . . . No, I already talked to Quanah and my brother. They say they can't afford to sell any horses. However, if I were willing to stay they'd be happy to *give* me some. Not a hundred head, but maybe a dozen or so, enough to start my own herd with Renegade."

"Stay—as in don't return to Fort Sill?"

"Stay as in 'stay and fight Mackenzie.' "

"So what are we going to do?" Grace released a sigh of dejection. "Wait until spring and try to escape with all of them?"

"If I had five Renegades, one for each of us, I might consider—but otherwise, no. We wouldn't make it very far, not with two kids and a sick woman."

"Ellie will be better by then."

"You hope. She isn't just sick physically, Boston. She's sick in mind and spirit. She may never get well. According to Three Toes, Spotted Lizard used to beat her frequently—"

"I know. Emily told me that, too."

"And rape her. He sometimes lent her to his friends and relatives. Because of the abuse, she lost the baby she was carrying."

"Oh, no! Emily *didn't* tell me that. No wonder the child is called Sad Face."

"All we can do is wait for spring and hope something happens to change the situation. In the spring I could go down to Mexico and try stealing some horses myself. However, if Mackenzie makes it too hazardous for that sort of activity—and he probably will—we may be stuck here even longer. And there's always the possibility that Three Toes and Buffalo Hump won't sell no matter how many horses I offer them."

"You can't offer Renegade. I mean it, Matt."

"Don't tell me what I can and cannot do." Matt scowled at her. "For you, because you need him, I would give him up and gladly."

It was the closest he had ever come to admitting he loved her. He might be the sort of man who could *never* actually say the words, but in offering to sacrifice his prized horse for her sake he had given her a gift beyond price. It didn't change anything—didn't fix their problems—but it was the most beautiful gesture, the most precious wonderful gift, Grace had ever received from anyone.

"Oh, Matt," she murmured, unable to say more.

"If you need him he's yours, Boston."

Blinking back tears, Grace reached across the fire to link hands with him. He entwined his fingers with hers, and squeezed once—hard—then released her hand before the fire could burn either of them. Their feelings for each other resembled a fire, Grace thought. A fire that smoldered and warmed them, enabling them to survive the coldest, most bitter winter . . . but one that could also flare up at any moment to consume and destroy both of them.

* * *

In the days following, Ellie grew stronger physically, but her mind and spirit remained the same. She did everything she was told to do, but she wouldn't look at Grace or speak to her, except to nod or shake her head. She never asked about her children or expressed concern for their whereabouts. When Emily came to visit, which wasn't often or for very long, Ellie simply hugged the girl and rocked back and forth. She didn't protest when Emily gravely announced it was time for her to return to Buffalo Hump and Black Antelope.

Ellie's behavior was frustrating, especially considering that as she recuperated, she began to look more like her old self again. Her blond hair shone with golden highlights, her strawberries and cream-color returned, and she lost the deep circles under her blue eyes. She was still thin as a stick and tired easily, but Grace started to worry that Black Antelope would soon come to reclaim her. Before that happened she had to somehow reach her sister.

She chose a cold blustery day when sharp winds and stinging sleet once again confined them to the tipi By Grace's reckoning, it was near Christmas, though she hadn't been keeping precise track of the days. Grace waited until Matt departed the tipi to go see his brother, with whom he'd been spending a great deal of time lately. In bad weather there was little for the men to do but clean their weapons and talk, and Matt wanted to make sure Stalking Wolf didn't spend all his time brooding over Summer Moon.

After Matt had gone, Grace sat down next to Ellie, who was idly brushing her hair and staring into space.

"Ellie, please listen to me. We really must talk. You know that I'm your sister, don't you? And that I've come here to take you, Emily, and Jonathan back home with me?"

As if she hadn't heard, Ellie kept brushing her hair. Grace cupped Ellie's chin in her hand and gently turned her sister's face in her direction. "Ellie, look at me."

Ellie dropped the brush and hid her face in her palms. When Grace tried to pry her hands away, she shook her head violently. "No! Don't make me look at you!"

They were the first words she had uttered since her arrival. "Why not, Ellie? Are you ashamed because of what the Indians have done to you? If you are, you shouldn't be. None of what happened was your fault. You didn't deserve any of it. When I take you away from here, I won't let anyone hurt you ever again. I promise."

"No," Ellie whispered. "Don't take me away. I don't want to leave the Comanches. They'll all be dead soon, anyhow, and so will I. It will be better that way."

"Ellie, don't say such things!" Grace seized her sister's hands. They were red, rough, and chapped, both from the work she'd been forced to do and from the cold she had endured. Once Ellie's hands had been soft, white, and graceful; they had never performed more taxing chores than arranging flowers or pouring tea.

"You don't really want to die, Ellie. I know you don't."

"Grace, go home," Ellie said, tossing her head so that her hair hid her face. "Leave us alone. The Comanches will never give up Jonathan or Emily, and I won't go home without them. Besides, there's nothing for me in Boston. I'd never be able to hold my head up among my old friends."

"Nonsense. Ellie, I'm going to find a way to buy you from Buffalo Hump—and Emily and Jonathan, too."

"I don't want you to buy us! Can't you understand? We're all dead. We died with William. These . . . these empty husks that somehow managed to survive aren't *us*."

"But you can all be yourselves again! Once I get you away from the Comanches, you'll forget . . ."

"I'll *never* forget! And neither will Emily and Jonathan."

"They're young, and they *will* forget eventually. You aren't being fair to them. If you won't think of yourself, think of them Do you want Emily to grow up and be treated the same way you were? As a slave, what else can she expect?"

This finally roused Ellie. She lifted her head, brushed the shiny, blond hair away from her face, and stared at Grace with such horror in her eyes that Grace was sorry she had mentioned it. "Then take Emily! I'll stay here with Jonathan. They'll never let him go—not without bloodshed. But Emily's loss won't matter as much. Buffalo Hump's too old to ride the warpath to reclaim her. She might have a chance."

"Ellie, dear . . . let me try to save all three of you."

"No, Grace, no!" Ellie hiccupped on a sob. "If you can save Emily, that will give me reason enough to keep living. If Emily is safe I won't mind so much what's happened to me."

Ellie wept then—great wracking sobs. Grace feared she'd become ill all over again. Nothing she said could calm her. Ellie wept until she exhausted herself, and after that she finally slept.

That night, when Matt returned, Grace explained the situation. "She doesn't want to leave the Comanches. She only wants Emily to go. I can't accept that, Matt, but I don't know how to change her mind."

He gave her a quick hug, then released her. "You have all winter to work on it—and you'll have to work on it, because I have some good news."

Grace couldn't imagine what good news he could possibly have on this bleak winter night. Her sister's despair was as catching as cholera. "What?" she asked warily.

"My brother has agreed to a plan I think might work. If it does we'll have Ellie, at least, and maybe even Emily. Then all we'll have to worry about is convincing Ellie to go and figuring out a way to kidnap Jonathan when we're ready to leave here in the spring. Maybe Stalking Wolf can help with that, too."

"Oh Matt! Do you mean it? What's the plan? Tell me. I can't wait to hear it."

Matt nodded at Ellie. "I don't want her to know about it," he whispered. "Not if she isn't ready to cooperate."

"She won't hear you. You don't have to worry. She cried herself to sleep, and now she's down for the night."

"All right, it's this. Stalking Wolf will pretend to court Ellie on the grounds that he needs a new wife. He'll offer Buffalo Hump some prime horses for her, but he'll bargain hard, as any prospective husband would. Buffalo Hump will eventually agree, because he hasn't much choice. Those two horses he brought with him won't last the winter. The beauty of the scheme is that the old man can't be nearly as greedy with Stalking Wolf as he'd be with us. Only Quanah commands more respect than my brother. And Stalking Wolf will insist on taking Emily, too, as part of the bargain. Once a bargain is struck, my brother will have the right to do anything he wants with his purchases, and he'll turn them over to us, of course."

"But what does your brother expect in exchange for all this? Surely, he expects something. He'll be losing many fine horses."

"For one thing, he wants all the money we brought with us so he can purchase more guns and ammunition in the spring from the Comancheros—the Mexican gunrunners. Seems your money may prove to be useful after all, Boston."

"That's it? That's all he wants—money?"

Matt hesitated, and she knew there was more. "What is it? What more does he want?" she prompted.

He shrugged and looked away. "He wants Renegade."

Before she could react, his green-eyed glance nailed her. "He wants to give the stallion to Quanah, in settlement of an old debt. . . . I don't mind so much if Quanah has him! Renegade is a fitting mount for the last great war chief of the Comanches. First, my brother intends to breed his best remaining mares to him, to replace what he's losing."

"It's not right," she whispered. "It's just not right you have to give him up."

His face hardened. "Are you refusing to accept the only thing of value I have to offer you?"

She swallowed hard and shook her head. What choice did she have? She *had* to accept the sacrifice of Renegade.

Dazzled by his generosity, she threw her arms around him

"Matt, I'll make it up to you! I swear. Some way I'll make it up to you."

Gently but firmly, he removed her arms from around his neck. "Not *this* way, Boston. Much as I enjoy our lovemaking, I didn't do this to buy your services."

"I know you didn't! And I didn't mean—"

"Don't sell yourself so cheaply! And if you *aren't* selling yourself, what do you want with a man who doesn't even own a good horse anymore? I did it for *you,* Boston, just for you . . . and I don't want to hear another word about it."

He grabbed his outer garments and started to tug them back on again.

"Where are you g-going?" she quavered, near tears.

"To spend the night with my brother."

"B-but why?"

"To escape temptation, both yours and mine. So you won't offer yourself in payment for my horse, and I won't accept the offer."

"But I said I didn't mean—"

"You can't stand the idea of being the needy one, *can* you? You still think you have to buy everything—and pay for it one way or another."

"That's not true! But what about you? You're every bit as bad—no, worse—than I am. You won't accept help, money, or any sort of payment, either, even when you've earned it. You'd rather be poor and proud than owe a debt to someone."

"That's true," he agreed. "It's the Comanche way to owe debts to no man—or woman."

"But even Comanches are willing to negotiate!"

"That's not what I want between *us,* Boston."

"Then what do you want?"

He paused a moment, considering. "Your respect, not just your gratitude. And how can you respect a man who has absolutely nothing to offer you?"

If he thought he had *nothing* to offer her, they were farther apart than she had thought. She had no answer to the question, at least none he would accept. For all his fierce pride, he didn't respect himself. He placed more value on his horse than he did on his ability to provide love, loyalty, and a haven from the world's danger and ugliness. How could she convince him he was wrong, that he himself—no matter how poor he might be— was all she would ever want or need?

Twenty-two

The very next day Matt invited Stalking Wolf to the tipi to share their meal. Comanches didn't observe regular mealtimes, but simply ate when they were hungry, so Grace kept food hot all afternoon in anticipation of Stalking Wolf's arrival. She understood that the invitation was the first step in Matt's plan for his brother to court Ellie; a man could hardly declare his interest in a woman if he had never laid eyes on her.

Early in the evening Matt and Stalking Wolf finally appeared. From the moment Stalking Wolf set foot inside the tipi and caught sight of Ellie kneeling by the fire and stirring the contents of the cook pot, Grace knew that he meant to court her sister in earnest.

For years, as she and Ellie grew up together, Grace had watched young men take one look at Ellie's fragile blond beauty and fall hopelessly in love. She had seen it happen too often in the past, including with William, to be mistaken in what she saw now.

Ellie's head was bent and her fine hair hid her features, but her hair alone made Stalking Wolf's eyes widen and his nostrils flare, as if he scented a rare fragrance. When Ellie gazed up at the tall muscular Indian, his eyes widened even more, and he expelled a long sigh.

Looking puzzled and surprised at his brother's reaction, Matt exchanged glances with Grace. It wasn't the right moment to tell him that Stalking Wolf had just lost his heart; Matt wouldn't believe it, anyway. Grace doubted he could imagine falling in love in a heartbeat; Matt was the sort to deny his feelings forever, especially if they inconvenienced him or didn't fit into his plans.

But Stalking Wolf was different. The fierce warrior melted on the spot, and a lovesick lamb took his place. Stalking Wolf ate, conversed with Matt if not with Grace, and lazed beside the fire for hours after he should have departed for the night, and in all that time never once took his gaze from Ellie.

If Ellie noticed him at all Grace couldn't catch her sister at it. Ellie remained locked in her own little world—present in the flesh, but absent in the mind. Twice during the long evening Stalking Wolf leaned over and lifted a strand of Ellie's blond hair. Rubbing it between two fingers, he studied it intently, then gently lay it on Ellie's breast. Once, and once only, Ellie returned his intense regard, as if wondering who he was and where he had come from.

Stalking Wolf seized the moment to say something to her but Ellie never responded. Grace was dying to ask Matt to translate, but she couldn't until Stalking Wolf had left, and when he finally did leave Matt went with him.

Just before he stepped out into the cold and followed his "brother," she touched his sleeve. "Matt? Are you ever going to sleep here again? You've nothing to fear from me. I won't bother you in any way."

His old grin flashed, and her heart leapt. "That's good to know. Maybe I'll stay tomorrow night. But tonight I want to hear what my brother thought of your sister. Before we came he said it might be hard for him to pretend to court her if he found her ugly and unappealing."

Good heavens, was he blind? Couldn't he see for himself what his brother thought of Ellie?

"Be sure and tell me what he says," Grace responded, tongue firmly in cheek.

"I will. See you tomorrow."

The next day Matt allowed as how his brother thought Ellie

was rather pretty—for a white woman. Grace wasn't fooled, especially when Stalking Wolf began showing up, on the pretext of visiting Matt but actually to stare at Ellie and try to entice her into conversation.

One day well into the new year, Grace returned from fetching water to hear Ellie speaking softly in Comanche, and a man's voice eagerly responding. Matt had gone to see Quanah, and Grace had left Ellie alone to straighten up the tipi. Not wanting to disturb the exchange, Grace paid a visit to Gray Owl instead. When she finally returned to the tipi, she found Ellie alone but quietly humming to herself and looking happier than she had since her arrival.

Another week slid by, during which Grace managed to speak with Jonathan. She surprised the boy alone near the stream, where the children were playing games on the ice. Someone— probably his Comanche mother—had darkened his hair and skin, but his bright blue eyes made him stand out like a blue jay among starlings.

"Jonathan?" Grace watched the boy closely to gauge his reaction to hearing his real name.

"I'm not Jonathan," he replied in English, his face mutinous. "My name is Small Toad."

He repeated the name in Comanche, but now that Grace knew he still remembered English, she intended to use only his real name. "Your mother misses you, Jon. You must come see her— and your sister. Emily stops by almost every day. Do you know where I live? I'd be happy to show you."

"I know where you live! But I'm not going to visit you. I'm Comanche now. I have a new mother."

Every word stung, but Grace doggedly persisted. "You can still be Comanche and come see your white mother. It's not wrong to love the woman who bore you, Jon. You were her little baby once, and she will always love you."

"I don't want to see her!" he shouted. Tears trembled on the tips of his long blond lashes. His Comanche mother had forgotten to darken his lashes and eyebrows.

Just then one of his friends called to him and he ran off, leaving Grace to gaze after him with all the hurt and longing Ellie must feel but didn't dare show.

Another week passed, and Black Antelope came to claim Ellie. Grace argued that her sister wasn't strong enough to work yet, but not until she fetched Matt and he stated her case did Black Antelope relent—and only afterward did Grace discover *why* she had relented.

"I told her she was welcome to take Ellie, but we wanted our food supplies back—the stuff you gave her when they first arrived here," Matt said. "I reminded her that we've been feeding Ellie all this time as a favor, and our own supplies are running low. So now we'd like some back to replace what we've given them and their slaves. Black Antelope then began to argue that Ellie should pay for her own food through her labor. . . . Therefore, we get to keep her 'til spring."

"You are exceptionally devious!" Grace declared. "I never would have thought of that."

"You don't know the half of it. She's also sending Emily over every day to help prepare our meals, so that they no longer owe us anything for the supplies we gave them. I grudgingly agreed to accept Emily's labor in exchange for the items."

"Oh, that's wonderful! It means Emily will get to eat with us. I've been worried about her, Matt. She works so hard for a little girl, and she's so thin."

Matt grimly nodded. "The hard months still lie ahead, Boston. You're wise to worry. Stalking Wolf has promised to bring over Summer Moon's cache of food, and with the two of us hunting whenever possible we should manage. . . . But I'm worried about some of the others, especially the newcomers."

His words frightened Grace, and she took extra care to make their food supplies stretch. Stalking Wolf gave them everything he had, and thereafter took his meals with them, openly wooing Ellie. When the time came, Grace wondered, would Stalking Wolf refuse to let her sister go?

Matt scoffed at the idea, claiming that his brother relished

the thought of presenting Renegade to Quanah, because Quanah
had once saved his life.

"You know how Comanches hate debts," he said to reassure
her. She knew how *he* hated debts, but she wasn't so sure about
his brother.

The rest of January and most of February were unusually
miserable, with bitter cold, deep snow, and high winds. Hunting
was impossible, and supplies ran low for everyone. It hurt Grace
to be so stingy, but she hoarded every single mouthful of food,
knowing that if she didn't she wouldn't be able to feed the
people depending on her. She thought longingly of all the abundance she had always taken for granted in Boston, and vowed
to be more charitable to those in need in the future.

One day Jonathan showed up at their tipi, his teeth chattering
from the cold and his thin limbs trembling. In a belligerent
manner he informed Matt that his Comanche mother had urged
him to come and pay his respects to his white mother. Matt
invited him to come inside, warm himself, and share the meal
Grace and Ellie were serving.

The boy accepted and ate as if he were starving, which was
entirely possible. Afterward, he consented to sit near Ellie and
Emily. As was proper, both had been ignoring him, but now
Ellie uttered a strangled cry and drew the child into her arms.
For a moment Jonathan resisted. Then he hugged his mother
fiercely and collapsed sobbing on her bosom. Emily threw her
arms around her mother and her brother and joined in the weeping. Everyone else looked away—even Stalking Wolf, who
seemed greatly embarrassed by the display of emotion.

When the time came for Jonathan to leave, Matt invited him
to return the next day or any other time he chose. Jon promised
that he would, but added almost guiltily: "Next time, I won't
eat anything."

"Of course you will! Why shouldn't you? If you eat here
instead of at your own tipi, your Comanche parents won't have
to struggle to feed you."

The logic of this apparently appealed to Jonathan, for after that he came at least once daily. Ellie, reunited with her children and basking in Stalking Wolf's attention, began taking more interest in her surroundings.

The rest of the camp suffered. Old people sickened and began to die off, as did babies and children. In March the weather improved, but no game could be found. Gray Owl and Night Hawk quit eating. They gave away all their food, lay down in their tipi, and refused to speak to anyone.

Grace took them hot broth, but they refused to touch it. Gray Owl shook her head and indicated that Grace should offer the food to someone with children. Grace pleaded with Matt to talk to the old couple; after all, they were his Comanche parents.

"It's the Comanche way," he told Grace. "They won't listen to me, or anybody. They've made up their minds to die. From now on only those with a good chance of surviving will accept food. The old ones will starve themselves. Nursing babies and children too small to handle pemmican stand no chance."

Soon after, death came for Gray Owl and Night Hawk. Beset by their own problems, the People barely mourned them. They shoved their frozen bodies into a crevasse, wailed a couple of times, and returned to their warm tipis.

Eventually Grace herself had nothing left but pemmican. The nuts, seeds, dried berries, flour, and other items were all gone. She steeped the leathery meat in melted snow water and boiled it to make it stretch. She herself ate sparingly, giving the watered-down fare to Ellie and the children and praying their supplies would last until Matt and Stalking Wolf found game.

March brought ice storms, and between the storms came heavy rains and sleet. Periods of beautiful weather followed, but sunshine, blue skies, and warming temperatures only mocked the inhabitants of the canyon, for game still eluded the hunters. An occasional rabbit or even an antelope didn't go far to ease the general hunger. After feeding their own families the hunters shared their largesse, but still it was a rare day when stomachs didn't growl with hunger. At least there were fewer burials the canyon crevasses.

Eventually the hungry Comanches had to consider eating the few horses still remaining in the Palo Duro. During a lull between winter storms, most of the animals had been led up the trail and turned out on the plain to fend for themselves through the remainder of winter. Because of the dwindling grass, only the best breeding stock and the war ponies and buffalo runners were kept below. To a Comanche, slaughtering horses was unthinkable; the animals were the lifeblood of the tribe. Without them warriors couldn't hunt, flee from their enemies, or round up other horses. A man would sooner lose his wife, child, or parent than his best buffalo runner.

But now, in the face of their need, the Comanches argued among themselves over which horses should be sacrificed. On the day the men went out to choose a victim the air was cold, but the sun was shining. The women decided to climb the canyon trail, spread out on the plain, and see if they could find any edible roots or new tubers.

Grace didn't know what she'd be looking for, so she stayed behind with Ellie. She and Ellie went to the stream to chip away the melting ice and fetch fresh water. The spot they chose was near the canyon trail. Grace suddenly glanced up and spotted a stranger making the descent into the canyon. Several women, chattering excitedly, accompanied him, and Grace motioned for Ellie to stop what she was doing and go with her to see who the young man was.

As the crowd trooped down into the canyon, the women shouted: *"Eeshatai! Eeshatai!"*

Grace turned to her sister. "Ellie, what does it mean? What are they saying?"

Ellie frowned. *"Eeshatai* has come. His name means Coyote Droppings, and I have heard of him. All the Comanches know him. He is a great leader and . . . and a prophet who can foretell the future."

"He is? What has he done to merit such adulation? The women are dancing around him as if he's a god. I thought Quanah was the band's leader."

"Quanah is the leader of the *Kwerharrehnuh,* the People of the Antelope. But *Eeshatai* is revered among *all* Indians. He once told of a comet's passing and claimed it would be followed by a period of drought. This happened. And Buffalo Hump says he saw him belch forth a wagonload of cartridges. It is said he can raise the dead and has performed many other miracles."

"Well, we have plenty of dead for him to raise," Grace muttered. "He could start with . . ." She was about to say Summer Moon, and bit her tongue. "Gray Owl or Night Hawk," she finished instead.

"Don't laugh, Grace. It could be possible. Stalking Wolf has told me about him and claims he has strong *puha,* or medicine. He has been hoping *Eeshatai* would come to us and tell us what we must do to defeat Mackenzie."

"We?" Grace stared at her sister. "Ellie, *we* want Mackenzie to defeat the Comanches. *After* we leave here, of course, and without bloodshed, if possible. Actually, we want the Comanches to surrender and agree to live on reservations, instead of attacking and enslaving whites"

"No . . ." Ellie shook her head. "That's what *you* want, Grace. The rest of us . . ." She let the sentence trail off, turned, and walked away from Grace.

Grace stalked after her sister. "Ellie! What are you talking about? You and Emily are slaves, and your son will grow up to be a Comanche warrior! In the spring, which is practically here, you're supposed to go back to Buffalo Hump. Is that what you want?"

Ellie paused, then faced her again, displaying a vibrancy and sense of purpose she had never yet demonstrated. "No, I want to be Stalking Wolf's wife. And that's what *he* wants. He says he will buy me and Emily from Buffalo Hump. He means to talk to him soon and offer him many horses, but first he must explain to Matt that he no longer wishes to have Matt's stallion or your money. He will find another way to repay Quanah for saving his life. He loves me, Grace, and I love him!"

"Love! Is that what you call it? He lusts after your blon

hair, Ellie. That's all he feels for you. If he really cared about you he would accompany us when we return to Fort Sill, marry you, and live as a white man. He wouldn't keep you among the Comanches to starve or to die fighting the soldiers."

"You can't manage my life for me, Grace! I'm grateful for all you've done, but I am no longer the foolish naive girl you knew back in Boston. I've told you I don't want to return there. I want to stay here. And maybe *Eeshatai* will make that possible. I've been given a second chance, Grace, to find happiness with a man I can love and respect. I will *not* let you ruin it for me!"

"Ellie . . ." Grace started to say, but she never had a chance to finish. A crowd of screaming, shouting, waving Comanches engulfed them, all hollering the name *"Eeshatai!"* and behaving as if the Great Spirit Himself had suddenly appeared in their midst.

Several days passed before Grace found an opportunity to tell Matt what her sister had said. For three days the Comanches feasted on horsemeat, drank horse blood, and smeared it on themselves and their children in an orgy of religious fervor. They danced unceasingly, and many sought visions through peyote. Every man, woman, and child vowed to grow strong again and defeat the white man.

Eeshatai's preaching whipped the despairing Indians into a frenzy, evoking memories of past victories and promises of future ones. The purpose of the young prophet's visit was to invite Quanah's band to meet him north of the Red River in May, where he intended to unite all the remnants of the once mighty bands of the Comanches with the remnants of the Kiowa, Cheyenne, and Arapaho.

All the Comanches had to do to attain victory over Mackenzie was perform the sacred sun dance, as the other plains tribes did, *Eeshatai* explained. They need not pierce their breast tendons and hang from poles like the others, but they must embrace the rest of the sacred rituals, and they would then become invincible to bullets.

On the fourth night of the orgy Matt stood up in council to refute these notions, but even his brother and Quanah shouted him down. Everyone wanted desperately to believe that *Eeshatai* had been sent to them by the Great Spirit to restore their past grandeur. There was no reasoning with any of them.

Matt left the assembly in disgust, and Grace followed him back to their tipi. After the hubbub of the fire, speeches, and dancing, the tipi's quiet was a welcome relief and gave Grace a chance to broach another unpleasant topic.

"Matt, I'm so sorry they wouldn't listen to you. I truly sympathize with your disappointment. I, too, am disappointed, not only in the Comanches but in my sister."

"I already know what you're going to tell me," Matt said, looking down at her in the pale, flickering light of the waning cook fire. "Stalking Wolf told me today. Tomorrow he's going to visit Buffalo Hump and offer him horses for Ellie and Emily. He wants to move both of them into his tipi as soon as possible."

"He's very confident Buffalo Hump will accept, isn't he?"

"The old man will have to. The band has just agreed to meet *Eeshatai* at the Red River in May. Unless he and his wives want to walk, they'll need horses."

"What are we going to do, Matt? We've come all this way and endured so much to rescue my foolish sister and her children—and now, none of them want to be rescued!"

Matt slid his arms around her waist and drew her to him. She rested her cheek against the curve of his throat and shamefully relished his nearness. "I never thought it would end this way. I'm happy you get to keep Renegade, of course, but . . ."

"I'm not keeping Renegade."

"What?" She raised her head to look at him. "But why not? Your brother reneged on his end of the bargain."

Matt sighed and passed a hand across his face. "It's . . . complicated. I'm not sure myself why I'm doing it, but earlier today, after I spoke to my brother, I presented the horse to Quanah.

It's right he should have him. If he rides a Medicine Hat Paint stallion, maybe bullets *won't* kill him, as the Comanches believe."

"But *you* don't believe it! You just argued against *Eeshatai's* ridiculous assertions."

"That's true. I don't. But I can't blame the Comanches for wanting to follow this . . . this fake. They're going to need all the *puha* they can get to avoid being slaughtered this coming season, especially Quanah. I think I should go with them to the Red River, Boston. If I keep arguing they might come to their senses. Maybe something will happen to prove to them that Coyote Droppings is a fraud and no better than his ugly name. . . . The question is, what will *you* do? . . . . If we leave now, I could take you back to Fort Sill and still make it to the Red River in May."

"Do you think I would let you get rid of me so you can continue this battle alone? No, Matt, I'm staying. If I go now I'll never see Ellie and the children again. As long as they're alive I still have a chance of saving them."

Matt pulled her to him. "We're a pair, aren't we? That's exactly how I feel about my brother and Quanah . . . and the rest of the Comanches." He nuzzled her hair and sighed. "As long as they live, I can't quit caring and just walk away from them."

Intoxicated by the warmth, scent, and feel of him, Grace pressed her body against his. Matt growled low in his throat and bent his head to kiss her. The kiss awoke all the passion they had so long been denying themselves.

When it ended, he murmured raggedly: "Boston, we shouldn't be doing this."

"No," she agreed. "We shouldn't."

She took his hand and placed it on her breast. "One more time, Matt. Just one more time."

His answer was to pull her down to the buffalo robe with him.

* * *

May came too soon, and the People journeyed to the Red
River to meet *Eeshatai* and the other Indians. Each band set up
their tipis on their own patch of ground. The *Yampahreekuh*
from the Arkansas came, as did the *Kuhtsoo-ehkuh,* and the
Tahneemuh. These were all bands of the *Nermernuh,* or Comanche peoples, but the other tribes *Eeshatai* had promised,
the Kiowa, Cheyenne, and Arapaho, also appeared. Only one
small band of Comanches, the *Pehnahterkuh,* refused to attend.

The *Pehnahterkuh* crossed the Red River and fled southward,
sending word that there were too many Texans to fight and no
magic could defeat the white men, not even *Eeshatai's.* Those
at the river scoffed at them and called them cowards, then made
ready to conduct the sacred rituals.

For three days and nights the People danced to drums, rattles,
and eagle bone whistles. The prairie rang with their songs and
boasts. The drums pounded far into the night and no one slept,
including Grace. She and Matt alone of all the hundreds gathered at the river did not join in the dancing and singing. Grace
was amazed to see Ellie, now Stalking Wolf's wife, swaying
and stomping in the wild throng. Holding hands with her children, one on either side, Ellie danced as if possessed by the
spirits, but by then all of the Indians were possessed.

On the fourth day the leaders sat in council while the warrior
societies continued the festivities. Criers rode through the
lodges, calling each band to stand before their tipis. Each band
chanted their own songs and performed their own dances. While
they were thus occupied, the leaders unanimously chose Quanah
Parker to be the war chief who would lead them against the
whites. The prestigious warriors—Lone Wolf and Woman
Heart of the Kiowas, and Stone Calf and White Shield of the
southern Cheyenne—agreed to follow him, and they voted to
deliver the first blow of their new alliance to the hated buffalo
hunters.

The festivities concluded with one more speech from
Eeshatai; he pompously declared that the Great Spirit approved
of the rituals performed over the last several days, and all the

warriors were now invincible to bullets. They could not fail to annihilate the whites and drive them forever from Indian lands. Soon, he promised, the buffalo would return, and all would be as it had once been; the Indians alone would rule the plains.

Once again Matt passionately refuted this logic, urging the Indians to send only one warrior against the buffalo hunters. If the whites killed him, the Indians would then see for themselves that the prophet's magic was false and none of them were safe from bullets. To Grace's horror, Matt volunteered to be the sacrificial warrior. He cited the many occasions when he had challenged the hunters in the past. This time, he offered to approach them openly and give them a chance to grab their rifles and shoot him.

Because he was the famed Painted Horse and was offering to die for them, no one killed him on the spot. They had all heard of his courage and didn't doubt his loyalty. But they refused to allow him to represent them. He was an unbeliever and a white man; therefore, the test would not be a true one.

No one else volunteered for the job, so that night the Indians made plans to attack a rendezvous point often used by the buffalo hunters. They selected the old Bent Fort at a place called Adobe Walls near the Canadian River in the Texas Panhandle.

Later that night Matt explained it all to Grace. "There will be seven hundred warriors against—I don't know—maybe thirty or forty buffalo hunters. No one knows for sure how many will be there near the end of June, the time they've set for the attack. I have got to go with them, Boston. The hunters may be few in number, but they'll be armed with Sharps buffalo guns, which very few Indians have. When the Comanches witness their comrades being routed by a much smaller force, they may be willing to listen to me at long last."

"Oh, Matt, I'm so afraid for you!" Grace flung her arms round him and hugged him, worried he might never return. "Who will you ride—Dunston? You need a good horse under you for such a venture. Will Dunston be fast enough?"

"Quanah's already told me to take Renegade. He prefers to

ride into battle on a horse with whom he's more familiar. He's not had time to get accustomed to Renegade, and other than you no one else has ridden him but me. Also, since I'm vulnerable to bullets because I don't believe in *Eeshatai's* magic, he thinks I need Renegade's *puha* to keep me safe."

"Faulty or not, I'm glad for his reasoning. I won't be so afraid if I know you're on Renegade."

"Don't tell me you now embrace Comanche superstitions! Renegade can't keep bullets from killing me any more than *Eeshatai's* rituals can save Quanah or my brother."

She hugged him tightly. "I don't care! I trust him to get you out of there safely and bring you back to me."

"Don't get too used to this, Boston," he warned, giving her a squeeze and kissing her temple. "What's between us can't last. You know that as well as I do."

"Yes, I know it," she agreed, fiercely clinging to him. If he didn't ask her to marry him when this was all over, she'd have no choice but to go back east to take up a life that no longer had any meaning for her. But while she still could, she'd give him anything—anything at all.

"Boston, don't hang on me like this," he said gently, setting her aside. "Don't make it any harder for us than it already is."

"But it doesn't have to be so hard!"

"Yes, it does! I don't fancy seeing you half-starved for the rest of your life, living with an outcast and trying to scratch out a living on the edges of Comancheria. Already, you're looking tired and worn—older than when you first came here. You belong in silks and satins, not buckskins, presiding over a lace draped table laden with delicacies—"

"I *am* older," she cut in. "I'm over a year older than when I first arrived. Age has a way of creeping up on a person, no matter where they live."

"But you'll live a hell of a lot longer if you don't make your home in Indian Territory."

But would it be living? Not without Matt. It would only be existing.

"I hope I survive long enough to see you change your mind," she told him.

"You won't," he insisted. "Not if you live another hundred years."

Stepping past her he began assembling his things for the return trip to the Palo Duro. The women and children were expected to wait out the warriors' attack on the Adobe Walls in the safety of the canyon.

Twenty-three

On the twenty-seventh of June Matt awaited the dawn in company with seven hundred mounted Indians, all of them painted, armed to the teeth, and eager to attack the old fort at Adobe Walls. On his right side Quanah sat patiently aboard his customary war pony, a cream-splashed brown gelding. On his left his brother radiated excitement, and could barely keep his piebald mare in check.

Glancing down the line of Indians, ghostly figures in the gray pre-dawn light, Matt was impressed. He thought it unlikely that the plains would ever again witness a gathering of so many different tribes in their distinctive war dress. For the most part the Comanches sported their usual buffalo-horn headpieces, but some had adopted the long, trailing, feathered war bonnets of the Cheyenne, who rode beside them.

Each band within a particular tribe had painted themselves and their horses in the colors and designs that identified them to savvy observers. The Indians had spread out to form a single line that was fast approaching a ridge overlooking the fort, from which vantage point the warriors hoped to intimidate and frighten their victims. Any buffalo hunter chancing to look up and see them would supposedly be overcome with fear and rendered helpless to defend himself or sound the alarm.

This weakening of the enemy's courage was an important part of Indian strategy; Matt had often seen it work. In his opinion no army composed of white, Negro, or Mexican soldier could begin to compare with the spectacle the Indians now presented. Even the horses—trailing feathers and emblazoned in exotic colors and designs—knew they were special; they arched their necks proudly and pranced in place, their quivering muscles revealing their eagerness to charge.

The plan called for the Indians to stop when they reached the top of the ridge and wait for Quanah's signal to gallop down the incline at breakneck speed. As they neared their destination Matt leaned over and said to his brother: "May the Great Spirit watch over you and keep you safe this day, Stalking Wolf."

He didn't know why he said it except that he had an uneasy feeling, and wanted to let his brother know he loved him even though he didn't approve of what they were about to do.

"No harm will come to me," Stalking Wolf asserted with typical arrogance. *"Eeshatai's* magic has made me invincible. I will prove it to you, my brother. This day not one of us will fall, nor will our horses. But before the sun sets every buffalo hunter in this place will die."

There was no time for Matt to respond, for they suddenly arrived at the top of the ridge. Quanah halted and held up one hand. Before he could drop it, a shout of alarm went up from the cluster of buildings known as the old Bent Fort.

The brightening light revealed two men outside the fort, moving among wagons half-loaded with hides and the paraphernalia of the buffalo hunters' trade. Hollering for help, the men raced for cover. Some of the Indians grinned, their painted faces grotesque in their amusement, but none of them moved. True to their agreement, they waited for Quanah to launch the attack.

Why is he hesitating? Matt wondered. *Doesn't he realize he's only giving the hunters a chance to reach their big guns?*

Quanah raised his hand higher. In the tense, expectant silence, Matt could almost hear the warriors' hearts beating with excitement. Just as the sun's gold rays pierced the eastern sky, Quanah dropped his hand, and the Indians tore down the ridge.

Whooping and hollering, they descended on the fort. Before they reached it the guns sounded, and two Cheyennes and a

Comanche toppled and fell. A moment later the guns sounded again, and Stalking Wolf and Quanah went down. In the commotion of the charge, Matt couldn't see what had happened to his brother. Quanah's horse had been shot out from under him, and he was crawling for cover beneath a wagon.

Startled by the unexpected casualties, the wave of charging Indians split into two columns and rode around the walls and wagons. To Matt, dodging bullets and frantically trying to locate his brother in the mass of churning animals, men, and wagons, it seemed a big mistake. The Indians should have pressed home the charge—engaging the whites in hand-to-hand combat, where their greater numbers guaranteed victory.

Instead, after splitting the charge the Indians doubled back toward the ridge to regroup. In the smoky hail of gunfire from the fort Matt couldn't see clearly, and Renegade nearly trampled his brother. Stalking Wolf was on his knees, a torn, bleeding arm dangling loosely at his side. As Matt skidded to a stop in front of him, he reached up with his free hand.

Matt turned Renegade sideways, leaned down, hooked an arm around Stalking Wolf's waist, and hoisted him onto the stallion's back behind him. The maneuver was a familiar one for picking up fallen comrades during an attack or buffalo hunt, but the relentless gunfire made it doubly dangerous. Crouching low over Renegade's withers, Matt wheeled the stallion around and raced for the ridge, with Stalking Wolf clinging like a leech to his back. Two solid thuds reverberated through his brother's body. As Matt reached the safety of the ridge, Stalking Wolf lost his grip and fell, landing almost at the feet of *Eeshatai's* horse.

The prophet had not joined the attack. He sat naked in yellow war paint on his pony on the ridge, watching from a safe distance. As Matt slid down to tend his brother the demoralized Indians converged on the man who had promised they would be invincible.

A Cheyenne warrior rode up, trembling with fury. "My son is dead! And no one can find our war chief. Your magic is false!"

"My magic is *not* false," *Eeshatai* insisted. "One of you

killed a skunk yesterday and displeased the spirits. That's why they are not protecting you."

"Then if the spirits are displeased with us, *you* must go down to retrieve the body of my son. Look for Quanah while you are at it. He, too, must be dead by now."

"Quit arguing, and take cover!" Matt snapped. "You're still in range of their guns."

No sooner had he spoken when a ball knocked a nearby warrior off his horse, instantly killing him. The Cheyenne who'd challenged *Eeshatai* raised his quirt and struck a resounding blow across *Eeshatai's* face.

Eeshatai howled in pain and outrage. "The Cheyenne are to blame for this disaster!" he screamed. "Not me!"

"It's not yet a complete disaster," Matt said, lifting his brother and placing him on Renegade. "You could still win the day," he told the ring of angry warriors now surrounding him and the prophet. Fury over his brother's wounds made him goad the Indians, in the hope they would overwhelm the hunters. "Today, you outnumber them. Tomorrow, you won't. Go back down there and kill them while you can, because the next time there will only be more of them."

"This was all a mistake—he lied to us! He has no *puha!*" the Cheyenne shouted. "We must flee before we all die!"

Ignoring the dead and dying on the field below, the warriors fled. Matt quickly tied his brother's arms around Renegade's neck and his legs around the stallion's belly. Then he swatted the horse on the flank. Renegade would return to the Palo Duro with the others, but he intended to find Quanah first and either bring him back alive or retrieve his dead body.

As the others, including *Eeshatai,* disappeared from sight, Matt grabbed the trailing reins of a riderless horse, leapt aboard him, and started back down the ridge toward the fort.

The Comanche women, including Grace and Ellie, were so eager to learn the outcome of the attack on the Adobe Walls that they climbed the canyon trail and camped near the rim, keeping watch on the horizon for the first appearance of their menfolk.

The warriors returned much sooner than anyone had expected. They approached the Palo Duro in a thin but steady stream—arriving with heads bowed and faces grim. When the women saw them they knew better than to ask questions; the battle hadn't gone well, and none of the shamed warriors wished to talk about it. How proudly they had set out! But now they returned like whipped dogs, with their tails tucked between their legs.

As the wounded began to arrive, the women saw with their own eyes the proof of *Eeshatai's* lies and deceit. One by one the warriors descended the canyon trail in company with their sad-faced women and children. The silence was eerie, broken only by the wails of mourning echoing through the canyon as news of the dead reached those who waited.

Grace remained with Ellie and the small throng of women staring out onto the plain. All day they waited, and occasionally, other braves appeared—some wounded—to be greeted with sighs of relief but no joyous acclamations. In the wake of the realization that the prophet's magic had proven false, the mood was one of utter despair. Quanah's wives began questioning the stragglers, and Ellie, too, begged for news, but no one knew anything—or else they wouldn't admit it. By late afternoon almost all the warriors had been accounted for one way or another Jonathan's Comanche father Three Toes, Quanah, Stalking Wolf and Painted Horse were the only exceptions.

"They aren't coming tonight," Ellie said. "We might as well go down. In the morning, as soon as it's light, we can climb the trail again. Perhaps they will come tomorrow."

"Or perhaps they'll never come," Grace said. "Ellie, we must face it. All of them may be dead."

"Oh, I know they're coming!" Ellie's face was serene, her eyes untroubled. "Stalking Wolf swore to me he wouldn't die today. Didn't he, Emmy?"

Emily gravely nodded. "Yes, he did, Mama. I heard him."

Grace's nerves were stretched taut as a bowstring. She wante to scream and shout at her sister. Wanted to force reality down her throat. If Ellie had faced reality years ago, with William, they wouldn't be in this predicament.

For the sake of the children Grace backed off from the confrontation. All day Jonathan had divided his time between his Comanche mother and Ellie. He didn't speak to either woman, but holding his small bow and a sheaf of arrows, he behaved like a young brave doing his duty by guarding his womenfolk. As angry as she was with Ellie, Grace didn't have the heart to tell the boy that he was probably now their sole protector.

"Why don't you take the children and go down?" she said instead. "I'll stay here a bit longer and keep watch for them."

"Really, it isn't necessary," Ellie insisted. "They'll come tomorrow. But if you must . . ." She motioned Jonathan to her side and held out her hand to Emily.

Quanah's wives and Jon's Comanche mother had already begun descending the trail. They, too, had given up for the night. Ellie, Emily, and Jonathan joined them, but Grace watched the horizon until darkness swallowed it. By the light of the rising moon she made her way down the rocky trail, and she was almost to the bottom when she heard hooves clopping on stone above her.

Turning, she hurried back the way she had come and met Renegade carefully picking his way down the steep incline. At first Grace thought that the unconscious bleeding figure tied to the stallion's back was Matt. The trail was too narrow to untie him, but she managed to lift his head to see his face.

When she saw who it was, her heart lurched heavily in her breast. *Where was Matt?* Why was Stalking Wolf tied on Renegade instead of his own horse? Only Stalking Wolf himself could tell her, but from the looks of him, he'd die before he could summon the strength to open his mouth.

Carefully, she led the stallion the rest of the way down the trail and took him straight to Ellie.

* * *

Three days passed and neither Matt, Quanah, nor Three Toes appeared. Stalking Wolf hovered near death, and could answer no questions from anyone. He had taken three direct hits. The balls had missed vital organs, but he had lost a great deal of blood. Two of the missiles had to be dug out, and one of Quanah's wives did the honors; she claimed to have had plenty of experience.

Stalking Wolf's left arm was shattered, and Grace favored removing it entirely. She couldn't see how it could possibly heal, but the Comanche women insisted it could, and Ellie agreed with them. Their tipi was crowded with women who seemed to know what they were doing, so Grace spent most of her time climbing the canyon trail and staring across the plain, praying for Matt's return, along with Quanah's and Three Toe's.

By the fourth day despair threatened. If they were coming they surely would have made it back by now, Grace reasoned but her heart told her she mustn't give up. She refused to think about living in a world that didn't contain Matthew Stone, her beloved Painted Horse. It made no difference that he didn't actually belong to her and probably never would; as long as he still lived she could nurture the tiny spark of hope that some day . . . some way . . .

Squinting at the horizon, Grace thought she saw a distant movement. Shielding her eyes from the bright sunlight, she sought to determine if her desires had produced an illusion or if two walking figures and a riderless horse were actually coming toward her.

Breathless and light-headed, she stood motionless, counting the steps it took for them to get close enough for her to recognize them. On they came, in no great hurry. . . . The horse was limping and seemed to be dragging something behind him— *yes!* Matt was one of the men, and Quanah Parker was the other. Sure of it now, Grace flew across the plain toward them.

* * *

In the privacy of their tipi that night, Matt told Grace everything that had happened. By then she already knew what had
taken them so long to return. With only one horse to transport
three of them Matt and Quanah had fashioned a crude *travois*
to bring back the body of Three Toes. Jonathan's Comanche
father had been killed in the battle at the Adobe Walls. They
themselves had walked the whole way, and even then the horse
had gone lame from an injury it had received during the battle.

Now Matt described how Quanah's horse had been shot out
from under him, how the Comanche war chief had been forced
to take cover under a heap of stinking buffalo hides to avoid
being shot or trampled. On seeing Matt he'd climbed out from
under the hides and jumped behind him on the horse to escape
the hail of gunfire.

They'd gone back that night with a few other daring souls to
recover bodies. Nine warriors had been slain. Only three whites
had died that day, and an unknown number of Indians had been
wounded, some of whom would surely die from the severity of
their injuries. Stalking Wolf was a prime example; for the moment he stubbornly clung to life, but his future remained in
doubt. If he lived he wouldn't be the man he had once been; a
one armed warrior could expect a short hard life.

"Matt, if he makes it, you must convince your brother to go
back to Fort Sill with Ellie, the children, and us. Maybe now
he'll be ready to listen. And what about Quanah? Has this been
enough to change his mind about taking the People to the reservation and surrendering?"

Grace handed a steaming portion of rabbit stew to Matt, who
ate a bite of it before answering. Some of the boys, Jonathan
among them, had 'gone hunting' the day before and managed
to snare a couple of large hares in the far end of the canyon.
Jon had been eager to boast of his accomplishments to Stalking
Wolf, when he got better, and Three Toes, when he came. The
death of his Comanche father had hit him hard, and Grace wondered how he would react if Stalking Wolf didn't make it. How

many fathers did a boy have to lose before he found one to see him through childhood?

Chewing and swallowing first, Matt said: "I had several days to argue with Quanah, but I still couldn't convince him to take the *Kwerharrehnuh* to the reservation. If anything, he's even more determined to deliver death and destruction to the whites. However, he's on his own, now. The alliance is finished. The Cheyenne, Kiowa, and Arapaho couldn't ride fast enough back to their own lands. Even the Comanches have split up, each band going its own way. By now the reservation Indians brave enough to join us have probably returned to the reservation, where they will pretend they never took part in this embarrassing failure."

"And what of that faker, *Eeshatai?*"

"That coward? He had painted himself yellow, a respectable enough color among the Comanches, but one the whites would say revealed his character. After the battle he disappeared. I doubt we'll hear from him again. If he values his life he won't return to this canyon any time soon." Matt paused a moment, and his green eyes sought hers. "Boston, you know we have to leave now, don't you? This time, it's really time."

Grace sat quietly, waiting for him to continue. She knew they had to go; it was really *past* time for them to leave the Comanches to their fate—and her sister, too, if Ellie still refused to accompany them.

"We only stayed this long in the hopes I could talk some sense into Quanah and my brother. That still hasn't happened. Quanah's already planning the next raid. I don't want to be part of it. It was bad enough participating in this one. At one point I actually urged the Indians to stay and fight. If they hadn't been so shocked by the discovery that bullets could still kill them, we *could* have taken that fort . . . and at the time, I wanted to take it. . . . A little taste of blood lust was all it took to turn me back into a savage."

"You're not a savage, Matt. None of these people are savages; I see that now. As you once told me, they have been *driven* violence and mayhem. We've lived with them almost a year now, and they've shown they can be quite civilized and compassionate."

"I'm afraid you haven't seen them at their worst yet, Boston. I'd like to get you out of here before some brave trying to prove his courage drags a couple of white captives into this canyon and turns them over to the women who have lost a husband or son in this battle."

"Like the wife of Three Toes?"

Matt nodded. "You won't want to be here if she's ever given the opportunity to take her revenge on a helpless white captive—male, female, child or adult."

"Will Jonathan be safe?" Grace was suddenly concerned for the boy.

"Of course. But she'll make him watch, and young as he is he'll learn to think that such harsh punishment and cruelty are justified. You've seen what happened to me and my brother. We became Comanches with a vengeance."

"Not you," she disputed. "You left them, remember?"

"Part of me will always be Comanche, Boston. Don't ever forget it."

How *could* she forget it? He sat across from her, still in his war paint, wearing nothing but a breechcloth and moccasins. Since she, too, wore Indian garb, clothing wasn't the thing that separated them; rather, it was something in their minds and hearts. An invisible barrier. She stood on one side and he on the other. They loved each other—of that she was certain. But she had about as much chance of taming him and making him her own as she had of breaking some wild stallion. She didn't know where to start.

There was always passion, of course. She could reach him through their lovemaking. But it wasn't enough. Whenever she tried it he accused her of trying to buy him with her body. He saw right through her efforts to bind him to her—and he still rejected her. Or rejected himself as unworthy of her.

"How soon do you want to go?" she asked, swept with misery.

"As soon as I can talk to my brother, and you can talk to your sister. If she still refuses, try to convince her to let the children—at least, Emily—come with us. If they stay, they'll either starve next winter or be killed when Mackenzie finally finds this place. Make her see that, Boston."

"It will all depend on your brother. She won't leave him, and I doubt she'll send the children, even Emily. They're all Comanches now, just like your brother."

Matt set down his stew near the cook fire. He lifted his hands to his face and sighed. "I'm so tired, Boston. I'm just so damned tired."

"I know," she whispered, realizing he didn't mean only that he hadn't slept since the battle, although he hadn't. "Sleep now. You need to sleep."

"Ha! I need to bathe. We wrapped the body of Three Toes in a couple of hides we stole from the buffalo hunters. But still . . . I can smell him. I can smell him on my skin and hair."

"Tomorrow, you can bathe. It's too late tonight. Lie down and sleep, Matt. I'll wake you if there's any change in your brother."

Nodding, he lay down and immediately fell asleep.

Six days passed before Stalking Wolf was in any condition for a serious conversation. Toward the end of that week he showed marked improvement, and Matt decided it was now or never. If he delayed much longer, Quanah would insist he accompany the warriors on the next raid he was planning. Matt didn't want to end his friendship with Quanah on a bitter note, which would surely happen when he had to refuse.

Grace accompanied him to Stalking Wolf's tipi, for they had decided to approach Ellie at the same time as Matt talked with his brother. When they entered, Matt couldn't believe the improvement in Stalking Wolf; he was sitting up and leaning

against a backrest while Ellie spooned broth from an iron kettle
into his mouth.

"Look at her!" his brother said by way of greeting. "My
yellow-haired wife thinks I am either an old man with shaking
hands and no teeth, or a babe too young to feed himself."

Matt laughed and sat down beside him. "For a warrior everyone swore was on his way to the happy hunting grounds,
you've made a remarkable recovery. How is your arm?"

Stalking Wolf grimaced. "It pains me day and night. I still
cannot move it—not until the heavy sticks tied to it are taken
away."

"And your other wounds?"

"They no longer bleed, and there is no bad smell, which
means they are healing. However, I must regain my strength.
Never have I been this weak."

"For what purpose will you now use your strength—so you
can get yourself killed the next time?" Matt tossed out for open-
ers.

Grace gave him a look. She had knelt down beside Ellie and
Emily, greeting them with a nod and a smile, which the two
had returned. To Matt's great surprise, Stalking Wolf lifted his
head and stared at him quietly. Instead of responding angrily,
as Matt had expected, he seemed deep in thought. "No," he
finally said. "I am done with fighting. Which means I am also
done with being a Comanche."

"Oh!" Grace and Ellie jointly gasped.

Even Emily looked amazed. Matt couldn't think of what to
say, but he finally found his voice. "Do you really mean it?
Quanah still intends to fight. So what will you do now?"

The corners of Stalking Wolf's mouth curved upwards. "You
have no suggestions? How is that, my brother? Always in the
past, you've had suggestions aplenty."

"You've taken me by surprise," Matt admitted. "I'll have to
think about it. I have a small ranch. It's not much, but you—and
our family—are welcome to stay there as long as you like. I'm

assuming, of course, that you intend to leave the canyon with us and return to the world of the whites."

"Where else would I go? To a reservation? I can't go there, because the man I was—Stalking Wolf—died the moment he discovered *Eeshatai* had no magic. Stalking Wolf fell from his horse, his arm shattered by a white man's bullet. He then decided it might be better to *be* a white man and live than to be a Comanche and die a fool. Like Three Toes, and someday . . . Quanah."

Matt couldn't speak past the lump in his throat. Tears streamed down Grace's cheeks as she beamed at him. He glanced at Ellie. Sobbing quietly, Ellie stared at his brother. Even Emily was grinning from ear to ear.

"Have you nothing to say?" his brother asked. "I have just restored . . . Thad . . . to you, but you say nothing."

Matt touched his brother's shoulder. "I'm overwhelmed. Grace and I came here today to try and talk you and Ellie into returning to Fort Sill with us. We didn't know how you'd react, but we suspected we might have a fight on our hands. If we had lost it, we'd have been returning to the fort without you, and leaving you to . . . more tragedy."

"Can you wait until I am able to ride a horse again?" Thad asked, with a wry gleam in his eye. "Also, if I'm to pass for a white man now, I need to practice my English. I've forgotten more than half of it. When Yellow-Hair—I mean, Ellie—speaks or Warrior Woman—your Boston—I understand well enough but speaking it will be difficult."

"You'll do fine. Don't worry. I'm sure Ellie will help you."

"What about Jonathan?" Ellie suddenly asked. "He must come with us. I can't leave him here!"

She spoke in English, and Thad touched her hand and responded in kind—haltingly but clearly. "We will buy him . . . from the wife of Three Toes. Do not worry. I still have horse left . . . to bargain with. I will keep only those we will need for . . . our journey, but she may have the rest . . . in exchange for him."

Grace took Ellie's other hand. "As long as Thad goes with us, you're willing to leave the Comanches now?"

Ellie smiled, looking surprised at the question. "Of course. And Jonathan and Emily, too. We must all go! . . . But I won't return to Boston, Grace. As long as I have my family around me, I can be a white woman again, but I'll never go back to Boston."

"I realize that," Grace said. "You don't have to return to Boston for my sake. I'll stake you right here—near Fort Sill, if you like. I'll build you a house, buy cattle, put up fencing—anything you and Thad want."

With each word she spoke, Matt's spirits plummeted another notch. His brother had the same reaction. "What do you mean—*stake* you?"

"Just what she said," Matt answered. "She'll supply anything you need or want. She has buckets of money. You'll never have to work or worry about taking care of your family. She'll do it for you. From now on all you'll ever have to do is sit around all day in the sunshine, looking handsome and content."

With each word he spoke Matt could see his brother growing angrier. "No!" Thad finally burst out. "We will accept nothing from you! I am still a man. I will regain the use of my arm. I will not live the life of . . . a cripple. I will care for my own."

Amazingly, his English was perfect.

Grace glared at Matt. "Your brother is cut from the same cloth as you are, I see. However, his pride will only cause Emily, Jonathan, and his own wife to suffer. Does that make you happy?"

"I'll help them get a start, Boston. It's not necessary for you to give them the sun, moon, and stars all at once."

Matt watched the crimson flush climb up her cheeks and wondered why she couldn't *see* what she was doing when she shredded a man's pride as only she could do. She would never wed him; she already had it all. What did she want with a man who had so little hope of attaining the luxuries she had always known?

When they returned to his ranch they'd be desperately poor. He and Thad and his little family would have to live as Indians—hunting for their food, making their own garments, rounding up and breaking horses. Accustomed now to hardship among the Indians, Ellie could find happiness in that sort of life, but Grace? How could he ask Grace Livingston to live in a crowded hovel, when she had a mansion and servants awaiting her back home in Boston?

There must be a hundred men in Boston more suited to her: men who were more educated . . . who dressed in fine clothes and rode in fine carriages . . . men who owned the factories where buffalo hides were processed and sold for huge profits.

He belonged in the wilderness, living out his life on the plains, but she belonged in that distant world where she would never know hunger or deprivation of any kind.

"I think I should be allowed to help my own sister and her children." Grace carefully enunciated each word. "If you don't want my help, Matt, that's fine. I won't give it to you. But please don't poison your brother's mind and set him against me. Jonathan and Emily deserve—"

"Please, Grace!" Ellie held up her hand, her blue eyes anxious. "Don't say any more. Thad will provide for us. Every day he's getting better . . . stronger. Soon he'll be as good as new."

"I will . . . work my bad arm each day," Thad said. "It won't always be . . . useless. If it never heals, my remaining arm is strong. I will be able to do everything I once did."

"Of course, you will!" Ellie fervently agreed. "And I have no wish for all the things my sister mentioned. So long as I have you I'll be happy living in a tipi, or wherever else you find for us."

"Jonathan and Emily must go to school . . ." Grace's eyes sparked. She set her jaw. "You're going to live as whites, now, not Indians!"

"I don't want to go to school!" Emily wailed. "I want to learn to tan hides and sew buckskins."

"Hush, now," Ellie whispered. "Don't worry. I'll teach you

"Small Toad—Jonathan—will have his own horse," Thad said. "I will teach him how to . . . train it. That's what he needs to learn—how to ride, shoot, and hunt. I am his father, now. I will teach him all he needs to know."

"He could have no one better!" Ellie exclaimed.

Grace jumped to her feet. As she passed Matt on her way out of the tipi, she hissed: "This is all your fault! You've turned them against me. Well, as far as I'm concerned the whole damn lot of you can live in filth and poverty for the rest of your lives!"

Matt knew better than to go after her; what could he say? She had as much as told him she was going back to Boston, and Boston was exactly where she belonged.

Twenty-four

Two weeks later, while Quanah and the other warriors were off raiding a distant settlement, they left the Palo Duro. Grace rode Dunston, Matt was on Tex, and Thad, Ellie, Emily, and Jonathan were mounted on the last four horses Thad still owned.

Not wanting to abandon the Comanches and his Comanche mother, Jonathan had given them some argument, but Thad's promise to provide the boy with his very own horse and teach him how to train it Indian-style had finally won him over. Grace felt as if she were the only white in their party of six. The rest were all Comanche; half the time, they still *spoke* Comanche. She had never felt more estranged from them—especially from Matt.

Since that day in Ellie's tipi when Thad had declared his intention of returning to the whites, Matt had avoided her. They maintained a polite distance and addressed each other only when necessary. It had nearly broken Grace's heart to watch Quanah Parker ride off on Renegade, but Matt had acted as if he didn't mind that he'd probably never see his friend or beloved horse again.

She had tried to say something to him—offer sympathy, comfort, or understanding—but Matt had walked right past her, and the words she had been going to utter died on her lips. Now as they left the Palo Duro far behind, he laughed over something with his brother, teased Jonathan and Emily, and told Ellie abo his ranch. How ironic that everyone in the group should seem so happy and relaxed but her!

This was what she had wanted—to bring Ellie and the children back from the Comanches—but now that she was doing it, all she wanted to do was weep. The thought of actually returning to Boston turned her stomach.

As she rode silently behind the foursome, she asked herself what she wanted to do now. No one needed her—rather, *wanted* her, and she was free to do whatever she pleased. She had a competent and trustworthy manager for her business affairs in her solicitor, Bartholomew Gumby. If she didn't want to, she need *never* return to Boston. If she wished, she could stay in Indian Territory.

Excitement rippled down her spine at *that* thought. Someday, when the Indian problem was finally resolved, this part of the country would become desirable. Settlers would flock to it. Despite the Indians, those already here were willing to endure all manner of hardships and dangers. Grace could envision towns springing up around the forts, and domesticated cattle grazing where buffalo had once roamed. Someone with enough money and the right connections back east could make a fortune in the region.

Those who'd had the foresight to invest in the first railroads linking the plains with the rest of the world were already making enormous sums. She had missed out on that opportunity, but there was no reason why she had to miss out on any others. Besides, no matter what Ellie and Thad thought about the idea of accepting help, they could hardly refuse to allow the children to visit her. And when Jonathan and Ellie visited she would do her best to exert her influence on them; the children must be prepared to face a changing future among white people. They mustn't be locked in the past with the doomed Comanches.

All the way to Fort Sill Grace made plans. She wasn't leaving. She was staying and casting her lot with the future of Indian Territory. It was also Matt's future—and Thad's, Ellie's, Emily's, and Jonathan's. Once they realized she intended to be a part of it, perhaps . . .

Grace knew she dared not hope for too much; she had to want to stay *regardless* of what happened to the rest of them. Whether or not they ever welcomed her into their lives, she must concentrate on her own reasons for staying . . . and those reasons were exciting enough.

The return journey proved to be much shorter than the journey going the other way. Matt took the most direct route, and in less than a week, traveling at a leisurely pace because of the children, they sighted the fort.

Soldiers rode out to greet them, but before they arrived Matt slowed Tex and motioned to Grace. "Boston, let me do the talking. Listen closely, and after I leave you here, stick to my story. The last thing we want is for the army to discover where we've been all this time."

"Give me credit for understanding the need for secrecy," Grace retorted. "You don't have to warn me to watch my tongue. . . . But what do you mean—after you leave me here?"

She had thought she would at least accompany them to Matt's ranch and help them set up housekeeping.

"My shack is small," he said. "There isn't room for all of us . . . and besides, I think it's best I get Thad away from her as quickly as possible."

"So you're just going to leave me here? Walk away and never look back?"

"That about sums it up," he said, looking straight ahead. "Write to me from Boston. Let me know you got there safe and sound. The mail will reach me eventually."

"Of course," she murmured, too hurt to mention her own plans or ask about his. This was indeed the end; whatever his plans might be, they didn't include her.

The arrival of the soldiers gave Matt an excuse to direct his attention elsewhere, and Grace somehow managed to act pleased to see them instead of collapsing into a fit of denial and weeping. Over the next several hours she even managed to pay attention to Matt's explanation of where they'd been. He described a canyon only vaguely similar to the Palo Duro, but gave it a strange name and claimed it was down in Mexico.

The soldiers—none of whom had ever been to Mexico—never suspected the lie; they found it amazing that all of them had been able to escape and make their way back home. They eagerly welcomed Thad, Ellie, Emily, and Jonathan as if they'd returned from the dead, and offered them the hospitality and protection of the fort. Matt told them that only Grace would be staying; the rest were continuing on to his ranch.

When they reached the fort the commander, Colonel Grierson, tried to talk Matt out of going home; it was too dangerous, he said. All over Indian Territory small bands of Indians had been attacking farms, ranches, and settlements. News of the Adobe Walls incident had already reached him, and he told them that only twenty-eight hunters and one white woman had been there, but for some reason the Indians had fled in disarray instead of overwhelming the compound. In his opinion, the surge in Indian attacks could be blamed on the fact that the savages wanted to prove they were still courageous. . . . Did they know anything about the incident?

Matt denied all involvement and attributed Thad's wounds to gunfire as they fled from Mexico. Grierson accepted his story as easily as the soldiers, and soon after, Ellie embraced Grace in a tearful farewell.

"Don't cry," Grace told her sister. "I may not return to Boston just yet. Whatever I do, I'll let you know."

Matt hardly said a word to her. His stoic behavior reminded her of the day he'd seen Quanah and Renegade for the last time. If he was sad to say good-bye, he didn't show it. He simply nodded in her direction and headed for the horses to help Emily mount her gelding. Leading the children's horses behind him, he rode away without looking back.

* * *

The fort held a fairly large number of women, Grace discovered. Some were the wives of local ranchers staying there for fear of attack by the rampaging Indians. Some were the wives of officers. They made Grace feel welcome and saw to her needs, even to supplying her with an army-issue tent and some bedding. The tent couldn't compare with the comforts of a tipi, but Grace hardly cared where she slept, what she ate, or what she wore. She had too much to do.

Soon after her arrival she befriended the wife of a rancher intent on returning east as soon as a buyer for his land and cattle could be found. The Vogelsons claimed four hundred acres south of Fort Sill near the Red River. The river skirted one boundary of their land. They had put up a clapboard house and a couple of outbuildings made of lumber hauled overland by train and wagon, and their cattle—a couple hundred head, including a prime bull—were roaming freely on the plain.

They had planned for many more improvements, such as barbed wire and more cattle, but the Indian menace had changed their minds. They'd found the bodies of their closest neighbors minus their eyelids and their scalps, staked out naked on the prairie.

Now, the Vogelsons wanted out. Grace made them an offer. They didn't think a lone woman should buy the place, especially sight unseen. Grace assured them it was only an investment. They finally agreed to a price, and less than three weeks after her arrival at Fort Sill, Grace owned her own ranch. She had also made arrangements to receive a shipment the following spring of a breed of domesticated cattle she wanted to try in place of the traditional Texas longhorns, and had purchased a wagon, a team of horses, some furniture, and various supplies and household articles from people who were fleeing the area and no longer wanted them.

She kept the telegraph wires humming to an extent never before seen at the fort. Now, while the weather was still warm, she wanted to move to her new home, but Colonel Grierson wouldn't let her. As the Indians rampaged from one end of the region to the other, all of Indian Territory and Comancheria were declared off limits to whites. Even the buffalo hunters ceased doing business. The stern-faced, bearded, fort commander wouldn't even permit Grace to visit Ellie and the children; he couldn't understand why Matt hadn't brought them into the fort until this danger was over. The Indians had never been so vicious, and President Grant was openly calling for the army to do whatever it took "to subdue all Indians who offered resistance to constituted authority."

As frightened ranchers streamed into the fort, demanding protection, Grace bought more land. She bought land on either side of Matt's. She bought land abutting her own land. She bought cattle abandoned on the plains, and longhorns from cattle drives that hadn't made it to the railhead at Dodge. She knew she risked losing them before she could have them collected and replace their brands with one of her own, but the price was cheap.

Accustomed to thinking in terms of empire building, Grace set about building an empire. It was all on paper, of course, but she didn't mind. When the dust finally settled she would emerge as an influential figure in the region. She'd hire men to round up her cattle, and she would personally ride out to inspect her holdings.

One afternoon she overheard one of the rancher's wives refer to her as "Amazing Grace," and she realized she had successfully shifted her life's focus from the east to the west. Once again she was building a legend. Unfortunately, she had no one to share her victories, and no matter what she bought, her possessions brought less joy than she imagined they would.

In early October word reached Fort Sill that Mackenzie had located and destroyed the Comanche stronghold in the Palo Duro. Before the details were even announced, wild jubilation broke out, and Grace had a hard time discovering the particulars. When she heard them, she became ill. Her head throbbed, her stomach roiled, and she was hot, cold, and dizzy all at the same time.

Mackenzie's scouts had discovered the trail leading down into the canyon, and on the morning of September twenty-eighth, the cavalry had descended it at dawn before the encampment was fully awake. A detachment of the mounted soldiers had struck out immediately for the Comanche horse herd, reached it before the startled Indians, and stampeded more than a thousand horses down the length of the canyon while the yelping Indians pursued them on foot.

With the Indians thus occupied, Mackenzie had led a charge toward the tipis. The warriors doubled back to protect their women and children, but by then it was too late. The Indians were forced to flee by scaling the canyon walls and disappearing into the plain. Most of them escaped, but Mackenzie gained control of all their horses, supplies, ammunition, homes, and virtually everything else they owned . . . and he had destroyed it.

Grace listened in horror as the stories circulated through the fort: Mackenzie had found over fourteen hundred horses, given a hundred or so to his Tonkawa scouts and retained some to serve the army. He had shot the rest—well over a thousand—in a tremendous fusillade that had rocked the plain.

Anything the army couldn't take with them, they had burned. Not a single piece of pemmican, not one buffalo robe, not even a tattered blanket, had been left behind. The incident had broke the backs of the Indians. Hungry, desperate Comanches were already trekking on foot toward the Sill agency. Quanah hadn't yet been spotted, but unless he surrendered before winter he would surely starve.

After hearing all this Grace retreated to her tent. While everyone else celebrated, she sat and wept. She wept for the People: for Quanah and his wives, for Black Antelope and Buffalo Hump, for the wife of Three Toes, and all the rest. She wept for the hungry Comanche children and the old people who had managed to survive the winter only to face this devastating loss . . . and she wept for the horses, the beautiful, solid colored and paint-splashed animals who had carried the Indians proudly across the plains.

Most of all, she wept for Renegade. Matt never should have left him with Quanah to face destruction—the stallion symbolized so much! That's why the soldiers had killed him, to crush the spirits of the Comanches and prove to them that not even the power of a blue-eyed Medicine Hat could save them from the white man's bullets. Now, he was gone, and like the buffalo and the Comanches themselves, the Painted horse would eventually disappear from the face of the earth.

In mid-October, Grace moved to a small cabin on a piece of land she had bought that abutted Matt's land. She didn't want to remain at the fort over the winter, and the Red River property was too far away and too isolated to live on alone. She hadn't even seen it yet.

The little cabin was close enough to the fort so that she had a safe haven should the need arise, and best of all she could ride over to see Ellie and the children whenever she had a day to spare. The fact that she could also see Matt hadn't influenced her decision in the slightest; until Matt wanted to see her, she didn't want to see him.

In the small cabin and animal shed that came with it, she stored enough supplies to last her the winter and beyond. The shed had a roomy lean-to attached, but there was no corral, and her team of horses could come and go as they pleased, seeking shelter whenever they needed it. For the first few days she kept them hobbled so they wouldn't roam very far. Once they learned that she provided them with grain and water at the same time each day, they promptly appeared every day at the appointed hour to gobble down her offerings.

Her only other company was a young dog who was part wolf. Someone had found it as a pup and brought it into the fort. He had a ravenous appetite, and the soldier who owned him was glad to get rid of him. Grace named him Pride, because pride was about the only thing she had to cling to these days—dog or no dog.

In early November on a crisp but sunny morning she loaded her wagon with things she thought Ellie might need—flour, coffee, sugar, blankets, and so forth—hitched her two horses, Gus and Walter, and set out with Pride to see her sister. All the way there she had to remind herself repeatedly that she had a perfect right to visit Ellie. As yet, Ellie didn't know where she was living or what she had been doing. It was time to tell her If Matt chose to eavesdrop, he was welcome to do so. If not that was fine with her, too.

The children spotted her first. They stood like startled dee watching her approach, but as soon as they recognized her the raced toward the wagon, calling her name. Associating youn humans with exuberant play and an occasional bone, Pride wa delighted to make their acquaintance. He bounded up to them barking joyfully. The yellow-eyed, gray-furred animal awe them.

"Oh, Aunt Grace! Where did you get a wolf?" Emily crie "We thought you had left and gone back to Boston by now."

"Well, I didn't leave," Grace said, activating the brake on th wagon and climbing down. She hugged Emily, but Jonatha was too busy with Pride to pay much attention to her.

"What's his name?" was all the boy asked as he knelt dow nose to nose with the dog, and plunged his hands in Pride ruff.

"His name is Pride, and he's only part wolf," Grace told hi "Emily, I assume your mother's inside."

She didn't see Matt or Thad anywhere about, and was su denly nervous at the prospect of confronting Matt again. T' girl nodded. She still wore her Comanche clothing, as did Jc and Grace hoped the children would appreciate the new g ments she had ordered for them by telegraph, along with ite for herself, Thad, Ellie, and Matt. Nothing had yet arrived, l she was hoping they'd come in time for Christmas. She h picked out all the items from the new Montgomery Ward a Co catalogue.

"Mama's resting," Emily added, "but Pa and Uncle Matt have gone hunting."

Matt wasn't there. She wouldn't have to see him—wouldn't get to see him.

Belatedly, Grace realized the importance of what the child had just told her. "Is your mother feeling all right? You said she was resting."

"Oh, she's fine! But Pa says she has to rest every day, because she has a baby growing inside her."

The news hit Grace like an avalanche of snow crashing down the side of the Palo Duro in the early spring. "A baby!"

No wonder Emily was calling Thad 'Pa'.

Emily grinned. "I'm hoping for a girl. Jon wants a boy. Mama just wants it to be healthy."

"Grace?" sang a familiar voice from the doorway of the little hack.

Turning, Grace saw Ellie. She hurried toward her, and they embraced in the middle of the front yard. Leaning back from er sister, Grace studied Ellie's glowing face and shining eyes; he also noted the slight bulge of her midriff beneath her buck-ins.

"Ellie told me about the baby," Grace said breathlessly.

"Yes! Isn't it wonderful? Thad is so happy. So am I. Come d see the house, Grace. Matt and Thad have been making provements. Thad's arm isn't back to normal yet, but you'd amazed at what he can do!"

Grace *was* amazed—amazed that her sister could be so happy ing in poverty, and expecting a baby! The men had dismantled att's outbuildings to add onto the house and create two new oms, a large one for the children and the new baby and a aller one for Matt. To Grace it was obvious Matt should move t and give the house to the expanding young family. It was o obvious they were all living like Indians, making do with at the plain provided and lacking the comforts a white family ght have expected.

The cabin was clean, but as barren as ever. Matt and the

children still slept on bedrolls on the floor. They had pushed aside the table and were using Comanche backrests and sitting on the floor to take their meals. What would Ellie do when she grew as big around as a buffalo?

Behind the cabin stood racks for drying meat, and a fresh buffalo robe lay pegged out and ready for scraping. Grace had a good idea who was doing the scraping, and she shuddered from the effort of trying to keep her mouth shut. She mustn't launch into a tirade on her very first visit!

Ellie was so happy to see her again—and so proud of each tiny improvement—yet the shack more resembled a tipi than it did the home of a white family. When Ellie had finished showing off her domain, she invited Grace to sit down on two barrels in the now warm sunshine to talk.

"So tell me what you're doing here? You're supposed to be in Boston." Smiling, Ellie tossed her blond braids back over her shoulders. In the distance the children were shrieking and laughing as they played a game of fetch the stick with Pride. "But I'm so glad you're not in Boston!" she added. "I've missed you dreadfully, Grace."

"I couldn't go back," Grace said. "I missed you and the children too much." *And Matt.*

But, of course, she hadn't stayed because of *him*. She told her sister a bit of what she'd been doing—not everything, but enough to let her know she'd been busy—and ended by admitting: "I brought all of you gifts. I assume I'm permitted to bring gifts to my own family."

"What sort of gifts?" Ellie's blue eyes clouded, and she suddenly looked wary.

"Flour, beans, coffee . . . things you can all use."

"We have enough to eat, Grace. Matt and Thad go hunting all the time."

"Then save the supplies I brought for bad weather, when game is hard to find. Don't deny me the pleasure of giving you gifts, Ellie. You can always tell the men I brought the stuff the sake of the children, if not for them."

"That's what I *will* tell them . . . and if they protest I'll remind them of last winter, when we watched so many old people and children die of hunger."

"Good for you! You've got to stand up to them, Ellie. Don't let their foolishness deprive Jon and Emily—or your new baby. You must eat especially well now, to feed that new life growing inside you." Having conquered her first obstacle, her own sister, Grace quickly changed the subject. "So tell me more about Thad."

"And Matt? Don't you want to know about Matt, too?"

Heat flooded Grace's cheeks. "Of course, about Matt."

"Thad is doing just fine. But oh, Grace, without you, Matt is miserable! He's just not the same man. Sometimes he broods so hard he goes for days without speaking. And he hardly ever smiles, except around the children."

That information heartened Grace—and *dis*heartened her. She didn't want Matt to be unhappy. She wanted only the best for him. But she was glad to know he hadn't forgotten her, and that he was paying a high price for his stubborn pride.

"I miss him, too," she murmured. "But I'm not about to scatter my money to the prairie winds and go around barefoot and dressed in rags to win his love. He has to accept me the way I am, Ellie, and I just happen to be a very rich woman who wants to use her money to help the people she loves."

Ellie leaned over and seized Grace's hand where it rested in her lap. "Oh, Grace, I'm sorry we've all been so cruel to you! Shutting you out of our lives the way we've done. I felt so guilty leaving you behind at the fort. But I didn't know how to make my husband or Matt understand that we don't have to be dependent upon them for food, clothing, and shelter in order to be dependent upon them for our happiness."

"Ellie, that's it exactly! You've stated the problem perfectly. Men must lack confidence in themselves if they think we only love them because they feed us! We aren't like Pride, after all, who only worships me because I give him a bone every now and then."

"Pride? Who's Pride?"

"My dog. The one playing with Jon and Emily." Grace nodded toward the children, and only then realized how late it was getting. She must unload the wagon and head for home if she hoped to make it back before dark.

"Goodness, I must quit talking and start working," she continued. "Maybe the children can help me unload the wagon."

"Of course they will," Ellie assured her. "They'll be delighted to help, especially once they know there are good things to eat inside it. But Grace . . . don't you want to stay and wait for Matt to return? You could spend the night. . . ."

Grace stood. "No. That's the last thing I want to do. It would be too awkward. Seeing Matt again will be too hard. He doesn't want me, Ellie, or he would never have let me go."

"You mustn't say that! He *does* want you. He just has to . . . to come to terms with how rich you are, and—"

"And what?"

"And . . . and how efficient. How good you are at making more money. You must admit, Grace, courting you must be a daunting prospect for a man—even Matt. Perhaps especially for Matt."

"I can't ride a horse like he can—or train one. I can't shoot or fight as well. I can't work cattle, build a house, father children, fix a broken wagon wheel, shoe a horse. . . ."

"Grace, don't tell me—tell *him*. He's the one who needs to hear how much you need him, and discover all he has to offer you."

"We've had some discussions in the past," Grace began. "However, all those things I just mentioned aren't what's really important. I could get by without them. I can be a great success in life without Matt. I can even be happy . . . but—"

"But what?"

"But we could be so much greater *together* than we could ever be apart!" Grace finished in a rush. "Some people think Grace Livingston alone is formidable. They have no idea how formidable Grace Livingston *Stone* would be. Matt is . . . the part me that's missing, Ellie. And I'm the part of Matt that's missing. We each have our own strengths and weaknesses, but my strengths make up for his weaknesses, and his make up for mine."

"Then you have to tell him that—make him *see* it!"

"I . . . I can't do more than I've done. I don't even want to see him again until he realizes all that for himself. We're both just . . . a little too proud, I guess."

"Do you mean you won't come to visit me again? As I get bigger, I can hardly come to see you."

"Of course I'll come to visit you! But . . . you'll have to . . . to send me a smoke signal or something, to let me know when Matt isn't here."

"A smoke signal!" Ellie laughed. "If I do that, the whole army is likely to appear. That's what they do half the time, now—run after smoke signals, hoping they'll find Indians sending them."

"Make it a very small smoke signal," Grace advised, smiling. "When I see it I'll hitch the horses—weather permitting."

Ellie rose and embraced her. "I will pray for you and Matt," she said. "Why should you both be miserable apart, when you could be so happy together?"

"I'm not miserable!" Grace denied.

"Aren't you—just a little?" Ellie leaned back and gave her a knowing look. "Pride must be a wonderful companion, I'm sure, but do you really want to snuggle up to a dog in the dead of winter?"

Grace wrinkled her nose. "Not really. He usually smells. And besides, sometimes I miss Matt so much I just want to . . . to give up. To quit trying. To hide my head under a blanket and never again have to face the world. Without him it's too lonely, and nothing I accomplish seems to matter very much."

"Don't do that, Grace. Don't quit. I know what despair is like. I've been there. Hope is the only thing that saved me. No matter how bad things got, I nurtured this little tiny spark of hope. And because I did, I got a miracle!"

They held each other and wept together a few moments, then dried their tears and went to unload the wagon.

Twenty-five

Every day about mid-morning, Grace stepped outside and watched for a smoke signal coming from the direction of Matt's ranch. Christmas came and went, and she still hadn't seen one She wondered when she would get to deliver the gifts that an army supply wagon on its way to the fort had dropped off to her. And she was eager for company.

On the eve of the new year frost covered the ground, but the sky was clear, a perfect backdrop for the little puffs of white smoke rising above the horizon's edge. Grace piled her Christmas gifts into the wagon, hitched the horses, and set out to see Ellie. She spent a wonderful day with her sister and the children left behind the gifts she had brought for Matt and Thad, and returned home without seeing either of them. But she felt content and at peace with herself.

At least Matt now knew where she was; anytime he wanted to, he could come and see her. The new clothes, boots, and has she had left for him were the perfect excuse. She just hoped he wouldn't refuse them.

Bad weather kept her housebound for most of January. February brought a short spell of relatively pleasant weather but no smoke signals, so Grace saddled one of her horses and rode to the fort. There she caught up on the latest news. Desperate starving Comanches were arriving daily at the agency—not Quanah, however. He remained hiding on the Staked Plains along with a few others too stubborn to yield.

Mackenzie had harassed the Indians all through the fall, covering thousands of miles and engaging the enemy on two dozen occasions. In mid-January, he had been assigned elsewhere. The Department of Texas considered the Comanches so thoroughly broken that it had recommended Mackenzie's transfer to fight the northern Cheyennes, Utes, and Apaches. Colonel Grierson was now in charge, and he had sent the 10th Cavalry, composed entirely of black men, into the field, along with the 24th Infantry. They followed Mackenzie's policy of destroying all lodges and stores of meat, horses, and supplies that might possibly be of use to the Indians.

"I expect cold and hunger to finish off the remaining holdouts, even Quanah," Grierson told her, stroking his beard. "This is the end. Why won't the man admit it?"

Grace had no answer to such a question—none the colonel would have understood.

Everyone at the fort was hoping for more bad weather—the harsher, the better. No matter how severe their own discomforts, they wanted the rebels dead.

Appalled by such callousness Grace hurried home to her snug little cabin. In March she visited Ellie and the children twice. Ellie expected her baby to be born around the end of April. In preparation she had taught Emily how to make smoke signals, so the child could alert Grace when her mother went into labor. Grace intended to be there for the birth, whether Matt and Thad attended or not.

Thad had accepted her gifts and was happily using them, but Matt's pile lay untouched in a corner of his room. Grace spotted them on one of her visits.

"I'm sure he'll wear them one of these days!" Ellie said lightly. "The garments he's wearing are in terrible shape."

"More likely, he would rather go naked," Grace retorted. Once again, Matt's pride was overruling his good sense. What would it take to banish his demons once and for all?

By the end of March the southern Cheyennes had surrendered. The army confiscated their horses and mules, gave some to the scouts, auctioned off 5,500 head, and destroyed the rest. On a visit to the fort, Grace saw some of the auctioned horses, a number of whom were Paints. None were for sale, but she conceived the idea of purchasing the best horses of the breed she could find, so that the line of color-splashed animals wouldn't die out entirely. Remembering that it had been Matt's dream to use Renegade to sire new offspring, she wished *he* could do the selecting of such prospects. Since he was still pretending she didn't exist, she had no choice but to go ahead without him.

Grierson promised to let her know if any more Paints arrived at the fort; he invited her to come and take a look at them before he had them destroyed. First, he tried to steer her toward the solid colored animals, using the argument that painted horses shouldn't be left alive to remind the Indians of their former grandeur. Grace easily overcame his objections. She had learned long ago how to bring 'round a reluctant man; the only man she couldn't seem to bend to her will in any way, shape, or form was Matt.

Ellie's baby arrived right on time—during the last week of April. Unfortunately, Grace didn't hear about the event until *after* it happened. During a heavy rainstorm Thad suddenly appeared at her door with the news that Ellie had borne another daughter, and mother and baby were doing well. Grace invited Thad to come in, but he shook his head, flinging water on her from the brim of the new hat she had given him for Christmas.

"I must go back. Ellie shouldn't be left alone. I would have sent my brother to tell you, but he's gone."

"Oh? Where is he?"

"He rode to the Indian agency at Fort Sill to plead for mercy for Lone Wolf, Woman's Heart, and many of the others who went with us to Adobe Walls. Your government is sending them away to Florida, where they will be locked inside four walls and never get to see the plains again."

"But—why? Why can't they stay here on the reservation with the rest of the Indians?"

"Because they might incite the others to violence. How that could happen I don't know. Even the reservation Indians are sick and starving. They have no horses and no weapons. No buffalo have been seen for a long time, and the game around here is gone. The Indians need another Painted Horse to fight for their cause. Now they have neither him or Quanah. It's . . . very sad." Grappling with emotion, he turned to go, and the movement splashed more water on Grace.

"Please, Thad. Won't you step inside for a moment? You're soaked."

"No, I'm leaving now. When the rain stops come and see my new daughter. She is as beautiful as her mother."

"I will. I can't wait to see her."

As Thad remounted his horse Grace rushed out into the deluge.

"Wait! What did you name her?"

Touching the brim of his hat, he grinned. "What do you think? She's so amazing there could really only be one name for her—Grace."

"Oh!" Grace said, and laughed.

In the pouring rain, she stood there laughing and watched him depart.

In May Grace visited Ellie, the children, and her blond-haired, blue-eyed namesake as often as she could. Sometimes Thad was here, sometimes not. Matt was never there. Either he had a lot of business elsewhere or he was definitely avoiding her. Grace hoped he was making himself scarce simply to give her the opportunity to spend as much time as she wanted to with Little Grace, as everyone called the baby.

Slowly, his corrals were filling—mostly with mangy, wild range cattle that wore no brands. Sometimes she saw new hobbled horses on his land; they, too, were sad specimens. If only he would give her the chance, she could do so much for him! Any day now she expected her shorthorn cattle to arrive from

the east. Where she would get the men to brand them she didn't
know; she was having no luck finding men willing to comb the
plains for the abandoned animals she had bought last fall at the
fort.

The families heading back east had already left, and there
was no big influx of newcomers. Except for the reappearance
of the straggly buffalo hunters, who had no interest in working
cattle, the region was oddly quiet. But it was only May, and
Grace expected to see a growth boom as soon as word spread
that the Indians were now subdued. People were probably waiting for Quanah to be captured before they flocked to the area.

In June Grace rode to the fort to inquire about her cattle.
There she learned that Quanah had finally surrendered at the
Sill agency. Bringing with him the last pitiful remnants of the
Comanches, he had arrived on foot only the day before. When
Grace heard the news from Colonel Grierson, she wondered
why the inhabitants of the fort weren't rejoicing; everyone had
been eagerly awaiting this.

"Do you know how Quanah survived this past winter?" Grierson asked her in his headquarters. "He and his rebels lived
on grubs, nuts, and rodents. . . . Well, it's over now. Thank God,
it's finally over."

Quanah had surrendered unconditionally, as the army demanded, but Grierson thought, if he behaved himself and caused
no trouble, he might find favor in time as a representative of
his people. He had killed many whites and burned their homes
but he had never broken his promises or reneged on treaties.
He alone of all the Indian leaders had never signed any treaties.

Grierson's change of attitude shocked Grace. She hadn't expected to find leniency in a man who had so diligently pursued
Mackenzie's harsh policies. However, the fate of Quanah and
the Comanches wasn't up to Grierson. His job was finished.

Outside, even the Buffalo soldiers who had spent months
chasing Quanah across the Staked Plain seemed unduly quiet
and subdued. Grace realized that Quanah Parker had earned
their grudging admiration for his courage and determination.

As she prepared to leave the fort, she spotted a bunch of newly arrived horses in a corral nearby. Among them were a few Paints, so Grace walked over to have a look. Since Grierson hadn't mentioned the horses to her, she assumed that some decision regarding their futures had already been made.

She asked a nearby soldier about the animals.

"Ma'am, you wouldn't want to buy any of these Injun ponies. Take a good look at 'em. They're in real bad shape. Half of 'em are lame, most have got broken wind, and the ribs are showin' real bad on the rest."

"You're right," Grace agreed, studying the animals, most of whom appeared too spent or badly injured to recover and be useful. "What will happen to them?"

"We'll hafta take 'em out on the plain and shoot 'em. We're just waitin' for the colonel's okay."

"Please tell Colonel Grierson that Grace Livingston would like to buy the Paint horses among them. I don't care what shape they're in. I want them."

"Ma'am, pardon me for sayin' so but I think you've plumb lost your reason!"

"Just tell him what I said, and that I'll be return in a couple days to get them. *I want all the Paints.* There are . . . let me see . . . five of them."

"Yes, ma'am," the soldier reluctantly agreed.

A commotion behind the corral suddenly drew Grace's attention. She stood on tiptoe and craned her neck to see what was happening. A half dozen soldiers surrounded a struggling horse. Four lassos were looped around its' neck, and the men were pulling on them, tightening the ropes and trying to regain control of the rearing animal. Up on its hind legs it went, pawed the air, and came down with a thud that Grace could feel through her own feet.

"What are they trying to do?" she asked the soldier as they both hurried closer.

The poor horse was filthy, lathered, and bloody. One man

had a long, black cattle whip, and every time the horse reared, he whipped it unmercifully.

"Oh, that's a killer horse—a wild stallion we found on the range along with this bunch. A couple of us tried breakin' him, but every time we touched a spur to his hide, he bucked us off. The last time, he turned on my buddy and damn near trampled him t' death. He's over in the infirmary now, and these guys thought they'd have a go with him. But it's no use. Looks like they're gonna hafta shoot him instead."

"No!" Grace cried, catching sight of the horse's wild eyes. They were blue. And he appeared to have a dark patch of color on his head, another covering one ear, and a shield of color on his chest.

She bolted around the side of the corral. Just as a soldier raised his pistol and drew a bead on the stallion's head, Grace threw herself between the man and the horse. "Stop! I want this horse. I'm buying him, and I'll pay anything you want!"

At the sound of her voice, the stallion planted all four feet and stood perfectly still, ears pricked in her direction, nostrils quivering as he scented her.

"Lady, this horse is a killer! You can't buy him."

"Name your price!" Grace snapped.

"It'll be up to the colonel, but you can't—"

"Yes, I can! Give him to me now. You gentleman haven't the slightest idea how to tame a horse. Whips and ropes won't do it." Grace turned to the animal. "Renegade?" she whispered softly.

The battered stallion gave a low nicker of recognition. As the startled soldiers watched, Grace walked up to him. He didn't move a muscle. She touched her cheek to his muzzle and patted his sweaty neck. Grabbing one of the ropes, she gave it a tug to tell the man holding it to release the tension. When he did, she removed the choking restraint from around Renegade's neck.

Now that she was close to him, she was sure it was he. He was the same size, and beneath the dirt and grime was the same color and had the same markings. But his behavior was the only proof she needed. When she had removed all the ropes but one he gave a long sigh, lowered his head, and briefly rested it on her shoulder.

Without saying a word, Grace led him away.

The soldiers parted to let her pass.

"Amazin'! Plumb amazin'!" One muttered behind her. "By God, you'd think she was a damn Comanche."

"Or related to that fellah—what's his name?—who used to break horses for us. Oh, yeah, Matt Stone."

When she got him home, Grace cleaned all of Renegade's wounds, doctored him, and then groomed him. Mindful of how thin he was, she fed him sparingly, then hobbled him and turned him out to graze. The hobbles were hardly necessary. When she entered the cabin, he stood outside the door, and when she looked out the window to check on him, he stuck his head in the window and whinnied plaintively.

He didn't want to let her out of his sight. If she retreated from view, he snorted and pranced. She finally went back outside and sat beside him on the grass, so he would feel free to graze. Pride playfully frolicked about him, and Renegade finally lowered his head and ate, leaving Grace to watch the sunset and think about Matt.

She had to go see him now. She had his horse. And if he didn't already know about Quanah's surrender, she had to tell him. First she would let Renegade have a few days rest, so he could heal and eat all the grass he wanted. Grass was plentiful, but Renegade had obviously been driven hard, chased, or herded across the plain, and hadn't had much chance to enjoy it. He and the other horses had suffered. She should have taken them. Maybe she could tie Renegade in the lean-to tomorrow, and return to the fort to tell Grierson she'd buy the entire bunch, not just the Paints.

Once they belonged to her she would start feeding them grain and keep the water trough filled so they would stick around. The bunch were probably all mares—Renegade's herd. Even the solid-colored ones might throw some Paint foals. The mares needn't be entirely sound to be good Mamas.

It was all so perfect. She had everything now, except for the most important thing: Matt. The time had come to set aside her own pride and try one more time to overcome *his* pride. Knowing Matt, she could count on it not being easy. He might refuse to accept even his own horse! All she could do was try—and pray that he missed her as much as she missed him.

On the day she had chosen to be *the* day, a messenger arrived from the fort to tell her that her cattle had arrived the day before. The drovers who had brought them from Dodge had already taken off; they had collected their money from Grierson, who had agreed to handle the transaction in her absence. The cattle filled all the army corrals, and must be removed at once. What did Grace intend to do with them now?

"I'll come get them tomorrow," Grace promised. "Today, have a more important errand."

"Miss Livingston, you'll need men to help you," the soldier warned. "Colonel Grierson said you needed to bring your own men, because he can't spare any soldiers. He needs them over at the Indian agency to help guard Quanah Parker. Beside it's . . . it's not—"

"It's not proper. I know that. Tell him not to worry. By to morrow night my cattle will have left the fort."

After the soldier departed Grace assessed her options. She didn't have many. She ought to spend the day recruiting buffalo hunters or newcomers at the fort to help her with the cattle tomorrow. She could not assume that Matt and Thad would willing; that would be asking too much. She would probably have more luck with Thad than with Matt.

But she couldn't bring herself to worry about the cattle today she had spent most of the night worrying about what she w going to say to Matt. If nothing worked out as she hoped, she would just have to open the gates of the corrals, let the cattle go their own way, and hope she could get them all rounded up and branded later.

Very carefully, she groomed Renegade, and, riding Gus, set out with him for Matt's ranch. Halfway there she spotted a lone figure riding a horse in the distance. Grace shielded her eyes from the hot sun and studied him. Today she wore typical catleman's clothing—better fitting and smelling than the awful garments Matt had once given her—but in her haste to depart he had forgotten her hat, and the summer sun was merciless.

The image of horse and man wavered in the heat haze, but Grace was certain she recognized him. It could only be Matt. His height and carriage in the saddle gave him away. She started toward him. At first he didn't appear to see her, then she thought he *must* have glimpsed her. Matt had always kept track of his surroundings. However, he didn't stop and wait for her to catch up to him. Instead, he galloped off in the opposite direction!

He was deliberately avoiding her.

Incensed, Grace gave chase, but Gus wasn't the sort of horse to enjoy wild pursuit. He lumbered along like a tired old dog. Coming to a halt, Grace gathered up Renegade's lead line and warily eyed the stallion. The distant horseman was already disappearing over the curve of the horizon; if she were going to catch him, Renegade was her only hope.

She pulled him close to Gus, took a deep breath, and switched horses. Too late she realized she would be riding Renegade with only a halter—no bit, no bridle, and no saddle. Entwining her fingers in the stallion's mane, she wrapped her legs around him and urged him forward. As if he were once again running a race, he bolted away from Gus and thundered across the sunlit plain.

In no time Grace caught up with her fleeing horseman. It was indeed Matt. His eyes widened, his jaw dropped, and he skidded to a halt. Renegade did likewise, and Grace tumbled off him to land in the grass on her backside.

She was too rattled and jarred to immediately jump to her feet. Matt didn't say a word. He stared down at her as if thunderstruck. Renegade nosed Grace, as if checking to see that she was all right, then plunged his head into the grass and started munching. He paid no attention to Matt or the horse he was riding—which happened to be Dunston.

Matt finally found his voice, but it wasn't exactly welcoming. "You never cease to amaze, do you? Where in hell did you come from, and riding Renegade, yet?"

"I came from my ranch—and don't act so surprised. You know very well where I'm living. You've done such a remarkable job of avoiding me that you *must* know."

Gritting her teeth against a few discomforts caused by her fall, Grace scrambled to her feet.

"You're supposed to be in Boston," Matt said, glowering. "Pouring tea in a flower garden or entertaining guests in your big mansion. You're not supposed to be dressed like a cowboy—with no hat, riding a stallion bareback with no bridle, and running all over a range where anybody could take a shot at you thinking you're a Comanche because you're riding a Paint horse."

"I never do what I'm supposed to do. I thought you knew that by now."

"So what trouble have you been getting into lately? I told your sister I didn't want to hear anything about you and I didn't want to see you, or accept your damn presents. I've been trying like hell to forget you. But now that you're here—riding my horse—you might as well speak up."

"I . . . want to talk to you," Grace began. She was trembling and suddenly couldn't think of a single word of all she had planned to say to him.

The reality of his presence after all these months was too overwhelming. She gazed up at him, drinking in his bronze face, his startling green eyes, the familiar width of his shoulders, the narrowness of his waist, the fact that he was wearing clothing similar to hers but none that *she* had bought for him, the length of his coppery hair—he had pulled it back from his face and tied it in place with a leather thong. . . .

"So talk. I'm waiting. Where did you find Renegade?"

"At the fort. They were going to shoot him. So I bought him—along with some other Paint horses. The others are still at the fort."

"So that's why Grierson won't sell any horses to me. You made him a better offer. As only *you* could do."

A wave of dizziness and horror swept Grace. "I didn't know you wanted them! If I had known, I never would have offered to buy them."

"I don't need you to do any favors for me, Boston. That's the whole trouble between us. You have everything. I have nothing. I can't give you a single damn thing."

"That's not true! You have plenty to give me, you big, stupid savage!"

"So we're back to that again, are we? Just what is it I have to give you, then? I'll grow old and die before I can gather up enough scurvy cattle and horses to make a go of my ranch, much less build you a house or keep you in britches. And I'll never be able to afford the silks I'd like to see you wear one day. . . . I've been working day and night, but I still haven't—"

"I don't need a house or silks or cattle or horses! I already have them! More than I want. More than I can handle. Right this very minute I have two hundred head of prime . . . lime . . ." She couldn't think of the name of her new breed of cattle. Mr. Gumby had researched the matter and sent what he thought might work.

"Prime what?"

"Shorthorns! Prime shorthorns I sent for back east."

"Shorthorns? For out here? In longhorn country?"

"Yes! And I have to get them out of the fort tomorrow. And need to get them branded. I also have hundreds of longhorns roaming the plain somewhere. I own cattle with six different brands on them. They all need to be marked with *my* brand, except I haven't got a brand yet. And I own land, too. You might as well know all of it. I own land all over the territory."

"How many acres?" he asked, frowning.

"Six—no seven—hundred by now. Maybe more. Before I'm finished I hope to own a thousand."

"A thousand." He sat and stared at her. "What are you going to do with a thousand acres, Boston? What will you do with hundreds of beeves?"

"Beeves?"

"Cattle! What cowboys call cattle. . . . How many horses do you now own?"

"I . . . I don't know! I haven't counted them. But not that many. I've got at least three houses, including one big one down by the Red River. They're all *empty*. Without you, everything's empty. It doesn't matter what I own."

"Appears to me you have a problem. Too bad I can't be bought—like Renegade and your shorthorns."

"Then I'll sell it all! I'll get rid of everything. Is that what you want? I'll come to you naked and barefoot, without a dollar to my name. I'll burn all my money or scatter it across the prairie. Tell me what you want, Matt Stone—or what you *don't* want. If I'm humiliating myself for nothing, tell me that, too. I need to know. To hear it from your lips. If nothing I do or say can make a difference, you owe it to me to tell me. If you don't love me, *say* so, and I'll never bother you again."

"I *do* love you," he countered, looking surprised that she doubted it. "I just hate your money—rather, I hate how it makes me feel. Inadequate. Incompetent. Unable to impress you, provide for you as I'd like. . . . That's why I've been working so hard. So that if you stayed, if you didn't go back to Boston, I could come to you with pride, with something to offer you—"

"Oh, Matt, nothing I own means as much to me as your love. Nothing you could ever *give* me means as much as that. If you can't *see* that for yourself, I don't how to convince you, Matt . . ." She stepped closer, put her hand on his knee, and gazed up into his eyes. "A woman isn't impressed by what man can *provide* for her—unless he's offering his heart, his commitment, his love, and his loyalty. Everything else is nice . . . but meaningless."

His hand covered hers. "Boston . . . I . . . I don't know what to say . . . or what to think."

"Say you love me!" she pleaded. "And we can work out the rest."

"Damn it all, Boston, I *do* love you!"

"How much? . . . How much, Matt?"

Her heart and soul waited on his answer.

"Like . . ." A grin hovered on his lips." Like a Comanche loves his horse!"

"Oh, Matt!" She burst out laughing, flung her arms around him, and pulled him off Dunston. He came willingly, and carried her down to the prairie grass.

They kissed until they were breathless. They kissed until the earth trembled, and nothing existed but eager hands, mouths, and bodies. They kissed until their clothing somehow disappeared, and they were one entity, straining together beneath the hot sun, gloriously reunited and unashamed to proclaim their love at long last.

They kissed until they were exhausted, and a large dog suddenly pounced on them. "What the hell . . . ?" Matt griped, pushing Pride aside.

"It's only my dog," Grace said "When I left he was off somewhere chasing something. He's finally caught up with me."

"Do I have to accept him, too?" The dog licked his face unceasingly, refusing to be denied. He tried to lick Matt's naked chest, but Matt elbowed him away.

"I'm afraid so. Like everything else you don't like that I own, he comes with the territory. He's part of the bargain."

Matt rolled over on her and pinned her to the ground beneath him. "What if I say you have to give him up?"

"Well, then, of course I will. I'll give him to Jonathan and Emily. Do I have to give him up? Must I give up my money and all I own to ensure you'll make love to me like this for the rest of my life?"

Matt gazed down at her for a long, poignant moment. "You really want me, Boston? You want me more than anything else in this whole wide world? If you lost it all, you could still be happy just having me?"

"Yes," she answered. "Yes, yes, and yes."

"All I have to give you is myself. I hope it's enough. From now on, every day of my life I'll wake up in the morning and try to figure out how I can love you that day and keep you happy."

"So will I," she whispered, tears filling her eyes.

When he kissed her yet again, she tasted the salt of *his* tears and knew their bargain was sealed forever.

They were married three weeks later, when a preacher stopped at the fort along with the first wave of new settlers arriving from the east. The ceremony lasted no more than a few moments, after which Matt and Grace returned home to collect their belongings for a journey to the Red River property Grace wanted to explore with her new husband.

Ellie, Thad, and the young ones were all waiting for them at Grace's little cabin, where she and Matt had been living—and loving—since their reunion. Ellie had prepared a small feast in celebration of their official nuptials. While Ellie was laying out food on a long table set up outside in a Comanche-style arbor where it was cooler, Little Grace began to cry. Thad started for the house, but Grace waylaid him.

"I'll get her," she offered. She hurried into the house to fetch her namesake, who had been sleeping in the middle of the bed with pillows piled all around her.

Little Grace quit crying the moment Grace picked her up. She cooed, smiled, and waved her pudgy little hands above her wispy, blond curls. Enchanted, Grace sat down on the bed play with her a moment before returning to the others.

"Need some help?" Matt asked from the doorway.

Grace looked up to see him watching her with a tenderness that turned her insides to mush. "You know me. I always need help."

She wasn't saying it just to soothe his pride. For three weeks Matt and Thad had been branding cattle, with the assistance of some Indian army scouts who were given a pass to leave the reservation for expressly that purpose. Only "good" Indians had received permission, and Matt had paid them in beef. The shorthorns were now finished and turned out on the plain to graze. They still had all the longhorns to do, as soon as they could be rounded up. While Matt and Grace were gone on their journey, Thad intended to start searching for them—and that was just the beginning. When they returned . . .

"Yes, I do know you—very well." Matt took a seat beside her on the bed. "You probably have ten more jobs lined up for me to do, not counting whatever help you might need this very moment."

"You're right. The new fencing should arrive any day now. And we need a new roof before winter. Also, I was hoping we could build a barn, and—"

"Stop!" Matt protested, grinning. "I'm worn out already. You don't need *one* husband, you need thirty."

"One will do fine, as long as it's *you*." Grace handed him the baby. "She's a bit damp. You can start with holding her while I find some clean clothing."

Matt took the baby as if he feared she might bite him. Stiff-ened, he held her away from him. "I draw the line at changing damp babies," he growled.

"There's nothing to it." Grace rummaged around in one of Ollie's *parfleches*. "Ah, here we are. . . ."

She took out a lace-trimmed gown newly arrived from Boston and held it up so Matt could see it. "What do you think? We're celebrating a wedding, so my namesake ought to be properly dressed for the occasion."

Matt narrowed his eyes. "She's only going to dampen it."

"Then we'll change her again. Change is good for a person. Wouldn't you agree?" She reached for Little Grace.

As he gave her the baby he pressed a light kiss on Grace's forehead. "I guess it must be. You've certainly changed me, Boston. I never knew I could be this happy—or this overworked."

She smiled and balanced the baby on her shoulder. "You haven't seen anything yet. I intend to make you even happier, and, of course, to keep you busy forever."

He groaned. She laughed. They kissed, while Little Grace drooled on her shoulder. "Oh, Matt!" she sighed, when it ended. "I feel guilty feeling this wonderful when I know how miserable the Comanches must be feeling."

Matt had tried several times to see Quanah, but hadn't yet succeeded. "I do, too," he said. "But I don't plan to forget about them. In time, the army will let me see Quanah. The wounds will heal. I have to believe that. I pray it will be true. Someday the whites and Comanches will all be one, sharing this great land."

"The wounds *will* heal," she fervently asserted. "We'll do all we can to *make* them heal. After all, they healed between us."

"I know. It's *amazing.*" He stopped and grinned. "And so are you, my Amazing Grace."

She shook her head. "No, not anymore. I've passed on my legacy." She laid Little Grace on the bed between them. The baby looked from one to the other, her blue eyes wide and wondering. *"This* is what's amazing—this new little life, given to all of us. Whenever I see her, I have such hope!"

"Me, too. . . . But are you going to change this baby, or do I have to do it? Everyone else is outside eating, and I, for one, am hungry."

She handed him the gown. "I think you should do it. You need the practice."

"The—*what!* Why do *I* need the practice? You aren't. . . Good God! Are you?"

"No, not yet. At least, I don't think so. I was just planning for the future."

"Boston, you'll be the death of me! I mean, I want children—more than anything. But I'd like to add on to the house first, get up the fencing, build the barn, brand all our cattle, train more horses—"

"Change the baby," she said. "First, change the baby. Let the future take care of itself."

That night, under a Comanche Moon, they left for the Red River country. Grace rode Dunston, and Matt rode Renegade. Pride loped along beside them. It was a beautiful night—a night made for lovers. It reminded them of nights in the not so distant past. Renegade pranced and snorted, eager for a long, wild gallop. He, too, remembered the old days, and wanted to run.

"Do you mind?" Matt asked.

Knowing what he wanted, Grace shook her head. "No, let's do it. This one last time, you can be Painted Horse—galloping fast and far and free beneath a Comanche Moon."

Matt took her hand. "Stay with me, Boston."

"Always," she said. *"Always . . ."*

Afterword from the Author

This story is fiction, but the historical incidents depicted herein are true. Following Quanah Parker's surrender in June f 1875, the Texas frontier rapidly expanded. Huge cattle herds replaced the buffalo, and new roads and railways crisscrossed the plains. In captivity Quanah continued to provide leadership) a people ravaged by disease, despair, and the increasing use f peyote. Through successive reductions in subsidies and reservation land, he tried to make the best deals possible. His descendants survive to this day.

Another survivor of the period is the American Paint Horse. similar color breed is the Pinto. I myself own a blue-eyed Medicine Hat, double-registered as a Paint and a Pinto. Whenever I ride him I think of the people who first cherished his ancestors and raced them across the plain beneath a full moon. He reminds me of the past and gives me hope for the future, r, unlike the buffalo, his kind survived and prospered.

If you have enjoyed this story, look for my other books involving different breeds of horses: "Windsong," "Ride the Wind," and "Race the Dawn." You may write to me in c/o Kensington Publishing, 850 Third Ave, New York, NY 10022.

Katharine Kincaid